DRAGON
HEART

DRAGON HEART

Peter Higgins

This paperback first published in Great Britain in 2019 by Gollancz.
First published in Great Britain in 2019 by Gollancz
an imprint of the Orion Publishing Group Ltd
Carmelite House, 50 Victoria Embankment
London EC4Y ODZ

An Hachette UK Company

1 3 5 7 9 10 8 6 4 2

A CIP catalogue record for this book
is available from the British Library.

ISBN (Mass Market Paperback) 978 1 473 21217 6
ISBN (eBook) 978 1 473 21218 3

Typeset by Deltatype Ltd, Birkenhead, Merseyside

Prologue

Or perhaps epilogue is better, and this first scene an ending, a fading coda to long centuries of war music outside human knowledge ... a war among the older peoples of the world, the cruel and beautiful and wise, their weapons the magic of wizards and mages who lived for a thousand years ... a war fought in regions where humans did not go, where ancient civilisations rose and then fell, war-ravaged, and altogether faded leaving only magic-haunted ruins and echoes of starlight voices ... a war that ends now in victory for none ... a war that ends in the shadow of final catastrophe, absolute and total ... and this the last sad day of that ancient war ...

The rumble of distant detonations. A flicker on the skyline, a sudden flare of dazzling lilac brilliance, the deep heart-rock of the mountain shuddering underfoot. Then the fierce wind came. It hurt the wizard Tariel's face and brought the scent of un-familiar magic, the taste of dark joy in destruction and a strange metallic burn.

Tariel narrowed his eyes against the lingering glare and when it faded the dragon Vespertine was a distant spark, a tiny speck of jewelled fire and glass against the bruised horizon. Tariel leaned on his staff, his left hand gripping the parapet, clenched fingers digging into flaking stone. Bitter cold seeped deep into his bones, but he could spare no energy to warm his body. He would need all his reserves and more for what he must do now. There could be no more delay; no more hoping for a different choice when none would come.

The overlook where he stood was a crumbling outcrop, a precarious jut of ancient masonry – broken paving and tumbled carvings worn smooth by centuries of ice and rain – leaning out over the edge of the mountain drop, dizzyingly high. Thousands of feet below him, armies were still killing one another on the Chelidd Plain: massed columns dark against the redness of the earth; the wheel and flow of horsemen, like birds flocking at twilight. They were too far below for him to hear the cries and screams and the clash of arms; too far and too obscured by smoke and dust for him to tell yet how the day would go. Not that the battle mattered any more. He had another purpose, and it was time.

The Deep War was finished. So many open battles, shedding the blood of uncountable numbers, entire regions harrowed into ruin; so many unseen vigils, secret acts and lonely heroisms; so many ambitions, betrayals and desires; the love and the magic and the sacrifices; all the generations of that. All of it had failed in the end, brought to an end by one foolish, wild and desperate act, the act not of an enemy but of one of their own, whose recklessness could not be restrained.

Far away on the plain the vain struggle continued, one last futile gasp, but what was approaching from the north was something else and could not be fought. A permanent rift had been torn between this world and another, decisively and for ever. There was no closing it: the wound was unhealable, and death would flow in from that other place, slowly at first, then faster and faster, the incursion spilling and spreading, scuttling, crawling, prowling, leaching out across the world. Alien light. Alien magic. Alien growth. Alien air. The strangeness and hunger of nameless things from a different, nameless place. And when they came everything of this world would die, and this world's life and magic would fail.

Tariel remembered how he used to wander long ago among the precincts of Far Coromance: remembered the sun-warmed grapes in the afternoon, the fragrance of cypress groves, the stillness of flamingos on the palace lake, the laughter and shouts of human children out of sight on the other side of a garden wall. He remembered, and his grief and sadness shone. This world's long Age of Life was over now, though much of the world did not know it yet: the war had been fought in regions far from where humans lived, among peoples they knew of only as rumours and ancient tales that few of them believed.

Yet we didn't fight only for ourselves. Always for them also. Always remembering them. At least for the best of us, that was true, though at the last we failed them. All of us failed.

There was yet one last thing Tariel could do, and he would do it. The price was appalling. It would certainly kill him, and what was worse – infinitely worse – it would destroy the shining intelligence of his friend, his love. The cruel desecration of that: it was an unbearable abomination. But in the hollow watches of the night Tariel had made his choice and he would do it. He would die and Vespertine would be destroyed.

And by their sacrifice they might leave one last small chance for the world. One tiny crack in the closing door. One single fragile seed. One throw of the dice in the whirlwind dark.

It was almost time.

The dragon Vespertine swept down upon him. Lacy and beautiful, delicate as refractions of colour in ice, brawny as the burn of the sun, she came so near to him that her bulk walled half the sky. She had been dealing death to her enemies on the red plain and the reek and joy of it trailed from her. The ache of Tariel's love for Vespertine burst and spread through him like the taste of a berry crushed against his tongue. He sent her a sudden, wordless, instinctive voice.

Hello, my beloved, I am so glad you are here with me.

The voice of the dragon in his head rattled his bones.

I FELT YOUR GRIEF.

Yes, heart. I know.

THIS WORLD IS OVER.

Yes.

THERE ARE OTHER WORLDS THAN THIS ONE. AN IN-FINITE ABUNDANCE OF WORLDS. WORLDS PRESS AGAINST WORLDS LIKE BUBBLES IN OCEAN FOAM, AND MANY ARE BEAUTIFUL.

Yes.

YOU KNOW THIS. YOU ARE MAGISTER. MAGUS PEREN-NIAL. MAGIC FLOWS THROUGH YOU LIKE A RIVER. YOU ARE STILL STRONG.

Yes.

WE WILL GO ELSEWHERE TOGETHER. COME NOW, BE-LOVED FRIEND. RIDE MY BACK AGAIN.

No. We cannot do that. There is something else we must do.

I KNOW. I HAVE SEEN YOUR HEART.

Vespertine ... I am sorry. So sorry.

I SHARE YOUR CHOICE, MY DARLING. I ACCEPT MY FATE AND YOURS. BUT DO IT QUICKLY. DO IT NOW.

Part One

Part One

I

Castrel could feel the child moving inside her: uncurling her arms and legs, opening her delicate fine-boned hands and pushing with her feet. Long, slow kicks. Waking and testing her strength. Castrel knew her child was a girl. She could feel everything about her. She felt the flutter of her heart, small and fierce as the heart of a bird; felt the hot thread of blood moving in her veins; the intricate, delicate articulation of tiny bones; the knot and stretch of muscle; the fluttering tongue. Her daughter's lungs, still slack and filled with fluid, were not moving yet, but to Castrel they were as present and vivid and obvious as her own body was. To know the interior of things; to reach in and touch the life there; to feel and understand and if need be to shape and heal: this was what Castrel could do. It was her talent, her born gift, and always had been. It made her what she was and shaped her life.

When she was thirteen years old, she sat at the table in Bremel's house in Weald and cupped a bird in her hands. A merle. Its heart fluttered rapidly, its small black eyes stared into hers. The sun came in through the doorway and splashed on the floor, bringing air that smelled of lilac and cut grass. She was inside the merle and Bremel was there with her.

See, said Bremel, *see how the threads that carry the blood spread like fine roots? Follow them. See? This is the liver. This is the crop.*

The merle was full of light and transparency inside. Its skin was like living glass and the warmth of the sun reached deep.

Now, said Bremel. *See this dark thing here? This twisted purse? That's where the problem is. What you must do is smooth it and ease it until it goes away. But gently. Slowly. Don't let it burst. Use the light and warmth that is in there. Use the bird's own strength, not yours, or you will be hurt. Help her to heal herself.*

Castrel tried. Carefully. Patiently.

Good, said Bremel. *That's good. That's very good. You learn fast and you have the right touch. Beautiful. You can do this.*

And afterwards Bremel had asked her:

'Will you be frightened to go away on your own one day, and travel alone and do this, do you think?'

'I don't think so,' said Castrel. 'No. I want to. When must I go?'

'Not yet,' said Bremel. 'Not for a long time yet. I have more to show you. But one day you will. If you choose.'

'Yes,' said Castrel. 'I choose.'

It was the golden day of her life, the seed-day for all the rest.

Afterwards, in long years of walking alone, Castrel helped many women give birth: she followed the growth and then the struggle, the bursting out into life of their children. But now she carried her own child, and it was different. Other women's children, she had wanted them to live, each and every one of them, but *this* child ... Her love for this tiny new life was fierce and total, a visceral force, deeper and earlier than thought. It was a love that wanted nothing for itself, a love without purpose or intent, absorbing and wordless.

Her daughter, still too fragile and unformed for the outer world, was not yet ready to come, but in a few short months she would be born. The crib was already waiting for her by the hearth: the crib Shay made while the evenings were still long, working with all the care and exactness he learned making boats when he lived by the sea. He made it in the shape of a boat, small and neat, with a curved up-rising bow and rounded stern, a vessel to ride out the storms and carry their daughter safe on the tide of their love. And when it was finished, a small thing of reddish oak, dark-grained and polished till it glowed in the firelight, Castrel had carved it with intricate signs of welcome and warding. She wove life and strength into it with the words Bremel taught her long before, in Weald.

She paused now at the crest of the hill to catch her breath and ease her back. Above her was the pale wideness of the sky, and all around her was tangled bracken and fern and the air of high places. Low outcrops of granite with a threadbare covering of heather. She put down her basket, stretched her shoulders and arched her spine. She'd done well: the basket was more than half full of mushrooms from the High Hedge Field, pale and milky, the underparts rich and dense and scented like the raw dark earth. She pulled her shawl tighter against the chill air, breathing its smell of wet wool and fire smoke. Autumn was always her favourite season.

'My autumn child,' she said quietly. 'We'll make you happy here.'

She felt the child respond. The answering touch of mind against mind. Her daughter had strength already, a force like water in flood: Castrel could feel it, as sure as the first heat of the rising sun still shrouded in dawn mist. When her child came into the world she would bring change, momentous and permanent. An earthquake. A landslide in their lives. Nothing would be the same, not for her, not for Shay. Everything would be changed, though she could not tell how. A fresh new person in the world.

She picked up her basket and walked on down the slope, making for the lane through the wood, and as she went she tried to see the world as if for the first time, trying to see it all with her daughter's eyes, breathe it with her lungs and feel it with the thinness and clarity of her child's new skin. Soft rain blurred the woodland in the valley below. A honey-pale buzzard wheeled low over the trees on broad flaggy wings, mewing, until a ragged handful of rooks rose in noisy irritation to sweep it away.

She pushed through a gap in the hedge and scrambled down the bank into the lane. From there the lane descended, soft mud and stones, under a canopy of low arching trees towards a dim, shadowed stream. It forded the stream and climbed again, steeply. She started down the lane but slowed. Stopped. Uneasy. In the north, behind the woods, the sky was not right. Along the horizon lay a damson-coloured bar, low above the trees, swelling like a bruise. She hadn't noticed it before. And there was a pony and cart standing motionless at the edge of the stream. She felt the pony's attention brush against her. It was a mare. A small cob mare standing in harness, patient and passive, taking occasional water from the shallow, muddied stream and grazing the grasses at the edge of the track. Castrel felt her weakness and exhaustion. The mare had come down the hill and then halted in the bottom of the dip because the climb out was too much for her.

And there were two figures in the cart. They were bundled and indistinct, and Castrel could feel nothing from them. No life. Only strangeness and death. There was something bad there, something momentous and dangerous. Her first thought was to stay away. Turn and go. There was her child to think of.

But she would not do that. It was important to know. Ignoring was not the same as being safe.

She approached slowly, trying to send reassurance to the cob mare as best she could. The mare whickered quietly and stirred from foot to foot but did not move. As Castrel got closer she saw the animal had suffered months of near-starvation: she was skeletal, her belly distended, her ribs painfully visible. Her coat was rough and matted, and on her sides there were angry, weeping sores.

The two figures in the cart leaned against one another, slumped together, shoulder to shoulder in death. It was as if one had died first and the other held on close to die as well, not wanting to go on alone, and eventually the cart had stopped, the pony exhausted, unsure and directionless, waiting. The bodies were thickly wrapped in clothes made from the pelts of some animal Castrel did not recognise. The furs were soiled and sour. There was a stained leather satchel on the plank beside them that contained raw meat. She could smell it faintly. The back of the cart was almost empty: only a few shabby belongings, and a couple of small barrels. Their clothes and scents and the shape and making of their things were like none she had come across before.

Castrel reached out to move aside the hood of the nearest body so she could see the face, and hissed in surprise. It was the head of an old man, but broader and heavier than human, the jaw massive, the face almost a muzzle, and there was a rough thickness to the texture of his skin. He was starved to an agonising gauntness, the strong bones of skull and jaw edged starkly clear. His brown eyes were open but blank in death. They showed no whites at all. Instinctively she tried to feel her way deeper into him but she could perceive nothing. There was no life there, and only living things were open to her.

He was of the bear-people.

It was a guess: she'd only heard of such people, descendants of human settlers who ventured into the far north long ago and joined their inheritance lines with fierce intelligent bears. The bear-people lived deep in endless pine forest where winter fell in months of silence and enduring night under impossible depths of snow. Their body temperature dropped in the freezing dark and they slept out the long winter in dugouts lined with pine needles. No bear-people had come this far south since the forests retreated, but centuries ago, in colder times when the forests spread closer, sometimes one or two might be woken by hunger and driven down out of the trees, arriving near death to ask for shelter at outlying farms. They kept their heads bowed between massive shoulders and watched warily with their round whiteless eyes. Sometimes the farmers let them sleep in a barn or a loft, but likely as not they drove them away and barred their shutters.

Castrel studied the dead man. She was curious. She'd never encountered anyone who was not human. Of course, he *was* human, of a kind, but not entirely. If there was a borderline, he was close to it but on the other side. Bremel had spoken sometimes about non-human people. The older ones, she called them. The others. Apart from the bear-people they were all gone now, but she had seen traces of them: strange ruins built long ago by minds that thought differently from humans and had skills that were lost now. Places where the feel of subtle ancient magic lingered. There was no trace of magic about this dead man, but nonetheless he was something different. From a world entirely outside her experience. She wondered what desperate need had brought him here to die. What had driven him so far south, to end his journey in this rarely used hollow lane that went only from one long-abandoned farm to another?

She went to look at the other body and realised her mistake. This one was not dead. It was a woman, unconscious, her breathing shallow and very slow. She was one of the bear-people too, but smaller and slighter than the man, and finer-featured. Her face was harsh and spare, her weathered skin creased, her long greying hair fine and smooth and tied back at the neck. She was emaciated but beautiful, like a wind-sculpted tree on a winter rock. She reminded Castrel a little of Bremel.

She was almost dead, but not quite. Not yet. She might be helped. Perhaps it could be done.

She reached deep inside herself, deep into the very core of who she was, and found the hot bright well of strength there. Then she opened herself out to the woman and shared, creating a link that let warmth and life flow. She did it instinctively, immediately and without thought, though it was an effort that cost her heavily. What she was doing wasn't like healing, where she could draw on the other's own resources to mend hurt and drive out sickness: this was a desperate push against exhaustion, despair and death. The dying woman had no resources of her own. As her strength poured out across the link Castrel felt herself weaken, tear and fray, and her child squirmed in protest.

I'm sorry, she told her. *You'll be fine. You come first. But I must do this. I must at least try.*

Castrel felt the woman – faintly, weakly, little by little, agonisingly slowly – coming back from very far away, but she could also feel herself weakening. The world around her was getting cold and dark. She was already near to sharing more than she safely could. Giving too much risked leaving her permanently sick and broken, even dying. Bremel called it *barrening.*

The ones you help the most will always be the worst danger to you, she had said. *They will cleave to you. They will drain you to the dregs. They cannot help it, they do not mean to, but they will suck you dry. Never forget this. There is a time when you can do no more. Then you must let them go.*

Reluctantly Castrel began to draw away and break the bond, but just at the point of complete separation there was a flaring surge from the other side of the link. It was as if she had touched and woken something wild and desperate deep within the woman – almost a rage, something that was more bear than human. Startled, she snapped out of the sharing. It left her giddy and exhausted, but life was flickering in the woman's face. She groaned and murmured. Then suddenly her eyes snapped open, glaring, and she seized Castrel's wrist. Her hand was broad, heavy and hard. The grip hurt.

'Who are you?' she said. Her voice was difficult to understand.

Hoarse, sibilant, barking, choking, strange. 'Where am I? What is this place?'

'You've come a long way from the forests. This country is Allerdrade. There are only hills and empty farms around here. The nearest village is almost a day's travel away. It's called Ersett. Is that where you're going?'

The woman looked at her blankly, as if she understood the words but could make no sense of them.

'Rest now,' said Castrel. 'Talk later. I don't think you're sick, but your strength is gone—'

'I said *who are you*?'

'My name is Castrel. Do you want some water? I'll fetch you some.'

The bear-woman hesitated, then nodded.

'Yes.'

Castrel found a wooden cup in the back of the cart and filled it from the stream.

'You don't need to be afraid,' she said when she came back. 'There's no danger. You're safe here.'

'*Safe?*' The woman's eyes hardened. Anger. Fear. '*Safe?* Nowhere is *safe*. Nothing is *safe*. You are not *safe*.'

She snatched the cup from Castrel's hand and drank deeply from it, choking, spilling half the contents down her chin.

'Paav?' she said suddenly. 'Paav? Where is Paav?'

She looked around in confusion. Then she saw that he was dead. The sound she made then was the saddest sound Castrel had ever heard. A long growling keening snarl that rumbled deep in her chest. She nuzzled her face against the dead man's neck.

'I'm sorry.' Castrel laid a hand on her arm. 'He was dead when I found you. There was nothing I could do.'

For a long time the woman said nothing. Then she raised her head, bleakness and grief in her eyes.

'Forty winters we slept in the same hollow,' she said. 'Shared our warmth. He with me and I with him. One scent. One warmth. One hunger. He is gone and without him I am emptied. Winter without him will be too cold.'

Castrel's heart went out to her. This was a kind of hurting she could not heal.

'I'm so sorry,' she said, and after a silence she added: 'Will you tell me your name? I know Paav, but I don't know yours.'

'Khaag. My name is Khaag. And you are Castrel.'

'Yes.' Castrel smiled. 'I wasn't sure you heard me before.'

'My wits are not so scattered as you may think. Nor am I so old, for my kind, though there is little fire left in me now.'

'I didn't mean ...' Castrel began, then thought better of it. 'Your strength surprised me. You'll soon recover. There's plenty of life in you.'

'No!' Khaag shook her head so fiercely Castrel flinched. 'This is not *life*! You have no experience of my people. We *burn*. We *roar*. You should have seen Paav in his prime. He was a waterfall at the flood. The dawn sun on a mountain. What you see there is not Paav, and what you see here is not me, not as I should be ...'

Khaag broke off, her eyes fixed somewhere far off. Castrel tried to bring her back to the present. She was conscious how far she was from home, this late in the day.

'Is there somewhere near here that you're trying to get to?' she said. 'Perhaps I can help you? Show you the way?'

'No.'

'Then you could ...' Castrel hesitated. 'You could come home with me. I mean, if you want to. My house isn't far, and you'd be welcome. You could rest with us a while and recover your strength. I'm a healer. I could help you, if you'd let me. And then we can talk more, later.'

Khaag turned her gaze full on Castrel, raking her with brown whiteless eyes full of anger and hurt and fear and a terrible darkness. And something else. Castrel thought it was warmth.

Pity. And acknowledgement too. She thought the strange, fierce bear-woman was acknowledging her. Accepting her. But she couldn't be sure.

'You mean kindness to me,' said Khaag. 'You are a good woman. I see the strength and wisdom in you. But you must learn different, harsher ways. What you're saying ... it's too late for that now. That time is over, that world is gone, and Paav's path is the better one. I have seen what is coming, and you have not yet seen what I have seen. You do not yet know.'

'But—' Castrel began, but Khaag interrupted her.

'You are with child?'

'I am.'

'Then I will tell you something. Mother to mother I tell you this. *Mother to mother.*' Khaag's voice was guttural and urgent. 'And as mother to mother you must hear me. You must listen.'

'What is it?' said Castrel.

'Will you hear me?'

'Yes.'

'You must run, Castrel. Run. Leave me here now. Leave your house and go, go far and keep running and do not stop. Ever. Look to your child, Castrel. Find a place. Keep her safe. Save her if you can. That's all that matters now. It's the only thing you can do.'

'I don't understand.'

Khaag struggled to sit up and lean forward, but her breath was suddenly failing her. She was visibly weaker. It was as if she had forced all she had left into the desperate urgency of what she must say to Castrel. Spending the very last of her strength on that.

'It is coming,' she said. Her voice was quieter. Hoarser. 'It comes from the north. It is behind us, but it is always coming. *Always.* The line of shadow. The bad darkening. It *follows.* Sometimes it slows and you get ahead of it for a while. But it does not stop. It never, ever stops. The fear …! It comes in the night—' She broke off in a fit of coughing. 'Are you *listening*, Castrel?' she said when she could continue. 'Do you *hear*?'

'It's all right,' said Castrel. 'There's plenty of time. I'm listening—'

But Khaag had already started to speak again, her voice so hoarse and breathy now that Castrel struggled to hear.

'… and then riders … terrible riders … and then … Hide! Run far, and hide! You must. You—'

Another fit of coughing, much worse. A kind of spasm. Castrel climbed up onto the cart next to Khaag. She sat close and reached out, trying to open some kind of way to her. Some healing way.

Breathe. Be calm. Breathe.

But she could make no contact now. The bear-woman's body and mind were so strange. All she could be aware of was Khaag's heartbeat slowing. It was ragged and weak.

'Khaag,' she whispered urgently. '*Khaag*.'

But Khaag's eyes were closed. She lapsed into sleep, or unconsciousness, Castrel couldn't say which. Nor could she say whether Khaag would live. There was nothing in her experience to tell her that, and nothing more she could do for her now except let her rest.

She took the cob mare's bridle and began the long slow walk home. The animal, so painfully thin and weak, limped slowly, glancing sideways at her from time to time. Brown eyes like water in a pool under the dim shade of trees. Castrel had no strength left to share with her.

You can do it, she told the mare wordlessly. *Courage. Your journey is almost at an end.*

They were descending the last hill in gathering twilight, wheels and slow hoof-falls clattering on the cobbles, making for the glimmer of firelight in the window that told her that Shay was already home, when Castrel felt Khaag's wild fierce life slip away.

2

Shay buried the bear-people near the apple garth under clear black skies and the bone-bright glare of the moon. Castrel was in the barn tending the cob mare, and when he rested he could hear her voice murmuring a song, rhythmic, quiet and gentle. The unfamiliar syllables of the hedge-witch tongue. It sounded closer than it was, carried on the night air with the scent of gorse from the hill and windfall apples rotting in the wet grass.

Her voice was beautiful and strange: he'd felt that the first time he heard it and he still felt the same. Her voice, her breathing, the warmth of her skin, the feeling of a room she was in … it was all part of her fluent gentle magic. She said it wasn't magic at all, but it thrilled and stirred him deeply as if it was. And what was magic if not that?

'What I do isn't magic,' she said. 'Magic is harsh and inhuman. Unnatural. Magic is wizards' work, it draws power by destroying something and it always leaves a hole behind. But what I do is part of being alive. I help living things do what I can do anyway, inside, slowly, without knowing they're doing it. It's feeling and sharing, that's all it is. There's nothing magical about it.'

Yet in the time he had known her, Shay had seen Castrel do impossible things, and in his heart he called it magic.

*

He laid the bodies side by side and covered them with earth. He did the best he could for them in death and mourned their loss, and not only because death was always hard. He wished he could have seen them alive and talked with them. He'd seen people who were not human once before, and now a trace of that otherness and wonder had come to him again, but dead, as strange bodies only, for him to bury in the ground; and that was a grievous loss.

He stood at the foot of the grave, adrift for a moment in memories of that other time, the time when the ships of the White Knives appeared one morning in early summer far out in the bay off Harnestrand. The sea was purple and the sun hadn't yet burned the horizon clear of mist, and when the great fleet appeared the bell of the Seilona rang, its hollow clang echoing off the cliffs. Shouts went through the village and people hurried down to the harbour. Shay left his tools on the bench in the boatyard and hurried with Galla and Moar up through the trees to the Rock, where they could lie on a flat place under the pines and see both the harbour and the bay.

He remembered everything about that day. All of it. The scent of warm earth and lemons and the sea, and how splashes of sunlight fell through the leaves and danced across his arms like reflections off a pool. The morning ground cool under his stomach and the sun hot and his feet bare and dusty, his toes scraping little furrows back and forth in the dust behind him. He remembered it because he was seventeen years old, and because it was the most important thing he had ever seen.

A forest of sails was emerging out of the haze on the skyline. Small in the distance, they caught the sun and shimmered silver and blue. The breeze was against them but they were coming in faster than any boat he had ever seen, their sails bellying forward taut as bowstrings. Galla tried to count them but she gave up after a hundred because they were too far away and always turning and crossing one another's wake. When the nearest had come so close that Shay could no longer stretch out an arm and hide one with his thumb, there were still more rising out of the horizon, their hulls long and narrow, their prows tall like sweeping blades, high as the masts. At last they let down sail and put out oars and rowed. Strange ships from elsewhere, with a strange purpose.

As Shay watched there was a hunger in his throat, an excitement that was new and he had no name for. It was like the first time he put his hand on Galla's bare skin, and she didn't push him away but turned and pulled him to her. Watching the ships come in, he knew he had come to a threshold and a new door was opening. The world was suddenly much bigger. The feeling was a kind of terror, but there was no fear in it.

The fleet beached on the long sands where the river entered the sea, and the line of them reached all the way to the eastern headland. Shay ran with Galla and Moar along the cliff path to another place closer to the long sands and all day they stayed there, out of sight between rocks, hugging their knees. They saw the White Knives disembark and muster. There were both men and women, thousands beyond counting. Shay drank them in with his eyes: they were head and shoulders taller than the tallest in Harnestrand, thin like young trees and strong like whips. He saw their fine narrow faces and straight hair, their armour, swords, quivers and bows, and the wondrous white knives at their belts. Some came so close to where they crouched that he could see their eyes burn and glitter and hear the incomprehensible language they spoke.

They led their horses through the surf to shore, and when Shay saw the horses he knew that the horses of Harnestrand were small, clumsy, stupid, ugly and weak.

Galla was holding his hand tight. He realised she was confused and afraid, and so was Moar. Shay could see it in his face. Moar was his friend because he always had been, because he was always there, but he was a dumb ox really. Shay wasn't afraid. His imagination was on fire.

A legation from the village came to the sands to offer the newcomers wine and food.

'We will take nothing from you,' the strangers said, 'or you will come to resent us after we are gone. Our way is to pass and leave no trace. Do not fear us: we go north into winter and mountain to join a great war. We do not hope to return.'

That same evening the White Knives rode away, fine cloths drawn across their faces and war bows at their backs, taking the steep road into the hills, and none looked back. The next morning their ships were gone and the tide had swept away all trace of them from the sand.

After the White Knives left, Shay woke every morning from the same dream, of which he remembered only that everyone in Harnestrand was dead and the earth itself was dry brittle cinders that broke underfoot. And beneath the thin crust of earth he walked on there were cool fires burning: the flames showed through, pale and bitter grey. There was no smoke.

The feeling of the dream stayed with him all through each day, and he became certain that Harnestrand was dying to him. When he closed his eyes he saw fleets at sea and the White Knives riding. Where did they go? What was the great war they rode to? He found himself thinking more and more of what lay beyond the hills, and traders' stories of the island cities of Far Coromance. His work in the boatyard grew careless and Hollin the yardmaster cursed him for it. He took the dream as a call to adventure, a sign that he must leave Harnestrand and follow the White Knives north.

'Come with me,' he said to Galla. 'We can't spend our whole lives here, growing old and dying, never seeing anything else. There's so much more in the world for us to find. I don't think the White Knives were even human.'

Galla snorted.

'What were they then?' she said.

'I don't know, they just felt ... different ... strange. It was like ...' He struggled for words. 'It was a wonder. Didn't you feel something like that?'

'No. I'm just glad they're gone. And you shouldn't talk that way. What will you do if Hollin throws you out? No other fishing master would take you then.'

'I wouldn't care,' said Shay. 'I'd be glad.'

And he meant it. He was on fire, his young will was iron and single-minded, he didn't weigh futures and considerations. After a week he told his mother he was leaving, shouldered his pack and went to look for the White Knives and whatever other strangeness and wonders were out there in all the hugeness of the world. After a few days he lost their trail among scree on the slope of a hill but he didn't turn back. His mind was set. For three years he wandered, finding work where he could, staying a few months here, a few months there, always making his way further north. At a town called Horrow he heard that fighting had broken out in Imbrel. It didn't sound like the great war of the White Knives but he had nothing better to do so he went, and in Imbrel, half drunk at some drab place on the road, he fell in with Hage and Ridder and Vess.

It pleased them to call themselves freebooters: resourceful fellows for hire to the commander who needed a discreet job done with cleverness and quiet. They told him they were attached to the army of a commander called Adma Corse. Shay liked them for their cheerfulness and wit, and they took a shine to him. By the end of the evening he'd agreed to join them, and the three became four.

He stayed with Hage, Ridder and Vess for more than a year and they became his friends, the best and closest he ever had. Together they acted as scouts, watchers, intelligencers and occasionally thieves for Adma Corse. Shay learned to move fast and silent. He was given a sword and learned cleverness and weapons and a little of the tactics of war. Adma Corse was marching slowly north-west, ostensibly to occupy and defend the Counties of the Hew, though it seemed to Shay and the others that she was more concerned with lining her pockets and settling obscure family scores on the way. He was in two battles, and hated it. He hated being shouldered and shoved, unable to move more than inches, breathing the stink of other men's fear while vicious blades came at him suddenly out of nowhere. It was exhausting, terrifying, and pure chance that he came through it alive.

'All this is just so much pointless shit,' he said to Hage after the second battle. 'Who gives a toss what Adma Corse does, apart from Adma Corse?'

Hage shrugged.

'Sell your sword somewhere else then,' he said. 'You don't have to stay.'

'Would somewhere else be better?'

Hage emptied his mug.

'Shit, no,' he said.

I've made a terrible mistake, thought Shay. *I'm twenty-two and I'm wasting my life. I'll go south where the sun shines. I'll live in a city by the sea. Maybe I'll sign on as a ship's hand and sail to Far Coromance.*

But he didn't leave, and he was still with Vess, Ridder and Hage and the army of Adma Corse when he walked down a hill and saw Castrel for the first time.

He was out on his own that day, scouting ahead, following the route out of a village called Ersett and up into higher moorland. The track dropped into a hollow almost wide and sheltered enough to be called a valley, and there was a low stone house there, standing on its own. It looked abandoned: a sagging roof shedding rotted thatch; streaks of black moss on the grey white-washed walls; a stand of lichenous apple trees overrun by bramble and thorn. But when he looked more closely he saw signs of recent small repairs, and a patch of fresh-dug earth among the nettles on the banked garden plot.

Castrel was working in the garden, though he didn't know her name then. She had dark hair, black and shiny as a crow's wing. She straightened her back and saw him there, and he went on down the slope to her, conscious of the knife at his hip and the short sword slung across his back. He sensed her wariness but knew straight away she wasn't afraid.

'That roof needs fixing,' he said. 'The purlin's giving way.'

'I know,' she said.

She was watching him with intense dark eyes. There was something harsh and self-contained about her. Physically, she was slight and not tall. Her narrow shoulders drooped a little under the weight of a heavy, shapeless satchel and her hands were coarsened by work and weather, but he felt a strange, fierce life and strength in her. She stirred something in him. Something buried somewhere deep.

'Are you a soldier?' she said.

'Yes.' He hesitated. 'Well. Sort of. Not exactly.'

He didn't know why he said that. It surprised him that he did.

'Oh.'

It was all she said. He couldn't tell what she meant by it, though he thought about it later a lot.

'Do you know how to fix it? The roof, I mean?' he said.

'I'll work it out,' she said. 'When I've got the time.'

'You should fix it before the snows come. It might not take the weight.'

She looked at him gravely, calmly, with those dark intense eyes.

'All right,' she said. 'If you say so.'

There was almost a smile there, but he wasn't sure.

He turned away and walked on down the track, aware of her eyes on his back as he went. Later that afternoon the army moved on from Ersett and Shay went with them, but every day he found himself thinking about her. Something about her had snagged him like a thorn. She had woken a need in him that he hadn't known he had. It made him unsettled. Disturbed by a restless, unconnected, unsatisfied energy.

Are you a soldier?

Yes. Well. Sort of. Not exactly.

He hadn't meant to say that, it seemed to come out of no-where. He'd been meaning to ask her for water because he was thirsty, but something changed. Going down the slope towards her he was a soldier, with a soldier's purpose, but now he wasn't a soldier any more: all of a sudden, between one instant and another, in some buried, essential heart-place, his whole idea of who he was had broken open. A kind of dullness had fallen away, leaving him raw, excited and full of confused energy. He saw ... he *remembered* – it felt like *remembering* – an entirely different life. The life he hadn't been living. The life that would make him real. She changed the world by being in it, and he wanted to be with her, only that.

After a week or so, hesitant and inarticulate, he said something of this to Vess.

'Go to her,' said Vess. 'If you've got a chance to grab hold of life take it, or you'll regret it for ever. Go.'

That same night Shay slipped away from the camp, leaving his sword behind, and went back south.

The roof still sagged.

He knocked at her door. When she opened it and saw it was him her eyes widened and he felt suddenly clumsy. Tongue-tied. Heart jumping.

'I'll fix that roof for you,' he said. 'And the door. And the other stuff. I know how. I used to build boats. I'll do it, if you'll let me.'

She hesitated.

'I'll sleep in the barn,' he said. 'You don't need to pay me, just something to eat.'

She looked at him without speaking for what felt like for ever. Shay felt his life held there, paused, suspended between one course and another: on the one side everything that was good, and on the other nothingness and waste.

'All right,' she said. 'If that's what you want.'

And joy burst open inside him, weightless and true and alive.

It was a year and a summer now since he walked down off the hill and stayed. Together they had built a life here, the two of them together, only seeing another human face when they walked the ten miles to Ersett. They had grown so close that sometimes Shay felt they were becoming one person.

He turned away from the bear-people's grave. Castrel had already gone back into the house and lit the taper. The window glowed.

As Shay was following her inside he glanced up at the strange bar of deeper darkness that hung across the night sky to the north, low on the horizon. It been there all day. Stars showed through it, but muted. Unbrilliant. Stained a dulled brownish copper.

The bear-people's coming had unsettled everything. He hadn't thought of the White Knives for a very long time, but now, unexpectedly, when he no longer looked for it, otherness had broken into his life again. Only this time he was older, their child was coming, and he knew to be afraid. Castrel had told him what Khaag said.

Run! Keep running and never stop. It's coming. It's always coming. Look to your child. Run. It's the only thing you can do.

They needed to talk. They needed to decide what to do.

3

Castrel pressed her back against the warmth of Shay's spine and wished she could stretch out her legs. The bed was too short: only a shelf under the loft where they stored their harvest. The one room where they lived was filled with the scent of apples and straw, honeycomb and the earthiness of potatoes and onions. Soon there would be turnips and cabbages too. Shay said their bed was a bunk in the belly of a trader ship, and the sound of the wind in the gorse was the sound of the sea. Shay said that. Castrel had never seen the sea.

There was still a fading glow in the hearth embers, which meant it was after midnight but nowhere near morning. The bed felt enclosed, familiar and safe, but outside the cob mare was uneasy. Castrel could sense her, way out at the periphery of her awareness, standing patiently in the lonely darkness of the byre. There was a tension in the night, a watchful prickling fear-scent in the air, and the mare knew it because she had felt it before. The feeling of something bad coming.

The child inside her was unsettled too. Castrel could feel her wakefulness and restless energy.

'Are you awake?' said Shay quietly in the dark.

'Yes.'

'What are you thinking?'

Castrel shifted to lie on her back. She stared up at the near-darkness.

'I was imagining us leaving here,' she said. 'I was working out what we'd take with us and where we could go.'

'Is that what you want?'

They'd talked about it all evening but they had to keep talking, over and over again, until they knew what to do.

'No,' she said. 'No, I don't ever want to leave. I've never felt I belonged anywhere before, not like this. It's our home, we built it together, ourselves, and every bit of it's ours. But what if we have to go? Khaag was terrified, Shay. Terrified. You didn't see her. They were running from something, running so hard it killed them. She said we should run, too.'

'She didn't tell you much,' said Shay. 'We don't know what she was running from. We don't know it's coming this way.'

'I know we could ignore her and do nothing. But what if we did, and then ... What if we could have got away in time, and we didn't? We have to be clever, Shay. We have to think. We have to react. The people who do that are the ones that survive. When I was sharing with her, trying to not let her slip away, I saw what she'd seen. I mean, not *saw*, I didn't *see* it, but I felt it. I shared what she was feeling, I shared something of what it was like to be her. Sharing happens like that ...'

She remembered the shock of Khaag's appalling grief and loss and fear. That bleak will for death that was dragging her away. Whatever she was running from, it was immense, and the experience of it had left a stain on her mind: an atmosphere of ruinous darkness and terror that was poisoning her soul. Castrel didn't know how to explain it to Shay so he would understand.

'She was struggling for words, as if she was trying to describe something, but she didn't know how ...' A bad darkening. Fear that follows and never stops. And some kind of terrible riders. 'Whatever it was, it was huge, it overwhelmed her, and it

29

wasn't … *ordinary*. It was bad. I'm sure of it. I *know*. You have to believe that. Please.'

'I do,' said Shay. 'Absolutely. Of course. Always. We'll do whatever you say. We'll leave now, if you think we must. Straight away. And we'll come back when it's safe, or we'll find somewhere else and start again.' He paused. 'There is that odd murkiness in the north. But that could be weather.'

'Yes …' said Castrel, frowning in the dark.

Do you abandon your home because you're frightened of a cloud?

Shay didn't say that, but he must be thinking it.

And do you abandon your home because a frightened stranger says something awful is coming?

If they left now they'd be travelling when winter came. They had no money to pay their way. And then there was the child. She was two months from giving birth, and every week the journey would be more difficult for her. She didn't want to go into labour at the side of the road.

But if Khaag was right? If she was right …?

'I don't know, Shay,' she murmured. 'I just don't *know*. How can we be sure …'

'We've got time,' said Shay. 'Tomorrow we could—'

A flash of appalling, bone-searing light burst the room wide open. Then came a heart-shattering shriek, long-drawn-out, terrifying, ragged and shrill: a scream from something neither human nor animal but something else. Not of this world at all. Castrel jerked upright, filled with sickening dread.

The sudden blaze of cold brilliance faded, leaving her dazzled. The darkness in the room seemed total. She was certain that whatever had made that terrible scream was somewhere high overhead, deep in the night sky.

'What was it?' said Shay, sitting up beside her. She could sense his heart racing.

'I don't know,' she said.

She realised she was holding her arms tight across her rounded midriff, protecting the child. She could feel nothing but stillness there. The child was alert but not moving. Listening. Attentive. Unafraid.

'That scream was a voice,' said Shay. 'It sounded like it came from above us, but it might have been out in the hills.'

'It was up in the air,' said Castrel.

They listened for it to come again, but there was only silence and darkness.

The fear. It comes in the night.

'We're too late,' said Shay. 'It's already come. It's here.'

There was no fear in his voice, only determination.

'It may not be that,' said Castrel.

Shay got out of bed.

'Hiding in the dark's no good,' he said. 'I'm going out to look.'

Castrel caught a glimpse of the soldier he had been. *Clarify uncertainty. Go towards the threat, not away. Do something about it.* It was part of the good man he was.

'I'm coming with you,' she said, and pushed the blanket aside.

'Don't you think you'd better wait here? The child … You have to keep her safe … I won't be long.'

'No,' said Castrel. 'We stay together. We keep each other safe. Always.'

She felt in the darkness for her knife on the table and gripped it tight in her hand.

There was nothing outside but the night. The empty sky prickled with darkshine between stars. Wisps of high cloud raced across the moon. Together they circled the house and the apple garth. Shay had a way of walking with absolute silence through the frosted grass, picking a path that never left them silhouetted in the gaps between buildings. Castrel let her awareness drift wide, open and alert, but she found nothing: there was no presence there except the mare in the barn, trembling with terror. Whatever had made that fear-shriek and blasted the darkness with that terrible flash of light, it had passed and left no trace.

'I think it's gone,' she said to Shay. 'There's no danger here, at least not now.'

'Perhaps,' he said. 'I want to scout around on the hill and in the lane, just to be sure. Let me go by myself, I can move faster and quieter alone. Please. I'll be fine. I know how to do this.'

Reluctantly she nodded.

'Be quick,' she said. 'Be careful.'

He moved away noiselessly out into the dark, the woodpile axe in his hand.

When he'd gone Castrel went into the house and dropped the bar across the door. Better not to light the taper. Show no light. She wrapped a blanket round her shoulders against the bitter cold and sat at the table to wait.

The darkness was almost complete, the house silent but for the night sounds of the wind on the hill. Except that no house was ever entirely silent. She listened to the movement of timbers. The embers cooling in the hearth. The scratching of beetles and mice in the loft.

We should keep cats, she thought. *Why didn't I think of it before?*

Parran had shown her a litter of kittens the last time she was in Ersett. Perhaps she could trade for one or two? It was the right time of year.

Ordinary thoughts to quiet the unease.

Shay would be all right. She was sure there was no unusual presence out on the hill. She would have known. Surely she would. The screaming thing had passed and was long gone now. But the night – the darkness, the wind, the house itself – was still alert with strangeness and threat.

Khaag's warning could not be ignored, that much was clear

now. Something big was happening. Something bad was coming. But the thought of leaving grieved her deeply. Every shadowy shape in the room was familiar. Intimate. Every scent and feel was memory. It was hers. Theirs. Home.

She remembered how she'd found the house a few days after she arrived in Ersett: a roof above the trees; an apple garth; a patch of land; all abandoned and subsiding under a slow tide of nettle, bramble and scrub. She asked in Ersett who owned it.

No one, they said. *It's been empty for years. You're welcome to stay there, if you think you can make it into something. It would be good to have you living there.*

Everywhere else she'd gone since she left Bremel, she found wariness and suspicion. Harshness. Worse. People accepted what she could do for them, but not her, because her gift frightened them. When she'd done what they needed they sent her on her way. But in Ersett they were different, perhaps because there were so few of them left. Ersett was a kind of frontier: beyond Ersett, all directions but south were emptiness and strange country.

You'll walk alone for years, Bremel said when she left Weald. *Then one day you'll find the place where you'll stay and you won't move on any more. The golden place. Know it when you find it. Don't make the mistake of travelling further. Everyone needs somewhere to be.*

This was her place: not only the house, but all of it – Shay, the life they'd made here together, their unborn child, their future, Ersett – and she would stay here. She would defend it. Whatever was necessary, whatever the enemy, she was not afraid. She was fierce. She would fight. She knew how. Oh yes, she knew how.

Her heart was made up then. She saw what she must do.

'I will not leave,' she said aloud in the dark. 'I won't be frightened away by rumours, or clouds in the sky, or lights and noises in the night. We will stay here.'

*

33

She didn't know how long Shay was gone. When his knock came at the door she unbarred it and let him in.

'Nothing,' he said. 'All quiet.'

Castrel lit the tallow taper. It filled the room with a warm golden glow and flickering shadows.

'I don't want to go, Shay. I don't want to run away.'

He looked at her and nodded.

'No,' he said. 'I feel the same. This is our place.'

'Are you sure?'

He grinned.

'Absolutely.'

Her heart went out to him then, just as it had that first time, when he came back and knocked at her door two weeks after walking away. How young he'd seemed to her, then. He wasn't much younger than her in years, but he was somehow still *open*, still raw to the world: his mind wasn't hardened and fixed like most people's were. And it wasn't weakness, it was his strength. A self-defining vividness. He had within him, right at the heart of him, a core of determination and will; an unconscious, implacable determination to be himself; a selfhood as deep-rooted and unbreakable as a tree.

And he trusted her. He shared his strength with her and never doubted.

She loved him so much it almost hurt, like grief or hunger. He was her world, and together they would hold what they had made. They would come through.

They went back to bed. There were still a few hours left of the night.

'Will you come with me to Ersett in the morning?' said Shay. 'We could see if they heard anything in the night. Maybe they saw something. I'd like to hear what Mamser Gean has to say.'

Mamser Gean was the nearest they had to a friend in Ersett.

No, he *was* a friend. Castrel liked him, and Shay talked to him often, spending hours in his workshop while Castrel traded and did what healing she was asked to do, if she could. Perhaps sixty years old now, Gean had set up in Ersett as a farrier but he'd been a soldier once. At least, that was how he described himself, though she doubted he was the same kind of soldier Shay had been. She'd always sensed something wild and wise and strange about Gean. It was in the atmosphere around him. If ever a man was a warrior, Mamser Gean had been, once. Ageing now, and hampered by an injured leg that made him limp, Gean was still immensely tall, broad across the shoulders, heavy as an ox, with thick wrists and big hard fists and an intimidating mane of greying shaggy hair. His smithy felt too cramped to contain him.

'Yes, I'll come to Ersett,' said Castrel. 'I'd like to see Mamser too.'

It would be a long walk, ten miles, and difficult with the growing weight of the child she carried, but she would go.

They set out in the first grey of dawn. The northern sky glowered with a dull coppery light. The ominous dark band of bruising still lay along the horizon, just the same. Shay carried the axe slung across his back like a sword.

The walk took them all morning and it was almost noon when they reached the top of a hill and looked out across a dip in the land to where Ersett lay hidden among trees, still half a mile off.

'That's odd,' said Shay. 'That doesn't look right.'

A sickly smoke hung low over the place where the village was. A greenish-blue stain, thin but not dispersing in the scant wind.

All the uncertainty and alarm of the night before came flooding back.

As they got nearer the village, the track widened and became a clear trodden road. By now the air was tainted with the smell of wet wood burning, and something else – something edgy, animal, sour and dark.

'Something's happened,' said Shay. 'Something bad.'

'We have to see,' said Castrel. 'We have to go there.'

'Yes, but carefully.'

They stopped at the edge of what had once been the village of Ersett: a couple of dozen buildings straggling around an open space, little more than a broad crossroads. When Castrel saw what had happened to it, her first reaction was blankness. Numbness. Disbelief.

We're in the wrong place, she thought. They had come somewhere else. Another village, not Ersett.

Shreds of low, bad-smelling mist clung to the ground. The light itself seemed dimmed and smeary. A sour, sickening smell under the copper sky. Whoever had done it had taken their time. It had been done with discipline. Care. Purpose. And pleasure. The buildings were all burned. All of them. Reeking ruins. Charred fallen beams. The contents of homes and barns scattered outside, broken and befouled. The ground itself was churned and gouged, grass ripped away to show the rawness of the earth. Plants rotting and foul. The smell of excrement and urine. And there were human bodies – corpses – everywhere.

The bodies weren't simply dead, they were destroyed. Hardened, bloated, blackened where they lay, the flesh flayed, burned, rotted. Bones snapped and protruding. There were dead animals too. Horses, cattle, pigs, dogs. Bellies ripped wide, guts and stuff spilled across the ground, heads broken open in puddles of their own contents as if the skulls had burst open under pressure from within.

And over everything settled a terrible, total silence.

Castrel's instinct was to run, to get away, to hide. Anything but stay and look at this horror any more.

It wasn't only fear, it was worse than that.

This cannot be! It must not be! No! Close your eyes! Shut it out!

She fought against the rising tide of panic that threatened to drown her. She had to clear her mind. She had to *think*.

'What . . .? What happened, Shay? What could have done this?'

'I don't know,' he said quietly. 'But whatever it was might still be around. We're not safe here. We should go, Cass. Now.'

Castrel shook her head.

'Maybe there are people still alive. They might be hiding. They might be hurt, and we could help them. We have to look.'

They went through the village, searching for the living, looking at the dead. They looked at all the dead. They checked every one for signs of life. None had survived.

They were people they knew. People they'd talked to. Traded with. Neighbours. There was Parran, who had the litter of cats. Castrel had helped her son into the world. Both were now dead. There was Davin, the tanner, who kept chickens and loved them all and named each one, and wept when one wouldn't lay and must be slaughtered. Many of the bodies could not be recognised. They were ruined beyond bearing.

Objects crunched horribly underfoot.

'Surely *someone* survived?' said Castrel.

Someone must have run, hidden, escaped. They couldn't all be here. Not everyone in Ersett. Not all of them. Not *all*.

But they found no one alive.

Some of the villagers had tried to fight back. At least, weapons had been drawn and lay scattered around the bodies, stained and broken. Shay looked for something he could use, something better than the axe – 'in case, just in case' – but every one he picked up was spoiled. All the iron was covered with a fine grainy substance, faintly bluish white. It was as if the dulled metal had sweated out some kind of mineral salt that had crusted on it.

When he tried a short stabbing sword against a post the blade broke, useless.

Castrel watched him kick around the cinders in the ruin of Mamser Gean's smithy, sifting through lumps of twisted, fused metal. There wasn't much.

'Is Mamser ...?' she said.

'I don't see a body,' said Shay. 'Maybe he wasn't here when it happened.' Mamser Gean lived in a cabin a few miles out of the village and walked into the village to work. Shay cast an eye across the ruin of the smithy. 'I hope not.'

He stooped to pick up a piece of iron out of the stinking ash, and broke it in his hands. It snapped easily. It was brittle. Fragile. Like charred wood.

'This is wrong,' he said. 'The burning of the building wouldn't have done this.'

'I know,' said Castrel.

She could feel something in the air and in the earth: a residue, a kind of sick dark energy. It was like nothing she'd felt before. Traces of the aftermath of some unfamiliar magic. Not just unfamiliar. Absolutely alien and blank to her touch.

'Some kind of power was here,' she said. 'I can feel it. Like an echo of magic-working, but different.'

The pressure of it was disorienting her. It was like a loud, distracting noise. She tried to shut it out.

'*Wizards?*' said Shay. 'Wizards in *Ersett*?'

'No. Not wizards. I don't think so.'

Castrel had never seen a wizard. Nor had Bremel. It was possible there were no wizards left in the world, and hadn't been for several lifetimes. But she had been once or twice in places where wizards' work had been done. It left traces, and she knew what it felt like: the trace of a personality left there; the characteristic mark of a purposeful mind and hand, like the individuality of carving or handwriting, or the clothes someone made for themselves.

'If it wasn't wizards, then what …?' said Shay. 'What could have done this?'

'I don't know. It doesn't feel like anything even partly human. It feels … I don't know, overwhelmingly strong, but empty. There's a kind of life in it, but … beyond darkness. Meaningless. Utterly wrong for this world.'

There were no readable signs in the churned ground. No tracks, no prints. No bodies that were obviously those of strangers. None who might have been an enemy. If any of the attackers had been killed in the struggle, the corpses had been taken away. She tried to open herself and let her awareness drift out, feeling for … she didn't know what.

It was a mistake to open herself like that. The awfulness of it – the grief, the cruelty, the foulness, the residue of strange dark power – overwhelmed her. She leaned forward with a groan and threw up where she stood. Again and again. It seemed to go on for many long minutes. When at last the worst of it passed, she managed to collect herself and put some kind of walls up against the onslaught. She raised her head, wiping her mouth with the back of her hand, and looked for Shay.

She could not see him. He was not there.

She felt again the touch of panic rising. She wanted to shout and yell and scream. Scream for Shay, for the people of Ersett, for herself. Scream to break through the numbness into something else. Scream to make it all go away.

But she must not panic. She fought it back.

Shay came round a corner, moving fast, his face drawn tight and dark.

'I saw someone,' he said. 'Riders. In the distance but coming this way, down the hill from the south.'

'How many?'

'I saw four. There could be more. We have to go. *Now!*'

… and then riders … terrible riders …

It was what Khaag had said, and it was upon them now.

Under the cover of the trees at the edge of the village they paused.

'Back to the house,' said Shay.

'You think it's safe there?' said Castrel.

He looked at her. It wasn't a fair question and she knew it. What else could they do? They had nothing, and nowhere else to go. They couldn't go on south past the village – that way the riders were – and east and west lay many days' walk though empty country and unknown danger.

'The first thing is to get away from here and out of the open,' said Shay.

There was no real choice.

They moved as fast as Castrel could manage with the child, staying away from roads when they could. Shay scouted ahead, alert and cautious, axe in hand, but never out of sight of her. She tried to let her awareness flow outwards, holding herself open for any trace of danger. She knew ways of folding them both into the world. She could make them harder to see. But it was a struggle to find the strength and calm concentration: the long morning's journey had taken its toll. Her mind churned with what had happened in Ersett.

She was shaken and sickened by the appalling ruination and death but also, more deeply and worse, by the alienness she had touched there. Her birth-gift talent, inborn and undeniable, was a joining with life: to her the whole world was one connected thing, brightly and transparently alive, all woven together with warm and shining threads of life and illumination, and she was part of it. It was as if her skin was permeable, and the borders of herself did not end there. There was a kind of shining deepness all around her that she breathed and swam in, always involved and submerged.

But in the desolation of Ersett the living weave that joined all things together was shrivelled. It was poisoned, destroyed, invaded and overwhelmed by something else: something absolutely bad, blank and strange. When she'd first brushed against it, the appalling pull of its strength had made her whole world lurch, queasy and vertiginous. It felt like she was falling sideways, all the angles of the world gone askew and wrong. The feeling was fading now, but it was still with her. She couldn't concentrate. She couldn't make her thoughts go straight.

She whispered words of comfort and reassurance to the child inside her, and more or less left it to Shay to take care of them all and get them home. She trusted him. She let him be her strength.

There was a heavy yellow light in the air and an oppressive silence, as if a storm was coming. The sky was still stained dull and coppery in the north.

They were at a crossroads a few miles out of Ersett, not yet halfway home, though the familiar, welcoming shoulder of high moorland was already rising into view, when Shay grabbed her arm and hissed in her ear.

'*Riders! Down the other road, coming from the left. Hide!*'

They scrambled off the lane and up the bank, pushing through a scrub of hazel and briar, and slid down the other side into the margin of a sparse woodland. There was wind among the trees, but Castrel could hear the riders now. The clanking of gear. The footfall of heavy beasts scuffing through mud and fallen leaves.

No voices.

Shay put his face next to her ear.

'*Did they see us? Can you tell?*'

She tried to feel outwards towards the approaching riders but it was impossible. She struggled to clear her mind.

'I don't know,' she whispered. 'I'm trying ...'

She knew how to calm panic and clear her mind. Bremel had

shown her. *Breathe deep. Open yourself slow and wide. Feel sky and earth.* She did it now. *Breathe.*

She let her awareness drift out again, gently, slowly, cautiously, edging towards whatever was approaching. It worked better this time. A little. She could feel the lane beyond the bank, the smell of it, the way the air moved there. But of the riders she could sense nothing, only a vague darkness and a sense of where they might be. She had to actually *see*.

She began to work her way back up the bank, crawling, turning on her side to squirm between thorn-bush stems. Shay put a warning hand on her shoulder. She turned and saw the look in his face.

What are you doing? Stay back! It is not safe!

Not daring to speak, she shook her head. It was hiding blind that was not safe. She had to know what they were hiding from.

Crawling was difficult with the extra bulk of the child. Some kind of branch or root in the ground dug into her side: she felt the spike of it gouging, dragging. It hurt. She eased herself slowly across it and edged forward, her face pressed close to the earth. Thorns snagged her hair and grazed the skin of her scalp. She paused to scrabble up a lump of earth and moss and smear her face and hair. The scent was strong and good. A strand of briar hooked across her back. She reached behind to pull it away and inched forward until she could see the lane.

Shay slithered up beside her. She hardly felt him come. She was glad of him next to her. The quiet sound of his breathing.

The riders were almost level with where they were. There were two of them, somewhat larger than human. They came on slowly, mounted on tall six-legged beasts. They were hooded. Dirtied grey cowls, shrouding their faces, making their heads look bulky and too heavy. They rode upright, alert, attentive, moving their heads from side to side, scanning. Castrel felt the pressure of their attention pass across her. It made her feel uneasy. Exposed. She

42

shifted cautiously backwards, deeper under the cover of thorns.

Of the beasts they rode she could tell little. Strips of dull black leather and studded hide hung from their flanks like trailing skirts. Their heads, long and snouted, hooded like the riders, swung low, below the level of their shoulders. Browsing the air. Snuffling. Large bags and dark-bladed weapons, notched, stained and unclean, were slung from their saddles, and behind them they dragged long bundles wrapped in cloth. The bundles were heavy dead weights, trailing furrows through the leaves and stones on the path. They could have been bodies. The beasts pulled slow and easy against the weight.

Castrel felt fear twist tight inside her. It squeezed her chest and made her heart struggle. She wanted to breathe clear air. She wanted to run. She wanted to be sick again. She forced herself to lie still and wait. Let them pass.

Long after the last sound of the riders had faded, Castrel and Shay lay without speaking under the thorns. The brush of that cowled eyeless gaze stayed with her. A foulness in the mind. But they had not been detected. She was sure of that.

They listened for any sign of more riders following, or the two returning. Long after it seemed safe, they still didn't move. Castrel stayed lying on her back, watching a spider moving slowly among the branches. Letting it absorb her attention.

'What were they?' said Shay at last.

'I don't know,' she said. 'I ... It wasn't ... normal. It wasn't *right*. They weren't *human*. Did you feel ...?'

A trail of wrongness and dying where they passed. A touch like the coldness of mist. The living connections of the world shrivelling and turning dark and sour and dead.

She tried to tell Shay what it was like.

'All wrong ... all dark and sick ... no, not sick, much more alien and strange than that ... The horrible opposite of life ...'

She struggled and stumbled for words, but he seemed to understand.

'I felt it too,' he said. 'I think so. A little. I couldn't see their faces.'

'I'm not sure they even *had* faces.'

'They were dragging bodies.'

'I think so, yes.'

Neither of them said anything else for a long time. The same thought churned round and round in her mind.

What's happening to the world? What is this? What do we do?

'We should get going,' Shay said at last. 'We should get back home.'

'Yes.'

Cold, stiff and aching, Castrel picked up her pack and they began to walk again. Shay didn't push on as before. They went side by side, and he kept stopping to look back or stare ahead at the point where the lane vanished into the trees.

They made faster progress when they left the lanes for the long climb up the hill to the moor, because they could see further, but Castrel felt horribly visible and obvious.

'Hurry,' she said.

'I think we're safe now,' said Shay.

'No you don't.'

He shrugged.

'Not really, no.'

'You just said that, to make me feel good.'

'It made me feel good too.'

She smiled, a little weakly.

'Well, don't. Please.'

He grinned.

'All right,' he said. 'Sorry.'

*

It was late when they reached the house. The last light was draining from the day, and a red sun hung dull and heavy in the sky. The child in her womb was not moving. Castrel knew she was awake, but she was watchful and wary. Keeping a quiet stillness.

As they came down the last slope together, Castrel paused to look out across the hollow. There was the strong new roof Shay had built. There was her garden patch within the ditch, the cabbages ready to crop, the purple and yellow of the turnips. There were the old trees in the apple garth, small and twisted and almost bare, only a last few leaves and some fallen fruit mouldering in the grass. The scent of that. The harvest in the roof space.

She loved it all.

It had been their happy year. Shay came in the last days of summer and now winter was coming again. Their second winter. This was their resting place. The end of their journey. The home for their daughter.

'We have to go,' she said. 'We have to leave. We do, don't we?'

'Yes.'

'I wanted to stay. But we can't.'

'No.'

There was no other choice. With Ersett gone they couldn't live here, isolated and alone. They could not stay near that place of death. And worse was coming. Something appalling. Some darkness, some terror from the north. They had seen something of it that day, but not yet all of what it was. What had happened already would not be the end of it. To stay where they were, to hide and hope that the danger had passed ... They could not do that.

But they would be all right. They would survive. She'd walked long and far before, and so had Shay. Travelling from place to place with nowhere that was home: they both knew what that was like, and they'd come through. They could do it again. This time there were two of them, and soon their child too, and those things were all that mattered in the end.

She felt Shay take her hand in his. He stood close by her, at her side.

'I'm sorry,' he said. 'This is a good place.'

'We were going to ...' she began.

Her voice faded. There was no point mourning lost futures. Lost hopes.

'It won't be for ever,' said Shay. 'This will pass, and when it does we'll come back here again, the three of us, and we'll be happy here.'

4

Shay sat awake and alert in the lampless dark, listening, axe in hand. There was no sound but the quiet, familiar noises of the night: the wind in the gorse; Castrel's quiet breathing as she slept. The gentle rhythm of her breathing.

His mind turned again to the desolation of Ersett, and then the riders, larger than human, riding high on six-legged beasts: those strange, hooded beasts – their long backs, the odd articulation of their gait, their heavy hooves split like goats' hooves and shod with iron (was it iron?) and dust. He imagined their thunderous charge at full pace. What were such creatures? Where had they come from? What was their purpose here? They didn't feel like they belonged in this world at all. They were discordant, impossible, absolutely *wrong*, as if they had walked in from somewhere utterly different, somewhere cruel and dark; they brought the atmosphere of that other place with them, spilling it, a foul icy breath. Their utter strangeness froze his heart.

I am afraid. No one could look at them and not be afraid.

If they came tonight he would fight them. If they came, he would die, Castrel would die, their unborn child would die, and their house would burn as Ersett burned.

And if they did not come, in the morning he and Castrel would leave: the two of them, travelling together. No, not travelling, running. Fleeing for safety, though they didn't know where was safe, nor how far they must go. Khaag and Paav had run far and hard, but they hadn't escaped, and when they died, what they ran from was less than a day behind them.

Sometimes it slows. You get ahead of it for a while. But it follows and it does not stop. It never, ever stops.

Khaag said that.

In the night he and Castrel had tried to make a plan, but what plan could they make? They had no friends they could go to, and no family: Bremel had already been an old woman near death when Castrel left Weald, and his own childhood home at Harnestrand was six months' journey away. They had no one and nothing else, only each other and what they could carry, and that was all. But they would manage fine. They would find somewhere to be safe and start again. Castrel was strong. She was all fierce hard courage and determination, all the way through. She was a wonder. Shay had seen her do impossible things.

And himself? His strength had never been tested, not really. But he would try. He would be a good man. The best he could be.

He listened again to Castrel's quiet breathing. He had said he would wake her to share the watch, but he let her sleep on.

I will protect her. I would give my life for her.

His love for Castrel was his strength, it was the core of him, it was his iron and his fire and his blade and his rock. In the end it was all there was of him, all that mattered. And it would be enough, because it must. He was afraid, but he had been afraid before, and he knew that fear was only a feeling, like hunger or thirst: they were only feelings that told you what mattered and what you must do.

In the first grey light of dawn Shay went out to make ready Khaag and Paav's cart. There was a lot to do, and quickly. Withdraw in good order before the enemy. He had done that before. He knew how.

He took only what they would need: the remains of their bread and the large cheese Parran gave Castrel last time they were in Ersett; their flour, their beans, apples and vegetables from the loft; the cooking pot; logs and kindling; axe, spade and hoe; their few wool blankets and the brass bowl he kept for himself when he was foraging for Adma Corse. The rest had to be left behind, though each decision a fresh small grief, a kind of bereavement. He had few possessions of his own: nothing but a leather jerkin, a pair of good boots and his knife. For the first time since he walked away from Hage, Ridder and Vess, he wished he hadn't left his sword behind and he missed his three friends: they would have been good companions on the road.

After much hesitation he took the crib he had made for the child and stowed it carefully on the cart.

When Castrel woke, Shay watched her move about the room collecting her own private things and putting them in her satchel. She took pouches of dried leaves, berries and bark; jars of earthy pigment; strange small artefacts of twig and fine bone and grass; a lump of some dark-scented waxy substance he didn't recognise. She was turned inward with her thoughts, calm, measured and determined. Doing what must be done. She said little.

When she was ready, she climbed up on the cart and sat murmuring to the unborn child. Shay couldn't make out the words. Strange whispered syllables – hedge-tongue, he guessed. There was a world inside Castrel that he didn't understand and could not share. She was still as mysterious to him now as she had been when he first came to live with her, when he first heard those quiet mysterious words she spoke and sang, first saw the strange things she gathered and kept on shelves or hung from hooks, first saw the marks and signs she carved into her house and sometimes drew on her skin. Castrel was connected to the world in ways that he was not: and that was his joy, because she was connected to him also and he was connected to her by a sharing bond that would not be broken, ever.

Shay finished loading the cart and went to fetch the cob mare from the byre. She was painfully thin and there was little strength in her, but she accepted the harness patiently, without complaint. When he had finished, Castrel rubbed fragrant grease into her sores.

'She's weak,' she said. 'She's not ready for this.'

'I know,' he said. 'But what choice is there? We need her, and she'll be better off with us than if we leave her behind alone.'

When they were ready, Shay took the bridle in his hand and they set out together. He walked beside the mare, keeping her company, letting her set the pace. Castrel rode in the cart.

'Ride now, walk later,' he said. 'Keep your strength for the child. We may both need to walk before the end.'

'Don't worry,' she said. 'I'm tired from yesterday but I'll be fine. We'll be fine.'

'Yes,' he said. 'We will. I know.'

She smiled then like she sometimes did, so that her whole face creased with beautiful life and warmth. There was courage and determination there but no grief, and she was not afraid.

The bar of ominous darkness still spread out on the northern skyline, distant behind the trees. It was a brooding shadow line, like an approaching change in the weather still far off. Was it closer than yesterday? Shay watched it until heavy cloud settled lower and obscured it from view.

They went without knowing where they were going, setting out with no destination except south, somehow south, because no other direction made sense; though first they would swing wide to the west for a few days, avoiding Ersett and whatever dangers might still linger there. Not a good plan, but the best they had. They would be all right, they would get through, they would find somewhere safe until this danger, whatever it was, had passed. And then they would come back.

Shay led the cart along narrow, sunken lanes. The fields in that part of the country were separated by ancient raised banks and hedges. The banks had been walls once, built of rocks and small boulders, and in places the foundation stones still showed through – blocks of grey and purple rock, crusted with yellow and rust-coloured lichen – but centuries of earth and turf had covered them, and ferns and small trees had taken root there. The banks were riddled with holes and entrances. Shay knew all the animals that lived there – the foxes, the badgers, the mice, the lizards, the labyrinth spiders – and he knew all the plants. Campion. Sorrel. Nettle. Hemlock. Briar. He knew the uses of them, their seasons, and which to avoid. He knew all this because Castrel had taught him, and the understanding she gave him had joined him to this place, it was like roots. But already he could feel those roots, a year and more in the growing, beginning to tear, loosen and separate.

It must be the same for her. But her roots go deeper than mine. This separation hurts her more.

At a crossroads they took the lane east towards Eaxten and Badget: villages that were names only; names and crumbling abandoned buildings. They passed the remains of derelict houses and barns, some of them fine and prosperous once. The fields beyond the hedge-banks lay waste and unused now, nothing but wide expanses of scrub, bramble and bracken. A winderel flew low and slow across the fields, spilling its liquid call, and the loneliness of that sound in the wide quietness cut him deep.

There were more people here once, many more, but they've all gone now.

So it went in all this raw borderland country, precarious and exposed between the southward woodlands and the strangeness of the high north. People moved in, settled and farmed and made villages for a while, and then something changed. Disease, storm, the failure of crops; they all came rolling through like tides and seasons. The people packed up and moved on and didn't come back. They found other lives elsewhere. That was how it was.

But we are not like those other people. One day we will return.

They had left the house neat and shuttered. It would survive.

All morning they followed the deep lanes, seeing no one. No sign of riders. No obvious danger. Once they saw a pall of yellow smoke: a single thread rising in the distance to the south.

'Something's happening over there,' said Castrel. She was sitting fierce and upright, back straight and strong, a blanket folded round her against the cold. 'It might be normal, just someone burning off stubble or clearing heather off a hill for grazing. Or it might be riders. It might be like Ersett all over again.'

'It's miles away,' said Shay. 'There's nothing we can do.'

Suddenly he wanted to be closer to her, and he climbed up on the cart to ride with her for a while. Castrel slid along the bench and took the reins. He felt her warmth pressing against him, shoulder and hip. Love and bleakness so full it hurt. The mare accepted the additional burden willingly and hauled on.

All the rest of that day they saw no one, and when dusk fell they stopped for the night at the side of the road, at a place where a small brook spilled through a broken, mossy culvert. They lit no fire, ate cheese and hard bread, and slept on rough grass in the lee of the cart.

Around noon the next day the sky cleared and lifted, turning a high, cold powdery blue. The bruising on the northern horizon stood out against it, a band of stark and lucid purple the width of Shay's palm when he held it at arm's length. The shadow had a clear-defined edge now: a thin crest of misty lesser darkness.

It looked like a mountain-high distant wave approaching – one of those gigantic single waves that could sweep in off the open ocean and smash against the coast, overwhelming and destroying everything.

'It's getting higher,' said Castrel. 'I'm sure of it. It's higher than yesterday.'

'Do you think so?' said Shay. 'Maybe it's just that we can see more of the skyline from here. It could be bad weather coming. Whatever it is, it's a long way off.'

Towards the middle of the afternoon the lane broke out of a copse at the top of a long shallow descent. Some distance in front of them was a lone figure, walking in the same direction as them. A bulky man, bareheaded, a mass of thick grey hair spilling across his shoulders. He was moving slowly, limping under the weight of a large pack.

'Gean!' said Castrel. 'Shay, it's Mamser Gean.'

Shay's heart lifted to see their friend alive. Someone at least had escaped the slaughter at Ersett. And he was going their way; they would have a companion on the road, at least for a while.

It didn't take them long to catch up with him. His limp was slowing him, and when they got closer he turned and waited for them. Shay was taken aback by how huge he was. Head and shoulders above the hedge-bank. Until now he had only seen Gean in his forge and smithy-yard in Ersett, and he had seemed a large man then, but out here in the open he was enormous, broad and solid as an oak, his face and his fists carved from chunks of stone. The sword he carried strapped to the pack on his back seemed longer and heavier than a normal man could swing.

Gean's face split into a broad grin as they came nearer. Castrel climbed down from the cart and ran to hug him. She looked small and slight against him, almost like a child. Shay shook his hand, smiling broadly. Iron-hard, Gean's fist smothered his: it was like shaking the paw of a bear.

'A grand meeting,' said Gean. 'I was hoping that whatever befell Ersett hadn't come through your way.'

'We saw what happened at Ersett,' said Castrel. 'Your forge was burned, but we didn't see you among the dead. There were so many, though ... we couldn't be sure ...'

'I wasn't there. The attack was before I came down from the cabin. I saw the smoke, but by the time I got there ...' He scowled darkly. 'I wish I had been there. I may be old and slow now, but I'd have made them pay a price. I'd have taken some with me when I fell. It's my shame that I did not.'

'There's no shame in that,' said Castrel. 'There was nothing you could have done. Whatever did that to Ersett, it wasn't ...' She hesitated, searching for the words. 'There was a power there ... I don't know what it was, but it wasn't ... natural. Not human.'

An odd look came into Mamser Gean's eye.

'You do not know me,' he growled. 'Not entirely.' He looked at Castrel thoughtfully. 'But you're right, there was a stench of foul, unnatural magic there. And you would have picked that up,' he added, almost to himself. 'Of course you would.'

It struck Shay as an odd thing for Gean to say, and the way he said it was odd.

'We saw who did it,' he said. 'A few of them, anyway.'

Gean looked at him sharply.

'You did? Tell me.'

They told him then about the riders, hooded and larger than human on their six-legged beasts. They told him about the blaze of light in the night, and the shrieking in the sky. They told him about Khaag and Paav too.

'This was their cart,' said Castrel. 'Their cob.'

'I noticed her,' said Gean. 'Didn't think you'd keep a beast in that condition. Not you.'

Castrel told him what Khaag had said. Her warning about the riders, and the fear, and the line of darkness that was always coming and never stops.

'So ...' said Gean thoughtfully when he had finished. 'This is a new thing to me, though there have been stories for some time about bad things in the north: rumours of stragglers on the roads; people in a poor state, running south. You hear a lot of talk, as a farrier.' He glanced at the darkening northern skyline. 'But it takes a lot to frighten the bear-people.'

'You've met bear-people?' said Shay, startled.

Gean nodded.

'In my time. One or two.' He looked to the north again. 'You're doing right to get away. Where will you go?'

Shay shrugged.

'South,' he said, 'as far and as fast as we can. We might be walking into trouble, but what else can we do? We don't know what the danger is, or where to go that's safe.'

'We need to know more,' said Gean. 'We must find news.' He considered for a while, then: 'Walk with me a while. I want to think.'

Gean walked a long time in silence. He seemed to be struggling with a difficult decision. Shay took the mare's bridle and they followed slowly, Castrel riding behind. Neither of them said anything. Shay watched Gean's broad, massive shoulders as he walked. He seemed changed, somehow. Different. It was a puzzle. There was more to their friend than he'd thought.

At last Gean seemed to come to a decision, and stopped to wait for them to catch up.

'Something is coming that I've never seen before,' he said. 'Something big. And when it hits, whatever it is, it will hit hard. I have decided to go somewhere I haven't visited for a very long time. I thought I would never go there again. It may be that the place is not even still standing any more, but if it is, the people there will know more of this. I will make my way there.'

He paused and looked at them thoughtfully.

'You are good people,' he said. 'And you are with child.' He took a deep breath. 'You could come with me, if you wish. And perhaps you might stay there a while, until your child is born. You should be safe there from whatever is coming.'

Something in the way he spoke made Shay think this was more than an ordinary offer. It was as if the decision to make it was costing Gean a lot. But Shay felt a huge weight lift from his shoulders: a place of safety to head for, and a strong friend and guide on the way!

'I should warn you,' Gean added, 'it will be no easy journey, though no harder, I suspect, than any other you could take.'

Yes! Shay wanted to say. He wanted to grin and embrace Mamser Gean. Of course they would agree to this. But Castrel? He wasn't sure how she would feel, and she must be the one to decide. He looked at her, the question in his face.

'What is it, this place you're going to?' she said to Gean.

'It's called Sard Keeping,' he said. 'A fortress, of a kind. At Sard they'll know what is happening in the north and elsewhere. They can tell us where is safe country and where is not. And they have their defences too. The Keepings have endured dark times in the past, when nothing else did. The Keepings have held firm for thousands of years.' He frowned. 'Though Sard is the most far-flung of them all, and their numbers were dwindling, the last time I was there. There was talk of abandoning Sard altogether and going somewhere less isolated. I hope they have not.'

'How do you mean, isolated?' said Shay. 'How far is it from here?'

'Hard to say,' said Gean. 'A week or two's journey, perhaps.' He looked doubtfully at the cob. 'Depends on her. We'd need to take a high route. Old drovers' roads, and then a track along a ridge of hills.'

'I've never heard of Sard,' said Castrel. 'I've never heard of anything east of here at all. I thought the land in that direction was all impassable wilderness.'

Shay had never heard of anything eastwards either, and he had scouted widely and thought he knew this country better than most.

'I've never heard of a Keeping at all,' he said.

'You wouldn't have heard of it,' said Gean. 'Sard Keeping is in the High Esh. One of the hidden countries. The High Esh is not a region where humans go. You wouldn't find your way there on your own. I believe no human ever has.'

Shay stared at Mamser Gean, astonished.

The hidden countries? Not a region where humans go? What is he, then? What is he talking about?

It crossed Shay's mind then that Mamser Gean was crazy, but one glance at that solid, massive man, and the calm frankness in his eye … he was not crazy at all.

'So,' said Gean. 'Will you come? I hope so. Frankly, I'd be glad of the company, and I wouldn't mind a ride on that cart, just now and then. My leg's not so good for a long haul any more.'

Shay fought back a kind of panic. He didn't know what he'd expected, but not this. When he and Castrel had made their decision to run, they didn't know what they were running from, or how far they must go, but at least he'd understood what running would be like. In some way he and Castrel were still in control. But now Shay felt even that was slipping out of his grip. The world was changing too fast around him. He didn't know what to do. He looked at Castrel to see what she was thinking.

'You do know, don't you, Mamser,' she said quietly, 'that we don't know what you're talking about at all.'

5

'Our way is the same as yours,' Castrel said to Mamser Gean, 'at least for a while, whether we take your road in the end or not. Come with us for today. We can talk more as we go.'

'Of course,' said Gean. 'You'll need to think about it. I understand that.'

Castrel caught Shay's glance at her.

'Yes,' said Shay. 'Sling your bag in the back. Ride a while. Take the weight off your leg.'

Gean looked doubtfully at the mare.

'Aye, well then, perhaps for an hour or so.'

He hauled his weight up onto the seat. Castrel made room but stayed on the seat beside him. Shay took the bridle and walked ahead, close enough to hear their talk.

'Tell us more about Sard Keeping, Mamser,' she said. 'You said it was a fortress.'

'It is a fortress, of a kind,' he said, 'but also more than that. When the Keepings were founded, they were outposts of the great empire of Oskhandy. They were places for lawgivers, clerks, intelligence collectors, engineers, soldiers; they were hospices for travellers and frontier fortresses in time of war; and most important of all, each had a group of wizards. A cabal.'

'Wizards?' said Castrel. What did Mamser Gean know of wizards?

Gean didn't answer directly.

'The empire that built the Keepings collapsed and disappeared,' he said, 'but some of the Keepings themselves survived, and without an empire to run the wizards gave themselves a different purpose. They set out to preserve the power and knowledge of their fading civilisation and diminishing peoples. They turned the Keepings into libraries of a kind, vast collections of everything important, and they set strong wards and protections about them to keep them safe. They called it their Great Work, and Sard Keeping was part of it. The remotest Keeping of them all.'

'And it's only a week for two from here?' said Castrel. 'But I've never heard of it. I've never heard of any of this. The hedge-witches know nothing. There are no stories. But we *would* know. We'd know *something*. It would be *important*.' Bremel would have told her. Such knowledge was always passed down. 'How is that possible?'

'Because all that I've said happened longer ago than hedge-witches can remember, or any humans. When the first human settlers came to this country centuries ago they were latecomers. This land – I mean the whole of this continent, all the thousands of miles of it, from the ice and forests of the far north to the shore of the great southern oceans – was already ancient then. There had already been civilisations here, vast empires, great cities and their dominions, rising and falling for thousands of years.'

'You mean the others?' said Castrel. 'The older peoples?' She had seen their crumbling ruins – the traces of cities and structures built by unknown hands, by people with other ways of thinking and crafts no longer understood. 'But apart from the bears in the north, they were all gone long before the first settlers came. They found the whole continent empty and deserted.'

'No,' said Gean. 'It wasn't. Not entirely. As humans spread out, the other peoples withdrew and diminished, until they lived only at the margins, in borderland countries where the new settlers never went. Those were the hidden countries – the Free Cities of Ost and Horrow, the Braided River, Sellaverane, the Dominions out of Khall, and many lesser names – and the other peoples lived on there, though their numbers continued to fall. They had ways of keeping the settlers out. Humans never even realised the hidden countries were there. The High Esh where I am going is such a place. Ersett was right at the boundary, about as far-flung a border settlement as humans ever made, though they never quite knew it.'

'But the bears weren't hidden,' said Castrel. 'Humans lived in the northern forests among them and even loved them. People like Khaag are partly human and partly bear. That's what I thought, anyway.'

'The bears were always different,' said Gean. 'They went their own way. There is no hidden country in the far north, and there never was. Few humans ever went there, anyway.'

'Are you saying,' said Shay, 'that the other peoples are still living in the hidden lands? They're still there, even now?'

Castrel could see he was excited. Mamser Gean had thrilled him. Stirred his imagination.

'There are still some,' said Gean. 'Yes.'

'What are they like?' said Shay.

'You would find them strange. They live longer and think differently. Some of them are extraordinarily beautiful. Tall and slender and strong. Others not so much.'

'I think I saw people like that once.'

Shay told Gean about the White Knives.

'That was a rare glimpse,' said Gean. 'They must have had a desperate reason, to show themselves like that.'

'But they were magnificent!' said Shay. 'Why would such people hide themselves away? They can't have been afraid of us.'

Gean frowned.

'They wouldn't have been hiding only from you. They would

fear other enemies. There has long been war in the hidden countries. Stupid, unavailing, desolating war. Obliviousness kept humans out of all that, and you should be glad of it.' He paused. 'But also, yes, they are afraid of you. Humans have never been numerous in this continent, but elsewhere it's been a different story. You do not willingly share your world with otherness.'

Castrel studied Gean as he sat beside her and talked. Opening herself to him. Observing. There was a profound, surprising strength in him. His life burned clear and deep and slow and strong. He was different, not like anything she had known before: a little like Khaag, perhaps, but it was difficult to compare. Khaag had been dying. What kind of man was he? His strangeness puzzled her, but there was no doubting the straightforward honesty of his heart as he spoke.

'If this is true—' Castrel began.

'It is,' said Gean.

'But how do you know so much, Mamser? You said humans never knew about the hidden countries, but you've been there, at Sard Keeping. How? Why you?'

'I did live among them, once. I was even a soldier in their wars. But I left all that behind a long time ago.' Castrel thought he looked sad. Grieving. He hesitated. 'But I've already said more than I should. Such things have always been hidden, and for good reason. These are not my secrets to keep or spill, as I choose.'

'You can trust us, Mamser,' said Castrel. 'You know that.'

She sent a flow of warm reassurance out to him, wordlessly, the way she did with wary animals. She did it unthinkingly, a reflex, but it washed over him and passed on like water over a rock in a stream. Castrel was taken aback. Some people were firmer and clearer in themselves than others and less easy to affect, but she'd never encountered such imperviousness before. Gean caught her eye and smiled wryly. She saw only goodwill and kindness there.

He did feel it, she thought, astonished. *He knew what I did. He simply brushed it aside.*

She felt almost ashamed, as if she had done something presumptuous.

'I've already decided to trust you,' said Gean, 'or I wouldn't have said anything at all. More than trust you: I am offering to take you there with me. It's right that humans should go there. The time has come for that. Old ways have to end. But I've said enough. Come with me to Sard Keeping if you wish. The choice is yours.'

He reached into the back of the cart for his sword, unwrapped it, and began to hone it carefully, silent and lost in thought.

Remembering, thought Castrel. *Sad memories. I'm glad he is our friend.*

The sun was sinking towards the western horizon. They came to a place at the crest of a slope from where they could see what lay in front of them. A little further on the lane veered sharply to the south for no particular reason, as if it were avoiding something, and disappeared into the distance.

'This is the border of the High Esh,' said Gean. 'The hidden country begins here.'

Westward, where the lane did not go, the country rose into low hills. Crags of bare rock pushed up through the grass there, raw and dark like the last stumps of ancient eroded mountains, and the crags glowed a dull red in the late afternoon sun. To Castrel they seemed to shimmer with quiet power, making the hills slightly hazy. It was difficult to gaze in that direction for any length of time: she felt an odd instinctive urge to look away from that inaccessible land. She'd felt nothing like that power before. It was strong but barely perceptible: she wouldn't have noticed it without Mamser Gean pointing it out, but she was sure that if they had come here alone, they would have given those hills a wide berth and turned gladly to go south with the lane.

'It's hard to look steadily at those crags,' she said to Gean. 'There's a strong power warding us off.'

'That's only at the boundary. Once you're inside the feeling will pass.'

'Do you feel it too?'

'Not the same. It draws me in. For me it feels like coming home.' He looked at the sky. 'The light will fade soon, and this is a good place to camp. Tomorrow I'll be leaving these lanes to go by other paths. If you choose not to come with me, our ways part here.' He climbed down from the seat and stretched his back. 'It's been a long time since I walked in the High Esh. It was wild, empty country then, and can only have become more so. I think it is our best hope, but I can promise you nothing. As I have said, I can't even be sure Sard Keeping still exists. I will go, but as for you ... the choice is yours.' He collected his pack from the back of the cart. 'You need to talk now. I'll return later. Tell me what you decide.'

He walked away down the hill towards an ash copse, where a stream was tumbling across rocks. He seemed to Castrel even larger now than when they had met him on the road, and already he was limping less. The open space of the landscape suited him. It was as if he was expanding into it and coming more fully alive.

'We've seen no sign of riders,' said Shay when Gean had gone. He was looking warily up at the High Esh. 'Perhaps we're out of danger now. Those hills look hard going, and we shouldn't drive the cob too hard. Nor you, either, not with the child coming. Mamser can go where he wants, but I think we should stick to our plan and carry on south.'

'You're avoiding the hidden country,' said Castrel. She smiled wryly. 'It has that effect on me too.'

Shay looked startled. He stared at the hazy ridge and the

shimmering outcrops of rock, red like rust and dried blood in the westering sun.

'You're right,' he said. 'Just looking at them makes me feel it's impossible to go there.'

'It's the wardings,' said Castrel. 'But that doesn't mean you're wrong. About sticking to our first plan, I mean. If that's what you think?'

'How can I know what to think?' said Shay. 'All those things Mamser was saying about hidden lands and people who aren't human … it's difficult to accept, difficult to know what to make of it. And Mamser himself … he's not who we thought he was …'

'No,' she said, 'he isn't. But there's nothing but truth in him, and he means us well, I'm sure of that.'

'So we go with him?' said Shay.

Castrel knew he would do what she said, because he believed she understood all this better than he did. She felt a pang of anguish. *But how can I know? What if I choose wrong?* Three lives hung on her choice.

Gean had opened a door for them, a door into strangeness, hidden countries and wizards' high magic. It would be easy to turn away from all that and go south, but if they did, they might be choosing to walk alone into suffering and death, like Ersett or worse. Or they might be safe; they might even go home and be ordinary again. But either way, the door Gean had opened would be closed, and no such door would ever open for them again. Whatever happened afterwards, they would always know that: always there would be this other path, which they might have taken but didn't, because she was afraid.

The braver risk is best. Courage chooses courage.

The northern skyline showed a dull copper shadow, tinged with veins of green at evening. That ominous darkness chilled her and made her feel slightly sick. She had to do what was best for the child. Only that mattered in the end. She felt her daughter move inside her, so full of new life and awakening future.

'Yes,' said Castrel. 'Let's go with Mamser.'

Shay grinned.

'Good,' he said. 'I think so too. I want to see this wizards' Keeping and this hidden land.'

6

Gean led them up into the moorland and fells of the High Esh. He took a path that seemed to wander, following the lie of the land, going nowhere in particular. They went by scarcely discernible tracks, grassy and rutted, along the tops of ridges and through wide, shallow valleys. He walked alert and massive alongside the cart with his vicious heavy broadsword across his shoulder, while Shay ranged wide, covering many miles, scouting ahead and behind like he used to when he was with Hage, Ridder and Vess.

Shay saw little life or movement on the hills. There were lone kites and ravens circling high, watching for carrion; pale day-flying owls like moths; and sometimes a yellow fox, or a distant buck disappearing over the horizon. Once he found a hill where berries grew low across the ground. Whinberries. Cloudberries. Tiny dark wild strawberries. He filled his pouch and carried it back like a prize.

Their progress was slow and the landscape never changed, and sometimes Shay wondered if they were going anywhere at all. But the days were fine, if bleak, and they saw nothing of riders or any other danger. Yet always the band of dull copper haze rose out of the skyline in the north and hung there all day, and he and Castrel watched it uneasily.

'I think it *is* getting higher,' she said. 'Yes, it definitely still is.'

*

Day followed day, unchanging, merging into one. They turned south to follow the spine of a ridge of hills and the track became a paved road, broken and overgrown. They saw no one, and no sign of settlement. No threads of smoke against the sky. All they had seen of civilisation since they entered the High Esh was a few deep grassy ditches, some mounds of fallen masonry lying in the grass, and once or twice the ruins of broken towers and walls on a distant escarpment. How long was it since anyone had lived here? When did travellers last pass this way?

Long after Castrel fell asleep, Shay lay awake in the dark of the night listening to the silent loneliness of the High Esh: all those miles of emptiness and nothing. He was worried. The food they carried was getting low, foraging brought nothing but berries, and fresh-running water was getting harder to find. They were cold and hungry and the long days of relentless walking were taking their toll. Castrel was thin, almost gaunt, and so was he; yet they would need to start rationing their food more sparingly soon.

Day after day the mare walked resolutely on, slow and patient, hauling the clumsy weight of the cart, stumbling in ruts and over stones, her bony shoulders leaning forward as if she shoved against a heavy wind. She was almost fleshless, the working of her haunches, her ribs, all the raw shapes of her skull, painfully visible, and her sores were not healing. She grazed when she could, but they were going into ever higher country where the grass was sparser. Castrel did what she could, and rode in the cart as little as possible, but she needed to keep her strength for herself and the child. The mare went willingly but the guilt of it pained Shay cruelly, and worse was the fear that she would collapse and fail. Without her they would be in serious trouble. He knew it could happen any time.

At least Gean seemed to get by on eating almost nothing, and if anything he grew even heftier. He didn't limp at all now and his thick mass of hair was more lustrous and less grey. And Shay's fear of the riders had receded, though he was still uneasy. They must always keep watch. They must be ready to fight. He kept his axe with him, always within reach. But day rolled into day, and still they saw no one, and seemed no nearer Sard Keeping.

'Where are the people?' Shay asked Mamser Gean one evening, when they had lit a fire and set out their camp. 'We haven't seen a single soul, only ruins.'

Gean frowned.

'It's as I told you,' he said. 'The hidden countries have been fading for hundreds of years, and the wars have killed many. All the same, I was expecting we'd have seen someone by now. I don't remember it like this.' He shrugged. 'Still, it's a long time since I was here. Perhaps the way is further than I thought. We'll find people when we get nearer Sard Keeping. I hope so.'

'How much further is it?' said Shay.

'A week or so, perhaps, if I remember right.'

'The wars must have been very terrible,' said Castrel, 'to empty the country like this.'

'It was bad,' said Gean grimly. 'Though war came because the lands were failing, rather than being the cause of it. The wars grew out of desperation.'

'What were they about?' said Shay.

This was the most willing he had seen Mamser Gean to talk, and he wanted to hear about the hidden countries and the peoples there. Coming here had stirred his old longings for otherness, strangeness and wonders. Pennants glittering in the sun.

'It was a wizards' war,' said Gean, 'fought between factions and cabals. They enlisted the other peoples, on various sides, for this pretext or that, but who understands the true purposes of wizards? It seemed to me that they were fighting for sources of power. They saw their civilisation waning and sought the means to stem the ebbing tide. One faction thought they had the answer, and then the other must have it, so they fought: but always it came to only one thing, which was destruction and weakening and loss. The wars had been going on for centuries before I was born, and they still are, somewhere, I suppose.'

He paused, staring into the thickening twilight. Shay stayed silent, hoping he would continue.

'I do remember,' said Gean eventually, 'there was a dispute once about what to do with the human settlers. Some were for engaging them in the struggle, some were for keeping you out of it entirely, and some wanted to turn on you and drive you out of the continent altogether. But nothing ever came of that, one way or the other. I don't think it was ever a crucial point of contention.'

'But you fought?' said Shay. 'You took a side?'

'Yes, I fought for one of the cabals for a while. There was no choice – we were caught up in it. I lost my friends. My family. My children. Everything. All lost in that futile destruction.'

Gean's face was shadowed in the deepening darkness. Shay couldn't make out his expression, but he could hear the pain in his voice.

'Mamser?' said Castrel. 'You had children? I didn't know. I'm so sorry.'

Gean grunted and changed the subject.

'After that I wanted nothing to do with the hidden lands. Let them destroy themselves and subside into ruin if they choose! I thought that then, and I think it now. The future is you. Your people. Your child.'

You? Your people? The same question came to Shay again. What was Gean, if not human?

'I had thought I would live out the rest of my life at Ersett among human folk,' Gean was saying. He laughed grimly. 'But now even that choice has been taken from me.'

'Do you mean that what happened at Ersett is part of the wizards' war?' said Shay. He looked towards the dull lurid copper in the northern sky. 'And that too? Is that the hidden lands' war breaking out into the rest of the world?'

Gean looked doubtful.

'My instinct is not. It feels different. Altogether larger in scale than anything I've heard of before.'

'There was some power at Ersett,' said Castrel, 'but I don't think it was wizards' magic. I don't know much about it, but to me it seemed something more ... I don't know, there are no words ... but not wizards' work.'

'The riders you saw and those six-legged beasts are new things to me,' said Gean. 'I hope we'll learn more when we get to the Keeping.'

If we reach the Keeping before the food runs out or the mare collapses, thought Shay, *and if we find a welcome there, and if its defences are stronger than what's coming from the north ...*

The next morning they crested a hill and the road began to descend sharply. Castrel gripped Shay's arm.

'Shay,' she said. 'Look!'

The road was lined with tall standing stones. They stretched for miles, all the way to the horizon, angular and rooted, stained black and crusted with ancient lichen.

When they reached the first one, Castrel hurried across to get closer. She stood in front of it, head tilted to one side as if she were listening. The stone loomed above her, three times her height. She laid her hands on it and leaned in to rest her forehead against it, gently. She stayed like that for a long time. Eventually she pulled herself away and passed on down the line, briefly touching another, and then another.

Shay and Gean watched her, saying nothing. When at last she came back her face was shining.

'They're alive,' she said. 'There's a presence in them, a watchful-ness, and each one is different. Every stone one has its own feel, like its own voice, they hum and crackle with it, and I can feel their roots reaching into the earth. There are slow strong tides of life down there, deep down in the rock beneath us, and the stones are rooted in it. I felt it. I shared it. The stones shared it with me.'

'Not many can feel that,' said Gean. 'I never have. I've been told it's like feeling the heartbeat of the rock.'

'It is,' said Castrel.

All the rest of that day they walked between the lines of tall standing stones, and when towards evening they left them behind, Shay could see she was deeply moved.

That night Shay and Castrel lay awake together under their blanket and looked up at the stars. Mamser Gean was snoring softly where he slept on the other side of the cart. Shay could hear the mare somewhere in the darkness, cropping the thick, coarse grass.

'Shay?' said Castrel quietly.

'Yes?'

'You didn't feel them, did you? The stones, I mean.'

'No.'

'Not even a little?'

'No,' he said. 'Nothing.'

'Nor could Mamser.'

'No.'

'But our child could.' She turned on her side to look at him. 'She responded. It was wonderful. The life of the stones was run-ning through her and she had a voice too, just like them. She was reaching out to them, and they reached out to her. She was so *alive*, it was like she was full of sunshine. It was a sharing, Shay.' He could sense her elation. 'Do you see? Do you understand what I mean?'

'I think so.'

'She has the gift, Shay, and much stronger than me or Bremel, I'm sure of it. She's going to be all right. Whatever happens she's going to be fine.'

She didn't say any more for a long time, until Shay thought she was asleep. Then her quiet voice came again in the dark.

'We did the right thing coming here,' she said. 'It was the right choice, wasn't it?'

'Of course,' said Shay. 'It was the brave choice, the only good one. We'll be fine. All of us.'

She moved closer to him, her warmth against his side, and he slipped his arm under her head so she could rest there.

'Can you feel the child?' said Castrel. 'She's restless. She's kicking. Do you feel that?'

'Yes,' said Shay, and he thought he did, though he wasn't sure.

The road descended into lower, waterlogged country, and became a track winding through lurid green bogs between tangles of sallow, alder and osier. They forded small rivers and followed the miry shores of shallow pools and small lakes. A misstep would sink them up to their knees in cotton grass or send them splashing through reed beds. Several times the cob stumbled and the cart had to be shouldered back onto the track. Gean did it with ease. In the distance they could see the steep jagged hills: upright blades and vertebrae of rock, blackened like the charred logs of extinguished fires.

'The Keeping is in those hills,' said Gean. 'We are close now.'

A staniel slid across the sky, low overhead. A slide, a pause, a flicker of wings; a slide, a pause, a flicker of wings. Patient and slow the cob mare bore on, and they went with her, at her pace. It seemed to Shay that the hills would take them weeks to reach.

*

Every day they watched with growing disquiet the bruised and copper-purple darkening in the northern sky behind them. Higher and closer, rising perceptibly each day now, it loomed above them, rolling onward at a discernible pace, swallowing the world as it came. A curtain rising out of the north. A swelling wall advancing. An immense approaching wave. It reached almost halfway up the sky, a thunderous damson weather, immensely, ominously deep.

All the birds they saw now were always flying hard, low and straight towards the south.

'How much longer till we reach the Keeping?' Castrel asked Gean.

'Not long,' he said. 'A few more days.'

But he looked worried.

'The air has changed,' said Castrel one morning. 'Do you feel it?'

Shay stopped and looked back. The cob mare shifted uneasily from foot to foot. Shay felt anxiety knotting his stomach and raising the fine hairs on the back of his neck.

'Yes,' he said.

There was a stress at the unseen edge of things, heavy and oppressive, as if the skin of the day prickled; an atmosphere like dry thunder building, tenser and tenser, rising to a lightning crash that never came.

At midday a current of warm, stifling air rolled down from the north. It pocketed them in enclosed quiet, in mists and soft downpours. Distances folded and horizons faded. Rain on earth. Rain on leaf. Rain on stone. Warm, brown, corroding rain. The ground turned to treacherous mud and flattened grass, greasy under foot. Muddy streams swelled and pooled behind shallow accidental dams. Rain trickled down Shay's face and stung his eyes.

73

Gean complained that his sword was rusting, dulling the edge of the blade. He sat in the cart and wiped it repeatedly with a damp rag, cursing under his breath. The same rust was on the mare's bridle, the bolts in the cart, the axe that Shay carried slung on his back. Rust that came back as quickly as he could wipe it off. He remembered the ruined, crumbling metals in the ashes of burned Ersett.

When the rain eased it left the world quiet and sodden and misty brown. Shrouds of rust-coloured fog drifted; they seemed to be rising out of the earth.

They came to a stretch of stagnant water, shallow and unreflecting in the mist. It smelled bad. Shay saw movement under the surface, a rippling wave that breached. The surge and lift of a huge aal in the shallows. It hurdled and thrashed, a sleek oily glisten of sliding, slate-shining muscle, thicker than a man's waist. The water was too shallow to cover it. Shay couldn't work out how it had got there. It seemed certain it must be stranded in the end. It would suffocate, drowning in air.

Castrel wrapped her arms across her heavy midriff in a gesture of protection. Shay wondered if she knew she had done it.

'Are you all right?' he said.

'There's strangeness everywhere,' said Castrel. 'A fraying … a closing … a decline … the sun is weak, the air … This isn't ordinary weather. It's as if the weather of the world's feeling has changed. What's happening? What is this? This horrible bleakness in everything …?'

'I don't know,' said Shay. 'But we're strong, and we're together. We'll be all right.'

'We'll reach the Keeping soon,' said Gean. 'But we must hurry.'

Shay scouted ahead, climbing a low hill that rose in front of them to see what lay ahead. Suddenly there was a shrieking from behind him. Castrel's voice in the fog, screaming harsh syllables, angry and frightened and fierce.

Shay ran.

Heart pounding, panic rising in his chest, lurching and jumping, stumbling, covering the wet and treacherous ground as fast as he could, always on the verge of falling, axe in hand, he ran.

Castrel! Castrel! No! Oh, please no, no!

There was nothing but coarse tussocks and mist and scrubby trees and Castrel's distant screaming. He was afraid he had lost his direction.

Then he crested the slope and the track was below him.

A prowling shape was circling the cart. A large beast, vague and shadowy, half-obscured at the edge of the fog. As Shay watched, it came nearer, taking form out of the mist. Solidifying.

At first he thought it was a rider, a six-legged beast. But it was not. It was a creature of this world, though he'd never seen one like it before. It was immense. Tall as a man at the shoulder, and twice as heavy. Its haunches were masses of bunched, sliding muscle. It was stalking the halted cart as a cat stalks, but it was heavy-chested and snouted like a dog, nostrils flaring to test the scents on the air. Angry and hesitant, a deep growl rumbling in its throat.

Castrel was standing upright in the cart now, screaming harsh hedge-witch syllables and making shapes with her hands. The beast hung back, uncertain. Glaring at her.

Where was Gean?

There was no sign of him.

'Castrel!' yelled Shay.

He began to slither down the steep, rough slope, shouting all the time, trying to distract the beast. But it ignored him. Its eyes were on Castrel. Shay could see it was gathering itself. Preparing to charge.

Suddenly Mamser Gean came lumbering out of the mist,

swinging his immense sword. There was a kind of joy in him. Even at that distance Shay could feel it. An incandescent careless fierceness. *Kill or die.*

And Gean was huge. Taller than the hunting beast, he made it look slight compared to him.

The creature spun, snarling, and charged at Gean, jaws open at the level of his face. Gean swung his sword wide in a two-handed sweep and slashed across the beast's exposed throat as it leaped, then stumbled aside, following the weight of his own stroke.

The beast collapsed heavily in a widening pool of its own dark blood. It lay there, moving its legs weakly. Trying to raise its bulky head.

Gean stepped in and flicked the sword again. Spilled its belly open. Eviscerated it.

The three of them gathered round the dead creature. Shay, standing next to Castrel, was conscious how small the two of them were compared to Mamser Gean. His own head didn't reach Gean's shoulder. Surely it hadn't always been so? It was as if their friend had grown taller and heavier.

Gean crouched to examine the massive carcase.

'I've seen beasts like this before,' he said. 'She doesn't belong here. Her home is the forests of the far north, at the edge of ice. She's been driven out of there like your bear-people were. She was desperate. See how bad her condition is?'

Gean lifted her head a little to look at her more closely. He was very gentle. Her jaw gaped wide in a death snarl. Yellow teeth. Her heavy claws were whited ivory, like a cat's. She was emaciated and obviously diseased. She had been beautiful once, her rough wiry pelt brindled yellow and brownish black, but now horrible greyish tumours crusted patches of balding skin. She must have been starving and in pain, and so very far from home.

'Brave courage mother,' said Gean. 'You died well.'

Giving her his respect, thought Shay. *There's something wild in Gean that answers her wildness. This is new. It wasn't there before. At least, I didn't see it.*

'The bear-people call them pinecats,' said Gean. 'I'm sorry I had to kill her. It would have been better to drive her away.'

'She would have stalked us always,' said Castrel. 'You had no choice.'

'Maybe,' said Gean.

Shay wondered how long the pinecat had been stalking them already, and if there were any others out there in the mist.

Gean stayed behind to bury the creature he had killed. When he caught up with them, they camped for the night and he built a large fire to roast a piece of meat he had cut from her. It smelled richly, darkly pungent as it cooked. The light of the fire made a small bright circle where they gathered, surrounded by darkness, night silence and walls of drifting mist.

'Will you share?' Gean asked them when the pinecat meat was done.

'No,' said Castrel. 'Thank you, no.'

Shay shook his head, though the scent made him hungry, and his hard bread, turnips and beans seemed thin fare in comparison.

Gean ate his meat slowly and with care.

'I eat her, and her strength joins with mine,' he said quietly. 'She continues through me, and her strength lives on.'

He spoke softly, as if it were a kind of offering. Almost a prayer. When he had finished he sat in silence, staring into the fire.

'What are you, Mamser?' said Shay quietly. He sensed Castrel grow still. She was listening intently. She didn't say anything and she didn't move. 'You're not human, are you?' he continued. 'You've as much as said that. But if not, well, what?'

Gean didn't look up from the fire.

'My father was human,' he said in a low voice. 'My mother ... well, she was different, she was from a place very far to the north of here, the kind of place where the pinecat came from. My mother's place was called ...' He made a guttural sound, not human syllables at all. Shay heard it as something like *Yoahk-rharhk-hkaym*.

'You mean she was one of the bear-people?' said Shay. 'Like Khaag and Paav?'

'No, my mother was not a bear. Her people were ... Well, they are all gone now, and their country is empty. She died a long time ago, and she was alone then. She thought she was the last of the ones like her, and she probably was. I never heard of another. There is a human word – not for what she was, but for a similar idea. But I will not use the human word, it's crude and wrong. My mother was wise and beautiful, full of elegance and grace and agility, although she was very large.'

A giant? thought Shay. *He means she was a giant. And he is a giant too.*

But he said nothing. He didn't want to speak clumsily.

'Mamser?' said Castrel after a while. 'There are many peoples in the world who aren't human. Or at least there were. That's right, isn't it? There are bears, and wizards, and people like your mother, and the people Shay saw, that he calls the White Knives. And ...' She hesitated. 'And others?'

Shay was taken aback by the intensity in her. The concentration as she spoke.

This means a lot to her, he thought. *This is leading somewhere.*

'That's right,' said Gean. 'Though there are few now, almost none even in the hidden countries, as you have seen.'

'And then there are people like you and Paav, who are partly human and partly not?'

'Yes, though I don't like to say *partly* human. It's as if a human who's also something else is less than fully human because of it.

I'm not *partly* human. I'm not part this and part that, or part anything. I am this and also that. I am myself.'

'So being human and also something else, that's always possible? It happens often?'

'Ever since the first human settlers came,' said Gean. 'Humans have this habit of drawing lines and making rules and boxes. So many of you like to say, only this is the way to be us: if you are not this, you are other; if you are this, you cannot also be that. But it's a stupid and fearful way to think, and also, as a matter of fact, wrong. Humans are the most porous and variable of all the peoples. If there is a defining characteristic of humanity, it's borderlessness: that's how humanity always grows and changes, even as other, older peoples like my mother's fade.'

'*She continues through me, and her strength lives on,*' said Castrel gently. 'That's what you said.'

'Life always goes on,' said Gean. 'Life flows and changes and learns and grows. Unless,' he added grimly, his voice filled with grief, 'unless the children die.'

I had forgotten, thought Shay. *Gean lost his family. He lost his children. They died and he's alone.*

His heart went out to him then, full of grief and love for this lonely giant of a man. Their friend.

Gean looked up suddenly from the fire and fixed them with a fierce glare.

'You must protect your child,' he growled. 'Above all else, that. Whatever comes, that. Look to the child.'

'Yes,' said Shay. 'We know.'

Gean nodded.

'I think you do. You are good people. That's why I brought you here.' Then he looked at Castrel and said in a softer voice: 'But that's not what you had in mind when you asked me about it. You were leading up to something else?'

'Oh,' said Castrel hesitantly. 'I'm sorry. I was thinking about myself. I've always wondered about … my gift … my sharing … and why hardly anyone has it. Neither my mother nor my father were like me. I had a friend called Bremel once, and she taught me a lot, but I never met another like her or me. So I wondered if … Well, if there might be something not human about us? Me and Bremel, I mean. And my child. Our child.'

Shay's mind lurched. That Castrel was more than human, and their child also … The idea crashed into his head and shifted everything. He felt a surge of love and joy.

Gean frowned.

'Perhaps so,' he said to Castrel. 'Does it matter?'

'I think it does,' she said. 'I want to know. I want to understand.'

'Maybe.' Gean paused, as if he was looking for the right words. 'Look,' he said eventually, 'I'm not one for giving advice. I've already urged more on you than I feel comfortable with, and I'm sorry for it. But I'd say, let yourself be who you are, if you can. You don't need to look for limits and definitions, and your child doesn't need the burden of your stories that you tell about her.'

Gean raised himself to his feet then, a shadowy bulk in the firelight, and carefully set the remains of his meat in the fire to burn.

'Too much talk,' he said. 'Rest now. Things turned bad today, and we must move hard and fast tomorrow. The Keeping is within reach, but we have to make haste if we're to reach it at all.'

Shay's head was still spinning with newness and a kind of excitement.

He is a giant! And Castrel is a hedge-witch. And our daughter … what is she? What will she become? And though I am only myself, I will be relentless: I will be their scout, forager, protector and support. I love them, and I am not stupid or weak, and together all of us will come through.

He felt a thrill of hope then. The obstacles that even a day ago weighed him down and seemed so huge – they could be overcome. There was magic in Castrel, and in their daughter who would soon be born; and a giant was their friend and would stand by them. The future was possible. Gean swept aside the pinecat with a single swing of his sword.

'Look to your child. Above all things, look to your child.' Gean is right. Nothing else matters compared to that.

Soon they would reach the magical Keeping in the hills and be sheltered there, safe from the coming storm.

7

Shay and Gean slept, but Castrel stayed awake in the night to keep the fire burning. She could sense things moving beyond the firelight, out there in the fog and blackness of the night. There were snufflings, low rumblings and grunts. Heavy footfalls, like weighty cold beasts padding at the hunt. Faint distant voices high in the air: inhuman voices; scraps of incomprehensible words in the wind.

Shay had gone to sleep brimming with new confidence and hope.

'We'll get there,' he'd said several times the night before. 'We can do this.'

Castrel had felt a surge of love for him then. It was like hunger and sadness, but warm and strong. He was a good man. But there was a wrongness here that she could feel deep in her bones, even if Shay could not. This hidden country was failing. The power she had felt in the standing stones had gone deep into the earth, though she guessed it had been everywhere once, and the magic in the border hills was very old. She had sensed that. But that was not all. The wrongness had got worse since the rain and mist came, and it was worsening all the time. The weather of the world's feeling. A terrible corroding bleakness at the heart of everything. Fear in the night. It was coming from the north.

She wove a net of safety around the unborn child, enfolding

her enclosed world in reassurance, welcome and love. Shutting all the bleakness out. She felt the small life stir lazily, sleepily, and respond. Her daughter was there, and she was well. She could feel the bright wholesome warmth of new life growing, eager, transparent and strong, and each day was bringing her birth closer, though she was still tiny and fragile, much too small to come yet.

The mare whickered unhappily and dragged at the bridle rope Shay had staked in the earth. Castrel went to soothe her and rub her down. Her coat was matted with sweat, though the night was cold.

'You have such courage, darling,' she whispered to her. 'These night-crawling fears aren't new to you, are they?'

Whatever was out there in the dark, Castrel saw nothing. Nothing ever crossed the line into their dim firelight. But she knew they must reach safety and shelter soon. The situation was getting desperate.

Next morning the mist was thick and chill. Castrel breathed it and tasted it in her mouth. It clung in her clothes. Her hair. Her face. Because of the mist she couldn't see the darkening bruise rising up the northern sky, but she knew it was there and coming closer. Closing their world.

Gean went striding ahead, showing the way, his sword on his shoulder, wrapped in cloth, a huge burly figure indistinct in the mist. Coming to the High Esh had released something in him: the hidden country was restoring him to strength, or making what he had always been more visible and real. Castrel wasn't sure which it was, but either way Mamser Gean was so much stronger now than he had been when they met him. He was a giant. He grew even as the world around him weakened.

*

83

The day was half over when the track lifted out of marshy country and became a long straight road: ancient paving, forging ahead into the distance, climbing gently. The mist thinned and they could see the spread of the land in front of them. Narrow bridges and causeways, engineered from weathered mossy blocks of stone, crossed a silvery threadwork of rivers, pools and bogs. Beyond that there were high hills ahead. Almost mountains.

'I know this place,' said Gean. 'See how straight they built this road? They drove it across the land, bridging and clearing. It's not just a road, it was meant as a sign. The Perpetual Empire of Oskhandy. There is only one road, and only one way. It's about certainty and purpose. A road built to last a thousand years. The Keeping is near. We'll reach it tomorrow.'

Castrel looked out across the wide emptiness.

'Mamser?' she said quietly, falling into step beside him. She had to look up to see his face. 'You said there'd be people when we got nearer the Keeping, and I thought we'd be seeing them by now, but we haven't even seen a building; only a few ruins, and all of them very old. Where is everyone?'

Gean's face clouded. He looked a little puzzled.

'I've been thinking about that, too. Things have changed here. There was more life in the High Esh when I was here last.'

'How long has it actually been?'

'About a hundred years,' said Gean vaguely. 'A hundred and twenty? Something like that. Perhaps a little longer. I'm not entirely sure.'

A hundred and twenty years? Castrel looked at him in astonishment: his massive body burning with strong slow life; his thick long hair, no longer greying as it had been in Ersett.

'How old are you, Mamser?'

'Not so old.' He paused to think. 'I was still a young man when I left the hidden country. I suppose I might be around a hundred and fifty now. It's not something I've thought about much. Counting a life out in years is a very human obsession.'

'So you haven't been in this country for more than a century?'

He shrugged.

'Thereabouts. Perhaps longer.'

Castrel's head spun. What might have happened in Sard Keeping in that time? He'd warned them he couldn't promise what they'd find there, but they hadn't fully grasped what he meant. How could they?

Why didn't he say this more clearly at the time?

He never meant to deceive us. Perhaps he didn't fully remember himself. He's changed so much since we came here.

Twilight gathered and fogs were rising again. They came to the brink of an expanse of dark water that stretched away to the horizon, and the road became a causeway, a low ancient bridge that ran dead straight for miles, out across the silent, misty waters. They could see no end to the causeway and no further shore.

Where the causeway began there was a single pillar of stone about thirty feet high at the edge of the road. It seemed to glow in the dusk, but not with light. The air prickled with its presence. It was watchful. It knew they were there.

Castrel was wary of going too near. Unlike the long lines of standing stones on the ridge of the High Esh, this column was not rooted in the heart-rock of the world. It stood on a square block of purple-veined stone, and it was covered with strange geometric patterns carved deep into all its faces. Not weather-smoothed, free of the lichen that grew on the parapets and cracked paving slabs of the causeway itself, it looked fresh as the day it was first set there.

'This is wizards' work,' she said to Gean. It made her feel queasy. She could almost hear the voices of those who made it, as if they were still there. 'This is harsh, strong magic.'

A damp cold breeze came rolling in from the lake. Castrel

shivered and pulled her blanket tighter around her. She was hungry and tired. She needed to rest soon.

'The first warding-stone of the Keeping,' said Gean. 'It has stood here unchanged for five thousand years. The bridge runs for miles across the lake and the Keeping itself is on the further shore, but this is the threshold. The protections begin here, and beyond this we are safe.'

He took a few steps forward past the high pillar and on to the causeway.

'Watch,' he said, with all the gauche pride of a child.

Suddenly all the miles of the low, straight bridge were illuminated with a weak bluish-white light. It was lined with widely spaced lamps: rust-pitted iron sconces holding globes of glass. The globes flickered with faint warmthless flames that reminded Castrel of marsh-gas fires.

'Come on,' said Gean. 'Follow me.'

The long lines of lamps created a tunnel of light in the thickening mist, and outside the tunnel across the water all was darkness. They walked on, their footsteps and the wheels of the cart echoing back at them from the stone parapet on either side.

'This is ... incredible,' muttered Shay. 'A miracle.' He took Castrel's hand, his face bright with wonder and relief. The long journey was nearly over. 'Isn't it something to see?'

'This is the Skywater,' said Gean. 'In a flat calm, the surface is so smooth and still that it reflects the sky like a mirror, though the waters are dark and deep and cold.'

'Is it salt?' said Shay. 'Are there tides? It's wide enough to be a sea, but it doesn't smell like the sea. It smells like the north, and faraway places.'

'A lake,' said Gean. 'It holds the meltwater from the ice of high mountains. Many small rivers feed it from the north, and one great river called the Arker drains it to the south, many miles from here. The Arker flows down out of the hidden country and all the way to the southern ocean thousands of miles away. Once, you could have taken a boat from here and crossed the entire continent. But that was long before the human settlers came.'

'I wish we could see it in daylight,' said Shay.

'Tomorrow you will,' said Gean. 'We won't cross all the way tonight, but there are places we can rest.'

Castrel walked in silence with the mare, listening to Shay and Mamser Gean's chatter. The faint wizard-light of the lamps made her uneasy. She had a strange feeling she was moving but making no progress, as if the long miles of the bridge were an illusion, and the lake not really so very wide. Perhaps the apparent length of the crossing was a magical defence, or it made reaching the Keeping a penance. A ritual labour.

'Last time I was here the Skywater was alive with waterfowl,' Gean was saying. 'Rain goose, ember goose, swan. Lairblade. Kirrmew. Lorin. Fish-eagle and harrier. Hernshaw and drumble in the reeds. Starling flocks so numerous they blocked the evening sun like clouds of smoke. But it's all quiet now.'

He described the wonders of the Keeping: the donjon tower of the Northwatch Oriel, with its immense bronze model of the heavens and its watch-glass trained on the sky. The Collection Rooms, where examples of all things, living and not, were assembled and studied. The Reading Rooms. The Beast Gardens. The Pharmacopeia. And he talked of the great bell Sounder, which must be rung at the same time each day, the same hour when all the bells in all the Keepings in all the hidden lands would ring at once, to harmonise with the Answering Bell in the Mother House, which was called Charm.

'No one may speak while Sounder rings,' said Gean, 'because that's when the wizards in all the Keepings join minds. That's how they share knowledge, so all the volumes in all the libraries become One Book.'

A sharp breeze rose and the mist thinned. Beyond the lamps there were stars in the sky, and the black waters glittered faintly. Ripples slapped quietly against the piers of the bridge. In the distance Castrel thought she could make out distant high towers and jagged hills, but she wasn't sure. She stopped listening to Gean's talk and walked on ahead.

She was wary of this high magic. What kind of welcome would they find when they reached the Keeping? But she could see Shay was caught up in it, and her heart went out to him. He looked so tired, his face drawn with constant worry and weather-hardened from the long journey, but his eyes were bright and keen as he listened. He'd left home as a boy to search for otherness, strangeness and wonders, and now in the hour of greatest need he believed he was finding it at last. But wizards' high magic had no place in Castrel's hedge-witch world, and she had no place in theirs. Nor did Gean's vision fit with the terrible darkness and change bearing down on them from the north. Could wizards' magic stand against that? The wizards had already retreated into these hidden lands centuries ago – hidden lands that were bleak and emptied now.

At last they came to a place where the bridge widened on both sides to form a platform. It was deep night.

'We'll stop here,' said Gean. 'This is about halfway across, I think. There are still miles to go, too much for the mare in this dark. She's exhausted.'

'So am I,' said Castrel.

'There's a watch-house a little further on. It'll be garrisoned. We'll get a good welcome there.'

Gean walked ahead, confident the long lonely journey was nearly over.

They came to a cluster of stone buildings and a gated wall

across the road. The windows were dark. The gate hung open on a broken hinge.

'We haven't been challenged.' Gean sounded disconcerted. 'There's no one here. They've grown slack since my last visit. No matter, we can sleep tonight and go on fresh in the morning. You go in. I'll see to the cob.'

They didn't argue.

'How are you?' said Shay, when they were alone in the starlit dimness of the guardhouse. There were bare wooden cots and a table in the centre.

'Tired,' she said. 'The child is very still. I can hardly feel her.'

'You don't have to walk tomorrow. You could ride on the cart. There's no rush now. We're nearly there.'

Castrel smiled wearily. She was hungry but too tired to think of eating.

'Mamser Gean's a good friend,' said Shay. 'I'm glad we came with him.'

'More than a friend. He saved our lives from the pinecat, and he's brought us where he said he would. He couldn't have done more. What comes of it next, though—'

'We'll be fine. I know we will.'

The wind was rising. It blustered and buffeted outside. Castrel slept heavy and deep on the chill flagstone floor.

She was woken by a heavy hand shaking her shoulder. It was Gean, his face tight with shock and fear.

'Quick!' he hissed. 'Quick! You have to go! Now! You have to *run!*'

'What—?'

Dulled with sleep, Castrel struggled to clear her head. The first grey light of dawn was trickling through gaps in the shutters and spilling through the open door.

'Now!' said Gean. '*Now!*' And then he was gone.

Castrel dressed quickly.

'What is it?' Shay muttered, alarmed, still more than half asleep.

'I don't know,' she said.

They followed Gean out onto the bridge. There was a hard wind swirling and gusting, and the mists that had shrouded their world were gone. To the south, the bridge led away across wide black waters towards a mass of towers and walls, and there were dark hills behind them. The Keeping was perhaps half a mile off, much closer than Gean had thought. But it was difficult to make out details. The whole edifice seemed to shimmer in a haze, a hidden place within the hidden land.

Then Castrel looked to the north, and her heart lurched with blank, sickening fear. The purple bruising loomed over them now. It had risen like an immense wall. It covered most of the sky. It was clearly and unmistakably a wave, many miles high. Impossibly high. Colours moved within its strange deep light like swirls of oil under water.

And it was moving. Surging unstoppably on towards them. Even as Castrel watched, it crept across the rising eastern sun and cast the whole world into lurid purple light. The sun showed dim and murky through it, a pale corroded disc like a tarnished coin. Closer and closer the great wave was coming, swallowing up the country, swallowing the sky. A scouring tide. It was travelling at the pace of charging horses. It would be upon them in an hour, maybe less.

It would swallow them whole.

'Go!' Gean was yelling. 'You and Shay, go!'

He had already put the cob in her traces. She was frightened, shifting from foot to foot, her ears laid back. Eyes staring wide and black.

'What about you—?'

As Castrel spoke, vivid blinding flashes erupted behind Gean at the northern end of the bridge. Incandescent blue light burning fierce. Although it was several miles distant, Castrel felt the air around her crackle and hum. The whole bridge vibrated under her feet.

'It is the defence,' said Gean. 'The Keeping's wardings. It may hold them back.'

'Hold what back? Who?'

'Don't you see them? There are riders. Many riders. They're already on the bridge, and they have some other creature with them.'

Castrel squinted into the distance, but she could see nothing but flares of bluish brightness and the vast loom of the approaching wave of sky. Then came a thunderous, deafening detonation that shook the whole bridge, and the brightness went out.

'They've broken the first wards!' yelled Gean.

As Castrel's sight cleared, she made out the tiny dark shapes of riders on six-legged beasts on the bridge, coming towards them. And following them, larger than they were, a heavy lumbering form was edging forward. Even at this distance, she could see it was being hampered by the narrowness between the parapets. The leading edge of the wave was close behind the riders, and racing closer.

Shay was standing at her shoulder. He had his axe in his hand.

'Come on!' he was yelling at Gean. 'We've got time. We can reach the Keeping before they're on us.'

'You go!' shouted Gean above the gusting wind. 'I'll hold them here. There are weapons and munitions here. I know how to use them, but you do not, and you haven't the strength. I can slow them down, at least. It will give you more time. Go now, or you won't make it.'

He began working a massive winch handle near the guard post. It took all his weight and strength. Heavy brass wheels set into the stone of the bridge turned slowly and there was a rumbling of heavy stone against stone. A row of pillars like the one at the bridge entrance, smaller but carved with similar markings, inched up from among the paving slabs, creating a barrier across the bridge. Castrel felt the tense shimmer of wizard magic gathering.

'We won't leave you,' said Shay. 'You can't stand alone against them. Come with us.'

'No. Save yourselves. Save your child. The Keeping is stronger than the bridge wards. It will hold them back, but you need time to reach it. Don't be fools. Go!'

'Mamser ...' said Castrel.

He looked her in the eye.

'Go,' he said again. 'You have to look to the child. Let me do this.'

And she went then, because she must, because she knew Gean was right. She climbed onto the cart and took the reins.

'We'll wait for you,' she said. 'Come when you can.'

But he was already unwinding the cloth from his immense, heavy sword. She could see in his eyes he didn't expect to follow them.

'I'll hold them as long as I can,' he said.

The cob was starting to panic. Castrel hauled on the reins and did her best to calm her, but she bolted as hard as she could, her hooves slipping and stumbling on the mist-slicked paving. The cart lurched off towards the Keeping, not at a gallop but faster than it had ever gone before. Faster than it was built to go.

'Shay!' Castrel yelled. 'Come on! Run!'

He jogged alongside and jumped aboard.

They turned to look back at Gean. His giant bulk was striding off the other way down the bridge, and beyond him the immense tide of squalling purple light rose high in the sky. Visibly closing in. Castrel could feel its pressure surging, a catastrophic alien wave. It was like a pursuit in a nightmare: slowly running from an enemy they couldn't escape. The cob scrabbled headlong, hampered by the clumsy weight of the cart, with the approaching wall of appalling change reeling them in. It felt like the end of the world coming.

Mamser Gean disappeared from view.

Castrel became aware that rain was falling. Thick pellets of sour rain, thrown in her face by the gusting wind like fistfuls of stone. It soaked her and blackened the paving. The cob was lunging forward. Castrel gave up trying to control her and hugged the unborn child in her belly in a vain gesture of protection. She channelled to the mare what strength and calmness she could muster. It wasn't much. The cart was jolting wildly. It seemed impossible it would not crash.

Shay jumped down and ran forward. He seized the mare's bridle, trying to calm her and keep her course straight. What he did made a difference. In the last extremity they would abandon her and the cart and all their possessions and run. But they still had time. They would make it.

The Keeping was closer now, and Castrel saw it more clearly. Walls, towers and domes rose out of low ground, surrounded on three sides by craggy hills. It was all built from massive blocks of slate-blue, green and lilac rock. Rock the colour of storm clouds. It seemed as ancient as the hills that nursed it, yet it had an insubstantial quality. Damp walls glistening in the wet, it seemed itself a thing made out of rain.

Castrel looked over her shoulder to see if there was any sign of Mamser Gean. As she turned, screams of rending, tortured stone shattered the air. There were blinding flashes like sustained lightning glare. Where they had slept last night, now she could see nothing but incandescent blue burning. Then a wave of prickling energy swept across her. It smelled of heated metal and rock and the strange tang of magic.

When the dazzle faded she could still see the riders advancing, much closer now, and that other massive beast still followed, loping eagerly forward, its heavy shaggy head swaying low between bunched shoulders. And behind them the terrible wave was consuming the bridge and surging on. Its leading face was a sheer cliff of dark light. She could not see the top of it. It disappeared up into the rain clouds.

'Shay!' she yelled. 'There he is! There's Mamser!'

He had appeared from nowhere, just in front of the riders. He stumbled towards them, stooping with the weight of something heavy and massive in his arms. She couldn't see what it was, but it was large. As Gean set it down on the bridge and stepped a pace back, the leading rider charged him down. Castrel saw the rider's weapon sweep wide and strike Gean's neck.

She felt a wordless, sickening despair as she saw him die.

Then, just as the riders came past it and on towards the Keeping, the thing Gean had placed before them erupted in a blinding, deafening detonation of wizard-tainted magic. When Castrel could see again, that whole section of the bridge was gone. She watched the last length of stonework, fifty yards of it, crumble and collapse into the Skywater. Taking the riders with it, and the greater beast that followed them, and the body of Mamser Gean.

A sickening wave of grief rose in her throat.

Grief struck her in the belly like a fist.

She wanted to weep.

The riders were gone but the worse danger remained. The wall of a different sky engulfed the break in the bridge and the disturbed water beneath and continued rolling steadily forward.

Castrel could see it clearly now and hear it above the wind. It was a sharp-edged cliff of plum-coloured, plum-heavy thunderheads, bruised and damson-swelling. A scouring, world-darkening blade of strange rain.

And then the alien sky rolled over them and took them in.

Castrel felt a deep, appalling, bleak sickness. It crushed her. She sensed its nature, this terrible new light that was darkness. She realised it fully and clearly now. It came from elsewhere. It was nothing to do with life at all.

This will cover the world. Nothing will be the same. Ever.

Our world is over.

Shay, their home, their future, their unborn child ... nothing could stand against this. Nothing would survive.

Castrel felt the child inside her twist and spasm in agony. The pain of her child cut her with a deep inward shock: it was a blade of horror in her belly, and the worst of terror and despair.

My daughter!

The shock and pain she felt through her child left Castrel weak and dizzy. Retching. A dry choking in her throat. They were engulfed in deep tides of alien air. Murky swirling winds and flashes of purple and copper lightning. Bruised light and pulses of bitter rain.

In the midst of it all she vaguely sensed the mare almost buckle and fall, and thought the poor suffering creature would collapse, but Shay held her bridle and hauled her on. He walked upright, purposeful and strong, half-dragging the stumbling mare, leading them forward. He would not fall in the darkness, he refused; still he went on while there was hope and life.

Castrel clung on as the cart swayed and lurched, fists of corrosive rain punishing her face. They were only a hundred yards or so from the Keeping. She could see a gate ahead of them. They were almost there. But the surge of poisoned sky would be there before them, and when it engulfed the fortress their last hope of safety would be gone.

Yet somehow the Keeping stood. The cliff of new sky swept over and around the walls and towers and passed on, engulfing the hills, but the haze that surrounded the Keeping sparked and crackled, brighter and brighter, a strange canopy of high wizards' magic. A protection that shivered but held.

At least for now, it held.

For a moment Castrel was afraid that the magical barrier the Keeping had raised against the onslaught would shut them out too, but it did not. As they got near the gate they passed through a shimmer of fizzing, disorienting light and into calmer air. The storm still buffeted them, the rain still fell, but it was less here, and the weight of the sky somewhat less terrible.

There was a gatehouse in the foot of a squat square tower. The walls of the tower were covered with intricate geometric carvings, lines and shapes and circles, crisp-edged as if cut yesterday. Spills of rain flooded across it from guttering high overhead. The bronze gates were forty feet high, smooth and featureless, wide enough to accommodate eight horses riding abreast.

The gates were shut fast against them.

So it ended here. They had come so far, and failed.

They could not go forward, and they could not go back because behind them the bridge was gone.

Their world was engulfed in the cruel darkness of elsewhere.

Mamser Gean, their only friend and guide, was dead.

And worst of all, inside her she could hardly sense her unborn child. The painful spasms had eased, and her daughter was alive, she knew that at least – but she did not respond when Castrel reached out to her. Something was badly wrong there.

She didn't say anything to Shay about that. Spare him that, at least.

Shay stood in front of the huge bronze gates and stared up at them. Castrel climbed slowly down from the cart to join him. Just to be with him. She took his hand in hers and stood close.

'We did what we thought was right,' she said quietly. 'You did all you could. Nobody could have done more. I'm glad I came this far with you. You are the best of men.'

Shay cursed under his breath and shook his head.

'I will not give up,' he said. 'Not so close. Not now.'

He groaned and leaned forward heavily, pressing his hands and forehead against the many tons of metal that barred their way. And the gates swung effortlessly inwards at his touch, moving in smooth silence but for the whispering hiss of some hidden mechanism.

When they were inside the Keeping, the huge gates swung back into place at a single push, as easily as they had opened, locking together with a sense of final permanence. The sudden calm and quiet after the terror of the bridge was a disorienting shock.

They walked ahead without speaking. Castrel struggled to focus on what was around her and get her thoughts into some kind of order, but all she could think of was the silence and stillness of her child and the discomfort she herself was feeling inside.

This is not right. What's happening?

She was vaguely aware they were threading a way through a warren of narrow streets, alleys and walkways: towers and buildings all crowded together, built over and against one another, layer upon layer. The protections of the Keeping were holding. She looked up at the surge of purple, green and copper light overhead. It was like being inside a bubble looking out.

The bubble did not keep out the storm. Rain fell inside the

Keeping, heavy and sour. Gusts of wind eddied and swirled, and it was dark as evening although only an hour after dawn. Lamps like the ones on the bridges were burning pale and bluish, glistening on wet stone. There were spiked iron railings everywhere, twisted and tortured, rusting. An open space at the foot of a round iron tower was crowded with the gigantic ruins of collapsed engineering. Rusted heavy cogs and gears, taller than Shay. The walls of the iron tower were stained with black slime and long streaks of orange rust.

So much iron. I've never seen so much iron in one place.

They walked side by side in no particular direction, leading the mare slowly across slippery cobbles. They saw no one. No lights showed in windows. No voices called to them. No footfalls echoed except their own. There was no wizard cabal here. She didn't think there was anybody at all.

'Where are they?' said Shay.

'I don't know,' said Castrel. 'I think the whole place is abandoned.'

'But Mamser—'

'He told us what he hoped to find, but he hasn't been here for at least a hundred years.'

'Oh ...'

They had travelled so long and endured such hardship and what they had come for was not here, and Mamser Gean was dead. She saw the grief and despair in Shay's face.

'Mamser ...' he said again.

She looked at him, and he looked at her, and they said nothing because they felt the same and there was nothing right to say.

'We're not safe here,' he said at last. 'We aren't safe yet.'

'Better than outside.'

Castrel was still focused inwards, trying to feel for her unborn child. Was there a faint thread of life there? An awakening? A recovering of strength? Perhaps. She was afraid it was wishful imagination.

'This is a big place,' said Shay. 'Perhaps it's not entirely deserted. We should keep searching.'

'Later,' said Castrel. 'First we—'

She broke off with a gasp. Cramps tightened low in her belly: bitter, cutting pains. Suddenly she felt a new and terrible threat closing in.

Not that, she thought. *Please, not that.*

Shay must have seen it in her face.

'Cass?' he said, alarmed. 'What's wrong? What is it?'

She shook her head and said nothing. She hoped it wasn't real. She wouldn't tell Shay in case she was mistaken. She could sense the sickly, fluttering race of her daughter's tiny heart.

Not yet! She's not ready!

'Cass?' Shay was frightened now. 'What is it? What should I do?'

She waved him away and started walking, but suddenly she stopped, bent forward in pain. The cramps in her belly worsened sharply. Tight agonies seared across her lower abdomen. One after another, coming too quickly.

This shouldn't be happening. I must be wrong.

But Castrel knew what was happening all too well. Her daughter was coming. The birthing time was upon her. And quickly. And bad.

'Shay,' she said quietly. 'The child is coming.'

He stared at her in horror, struggling to take it in.

'Now? What? *Now?* Are you sure?'

'Yes. I'm sure. She's coming, and quickly.'

She felt another sudden lurch of pain. Too much pain. It wasn't right. Something had happened to bring this on. The storm. The wave of sick horrible light. It must be that.

I feel so weak.

She was too weak for this, and so was the child. Nothing was prepared.

I've been so stupid. I didn't think. I've done it all wrong.

We'll lose her, and it will be my fault.

The darkness was deepening. The storms in the upper air were loud and wild.

Part Two

8

Shay knew little of birth, but he knew the child had come too early and too small. He held her, this tiny crumpled shock of life, in trembling hands. She was a hot slippery thing of bird-bones and air. She had no weight at all. Wisps of hair were slicked across her little skull and her eyes stared wide in the half-light, soaking up the world. Shay was a heart pumping in darkness and firelight, so filled up with love and fear he could not think at all. How could she live? She could not live. How was it possible? And yet she must, and that was all there was.

Blood was drying on his hands and the child was smeared with it. He had cut the cord cleanly with the sharpened knife and tied it off, as Castrel said he must; but he had done it clumsily, hands awkward, numb with cold, fearing to touch, fearing to get it wrong. The birth-sac lay glistening and heavy where he had laid it aside. He could smell the blood, chill and heavy as iron in the enclosed space. There was too much blood. Castrel should not have spilled so much blood.

Castrel was a reef of silence. She had not moved since the child came. He reached out and put his hand on her brow. Hot and damp. She was burning. He touched her shoulder.

'Cass?' he said quietly. 'Castrel? Cass?'

But Castrel lay on her back, eyes closed, unresponsive, as if she were asleep, her face smooth and flushed with fever-shine in the firelight, her hair a heaped abundance of damp rope spread across the blanket. Her mouth was slightly open. Her breathing came and went, ragged and irregular.

'Please wake up,' he said. 'I need you. Please.'

She did not stir.

The child was making small sounds. She had a voice now: a faint throaty mewing, thin cries like no human sound, yet more human than anything before ever was. It was *her* voice, and it flooded him with desperate love and wonder like nothing ever had. It filled him, it choked him. His daughter was fully there in that voice; a whole new person come into the world, complete, raw and perfect, the essence already of everything she would be. Shay held her tight and close, sitting on the hard flagstone floor and hugging the frail body to his chest. She was so soft he could feel the bones inside her, rib and arm and hip, the articulation of every one. He put his mouth close against her tiny perfect ear. The beloved smells filled his nose and the taste of her was in his mouth. He would protect her for ever. He would keep her alive.

'Please,' he said. 'Hush. Don't cry.'

He put the tip of his little finger to her mouth and felt her lips and gums close on it urgently. A pad of flesh on her upper lip like a gentle tooth. She latched on to his finger and sucked at it, a rhythmic haul that got nothing but dryness. She grunted and squirmed. Dismay filled her whole tiny body. She was all writhe and silent squall.

He couldn't do this. He didn't know what to do.

She would die and Castrel would die.

He would lose them both.

He crossed to the waning fire in the hearth, the child tucked inside his shirt, close against his chest for warmth. The room was so cold. The stones of the walls and the floor breathed out a bitter chill that clamped his face and hurt his lungs. It passed through flesh, seeking bone. He put another piece of wood on the fire. It was damp, and smoked but gave no heat. The meagre woodpile in the corner was almost used up – soon he must go and fetch more. But not yet. The warm fragile bundle of bones stirred against him. He felt her pressing at him with her tiny, perfect fists. He felt her open mouth grazing across the skin of his ribs. She was making small sounds in her throat. He scooped a palm full of water from the bowl and tipped it against her lips. The coldness of it angered her, but perhaps she swallowed a little.

Castrel had not moved. Sound and touch did not wake her. Whatever had taken her, wherever she had gone, this was not sleep.

He crouched next to her and pulled the rough cover aside, smelling as he did it the sourness of her fever. She was damp with sweat and her skin glistened. The shine and plumpness of her face made her look so young, almost a child, erasing the signs of the last terrible weeks that had aged her and made her gaunt. He moved some strands of hair from her face and made her comfortable under the blanket. Kneeled and kissed her hot brow.

He loved her so much. She was everything. He had surrendered all of himself to her and loved her with an absoluteness that felt like hunger. Desperation. Sadness. Grief. And now he must turn all of it into strength, because although Castrel was stronger than he was and he had seen her do impossible things, for now there was only him.

He put the child against her mother's breast and guided her small mouth. The child grasped eagerly, moaning and pushing at her mother with those miniature hands. A dry, fruitless nursing. The thinness of Castrel's body pierced his heart. He was responsible for her now, for every visible rib, for the too-obvious shoulder, round and smooth like a pebble. Love. Protect. Defend.

'I'm sorry,' he said quietly. 'So sorry. I wish this wasn't happening. I would change it, I would give my life to do that, if I could. But nothing will change it now. All we can do is go on. Please come back to me. Please wake up.'

He lay down next to her, his cold body against her burning, and pulled the rough blankets up over the three of them. He put his arm across Castrel to hold the child in place at her breast, because that was better than nothing and there was nothing else to do. His daughter was so small he could almost cup her tiny satin spine in one hand. He stroked the curve of her vertebrae with his thumb. It was a fragile, wave-smoothed conch, cast up on the shore.

The embers of the fire were fading. Shay lay awake in the dark and listened to the storm. Wind gusted down the chimney, driving smoke into the room, scattering the embers and making the fire flare.

Three days the storm had raged. Three days while Castrel struggled and laboured, weakening, drifting in and out of consciousness, fighting to give birth to the child who insisted on coming but would not come. She had done what she could: marking her skins with signs and patterns; murmuring the ancient hedge-words as she worked, weighing each syllable, conscious of every breath; weaving the child ever closer into the core of her own life's strength. But she had been so weak herself, so sick. The struggle was costing her more than she could pay. Sometimes she shouted and screamed, and Shay was afraid of what the noise might bring. Were there hunters out there in the dark and the storm, prowling the strange alleys of the Keeping? The storm was no natural weather.

Sometimes Castrel would lapse into sleep, and Shay would cover her with blankets and lie next to her, cradling her head under his arm, feeling the fever-heat burning her as she slipped into darkness. And when she slept, he went out, forcing his way against the wind to find firewood and water, fetch food from the cart and tend the terrified mare in the stable. Their basement refuge was just inside the massive outer wall, and all around was a warren of what had once been yards, dovecotes, granaries and barns. There were laundries, the remains of kitchens, and walled spaces where herbs and vegetables had once grown. But there was no one there. Sard Keeping had been abandoned long ago. Whatever power protected it still held, but the world outside their underground room was deserted and submerged in bruised greenish-purple light.

And then on the fourth day their child had come – the wonder and terror of that! – but Castrel was hardly aware and fell immediately, before it was even fully done, into the deep inertness that still held her.

Shay huddled under the blanket, closing his body tight like a fist around Castrel and their tiny newborn child. The dim underground room was the single last fading point in a vast and aching darkness. He shut his eyes and pressed his face against Castrel's neck and slept.

And in his dream the whole world burned with pale cold fire and everything was ashen grey, licked with the flick and shimmer of small white flames. Whatever he touched was brittle and crumbled to dust in his hands. The world was prowled by hooded hunting riders on six-legged beasts. They moved slowly but never stopped. They followed him always, and though he hid behind walls and trees they were no protection; everything was brittle and the followers smashed through as if it was not there. He had lost Castrel, he had lost the child, he didn't know where they were. He ran and ran till his lungs felt they would burst but he could not find them. He panicked. He was alone, and they would die, and he would not be there.

*

He woke in terror to the sound of his own voice shouting. Heart pumping hard. He sensed the nearness of another dawn. Somehow, though no daylight reached them in the underground room, he always knew. The child was sleeping and Castrel lay still. He listened to the roughness of her perforated breathing and felt the heat of her furnace body.

Burning what fuel?

The basement room was so cold. Bitter and chill, far colder than before. Icy air clamped his face and hurt his fingers. There was white ash in the hearth and a few last glowing embers. The child could not live in this. She must have a fire. Wood for a proper fire.

He didn't want to leave them, but he must.

He stepped out into the freezing stillness of the Keeping and felt the emptiness of it pressing against him. It was colder than before. The three days' storm had ceased. Between crowded roofs and towers, shreds of copper light scudded across the first bleak greyness of dawn, moving fast. Dead silence echoed: he could hear his own breathing and the scuff of his boots on cobble and slab; the very ground seemed hollow. Everywhere was covered with a thin layer of grey ash. It must have fallen in the night like snow. Then he realised it was snow.

His anxiety was the settled surface of a deep lake: dark half-seen shapes moved beneath it.

Anxiety is a whetstone. Sharpen yourself against the stone of fear.

He hefted the axe in his hand; felt the smoothed shaft in his palm, the heaviness of the blade-head.

There was a patch of bare ground between broken railings. Sparse yellow grass and frost-hardened earth. With the axe he chopped a pit and buried the birth-sac and the bloodied rags.

*

He climbed a winding stair to a high place, as he did every day, and scanned the roofscape and the distant hills beyond the Keeping's outer wall. Slowly. Methodically. All the quarters of the compass. No thread of smoke. Nothing that moved. No sign.

Then he went to the stable block.

The chilled air in the stable was thick with the odour of mouldering straw and rotting beams. The mare stirred and whickered and took a step towards him, muzzling the distance between them, sifting the air for his warmth and scent. In the dimness she was pale and skeletal, her belly a distended barrel, the vicious crusted sores on her skin a weeping crop. Her huge passive eyes, shining like berries, black and slow, never left him. Shay ran his hand along her neck and resettled the useless blanket. She leaned in to his touch.

'Poor brave girl,' he said.

He looked away from her eyes. Those dark pools of trust and dependence. She watched him break the ice in the barrel and heave the last buckets of water into her trough. Then he swept the flags and scattered an armful of straw. It was grey and dusty. She browsed at it for something she could eat. Shay put out a few apples for her. There weren't many left.

When she had finished, he led her out into the grey light and bitter cold and hitched her to the cart. A scant wind stirred the grey snow and mouldered dust.

They clattered echoes as they wound through ancient streets, all rough brick and weathered stonework slick with ice and damp. Weather-blurred gargoyle faces crusted with lichen. Narrow passages and stone stairways leading into shadow. Mossy corners. Moss on the roofs. Slimy lead cisterns in the guttering. Wooden casks at the foot of long lead pipes, there to collect rainwater but frozen, rotted and broken now.

The water in the culvert ran black and fast. Slipping on ice and weed he lay outstretched, wetting his shirt front, and reached down to dip the bucket. Carried it back to the cart and emptied it into the cask. Time and again he did the same while the cob cropped at meagre sproutings of frozen grass between cobbles. His clothes were soaked and the strengthening wind was an ice-blade against his chest. His fingers were bone-white, numb like iron. Like thin stone.

The door was damp at the bottom and rotted soft, but in parts the timbers were sound. Shay swung the axe with a boat-builder's precision. This he knew how to do. It felt familiar and right. The blade bit near the hinge.

Five more hefts and the door fell inwards. He pulled it free, split it into plank-lengths and piled them on the cart. Then he moved to the next door and did the same. The third time, he split the planks smaller, lengthwise, into a heap of kindling.

Absorbed in concentration, warmed by the work, he went along the row, harvesting doors. Leaving a line of gaping thresholds like silent open mouths. Sometimes when he broke into long-shut rooms he surprised the scents of people who had lived there, still caught in secret pockets of air. It was as if they had just stepped out and were perhaps only in the next room. Such traces vanished when he entered.

With a full load of water and firewood, exhausted, soaked, chilled to the bone, he turned for home.

Home?

Fear gripped his belly and squeezed. Imagining Castrel dead.

Imagining the desolate lonely wailing of his naked child. And worse than that. Much worse.

I have left them too long.

Back in the basement Shay lit a fire, filled the bronze bowl with water and set it in the hearth to warm. Castrel was unchanged: unresponsive and hot with fever. He didn't think she had moved at all.

The child had kicked her cover off and lay with her eyes open, quiet and watchful, in her own soil, the smell of it oddly sweet. To his eye she was weaker: tiny, thin and frail, her skin mottled, bluish and purple-pink. When he lifted her she was ice-cold to the touch.

He warmed his hands in the dish of water he'd left in the hearth-ash, then cupped some in his palm and trickled it over the child on his knee. He washed her small body. With his fingers he touched the creases inside her elbows and knees and the soft folds of skin under her arms. Ran his palm across the smoothness of her skull. Held her face against his. An unresisting fragile animal. He wiped the crust from her eyes with a dampened corner of rag and dried her with the cleanest scrap of blanket he could find, and when she was dry he tucked her inside his clothes against his skin for warmth. She was so cold she chilled him.

He knew her face now. When he closed his eyes he saw her still.

The shock of the sudden existence of this child: nothing had prepared him for it. Everything inside him was moving. Rearranging itself. Structures that had always been there were breaking and shifting into new patterns. New things coming. A fierce new kind of love flowed up from somewhere deep: hot, raw, strange and unsettling. And fears, new kinds of fear. Fears he had not known before. There were strange expectant blanknesses too. What to do next had become urgent and mysterious.

He wanted someone to tell him how. He wanted Castrel. His need for her and the roaring ache of her absence dinned in his heart. His loneliness was a shining loudness in the dim room under ground.

The child shifted comfortlessly against him.

Hunger.

He laid her again at her mother's breast. She struggled without result to feed.

How long can a child live like this?

Not long.

Castrel was sticky and sour with sweat, and still smeared with traces of dried blood. He soaked a rag in warm water and washed her as best he could, cautiously, tender and awkward, conscious of the trespass. Gently touching the marks on her skin: those wild and strange interlacings of leaf and stem she had drawn on herself with red earth when she knew the child was coming.

Castrel understood mysteries. She had known and suffered things and been to places he would never know, and she would not tell him. He had seen her make things happen that astonished him and he had believed impossible. Her resources humbled him, yet there were darknesses in her that sometimes frightened him and made him shy.

Her eyes were closed. Her face without expression. For a moment he allowed himself to believe she had withdrawn inside herself deliberately. Gone on a journey to find the strength and healing she needed, for herself and for the child. He held a cup of water to her lips. Maybe a little went down her throat, he couldn't tell.

Cass. I need you to wake up now.

The rest of the day he watched over mother and child. He would do whatever it took to keep them safe. He would fight and kill.

There was no crime too terrible, no sin, no sacrifice too far. No suffering he would not gladly bear. What was needed, he would do. No limit.

That night he built the biggest fire he had ever made in the room. The wood burned hot. Flames roared up into the gaping mouth of the chimney: flickers of red and green and blue, sucked upwards in the brightness of the blazing heat. It was a furious, abundant, racing consumption of wood: breaking, snapping, bursting, flaring. The heat pressed its hands against his face, and draughts rattled the door and stirred and scattered the dust and litter on the floor. It was a mistake. Glowing flakes went flying up the chimney in a rushing pillar of heat and smoke. The pall of sparks and woodsmoke would billow out over the roof and trail for miles on the wind across the empty dangerous city. The fire was a shout. A clanging bell.

Here are here! We are here!

Fear welled up inside him.

What have I done?

But he could not be always afraid. Not always only afraid.

When he slept he dreamed of the giant man Mamser Gean.

I did what I could, boy, Mamser Gean said to him in the dream. *They're tough bastards, and quick, but I took the fuckers down.*

You did fine, Shay told him. *Best of the best. Thank you. I'm proud you're our friend.*

He woke. It was a lie. He had said no such thing to Gean before he died.

Before dawn, the second day in the life of their child, he woke when Castrel shifted under the blanket. She made small sounds in her throat, but if they were words he could not hear them. Perhaps the mumbled broken syllables of the hedge-tongue he did not know. Perhaps. Heart pounding, he cradled her close.

She was a slack warm weight against him, all aching thinness and bone, and the wool of the blankets smelled of her sweat. He saw how the skin was drawn tight across her face. He watched the pooling and flickering of shadows in the hollows and sockets of her too-perceptible skull. These days and these nights. It was impossible that she clung so fiercely to life. And yet she did.

'Castrel,' he said. '*Cass*. Our child is here. She needs you. I'm not enough. I can't … I'm not … She needs you. Come back now.'

He managed to get a little water down her throat. It spilled over her chin and soaked her chest. Cough and swallow. Cough and spill. Swallow. Not enough. But some. Did her fever burn less? He could not tell. In the roaring heat of the fire, perhaps it was only that he was warmer, and so she felt less hot to him. The intricate markings on her skin stood out livid and fresh. Almost it seemed to him that the room hummed with quiet magic, and they moved.

He ate a little food, his one scant portion for the day, then bathed the child again, cupping her fragile head in his palm. The skull was as small as an apple yet her neck could not hold its weight. There was a place at the crown of her head, a delicate opening in the bone. He could smooth it with two fingers and feel nothing but peach-soft skin beating with a quick rhythm, like a flickering second heart.

When he held her, all her bones seemed more prominent now. Those tiny bird bones. Her flesh was translucent in the fire glow. She lay quiet and passive in his arms, accepting the obviousness of how things were. Her wide, liquid, unfocused eyes reflected the roar and flicker of the fire.

The need and the trust.

How small should a newborn be?

He didn't know. But not this small. From somewhere, she drew a little life and strength.

But how much longer?

Always the same question. It came down to that in the end. How to measure this slow ebb? This agonised prolongation? His daughter had lived her whole life so far in darkness underground. She had never felt the spaciousness of air and light. And what if she never would? What if this brief passage in a dark smelly hole was the entirety of their gift to her, before she died?

When dawn came he went out into the Keeping again, and this time he took the child. The risk terrified him, but at least this way she would have one day outside, and if it were her last, then she would have seen the world.

By the light of the ashen sky he saw how weak she was. How freakishly tiny and pale. Thin and chalk-white and angular and strange. His love for her was an unappeasable hunger – a joy that would hurt him for ever.

She stayed quiet in his arms but her eyes were wide and avid. A pinched face peering from a clumsy bundle of rags: a tiny pale face he could have covered with four fingers. She was not puzzled. She seemed to *know*. She was open to the world and let it pass through her like a river.

She was a new thing that had come, unexpected and impossible, begotten out of love after everything else that was alive and good had died.

Holding her tight against his chest he walked with her through the winding alleys of the Keeping, past broken and decaying things skimmed with a scurf of snow, and as they went he kept up a constant flow of quiet talk in her ear. He told her about her mother. About the sun and the sea and grass and boats and how fruit grew on trees.

'We're travelling now,' he said, 'you and Castrel and me. We've a long road yet to go. We're resting here, but soon we'll set out again. And one day in the end we'll come somewhere, and we'll be safe there, and we'll have a house with windows, the three of us together, and I'll show you how to make things. I'll teach you to have clever hands, my beautiful sweetheart. I will.'

She couldn't know what he was saying, he knew that well enough. He talked so she would hear a stream of kind words flowing round her; so she would feel the warmth and welcome and loving gentleness of that. At least once, that. And he did it for himself, for the comfort of it, almost believing the tissues of hope he wove, though they were as flimsy as the child's fine dusting of hair.

A bank of heavy cloud-mass rolled low across the sky, closing it slowly like a lid, dimming the day to almost twilight. Shay looked up at the high tower that loomed massive and black over the rooftops, deeper into the Keeping than he had ever been. It was round and bulky, seemingly squat, but twice the height of any of the other towers. With its pinnacled dome-structure of iron and glass at the top, it was surely the donjon tower that Mamser Gean had talked of. The Northwatch Oriel. At least Gean had been right about that.

Shay's heart lurched.

There was yellow light in one of the high windows. It had never been there before. Someone up there in the tower had lit a lamp against the sudden gloom.

They weren't alone in the Keeping. He had to find out who was there.

He hurried with the child back to the basement room. Castrel was unchanged. Her skin was hot, her breathing ragged. The fire in the hearth had died and he dared not rebuild it.

He laid the child under the blanket with her mother in the dark.

'Please sleep now, sweetheart. Please don't make a noise.'

Leaving them alone hurt him so much. The fear and the grieving.

Something terrible is happening in the world. It feels like everything everywhere is dying. But while these two live, there is life, and if I lose them ... None of the rest matters, compared to them.

Outside the lamp in the tower was still showing, a tiny yellow light in a high window against the darkness of the sky. He navigated by it.

At first it was easy. The pinnacled height of the donjon was visible from everywhere, and all ways seemed to lead towards it. Avenues and lanes turned inwards from gates and towers, all striking more or less directly for the tower at the heart of the Keeping. He went cautiously, axe in hand, listening and watching, checking behind. Anxiety fighting with hope. But the nearer he got the harder it was to find his way; he seemed to lose his sense of direction and get turned around, confused. The Keeping was many layers of building and rebuilding. Fragments of older structures incorporated and reused for different purposes. Features no longer acceptable had been obliterated, but only ineffectively, and still showed through. Old buildings that had partially collapsed left fragments of half-buried masonry, and newer additions had fallen off, revealing what lay underneath. He tried several doors and alleys that went nowhere. Always he could see where he was trying to go, and the light still showing, but he couldn't get there, and he began to be afraid he wouldn't be able to find his way back. It was hard to keep track of time. He didn't want to leave Castrel and the child alone too long.

How long is too long? Any time alone at all.

At last he was near the foot of the tower, and through an archway he found himself no longer outside at all. This must be the precinct of the donjon. Dim daylight filtered down from high smeared windows and fell on flagstones and tiles. The floors were geometrical patterns of black and white under a litter of dust and dried leaves. An eightfold pattern of repetition. Where the daylight could not reach there were perpetual flickering globes. Lamplit passageways led deeper inside and arched stairwells went down into shadow. He lost all sense of direction, but he knew that where he wanted to be – the stair that climbed the tower – must be further inside. At the centre. The heart.

He entered a vast, high-ceilinged hall. There was a strange, rich smell. Sweetness and silence and dust. Echoes of his own footfall. The hall was filled with row after row of towering cupboards, taller than he was: rank on rank of them, diminishing into shadow and distance, so many he could see no end. They all had glass doors to show what was inside. Squeezing down the narrow passages between them, he saw they contained trays of beetles and rocks and stones. Eggs and nests. Skeletons. Skins. Horns. Antlers. Dried lizard skins and snake sloughs. Waxy dead creatures and parts of creatures in jars of straw-yellow liquid. Moths and spiders mounted on slivers of wood. Uncountable thousands and thousands of objects and fragments and dead things. Against each one was a parchment square with neat ink writing that he could not read. He did not know how. The carcases and skeletons of large creatures were suspended in shadow from cords and wires high above.

The massive cupboards themselves were built with a precision and fineness of work he hadn't known was possible – delicate hinges and almost invisible joints, glass thin and fragile as the first ice of winter, dark reddish wood polished to a perfect lacquered sheen – though they had been long neglected. There were clusters of tiny wormholes in the wood and spatters of chalky mess from birds in the rafters; rodents had gnawed their way in and left musty pellets and stains; many of the objects were chewed ragged and holed.

This was one of the collection rooms Mamser had told him

about. But what kind of people collected such things, and so many of them, and built for them such beautiful cabinets? What purpose could they have? Shay felt he was in the presence of strangeness and incomprehensible thought – he found it stranger than magic; stranger than giants and bear-people and pinecats; a way of dealing with the world he couldn't understand at all. He wished Castrel was with him, so he could show her and they could talk about it. They talked about so much. They always talked. Her absence now was a hollowness inside him. He was afraid that she was dying. He could not bear that.

As he walked on he saw in the distance other archways that led through to further shadowy halls and further collections. It grieved him that these huge collections had outlived the collectors. He wished he could have known them. In another world, he would have loved this place. He would have spent days and weeks here. Months. He would have learned. He wanted to do that.

Perhaps some few collectors still remained, and it was their light that showed high in the tallest tower? He imagined a small group of aged men and women – wizards, scholars, priests – gathered at a table to examine their ancient, precious items by candlelight. Scratching words about them into a book. He had to press on. He had to find the stair that climbed to the Northwatch Oriel.

He went out by the widest archway, the one that breathed draughts of colder air. Steps led upward to a lofty, high-windowed area filled with barred cages. The collection had kept living creatures too. It imprisoned their corpses now: desiccated, collapsed, unidentifiable assemblages of bone and skin and dust.

At the far end of the hall of dead animals the passage led him into a darker place, where there were no windows. The only light came from a few faint globes. As he stepped through the door his heart jumped in sudden, startled fear. He shouted out loud, a shocking sound in the deep silence. Inside the darker hall, in cold recesses and dimness, caged creatures were living still.

Large, sorrowful dark-adapted eyes gazed at him patiently. Strange animals prowled in shadows behind bars, chill and scentless. Delicate papery forms almost without colour. Some watched him avidly. With hunger. Bat-like things and large birds the colour of ash, all talon and beak, hurled themselves at screens, screeching hoarsely, trying to reach him. They seemed almost weightless.

These were not alien, unnatural things from altogether else-where, like the riders and their six-legged beasts, but they were somehow not right either. They were living, but they should be dead. How long had they been here? Decades. Perhaps centuries. How did they survive? What nourishment did they find, impris-oned under the pale light of the globes? They were uncanny and disturbing.

Briefly, he thought it would be a kindness to release them. He paused to examine the locks and chains on their cages, but the sudden beady eagerness of the creatures inside when he approached made him think better of it. The idea of these in-comprehensible beasts loose and stalking the deserted Keeping, while Castrel and their child were defenceless and alone in that basement ...

Shay broke at last out of the halls of collection, onto a paved area open to the sky. The foot of the great tower itself. He pushed open a door and stepped in. It was like being at the bottom of an immense well-shaft: there was no ceiling. The walls of the shaft were ringed with tier after tier of lamplit windowless galleries, dizzyingly high. A steep zigzag stairway ascended from one to the next. At the very top, tiny in the distance, the grey daylight of the glass dome was like a single cataractous eye.

He began to climb, cautious and slow, setting his feet softly. Each gallery was lined floor to ceiling with books. Level after level he climbed through books, uncountable thousands of volumes, their spines all lit with the same flat, pale lamplight.

He seemed to be climbing for hours. His fingers ached from gripping the axe tight for so long. He fought to breathe calm and shallow, though his heart was pounding. In some of the galleries, narrow doors in the shelving opened on to small rooms with desks and lecterns, pens and inks and unlit candles, and narrow windows. And from one of the doorways, high in the tower, yellow candlelight spilled.

Shay knew how to make a quiet approach. His time with Hage and Ridder and Vess had taught him that.

If need be, he knew how to quickly and quietly kill.

A man was reading a book by the light of two stubs of candle. Absorbed in his work, he had his back to the door.

'You don't have to lurk in the shadows,' he said without looking up. His voice was subtle and clear and warm and light. Running water under a summer sky.

He turned and smiled. Golden yellow eyes in a fine-boned youthful face. Not youthful. Ageless.

'It's quite safe,' he said. 'Please. Come in and talk.'

His skin was gold, the colour of old honey, and candlelight flickered on the smooth paleness of his long fine hair. He smelled beautiful and wore beautiful clothes: fine wool and green polished leather; an undershirt of silken cloth that glimmered shifting colour.

He is not human.

As soon as he thought it, Shay knew it was true. There was a glimmer of ancient starlight in the stranger's golden eyes. A glow of immortality in the candle-shadowed, book-lined room.

'Come in,' the stranger said again. 'I'd welcome company. I've had no conversation for a very long time.'

Shay hesitated. He had no bearings. He didn't understand this situation at all.

'I saw the light,' he said. 'I thought the Keeping was empty. I thought I was the only one.'

The stranger held up a neat leather flask inlaid with decorations of some bright metal.

'Wine,' he said. 'Have some. You look cold.'

Shay stayed in the doorway, the axe in his hand. The stranger shrugged and poured himself a cup.

'You're welcome, if you change your mind,' he said. 'It's good. It's from Arrogane.'

'Who are you?' said Shay. 'Are you one of the collectors?'

'No, I came here to read the books in the library, that's all. The collectors are long gone, alas.' He glanced at the axe. 'Won't you put that thing away? Don't you think we should talk?'

Shay considered, then grunted and nodded. He had seen the stranger's scabbarded sword propped in a corner out of reach.

'Fine,' he said, and pulled up a chair. He sat at the other side of the table, positioning himself between the stranger and his sword.

The stranger offered the wine again.

'Have some,' he said.

'A little, then. Thank you.'

The wine was light and slightly sweet on Shay's tongue. His whole body was flooded with warmth and a gentle wakefulness. Clarity and returning strength. He felt stronger than he had since ... since he couldn't remember when.

'Good, isn't it?' The stranger swirled his cup thoughtfully and emptied it. 'There'll be no more when what I have is finished. Never again. *The last vintage of Arrogane*. There's a melancholy ring to that. Do you read poetry?'

'No, I don't read. I never learned.'

'Ah. Sorry. Clumsy of me.' He looked genuinely ashamed.

'One forgets that lives take different paths. Please, forgive me, I've been alone for too long. In fact I wasn't expecting to meet another person at all, not this far north, not any more. I thought the time for such meetings was over, like the wine of Arrogane.' The stranger paused for a moment and studied Shay frankly. Candlelight glittered in golden eyes and cast shadows on golden skin. 'And yet here you are. A human in the hidden countries. In the High Esh. In the innermost library of Sard Keeping itself. This is a new thing in the world, an authentic wonder, and just when I thought all the surprises of this world were finished for ever. So, how did you come here? That must be a story worth hearing.'

'A friend showed me the way.'

'Really? Curious.' He sat forward in his chair, eyes widening. 'What brought you here?'

The golden stranger seemed so calm and unconcerned. Reading? In the middle of all this shadow, emptiness and ruin? Yet there was warmth and honesty in him. He seemed genuinely *interested*. Shay wasn't sure how to react: he didn't trust him, exactly, he didn't understand him enough for that; but he was beginning to like him.

And he was ... beautiful.

He is not human. He does not feel as we do. He does not see what we see. He is similar, but not the same.

'Please,' the stranger said again, pouring more wine. 'I'm sure your story is an intriguing one. Perhaps even important. If you tell me, perhaps I will be able to tell you something useful in return.'

Information for information. A trade.

'All right,' said Shay. 'It's a deal.'

He told him about the desolation of Ersett, and the riders on six-legged beasts, and the rising darkness in the northern sky, and the long walk to Sard Keeping with Mamser Gean. And then the terrible wall of alien light and air that overwhelmed them at the end, and Mamser Gean's stand at the bridge, and how he had died. He didn't say anything about Castrel and their child and their basement refuge.

'Your friend did a great thing for you,' said the stranger, when Shay had finished. 'A remarkable thing. Did you know that no human has ever been in Sard Keeping before? Only a very few have ever walked in any of the hidden countries at all.' His golden eyes rested on Shay's face, openly studying him. That curious, warm, detached inhuman gaze. 'Your friend must have seen great qualities in you.'

Not me, thought Shay. *Castrel. And the child.*

'I don't know about that,' he said. 'We came here to find news. We wanted to find out what the riders are, and what other dangers are coming from the north, and where we could go that would be safe.'

'Your friend did the right thing, coming here. Too bad the Keeping is long abandoned, but he wasn't to know that. I'm sorry you didn't get to see this place in its prime. It was very fine, extraordinary, though you wouldn't know it, to look at it now. It began to go sour centuries before the last of them were forced to leave. They left in a rush, of course, in the end, and took very little with them, which was fortunate for me.'

'Tell me something I don't know,' said Shay.

'Of course. That was our arrangement. Just ask me, and I will answer if I can.'

'Tell me about the riders. What are they? Where do they come from? Tell me about the weird storm and the darkness in the sky.'

The golden stranger hesitated. He looked grave.

'Do you know about that?' said Shay.

'Yes, I do know. I'm afraid I do.' He emptied his cup of wine and poured another. 'I'm trying to think how to explain it.'

'Just tell me,' said Shay.

'Very well, then. This world of yours,' the stranger began, 'is only one of many. The sun in the sky is many suns. There is the one you see and also others, a thousand thousand other suns, all in the same place, all contained by and containing your visible sun, yet their light falls on other worlds. Different worlds that are also there.' The stranger made a broad gesture that embraced the room, the Keeping, the High Esh, everything. 'Or rather, *here*. It's impossible to say how near those many other worlds are to this one and to each other, yet each one is oblivious of all the rest.' He paused. 'Do you see what I mean?'

'I understand the idea,' said Shay. 'But what has it to do with the riders?'

'There has been a catastrophe,' said the golden stranger. 'An absolute and irreversible catastrophe. Something, or someone, somewhere in the north has torn a huge and permanent hole between this world and another. I don't know who has done this, or how – I suspect it has something to do with the endless wizards' warring in the hidden countries – but it doesn't matter. All that matters is, it has been done, and it cannot be undone. The tear between the worlds will widen and widen. It can never be closed. And that other world ... It's strong, it's dark, it's cruel and terrible, and it's flooding into this one. Tumultuous tides of other light and other air and other life. You've seen a little of this already, and you were lucky to escape. It spreads. It spoils. It contaminates and invades and desolates. I don't know what will come of it, when the two worlds are joined completely – they might destroy each other utterly, or some new world might come out of their joining – but what's certain is, nothing of this world as it is – *nothing* – will survive. Your world is lost. All of it. Desolation is coming. The utter and permanent ruin and death of all things everywhere.'

The golden stranger studied Shay when he'd finished. There was a look of sadness in his inhuman eyes.

'I'm sorry,' he said. 'Truly sorry. You probably don't believe what I've said, I understand that. I'm not trying to convince you. Frankly, it makes no difference: what's coming will come, regardless. But for what it's worth, what I've told you is true.'

Shay didn't know what to believe: the words connected with nothing he understood of the way things were. And yet he had seen what he had seen, what had happened had happened, and this stranger was here, his skin and his eyes were all golden and he was not human at all.

'There's always something that can be done,' he said. 'Always.'

'No,' said the stranger. 'I really am sorry. This world is over. All of it.'

'Mamser Gean killed the riders on the bridge. They're not invincible. They can be fought.'

'Those are nothing. Outriders. Scouts. The first few straws in the wind. You can't even imagine what's coming behind them. Neither can I.'

'An army's coming?' said Shay. 'Then they must have a plan. They can be outmanoeuvred. Defeated.'

'I'm sorry, I used a bad image. This isn't a stratagem. There's no intelligence at work here. This is a cataclysmic natural event – an earthquake, a tidal wave, a forest fire – except it makes no sense to call it *natural*, because it's not natural to this world at all. I'm talking about an entirely different nature, the total transformation of this world, flooded by the poisonous light and air of another, darker sun.'

The golden stranger emptied the wine flask into Shay's cup.

'Finish it,' he said. 'It's only fair.'

Shay hesitated.

'But it's your last ...' he said.

'Please, go ahead.'

Shay glanced at the window as he drank. All he could see was a narrow rectangle of darkening grey watery sky. He felt a lurch of fear. Almost panic. *I've left Castrel alone too long.* If anything happened to them, the whole world could die and he wouldn't care at all. Suddenly he was overwhelmed by frustration and helpless anger. He felt himself on the brink of black despair. There had been too many deaths and disasters. Too many choices that hadn't helped at all. He tried. He kept on trying. He did the best he could, and so did Castrel, but their whole world had been turned upside down too many times, and everything always got worse and worse.

'What can we do?' he blurted out. 'Where can we *go*?'

The golden stranger looked at him with interest.

'We?' he said curiously. 'I thought you said your friend was dead. I assumed you were alone?'

Shay realised the mistake. He felt he had to keep Castrel and the child secret, though he didn't know why.

'I mean, you and I,' he said.

'Oh. I see. Actually, my position is not the same as yours. It's a little ironic in the circumstances, but I am from another world myself. I've been in this world for a very long time, and I've come to love it, and its destruction saddens me immensely. But, practically speaking, it's an inconvenience, nothing more. When I've finished my work here, I'll go home. It is possible to cross from world to world safely, without causing rifts like the one in the north, but it must be done only rarely and gently. A crossing is a delicate thing, to be made with infinite subtlety, knowledge and care. I do not myself know how. Others open the crossings for me.'

Shay stared at the stranger in astonishment, and the stranger returned his gaze with glittering golden eyes. The candlelight kindled his face to a deep shining gold and glinted on the fine decoration in the green of his jacket. How old was he? It was impossible to say. He was ageless, shifting and changeable, shimmering and deep and endless and simple, like shadows of cloud and sunlight on the surface of a summer sea. Not human at all.

'You're serious, aren't you?' said Shay.

'Absolutely. I'm a traveller from elsewhere. An observer, nothing more. I came to Sard Keeping to read the books in the library before I leave, because I thought there might be a few worth taking with me when I go, so that something at least of this world might be not altogether lost.' He smiled wryly. 'So you see, there's no *we*, I'm afraid. We have our separate roads to follow, you and I.'

'I didn't really mean—'

'As to what you might do, I think you should leave here as soon as possible. The wards on the Keeping protected you from the three days' storm, but those wards are broken now. The riders will come here, and worse will follow. I don't know what you'll find outside the gates, there was no protection there and the darkness has already begun to fall. But if you keep running, perhaps you may still have a little time.'

'How long?'

'Who knows? The world is large, and the darkness does not spread steadily. It seems to progress in bursts and surges. In some places it has already reached far south of here, but there are also still countries that know nothing of it. Not yet. Have you somewhere in particular where you wish to go?'

'Not really. South seems the best choice, but my friend is dead and I don't know the way.'

The golden stranger thought for a moment.

'Can you read a map?' he said.

'No,' said Shay. 'But I saw a sea chart once.'

'Come with me. I'll show you something.'

The stranger led him to another room where a large map was fixed to the wall. He held a candle close so Shay could see it.

'The green is forest,' he said, 'the blue is lakes and seas. The threaded lines are roads, and sometimes rivers.' He pointed out the clustered marks that meant mountains. 'And here, near the top, is the High Esh, And that is Sard Keeping.'

There was so much of everything on the map. Shay hadn't known there was so much world. The stranger traced a single thread that ran down from Sard Keeping. It went more or less straight across empty yellowing space and through a sprawl of mountains.

'When you go from here,' he said, 'you should follow this road. It's the only road south, and it will take you across the Chelidd Plain – you see that red area there? – and out of the hidden country. Those mountains are the boundary of the High Esh. If you get through there you will be in the human lands again. There. Do you see?'

'Yes,' said Shay. 'I understand.'

'Remember, you must follow the road across the Chelidd Plain. It will take you through the High Passes. It's the only way to cross the mountains without a guide.'

Beyond the mountains the map showed much green and the road divided in many directions. The muddled patchwork of enormous lands spread out beyond reckoning, and south and east of that were the areas of blue that meant sea. It was too much for Shay to take in and commit to memory. He pointed to many small marks scattered like a fistful of seeds across the faded, stain-mottled blue at the map's bottom edge. It was the most distant place from where they were now, which made it the farthest from whatever was coming from the north.

'Where's that?' he said.

'The archipelago of Far Coromance. All those marks are islands. I was there once, and it was very beautiful, but that was long, long ago. A bright memory of days that have passed. All is much fallen away since then.'

Far Coromance! Shay's pulse quickened. He had heard stories of Far Coromance as a boy in Harnestrand, and they had always made his imagination shine, almost as much as it did when he saw the White Knives.

'I'd like to go there one day,' he said.

'It's a journey of many thousands of miles, much of it across the sea.'

'I know boats,' said Shay. 'And I can walk. All it takes is time.'

The stranger looked at him kindly. Grief and sorrow in inhuman golden eyes.

'I'm sorry,' he said. 'Time is what this world does not have. There are no safe places. Please believe me. Do not hope for that.'

As Shay was leaving, he paused in the doorway.

'One last question,' he said. 'Those creatures in cages? The ones that are still alive? What are they?'

The golden stranger frowned.

'Those? Those are wizard-made experimentations. Constructed things that were natural once. Cruel, deathless abominations, imprisoned here to keep them out of the world. You should stay away from them altogether. Always stay clear of wizards' work.'

'Didn't wizards make this place? That's what I thought.'

'There are wizards and wizards. They have purposes of their own. Wizards make themselves what they are: some start human, some not; all of them refashion themselves and follow their own ambitions and desires. They cross all boundaries and go where they will. Some are wise but most are not, and they're all dangerous. If you encounter one, keep away.'

'You're not a wizard then? I thought you might be.'

'Me? No, I'm a curious traveller from somewhere else, that's all. Just passing through and taking a look.'

'And you're not a healer?'

Perhaps it was a mistake to keep secrets. Perhaps this man could help Castrel and the child.

The golden stranger looked at him, surprised.

'A healer? Alas, no. I have no need for that.'

It was later than Shay had thought. By the time he found his way out of the tower precincts, twilight was closing on the Keeping. He hurried through winding lanes as fast as he could, his mind churning. Wizards and pale deathless creatures. A gold-skinned inhuman traveller from a different world. There were many other worlds. And this one was dying quickly. Or maybe it was not. How could he know?

Even if the world was not dying, everything was changed. Nothing was as he thought it was. The world was much larger and stranger than he had imagined, and it could not be controlled. It could not be understood. He could not know the right place to go or the right thing to do. All he could do was love Castrel and their beautiful child, do everything for them, keep them alive, and try to keep going as long as he could. Try to be a good man.

As he got nearer their basement room a wonderful thought grew stronger and stronger until it was overwhelming, until it pounded his heart breathless. He imagined how he would go down the steps and push open the inner door, and Castrel would be there, awake and sitting up. She would be nursing their beautiful daughter and when he came in she would hold the child out towards him.

Shay!

She would say his name, and her face would be all brightness and shine, brighter than the embers of the fire.

Shay! she would say, and she would smile. *You're back! And isn't she lovely! Isn't she perfect?*

And *yes*, he would say: *yes, she is.*

*

But the underground room was cold. He entered again into the sourness of sweat and fever, the sweetness of the child's soil, and the sound of his daughter weeping in the dark.

It was a hoarse, frail, heart-wrenching little sound. She was forlorn. Bereft.

Shay felt so helpless. Guilt at leaving her tore him inside. There was nothing he could do but pick her up and hold her, and try to help her take a little water.

'You want your mother,' he said to her. 'I know. I'm sorry, she's sleeping. She isn't well now but she'll be fine soon. All will be well, my poor sweet beautiful child, but for now there's only me.'

Castrel was breathing shallow and fast. She was hot. It worried him.

She isn't right.

He lay down under the blanket next to Castrel, holding the child tight and trying to soothe her to sleep. Breathing the beloved smell of her.

Tomorrow might be the day Castrel wakes.

And one day he would make things good again. He would find a way. One day they would all go home again together. That would be a golden day. Or perhaps he would take them all to Far Coromance. What did he care of other worlds? This was his one world, and Castrel's, and it was his daughter's world too. No matter how little time they had, she would see more of it than just a hole in the dark. He would make sure of that.

The next morning Shay took his daughter outside to see her world again. In the stable he held her close against the mare's neck. Put her hands where she could run her fingers through the rough dry hair. Get the smell of her in her nose. He wanted her to feel those things. Things that had life.

Then he carried her up to a high place to show her wideness

and sky. He wanted her to see the expanse of rooftops, and the towers, and the dark misted rise of hills. He held her at the parapet, his arms around her, his chin resting on her bundled shoulder. There was no light in the high tower window that morning. Perhaps the stranger slept late, or worked in another room.

A sudden terror like vertigo dizzied him. He heard the clatter of harness off echoing walls. The strike of hooves on cobbles below. Panicked, heart pounding, he crouched below the parapet and hugged the bundled child tight.

There were riders in the lane below. Two of them. Foul riders on tall, pale six-legged beasts, moving slowly. They were searching. Moving their shrouded heads from side to side. Listening. Lifting their heads to test the air. The long blades of their weapons were flat and wide and blackly stained, the edges heavily notched, almost ragged. Not battle weapons – more like tools for a harvesting.

He saw them turn in his direction. Saw their long, narrow, pockmarked and ragged faces. Their white eyes like chalk and bone.

He ducked away.

Was I seen?

He gripped the haft of the axe. But he could not fight them. Not two.

Probably not one.

Hugging the child he backed away. Down the stair off the roof and out through another door into another narrow street. And ran.

To run and run and make no sound.

The labour of his breathing scoured his lungs. He retched and stumbled. Fear made him weak.

*

When he reached the basement he closed the door and wedged it with a plank. Pushed heavy things against it. All the heavy things they had. There wasn't much. It was a last flimsy barricade.

He lay pressed against Castrel in the dark that was their best protection, his warmth against hers, and their child between them. He listened to their breathing and tried to make it rhyme with his own.

Under the blanket with them he kept knife and axe.

Time passed, unmeasurable. Long slow hours. Sometimes he burned a candle and sometimes not: his instinct was to spare them, to eke out the supply. The cob mare alone in her stable would eat the last of her meagre rotted hay and apples. She would lap the last of the water from her trough, and then she would die. Perhaps that had already happened. He could not know.

He would go out when he must. The time would come when he must leave them again. But not yet.

He lapsed into a strange half-sleep. A bitter drowse.

He woke and lit another candle. The dream he woke from was raw in his mind, the emotion of it stronger than the cold darkness of the empty room. It pulled him back under again. Always the same dream.

In the dream, Castrel was with him and they were in a tangled forest and he was walking behind her and the trees stretched out around them in all directions. A long path through trees. The illimitable silence of trees. In the dream he watched her go ahead of him down the track, carrying the child, and he was following. The knife in his belt, the weight of the axe strapped across the pack on his shoulders. He would protect her, he would keep her safe – though in the end she was stronger than he was, and she would be the one to lead them back, and without her walking ahead of him he would have stopped already and found a crouching-place to wait and die.

He came awake once more. He was lying on his back, wet with sweat, cold as ice, and the room was unbearable. And then he realised that her hand was holding his.

And that was not in the dream.

He looked at her and her eyes were open and she was watching him by candlelight, nursing her daughter at her breast.

And the noise he made in his throat then was not a word, not a shout, it was a breaking of walls: an impossible explosion of joy, more than his heart could hold.

It was a long time before he could find words, and when he did: 'We have to go,' he said.

They were the first words.

'We have to leave. I'm sorry. We have to do it now. Today.'

'Yes,' said Castrel, though her mouth was dry, her lips chapped and painful. 'Yes. I know.'

Shay went to find the cob in the stable. She was still alive. It was another wonder, but she was. He harnessed her to the cart and she tested the air and knew there was a change, and she was happy.

He loaded the cart with all they had, which was very little now, and when it was ready he helped Castrel up the stairs and she carried their daughter with her. In the grey daylight Castrel was so thin and spent it hurt him to look at her. She had burned herself up from the inside.

Shay helped her up onto the cart with the child and they set off, he going ahead and leading the mare by the bridle, winding their way through the lanes of the Keeping, looking for the road that went south, always further south, into the broken world.

*

They named their daughter Hope. The name was their gift to their child, the only one they could give, because they had nothing else. They walked out alone into scoured desolation and loss; but you, they said to their tiny, fragile, beautiful child, you are Hope. *Who are you?* people would say to her, and she would say, I am Hope. And so the thread of hope would run through her life and bind her to it. Frail, tenuous thread. She would say it and she would hear it, again and again: a small word spoken in bleakness; a thin bell chiming against the wind and the dark.

9

Once broad and paved but neglected and ruinous now, the remains of the ancient road ran south from Sard Keeping through a cold empty country. It wound between crags of sharp rock and descended into moorland, wide and barren. Everything was grey and hollow, with a quiet ashen brittleness. The aftermath of strange storms.

The days were short and the nights were long and winter followed them south, though they kept moving long into the night. They travelled slowly, letting the mare stop when she would to graze the scant, rough margins. Castrel rode in the open back of the cart, cradling Hope in her arms and watching the road behind them for pursuit. She saw none. They camped by the roadside and eked out their food – shrivelled grain, grey flour, ageing dried beans – some, but never enough. Castrel was always hungry. It was a numb aching want. She slept in the day when she could.

She was still healing inside. All those days in the underground room she had burned herself up inside, exhausting last reserves she did not have, fighting to reknit her own torn tissue and keep a tight grip on the life of the tiny newborn child. And now the damage done by her illness and the birth of her daughter must all be repaired and restored. Where was the strength to come from for that? It must come because it must.

Hope was so small and weak. She had almost died – Castrel never told Shay how close that had come – but she had lived, and now, day after day, Castrel nursed her with a fierce passion. She wrapped her daughter and herself against the world in a hot and intimate closeness, a narrow urgent concentration that went deeper and darker than love. Time took on a different, slower shape. Hope's fine wisps of hair and her watchful eyes – their perfect and depthless clarity – filled Castrel with an instinctive, visceral joy. Wordless and constant the thought flowed from mother to daughter.

I am here. I am your mother. I am with you and always will be. Always. Always.

And Hope responded. Castrel felt her daughter reach out for her. She sensed the child's searching awareness brushing against the edge of her own mind, light and gentle, feeling her feelings. Absorbing. Wondering. Hope's quiet, curious touch was so young, it was almost without any identity at all.

Castrel opened herself and let Hope in, mother and daughter merging till the borderlands between them were ill-defined and doubtful. It was a kind of wordless conversation that went on for hours. She took Hope's small hand and held it in hers, feeling its fragile gentle warmth.

'I'm sorry,' she said softly. 'I wish it wasn't like this. It wasn't always so. Something happened. But we'll keep you safe. I promise.'

Your world is lost, the golden stranger had said. *All of it. Desolation is coming. The utter and permanent ruin and death of all things everywhere.*

Castrel told Shay she wouldn't believe it.

'All my life I've known the warmth and light of living things,' she said. 'I've touched it and held it. It comes from rock and water and air, from heart and bone and blood. Life is bigger and stronger than anything. It can't just be ruined and destroyed. It's too *real*. Whatever is happening will pass, and the world will come good again.'

'Of course it will,' said Shay. 'All we need to do is follow this road south and cross the mountains, then we'll be out of this hidden country, and we'll be fine.'

'And anyway,' said Castrel, 'even if all of what the stranger told you was true, what difference does it make? If he's right, then it will happen and there's nothing we can do. It doesn't change anything, not for us. We can't give up. Never. We have to keep Hope safe and keep going south. There isn't anything else. There isn't another choice.'

But even as she said it, in Castrel's heart a part of her was not so sure. There was something wrong, deep down wrong. It was everywhere. A constant sourness in the mouth. A foulness against the skin. A jangling in the blood. A thing in the bones that crouched in the spine. Unhealable.

Day after day they walked slowly south through wide emptied country. The road followed a high ridge between expanses of greyish-brown moorland grass. They came to a place where it was lined mile after mile with standing stones like the ones they'd seen before, when they were with Mamser Gean. But those stones had been rooted in the deep strength of the rock – it had flowed through them and when she touched them it flowed through her – and these stone now were dead.

'They're silent,' she said to Shay. 'Empty. Hollow. Nothing but big lumps jammed in the grass. They're scarcely there at all. It feels like if I kicked one it would echo, or crumble to cinders and dust.'

That night they camped among wind-bent scrub in a hollow away from the road. Shay built a fire and cooked beans. Fried flats of hard bread on the skillet. She ate what there was, but it wasn't enough.

Afterwards Castrel sat cradling the sleeping child while Shay saw to the mare. The warmth of the fire played across her face. She was so tired she hardly thought at all.

Shay came and sat beside her.

'How are you?' he said. 'How's the little one?'

'Fine,' she said. 'We're both fine.'

She took his hand in hers. His skin, hardened with work and weather, felt cold and smooth to her touch. He had a straggle of young man's beard, and his hair had grown long so he tied it back. Sometimes she forgot how young he was.

She reached out to him, the way she reached out to her child, feeling for his mind with hers. It wasn't the same as with Hope – there wasn't the same surge in response, not a real communication, Shay wasn't even aware she was doing it – but she could feel the core of him, what he was like inside. He was warm like a fire, wholesome and nourishing and good. Shay had kept them safe in the Keeping when she was ill. He was all in the world that she had, and she was sure of him. She loved him so much it hurt.

'You're doing fine too,' she said. 'We're going to be all right.'

'Yes,' he said. 'Yes we are. We'll make it in the end.'

They forded a shallow stream edged with slivers of ice. Shay waded, soaking his legs to the knees. The mare hesitated, then went after him, the wheels of the cart jerking and sliding. Pitch and creak. Sway and yaw.

Castrel felt the mare's hunger and weakness, the hurt of her sores, the pain of her knees and back, her dogged haul and trudge. All accepted: for the mare, this moment was all there was. No before and no after. Knowing the past only vaguely and the future not at all, she dragged patiently on through a perpetual now.

*

The road climbed slowly higher. Brown expanses of dead twisted bracken rolled away to the horizon under a wide sour sky. Nothing lived there. The sun was a patch of brighter paleness, watery and indistinct. Shay walked ahead leading the cob and Castrel rode, swaying with the motion of the cart, the child at her breast, a blanket pulled up over them both like a hood. The blanket was rough against her cheek and reeked of woodsmoke. There was pain still, in the place below her stomach, and her arms and legs were weak.

Thunderous purple storm clouds were building in the north, darkening the sky as if night was coming early. White lightning flickered. A ragged bitter wind rising. The first fat raindrops fell like bursting pebbles, ice-cold and heavy. Looking back from the crest of a low hill Castrel saw two black specks in the distance, moving along the road. And there was a third, working fast across open country some way to the west, keeping a parallel course with the others but hidden from their view by a rise of the land. The third seemed to be leading another mount that had no rider, but they were too far away to see clearly.

'There are riders behind us,' she said to Shay. 'Look.'

He squinted into the distance and the gathering dark.

'I see them,' he said.

'I think they're following us. We should get out of sight.'

'How?' said Shay. 'Where?'

It was a rolling, featureless country. There were dips and hollows and a few scrubby stands of tree and thorn, almost leafless. Shay tugged at the cob's bridle, urging her off the road and down the shallow bank.

'Hurry,' he said. 'Hurry.'

It was the weather that hid them. There was no sheltering from it. Night fell quickly and a hard screaming wind, shredding and punishing, drowned out the thunder. Rain poured like a river. Torrents of roaring dark. They crawled under the cart and huddled there to wait out storm and night, the blackest of nights, rain-blinded under sodden blankets.

'I think it's just ordinary rain,' said Castrel. 'Not like before.'

She held Hope close to protect her and keep her warm. The child made no sound but Castrel knew her eyes were wide. Every time the immense lightning crashed, illuminating the black arc of the sky, she felt her daughter's tremendous answering wordless surge of joy.

Castrel woke late the next morning. The wind had fallen and snow was veiling from a sullen sky. Thin grey bitter flakes dusting frost-hardened earth, the ground iron and unforgiving under her boots. So *cold*. Her clothes were drenched and her whole body trembled, shivering to the core. She winced at the cruel ache in her lower belly, deep inside where the healing was not yet complete.

Shay had built a fire. Pale smoke drifted upwards and merged with the falling snow. Flatbread on the hot iron pan. The smell of that. He was holding Hope in his arms, kneeling to bathe her in a bowl of water he had set to warm in the glowing ashes of the fire. Faint wisps of steam curled and drifted.

'We shouldn't have a fire,' said Castrel. 'The smoke – it will bring the riders.'

'They won't see, not through this snow.'

'They might smell it.'

'They're long gone. They won't have stopped for the storm.' He smiled. 'We can't be frightened all the time. And you need to get warm, or you'll be sick again.'

He brought her black tea, a porridge of barley and a slab of warm flatbread, slightly burned.

'Thank you,' she said. 'Thank you.'

While she ate she watched Shay walking with Hope, carrying her in a bundle against his chest and talking to her quietly.

'This is the mare,' he said to her. 'See? You know her. She should have a name, don't you think? Like your name is Hope. I think we should call her Stalwart, how about that? Stalwart, because she is brave and patient and keeps on going and going and never stops although she wants to rest. Yes, Stalwart, that's a good name for her.'

Day followed day, unwinding slowly from the store of days that were all the same. Castrel rode in the cart and Shay walked ahead, back straight, head up, chin forward. Into the darkness. There was a hitch in the way he walked that was the essence of him. He was courageous and her heart burned to watch him going into the dark. She pictured the four of them – Hope, Shay, herself and the mare Shay had named Stalwart – as if she were looking down from a great height. Four figures on the long road, going onwards because it was the only thing to do, because it was better than stopping. Four tiny flames moving through an immense shadow that stretched away for ever on all sides, the terrible shadow that soaked into the very light and air. Shadow that had no boundary and no centre but was everywhere and always.

And in all the days of their walking they saw no one, no other living person, and scarcely an insect or bird, almost no living animal that moved.

'We can't be the only ones left in the world,' she said, one time when they were sitting by their meagre fire in the night. 'We can't be, can we? There must be others somewhere.'

'We're not the only ones,' said Shay.

The road crested a steep ridge and they stopped. They were look-ing down from the edge of steep, high rocks on to a rust-coloured plain many miles wide: a vast shallow depression of reddish earth, empty and featureless except for some scrub woodlands far away to the south. Castrel could see the dull glint of distant waters there; and further away, beyond the plain, a line of mountains rising against the horizon.

'That must be the Chelidd Plain,' said Shay. 'Those mountains are the end of the High Esh. We're almost out of this.'

The nearer foothills were brown and sombre, and beyond them were further, higher, paler shapes of grey, and finally the glimmer of white peaks merging into cloud. And in all the vast red plain between them and the mountains, nothing moved. No birds crossed. No distant threads of smoke rose from among clumps of trees.

Castrel's heart lifted. A sudden weightless surge of relief and hope. Once they passed though those mountains they would be out of the hidden country and back where humans lived.

They descended the southern side of the ridge, down towards the plain. The road zigzagged precariously through narrow clefts between the ruins of grass-grown walls, deep ditches, steep banks, the burned remains of works of earth and stone.

Halfway down, Shay halted the cob.

'Something happened here,' he said. 'I'm going to have a look.'

Castrel watched him scramble up the slope at the edge of the road onto a high ledge. He crouched at gouges torn in the earth. Ran his hand across soot-blackened slabs of broken rock and examined his palm. Lifted a piece of rusted iron from the mud, hefted it and let it drop. Then he slithered and slid back down to her.

'There was a battle here, I think,' he said. 'Something like that. Explosions and fire. A lot of burning. But it was a long time ago. The damage isn't fresh.'

'Not a human battle,' said Castrel. She could feel the faint residue of wizards' magic in the rock and earth. 'The wars of the hidden countries.'

As they went down towards the plain the signs of battle were more obvious and the taint of wizards' high magic was stronger. It was in the air, in the earth, in the stones and the trees. Castrel felt it against her skin and tasted it in her mouth. It prickled at the roots of her hair and the tips of her fingers. It was as if none of the angles and corners of the world were quite straight any more. She'd never felt wizards' magic so strongly before, not even on the Skywater Bridge when Mamser Gean destroyed the bridge.

'Terrible things were done here,' she said. 'It's left traces and stains. Can you feel it, Shay?'

'I think I can, a little,' he said. 'It's a kind of edginess. I don't want to go any further, but I don't know why. It's a bit like when we first saw the hills of the High Esh, when we were leaving Allerdrade with Mamser. Maybe that's what it is? We're coming to the border of a hidden country again.'

'It's more than that. Wizards have done huge catastrophic things here. It's like the country itself is in pain.'

Hope was feeling it too. She was squirming in her arms.

'We should go no further,' said Castrel. 'This is a bad place.'

Shay looked at her. His eyes were full of concern.

'Are you all right?'

'We should find another way,' she said.

'There is no other way. I'm sorry. This is the only road out of the High Esh. What else can we do? We can't go back the way we came.'

Castrel knew he was right.

'Then we must cross it,' she said, and forced a thin smile. 'Don't worry. I'll be fine.'

But the closer they got to the edge of the Chelidd Plain, the stronger grew her urge to turn back. The very earth and sky were a silent scream, a writhe without motion.

*

They camped early at the foot of the ridge at the edge of the plain, under the roots of a fallen tree. Its timber was brittle and covered with a dusting of what looked like bluish-grey salt. They didn't build a fire.

Castrel lay in the dark of night under a blanket on the hard stony ground. Wind hissed in the pale dead branches of trees, streamed shreds of cloud across blank spattered stars, and howled away across the empty miles of the Chelidd Plain they would have to cross tomorrow. She could see Shay nearby, sitting up to keep watch. The straightness of his back was a shadow against the sky. Hope nestled against her, feeding drowsily. At least the child seemed to have got used to the feel of wizards' work that saturated this place, though Castrel couldn't shut it out. It was a continuous jangling noise in her head, and the fragile, uncertain ground she lay on was streaming with it like the wind across the sky.

Was there a wizard actually out there now, at work somewhere on the Chelidd Plain? She opened herself and let her awareness drift across the open spaces to investigate. As soon as she reached out she was shredded and torn and lost control, and withdrew hastily, giddy with shock. She felt queasy, as if she wanted to be sick.

There was no intelligence working there, no living wizard, only mile after mile of chaotic echoes and disturbances left by what had once been done there long ago – but what that was, she couldn't tell. The only thing she knew was, it hadn't been the work of one wizard alone but of several. The wielder of a powerful magic always left a mark – a characteristic, a feeling of personality, a kind of stain – and in the aftermath of what had been done here, she could identify the individual feel of at least three different wizards, perhaps more. But everything they had done had the one same purpose: to kill, to tear down, to destroy.

She had never encountered such cataclysmic magical strength before, and it shook her to the core. She tested her own strength against it, but could make no impression at all. A moth fluttering against rock.

The thought of walking out into it tomorrow terrified her, for herself and for what it might do to Hope. Perhaps even Shay would be affected, though he seemed all right now. In the hour before dawn, she went a little way off by herself to prepare for the crossing.

She found a place where she could squat on the ground under the bleak glimmer of the last of the stars, and lit a small fire. Then she took the small pouch of dried bitter herbs that she had carried with her for years. She used it rarely and sparingly, because it was dangerous. There was always a price to pay, and using too much could do permanent harm, but she had taken a little when she knew the child was coming, and she must use it again now. She set water on the fire to make the infusion.

While she was waiting for the water to heat, she scored the flesh of her arms and legs very gently with a knife to draw fine dark lines of blood. She mixed some of the blood with red earth and daubed careful marks on her skin, murmuring quiet careful words in the hedge-tongue as she worked. Patterns and weavings. When she was ready she drank the warm bitter infusion.

She had done all she could. It didn't feel like enough, not nearly, but there was nothing more to be done. Whatever waited out on the wide red Chelidd Plain, she would go to meet it soon, and she would protect her child as well as she could.

The road ran straight, mile after mile across flat rust-coloured earth. A cold, sullen desert. The cart swayed and jolted, its wheels raising dust that blew behind them on the wind. The mare bowed her head and hauled.

There was no visible sun, but the brighter paleness in the sky was almost overhead when they reached the first signs of the aftermath of a great battle fought with the high magic of wizards. Deep scars and craters had been gouged and blasted in the rock of the ground, huge boulders torn loose and hurled about, and the deep wounds in the earth were filled with a thick, viscous liquid that was not water. Pools of chalky purple and blue, of a colour the sky never was, wreathed in scraps of drifting mist, reflected nothing. The smell of them was bad, and when the road passed near Castrel felt light-headed and confused, as if the world was far away and time passed too slowly and all directions were no longer right. Everything became slant and slope.

'This is what the battlefield in a wizards' war is like,' she said.

The taint of it sickened her, but Shay was looking about eagerly, taking it all in.

'Such power,' he said. 'Such awesome power.'

In places the road and the stones on the ground on either side were shattered and crusted with deposits of crystal: seeping chalky outgrowths of white and blue like tumorous crystallised moss, the residues of exhausted magic that crunched underfoot. The same deposits edged the deep splits and cracks in the earth.

Then they began to see bodies, a few at first, then more and more, lying where they had fallen or piled in large corpse-heaps for pyres never lit. For miles they passed between the unburied, untended harvest of the fallen dead. The field of battle was scattered with ruined weapons and broken banners and shreds of beautiful many-coloured fabrics fluttering in the wind, brittle and stained with dirt and blood. Shattered skulls in crested broken helms spilled flags of fine pale hair.

The dead were all taller and more slender than human, and among them were giants. In life the giants must have stood twelve or fifteen feet high. There were thousands of dead horses too, armoured and caparisoned, stained with filth.

Castrel had the feeling that the dead had not only been killed by the wizards' magic: their deaths had been used to power it. Their lives had been consumed like fuel. She walked on into the dislocated, terrible aftermath of all the magic desolation and death as if into a headwind, mumbling words of warding and defiance, feeling the patterns she had drawn on her body come alive and tighten.

Shay was feeling the onslaught of it too, she could see it in his face and the hunch of his shoulders, but he walked on. Against this strangeness he had the strength of a bear, a resilience that astonished her. As he went forward he looked about with bright-eyed interest. This was a new thing. Otherness, strangeness and wonders.

Stalwart whickered and trembled in terror. The mare's sensitivity to the presence of magic surprised Castrel. She felt something break in the poor creature who had endured so much for so long. This new strangeness and suffering was too much for her. Stalwart bowed her head and hauled on, allowing herself to be led by Shay, but Castrel knew that in some permanent way her heart was gone.

Terrified that Hope would suffer as Stalwart did, Castrel hugged her closer in a gesture of protectiveness. The tiny child in her arms was so defenceless, so gossamer-frail and completely open. She was a delicate touch against the world, a tissue of airy translucency without blemish that these echoes of magic war would shred and shrivel and tear.

But Castrel realised with a shock that she was wrong. Hope was responding with joyous elation: she was revelling in the spilled lingering magic, soaking it up, drinking it in, avid for more. The child could feel it as deeply as her mother, but she met it only with her father's openness and curiosity for more of the new. Then Castrel realised something of the true strength of their child. The wonderful impossible daughter they had brought into the world.

*

There were places where large swathes of the ground had been burned by a fierce heat. Narrow licks of incinerated earth hundreds of yards long. The smell of ash and searing incandescent flame still lingered. Charred corpses flung limbs wide in unnatural twisted shapes, skeletal cinders caught and exploded in sudden flakes of fire.

'What happened here?' said Shay. 'This is different.'

'I don't know,' said Castrel. 'Not wizards' magic. Something else, but just as powerful.'

They walked on, Shay leading the broken, exhausted mare, through the chill red country of the fallen dead. Eventually the oppressive heaps of bodies were left behind and the assault of spilled high magic faded and fell away. Still the road rolled onward across expanses of earth and stone.

Everything around them now was scorched by a great heat. Their feet scuffed through ash and cinders.

Shay stopped and pointed.

'What's that?' he said. 'Do you see it?'

A long low shape, spiky against the skyline in the distance.

'I see it,' said Castrel, uneasy. 'I don't know what it is.'

They went on. The mountains rising in the south seemed closer now.

'We'll be off this awful plain soon,' said Shay.

Castrel said nothing. The shape near the road ahead grew larger as they approached. As they got nearer she understood its true scale, and what it was.

'It's a dragon, Shay,' she said. 'A true dragon. I never imagined such a thing was real.'

'But dead,' said Shay. 'It's only a dead one.'

Castrel heard the disappointment in his voice, but she was glad it was dead.

*

The vast carcase lay on its back, belly to the clouds, scoured by wind and sand, higher and longer than a row of houses. The white bones of its broken wings were splayed wide, spread out across the ground as if it had tumbled from the sky. Gaps were torn in its hide. They showed ribs like the bleached and arching trunks of tall trees. Castrel stared at the massiveness of its long, bleached skull: unfleshed, intricate, grinning and cavernous. She could have climbed into its jaws and stood upright there.

'It didn't just die,' she said. 'It was killed.'

She sensed all around them the residue of the catastrophic destructive attack that had brought this immense creature down. The power of what had been done here was unimaginable. The presence of high wizards' magic hung in the air again, a quality in the silence, a tense and buzzing stillness, but this had a different feel from the chaotic, crazed disruptiveness of the battle they had left behind. The wizard who killed the dragon was not one of those who had fought there: this was someone else, with a different – more measured and controlled, but in the end more terrifying – touch.

Castrel went closer and closer to the dragon, until the immense dead creature towered over her. It would have been magnificent to see in flight: sweeping out of the sun on broad blazing wings, screaming roaring fire. Now that she was near she could see the scales on its hide. Dulled and ruinous though they were, they still shimmered with a faint and subtle colour that changed as she moved. Blurred jewels in the rain. Even now she felt the glamour of its magnificence. A living intelligence of such calamitous hugeness, it was utterly strange and wonderful. In all the desolation of the world around her this was the one true beautiful thing, even in death.

'Be careful!' said Shay. 'I don't think we should go too near, even if it is dead.'

His voice reached her from very far away, like a memory of long ago. She let a faint edge of her awareness drift out to the ruined body. She was curious. How was it made inside? What were the elegant secrets of anatomy that would give such a monster quickness and grace? She pushed cautiously through the lingering shreds of the power that had killed it. Gently, carefully, she felt her way, brushing against the silent bones. Breathing the airy darkness of the empty, caverned skull. Imagining the cold inhuman fire of mind that must have burned there once.

And reaching inside there she touched something that woke.

A trap snapped instantly open.

Something appalling surged.

'*Shay!*' she shrieked. '*Shay! Shay!*'

Panicking, screaming, she snatched every thread of her awareness instantly back into herself and threw up around her what barriers and defences she had, which were nothing and too late. The speed and the strength of what came at her ...

The small child in her arms spasmed and thrashed and struggled. Rigid. Squirming. A thin ragged wailing shriek.

And then the thing that had woken in the dragon, whatever it was, had gone.

And Hope was still.

Everything was still.

'Castrel! Cass! What is it? What *happened*?'

Shay was crouching beside her on the bare burned earth, and she was kneeling, tearing at the bundled blankets that wrapped the child, pulling them from her, trying to free her from them so she could hold her and love her and make her safe.

'Hope?' she was saying. Murmuring. '*Hope?*'

It was barely a name at all. A low continuous moan, desperate and appalled.

'Oh, no. No. Please. No.'

The child lay limp and quiet. There was no strength in her. Her eyes were closed. She was empty. Castrel could not reach her at all.

Shay touched her shoulder.

'Castrel? Please. Tell me. Hope … Is she …? What happened, Cass? Please …'

And then the moment passed. Her wonderful daughter was alive. She was breathing. She was warm. Her eyes were open again. Terrified, Castrel reached out to her, trying to find the connection again, that communicating openness, that beautiful wordless sharing. It was there. Hope seemed fine.

Yet something had happened. Castrel was sure something had passed then between the dragon and her child, but she didn't know what, and whatever it had been, there was no trace of it now. Perhaps she had imagined it. She decided to say nothing to Shay. What could he do? What could either of them do? But she would be watchful.

IO

They pushed on south towards the distant mountains. Shay walked with Stalwart, encouraging her with quiet words, but each step was a slow dragging hurt for her now. There was something badly wrong.

'She's not well,' he said. 'I mean really not well.'

'I know,' said Castrel. 'The magic on the plain hurt her, I think. It was just too much. She's so brave but it was the last straw, it broke her heart.'

'She might get over it.'

'Maybe. I hope so.'

He heard the doubt in her voice and it worried him: if they lost Stalwart they would lose the cart too, and that would be a disaster. They would have to walk then, carrying what they could as well as the child, and the High Passes would be barren rock and bitterly cold. He didn't know how long the road would be, but many days.

He ran his hand gently along Stalwart's flank and stroked her muzzle and neck.

'Come on, my beautiful girl. There's green grass the other side of the mountains. Think of that. Soft grass to walk on and a warm blue sky on your back. You can rest then, you can have a really long rest. It's not far now.'

She was so thin and tired, but she never gave up. She had been his sturdy companion for so long. He thought of Mamser Gean, and Khaag and Paav, and all the people of Ersett, and all that he and Castrel had already lost, all the bleakness and darkness that had overcome the world.

'We can't lose Stalwart too,' he said to Castrel. 'There've been too many deaths already. We can't have another.'

Even thinking of it, grief welled up inside him and he felt the prickle of tears. They couldn't have come this far without her.

Castrel looked at him, and the hurt in her eyes was the same as his own.

'She likes it when you walk with her,' she said. 'She feels safe then, and the world for her is good. You make her stronger, I can feel that in her, but she's very weak now.'

'Is there anything you can do for her?'

'I've tried,' she said.

'We'll look after her. We'll give her more rest. We won't push her so hard.'

The corpse of the dragon was already small in the distance behind them, but something made Shay keep glancing back. He wanted to look at it for as long as he could. The dragon's awesome power and absolute, impossible strangeness filled him with terror, yet it must have been so beautiful. Even its corpse called him back with a glamour that pierced his heart. It made his imagination shine and burn.

'Castrel?'

'Yes?' She was walking beside him, nursing Hope.

'When we were looking at the dragon, what happened there? To you and Hope, I mean. It seemed like she was hurt, and so were you, and I thought ... I don't know ... It scared me. What was that?'

'I'm not sure anything happened at all,' she said. 'Everything went far away and faint for a while, and all I could see was the

155

dragon, and it seemed like something was waiting there, and then it came out. It was all very quick. I reacted, and so did Hope. She went so still she was hardly breathing.' She gave Hope a hug. 'But then it passed, and she seems fine now. I'm not sure it was anything, really. Maybe just seeing the dragon. It had a powerful effect.'

'And you're all right now?' said Shay. 'Both of you?'

'I've been watching her, but there's nothing wrong, not that I can find. I've never known a child so strong. I know she's small and born too young, but her gift is deeper than mine or Bremel's was – sometimes it's almost as if she and I are talking. I know what she's thinking and feeling, although she hasn't got any words. She'd let me know if something wasn't right.'

It was getting cold fast. Bitterly cold. The road failed at the margin of a sullen lake, losing itself among brittle frost-edged reeds and marsh pools crusted with ice. Shay could see no further edge, only twilight and gathering mist. They stopped, at a loss.

'This isn't right,' he said. 'The road should go on, all the way to the mountains. That's how it was on the map. We must have missed a turning.'

He saw how thin Castrel was, standing next to him and hugging Hope bundled in a blanket. Her hands were raw with cold, and he could see the fine anatomy of her bones.

'This is the road,' she said. 'There's no other. This lake must be new since the map was made. Maybe a river flooded. Maybe something happened during the battle that blocked it. If we go round, we'll find the road again on the other side.'

Shay looked doubtfully at the rough ground on either side of the road. There was no track to follow, only hard-frozen earth and tussocks of rough grass as far as he could see.

'The cart won't go easily over that,' he said. 'It'll be tough for Stalwart. We should look after her.'

'There's no choice,' said Castrel. 'We have to keep going. We can't go back.'

Stalwart was cropping hesitantly at the frost-hardened grass, and the grass was like her mane. Colourless, lifeless and brittle.

'You hold Hope for a moment,' said Castrel. 'I'll go to her.'

He watched her lay her head against Stalwart's skeletal neck. Those weeping crusted sores. She smoothed the mare's muzzle and whispered in her ear. She stayed with her for a long time.

Shay walked around to keep warm, holding Hope sleeping in his arms. He put his face near her and breathed her warm scent. She was so tiny. She was a beloved wonder, a resilient, impossible thing, and every day, every hour of her was a golden treasure. Although sometimes it seemed that all good things had abandoned the world, while there was still Castrel and Hope, that was enough for him. Even one moment of that was enough.

Castrel came back, her face crumpled and wrong.

'She's weak, Shay, weak and sick and there's nothing more I can do. I haven't got the strength, I've used it all up. And even if I did ... I have to keep what I have for Hope and me. I don't have anything left even for that.' She turned her eyes away. 'I'm sorry. I can't.'

He held her close. Buried his face in her hair. His love for her was an ache and a burst of bitter joy. It was his only purpose. Castrel and Hope.

'It's all right,' he said. 'It's fine. You're doing fine. We'll get through.'

They camped that night and set out in the first light of dawn to follow the edge of the lake in search of the road. The going was painfully slow. The cart jolted and lurched and Stalwart had to stop every few paces to rest. From time to time Shay broke the ice on a black pool with the axe so she could drink. After a few hours of this the axle of the cart broke. A wheel leaned painfully, angled and useless.

Shay crawled under to look.

'I can fix it,' he said. 'At least, I think I can patch it up.'

The work absorbed him. It felt good. It was something he could do, and competence was peaceful. He remembered Hollin's boatyard in Harnestrand: the heft and swing of the mallet in his hand; the smell of cut pine and caulk and hot pitch; the noise of the gulls; how shadows fell across his bench and dust danced in bright shafts of sunlight; the stream of Galla's happy chatter in his ear. Every hammer-strike and chisel-cut was a moment mastered – easy, thoughtless, sweet – carving out the form of what a day should be.

Stalwart hauled them on through another day, following the edge of the lake. Shay knew by the stars when they swung south and then west, but Stalwart's breathing was hoarse and shallow now, and she coughed, dry and hurting. At dusk they found the road again and turned right, letting it take them to the mountains.

The next day the road began to climb out of the Chelidd Plain. The way was wide but broken and strewn with stones, and the cart clattered and juddered worse than before. Stalwart had to drag it uphill against the steepness, picking her footing carefully between ice-filled holes and across shallow streams. Shay held her bridle tenderly and stroked her muzzle and neck, talking to her quietly all the time.

'I'd give you apples if I had some. You deserve apples. Perhaps there'll be orchards on the other side of the mountain.'

Stalwart stumbled and fell hard, a sagging weight in the harness. When he cut her free she collapsed and struck her knee on the road. Her head cracked against sharp stone and she lay there, not moving, her ribs rising and falling like the long swell of the sea, less and less. Her eye looked into his, wide and lost and surrendered. Her foreleg was twitching.

Shay ran his hand along the ruined, sickening angle of her fetlock. The jut of snapped bone against skin. He didn't need Castrel to tell him this was past all mending and there was nothing to be done.

Oh, Stalwart. I'm so sorry. What did we do to you?

They stood together looking down at her dying.

'We can't stay,' said Castrel. 'She'll lie like that until she dies.'

'How long, do you think?' said Shay.

'I don't know. It could be an hour or a day. Or days.' Castrel gave him an agonised look. 'We can't wait. We have to keep moving, Shay.'

'We can't leave her here. Not like this. Not on her own.'

'No,' she said. 'We can't do that. She's in a lot of pain.'

'So what then?' he said fiercely. 'What do we do?'

He knew, but he didn't want to say.

'I'm so sorry,' she said, and there was grief in her eyes. 'You know what we have to do. It's the best thing for her. I'll do it. I know how to do it kindly. You take Hope out of the way.'

'No,' said Shay. 'Let it be just me and her.'

Castrel walked on up the road, carrying Hope in her arms. Shay saw tears in her eyes as she turned away, and he had tears too: he wept for Stalwart, and for all that had happened. He did what he must do, but it was the darkest hour in all the darkness and he hated himself for what he did.

After it was done, he stood by the wreckage of the cart and took stock.

Don't feel. Not now. Don't look back. Keep moving on. Think.

The loss of the cart was a terrible blow: now they would have only whatever food they could carry themselves, and if they were still in the mountains when it ran out then they would starve.

There was snow on the summits. He didn't know how long the road was, or even if the High Passes were open so late in the year, but south of the mountains the weather would be warmer, and things would grow, and there would be animals and birds. There would be people.

Roads didn't climb into mountains and end there.

Did they?

Shay made larger packs for him and Castrel to carry on their backs, using strapping from Stalwart's harness. The new packs were heavy even when they were empty, and the straps rubbed sore, but they were strong and made of canvas that would keep out the rain, and they would be able to carry more. He made a sling as well, so they could carry Hope and still have both arms free.

While he worked, Castrel built a fire. There'd be no more fires once they were in the mountains because there were no trees there, and they couldn't carry their own firewood. They cooked and ate what they couldn't take with them: beans and a porridge of oats and barley with flatbreads of rye and corn. It wasn't much. Shay hadn't realised how little food they had left.

After they had eaten, Shay tried to dig a grave for Stalwart but the ground was frozen hard and he only had an axe, so he built a cairn to cover her. Darkness fell while he was still gathering stones and small rocks for the pile.

He took from the wrecked cart the crib he had made in the summer for Hope, and left with Stalwart under the stones. It struck him then that he didn't think of going home any more. Whatever became of them all in the end, they wouldn't see the house in the hills near Ersett again.

When the cairn was done, Castrel came and stood next to him, looking at it. She didn't say anything. The loss of Stalwart was a bleak absence, a ragged hurting wound torn out of their small private world: the fourth of them gone.

Grief and guilt: Shay couldn't tell them apart.

'We pushed her too hard,' he said, 'and she died. We used her.'

'It wasn't like that,' said Castrel. 'With us she had company and a purpose, she had somewhere to go, and you walked with her and cared for her, and she was glad for that. What else would she have had, if not that?'

She took his hand and held it. He didn't look at her, but he was glad she did. Side by side they stood in the dwindling firelight, and their daughter Hope was a tiny bright presence between them.

They set off on foot in the first grey before dawn, Castrel going ahead and Shay following, watchful, hand on knife-hilt, axe strapped across the top of his pack: all the preciousness of the darkening world walking five paces in front of him.

A great stone wall was strung out along the foot of the mountains, mile after mile, east and west from horizon to horizon, vanishing into the distance, and every mile there were hill forts: but the forts were ancient ruins and the wall was broken in many places. Tumbled blocks of stonework spilled down across the lower slopes. Where the road passed through the wall, there was an arched gateway with high towers, and columns to support massive gates that were no longer there. They camped in the shelter of the gateway, and in the morning they hoisted their packs on their backs and began to climb.

The summits ahead were hidden in cloud. Every hour they climbed, the going got steeper and the air grew colder. By midday the road had narrowed to a precarious ledge cut into the flank of the mountains. On their right, cliffs plunged steeply down into black ravines, and on their left iron-black rock rose sheer and covered with ice. Ice hung suspended from ledges high above them: immense spikes and sheets of ice; frozen tons of iron water ready to crash and fall. Thin freezing air rolled down off the peaks. It hurt his lungs. His breath froze in his beard. He stuffed his hands inside his clothes but still they were numb.

And the nights would be worse: Shay pictured himself huddled in the dark against the cliff without fire or shelter in the terrible worsening of the cold, always only a stumble away from the appalling plummet of the icy brink.

How many days of this? How many nights?

On. Always on. Somehow on.

All there was for them now was onward and climb. That was all.

The road turned sharply east, following a fold in the side of the mountain. They came to a structure of cracked and fissured stone, the ruin of an ancient bartizan leaning out from the road-edge, high above the precipitous drop. It was a watchpoint, built long ago to guard the approaches to the pass. From here they could see the whole of the Chelidd Plain laid out, dizzyingly far below. There was the lake they had skirted, a long narrow arm of dismal water made tiny by distance, and beyond it the faded levels of the plain, reddish like rust or dried blood. The place where the dragon had fallen was a distant circular splash of burn, almost at the horizon. Shay thought that perhaps he could see the speck in the centre that was the carcase itself.

I'm imagining. It's too far.

But the movement at the edge of the lake, that was not imagination.

'Do you see that?' he said to Castrel.

There was a rider. A tiny speck many miles behind them, following the shore of the lake as if looking for the road.

'I see it,' she said. 'I think it might be a horse. It's moving like a horse.'

Only four legs. That was good. But too far away to be sure.

'It's several days behind us,' said Shay. 'It might not even be coming this way.'

The watchpoint had no roof – it was only a platform edged by the rubble of collapsed columns and a broken wall – but the short day was already darkening.

'We could camp here tonight,' said Shay. 'It'll give us some shelter, at least. What do you think?'

'Let's have a closer look,' said Castrel.

She walked out onto the apron of stone to look over the edge.

'Shay,' she called. 'There's something here.'

It was a corpse, lying in the lee of the parapet, almost covered by a heavy wool cloak and thinly drifted grey snow.

The corpse had been there for a long time, a year at least and probably more, but it wasn't like any corpse he had seen before: not swollen and collapsed, not discoloured and decayed to dust and bone, but strangely preserved. The waxen skin was somewhat loose and sunk against the skull, but the features were still clear, barely changed by death.

He had been a tall man in life, old before he died, his hair and beard gone long ago from grey to white: hair and beard that he had let grow almost to his waist, and smoothed to a silken straightness, though it was brittle and faded now. Under his cloak he had worn a coat of fine weave, its colour a shimmering blue, blue and yet not blue, rippled with subtle shades, and he had a leather bag, a kind of satchel, clutched in one hand. He had leaned on a staff to walk: a staff made from two different woods wound together. The staff lay some distance from him now, split and shattered in many pieces.

'Shay?' Castrel's voice was quiet. Tentative. 'Do you feel that?'

'Feel what?'

'A power was used here. High magic. It's gone, but the stones remember. An echo that never stops.' She was looking at the corpse. 'It was him. He did it.'

'Did what?'

'He was the one who killed the dragon. He did it. I know it was him. I know. He was a wizard. A very powerful wizard.'

Shay studied the corpse carefully, with curiosity. Deep creases in brow and cheek, veined and knotted hands, the suggestion of a stoop. The wizard had been an old man, yet the expression preserved in the dead face and the pale granite eyes that still glared from under thick-grown eyebrows didn't belong to an old man. It was the face of a man who had lived many, many years, but a man to whom ageing had meant little, to whom it was merely an accumulation of time left behind.

'I can't see a wound,' he said, 'and he hasn't starved. Maybe he died of exhaustion. Or old age.'

Castrel shook her head.

'I don't think wizards die of exhaustion or age.'

Ignoring the glare in the corpse's clear empty eye, Shay prised the leather satchel from its grip. He was taken aback to find himself uneasy as he did it. He realised he was feeling ashamed, as if this was a trespass and a desecration, a touch that should not be touched. A thing that should not be done. He hadn't felt like that before in dealings with the bodies of the dead. He pushed his reluctance aside.

This must be done.

He unbuckled the wizard's satchel and went through the contents. Nothing but a sheaf of parchments and papers covered with script. They meant nothing to him.

Castrel had been scuffing at the remains of the broken staff with her toe.

'Can I see those papers?' she said.

'Take them. I'm going to do something with him.' A corpse was a corpse. An empty thing finished with. It had to be got rid of. 'If we're going to stay here tonight we can't sleep next to this.'

He bent to take the dead weight by its boots and drag it away.

When it started to move he saw there was an object hidden underneath. It had been tangled up and shrouded in the cloak.

A sword.

II

There was not one pass but many, each higher than the last, winding between the high peaks of many mountains – mountains behind mountains, an endless unfolding of height after height – and the narrow precarious road always climbing, threading between high gaps, and always the summits lost in cloud. Nights they found no shelter at all. They made the food they carried with them last for five days, and then it was gone and there was nothing but ice and rock and swirling wind.

Castrel unslung her pack and crouched in the shelter of a shoulder of rock to feed Hope. The wind was less there, the hard bitter wind that was always against her, her face raw with it, her eyes dry and painful, her lips chapped sore. She could no longer tell her daughter's hunger from her own.

When she was sure Hope had finished and was sleeping, she leaned back against the wall of rock, resting the back of her head against sharp vertical blades of rock, and reached into her pouch for a leaf of the bitter herb. She chewed it slowly. The juice was dark and bitter and burned the back of her throat. She swallowed, and felt the heat roll through her. Inside she burned like a furnace and the fuel she consumed was herself.

In the last few days she had done this more and more, until now she relied on it totally. Unable to make infusions without a fire, every few hours she took a fragment of raw dried leaf, though she knew that raw leaf was dangerous: it made the dose unpredictable and the effect much stronger. Her heart fluttered and raced, she was always anxious, and strange visions troubled her. It was reckless and foolish to keep on taking it again and again, but what other choice was there? How else could she keep moving and also feed the child and wrap her in warmth, while she herself walked all day and ate only snow?

She didn't say anything to Shay about the herb and took it furtively. She'd never kept anything from Shay before, and she wasn't sure why she did now. It troubled her. She told herself it was because he could do nothing to help and had burdens enough of his own, but part of her suspected it was because she was ashamed, and afraid he'd think less of her, though she knew he was better than that.

And then there was the other thing that she wasn't telling Shay, and that was far, far worse.

There was something wrong with Hope. Something had got inside her, something that was ancient and strong and alive, but not in the way humans are. It had crawled inside her and taken deep root there. Castrel didn't know what it was, but she knew it was there and nothing she could do would drive it out.

It wasn't sickness. Hope was growing faster and stronger than ever, more than any child she had ever known, more than seemed possible when she was always half-starved and half-frozen, but when Castrel opened herself to share minds with her it was no longer like it used to be in the early days, before they crossed the Chelidd Plain and went up into the mountains. Being with Hope then was like walking in a clean, sunlit country. It was like a clear pool to swim in and see the depth of the sky. But now there was a hidden place deep inside the child, walled and defended, that Castrel could not understand or approach, and when she came close to it, that appalling, alien thing knew she was there and it studied her, attentive and intelligent and without concern. She feared it and hated it. It was her mortal enemy because it was inside her child.

Two days after she had first felt the horror in Hope's mind, she had opened the blanket to bathe her and almost screamed. Along the tiny child's spine, spreading across her shoulders and up the back of her neck, there was a fine iridescent scaling, blue, purple, crimson and grey. Castrel bundled Hope back into the blanket and said nothing to Shay.

Most of the time she couldn't bring herself to even think about it. She couldn't think about anything at all, except that everything would somehow be better on the other side of the mountains, and that getting through the High Passes was the only thing to do. All she did was walk in silence and chew the bitter leaf to give her strength and numb her mind.

The leaf gave her strange dreams and waking visions. Sometimes it seemed to Castrel that Hope was a dragon, skinned with enamel scales, her eyes flecked with slivers of purple slate and tawny gold. One night she dreamed that Hope slithered out from under her arm and swarmed up the rock face and crouched on a ledge and gazed down on her with wide lidless eyes, and Hope's bright and many-coloured face was not ancient but immortal.

Sometimes Castrel knew that what was happening was terrible, and it was terrible that she wasn't telling Shay, but when he asked her what was wrong she told him it was only that she was too exhausted to talk, and he understood that because he was the same.

'What you're doing to keep Hope alive is incredible,' he said then. 'You're a wonder. I love you.'

And he turned and walk on ahead alone, shoulders down against the wind.

Oh, Shay. My darling, you do not know.

Sometimes it broke Castrel's heart to see Shay struggle on

oblivious, and to know that if he found out it would be worse because she'd kept it from him. But then the leaf-juice would take full hold and she didn't care any more, but only laughed at the strangeness in her daughter. Laughed at darkness and despair and the ending of everything.

Snow came suddenly, blank and tumultuous, closing the horizons and shutting the mountains away in a grey box. Shay walked ahead of her and she always knew he was there. Always pushing on. She let the ceaselessness of him, his relentlessness, carry her forward, and she carried Hope, riding his strength as she walked behind. But every time the snow swallowed them or night fell and they had to stop, the cold crept deeper into the bone. And every time they went on again they were slower and weaker, too weak to even be hungry any more. The days were short and the nights were long.

Every day now the walled area in Hope where she could not go was larger, and the presence squatting inside it grew. Its roots went deeper. It changed her daughter more. Castrel struggled against it. She tried to hold on to Hope and drive the alien thing back. She hated it and feared it and fought it alone.

On. Always on. Always weaker. Each step a struggle and a failing, each dawn harder to wake from sleep. Hour after hour, day after day, Castrel took all the life and strength from inside herself and drove it into the child. Pushing. Fighting. Scrabbling for a grip and holding on. She was being drained. Fraying and diminishing. Using herself up, right to the core. It cost her all she had. All she was. She used the bitter herb all the time, a leaf always kept in the corner of her mouth, though it no longer made her laugh at dragons and mountains and darkness. In the end – the end that could not be long coming now – there would be nothing left, and she would die.

Don't think about it. Don't think about anything. The time for thinking is gone.

I will not let my baby go, lost and alone in the cold and dark.

And then she would somehow find more. She would do it again. Do it *now*. And then after that there would be another *now*, and she would do it again. And she would keep on doing it, now, and now, and now, and now, and now. She would win the fight against despair not once but always, over and over again. She would hold on tight to *now* and never let it slip into the past. *Now* following *now* following *now*, just one more *now*, until they had come to the end of ice and wind and high darkness.

Stay with me. I will not let you go.

Oh, Shay.

It was her fight, hers alone, in a place where Shay could not go. And she didn't tell him about Hope because she needed his strength for the walking, not for this.

There was a sound coming from somewhere far away in the dark, the saddest, most wrenching sound, the sound of a soul that was frightened, confused, inconsolable, utterly bereft. The sound of her baby crying. Castrel touched Hope's small crumpled face with ice-numbed fingers, and pressed her cheek against the child's. The world around them was shrunk now to this.

You are beloved. You are not alone.

'Let me carry her sometimes,' said Shay. But she wouldn't let him.

'I'm her mother. She needs me.'

'Not all the time. I'm here too.'

'Yes, all the time, Shay. Always. That's how it is.'

She could see the concern and love in his face, and the exclusion he felt. The hurt of it. Hope was his daughter too. She knew it, but it couldn't be helped. This was not his fight. She could only do one thing, and it needed to be this.

'Cass—'

She turned her back on him and stared up the road.

'I do what I can,' she said. 'Every *day*. All the *time*. I *try*.' She made a wide, desperate gesture that included everything. 'Look at all this. I do what I can.'

He was standing close behind her. He put his hand on her shoulder and pressed his forehead against the back of her neck. She shook him off and took a step away from him, forward up the narrow road between precipice and cliff.

On she walked, always on, into the hunger and weakness and wind and cold, and it seemed that the climb into hurt and darkness would go on for ever, and there would never be anything else for her ever again. The whole world narrowed to that. She used the last of the bitter leaf and threw the empty pouch away. There was nothing left for her now except her own failing strength, and always she poured all she had into her daughter, maintaining the connection, keeping her there, fighting the thing that had lodged itself inside Hope – trying to destroy it, trying to drive it out. Trying to find a way to do that. But she could not. She could find no way to grip on it. Whatever the thing was, it was elusive. Untouchable. When she reached for it or tried to confront it full on, it was almost not there at all, and yet she knew it was. She fought it alone, because she must. Still she said nothing to Shay. All she needed him to do was keep walking and leave her alone.

Castrel tripped and fell hard on her face. Breath smacked from her lungs. Elbows and knees crashed against hard rock and exploded into pain. She was dizzy with panic.

Hope! Hope!

The child was gone. Castrel scrabbled around but could not find her. She tried to get up but could not.

Where is she?

She felt Shay trying to lift her and shook him away.

'Leave me! Find her! Look after Hope!'

Shay picked up the child. She had not cried. He held her and talked to her gently.

'She's fine,' he said. 'She's fine.' He crouched at Castrel's side. 'Are you hurt? Don't try to get up. Let me see.'

'Leave me alone!'

She tried to stand but the ground slipped sideways. She crawled to the side of the road and pulled herself up to sit with her back against the cliff. Shay was holding Hope. Looking at her closely.

'Give her to me!' she screamed at him. 'Let me have her back!'

'Cass?' he said quietly. 'What's this? What's wrong with her?'

He turned his back against the wind and unwrapped the blankets to see the child better. She was so small in his arms.

'Give her back to me please. She's cold.'

Shay saw the beautiful iridescent scaling across Hope's shoulders and back.

He wrapped the child in the blanket again and carried her to Castrel and handed her gently back.

'Here,' he said. 'Hold her tight. She's getting cold.'

Then he sat next to her on the ground. Shoulder to shoulder.

'I'm sorry,' he said quietly. 'I should have realised something was wrong. I should have seen this sooner. You shouldn't have had to deal with it all alone. What's happening to her? Is she sick?'

'I don't know.'

'How long has she been like this? And what about you? Are you all right?'

She told him then. She couldn't keep the dark and appalling secret any more.

She saw his shock and incomprehension. He was struggling to understand.

'It's not a sickness,' she said. 'It's ... something, a power, a presence, something that's not her but it's found a way in, and all the time it's getting stronger. It's spreading and growing. I can feel it taking her away. It's pushing her out of her own body, and I can't stop it. It knows I'm there, and I try to fight it. I try to drive it out! But I can't. It's too strong. I can't do anything.'

She was a healer, but she couldn't heal this. She couldn't heal her daughter, her beautiful daughter who was being taken from her, and she must watch her go and know that there was nothing she could do. Shay tried to understand but it wasn't easy for him.

'Are you sure?' he said. 'I've let you do too much and bear too much alone. I've been stupid, I should have ...' He paused. 'Maybe she's just ill, and we can—'

'No, it's not that. This is real. I know. I *know*. I've been fighting it, I've been trying to drive it out. But I can't.'

'It's not all on you, Cass. You don't have do it all by yourself. Let me help you, we'll keep her safe. You can drive this thing out, you'll find a way. I know you can.'

'You believe me, Shay, don't you? You don't think I'm inventing it? You don't think I'm crazy?'

'What?' He looked genuinely taken aback at the thought. 'No. Not that. Of course not. We'll do this, Cass. Together. Whatever this is, we'll get through.'

They walked on up the narrow road. Scarcely a road at all. A broken path between closing cliffs.

'Let me carry your pack,' said Shay. 'I can take two.'

'Thank you,' she said. 'Yes. That would help.'

The pass rounded a steep shoulder and went into the cliff face.

And then there was no pass between the mountains any more, only sheer walls of rock and ice and terrifying edges of fall.

*

The builders of the ancient road through the High Passes, reaching these walls of rock and having nowhere else to go but refusing failure, had cut a tunnel. It entered, wide and black, into the root of the highest mountain.

Immense bronze gates hung across the entrance, skewed and scarred and broken from their hinges. They had been smashed inwards. When they got nearer they saw there had been some attempt to defend the tunnel from within – massive spars of timber used as barricades – but the timbers were splintered and cast aside, charred with a strange burning.

'There was a battle here,' said Shay. 'Whoever was inside the tunnel, they were trying to hold it against attack but they failed, and whatever they were fighting to keep out broke through.'

There were no bodies. No sign of who the fighters had been. Shay crouched to examine the damage to the gates and touch the ash of the burned barricades with his fingers.

'This is recent,' he said. 'Not more than a few months ago. Probably only weeks.' He stood up. 'Come on. There's nobody here now. We have to go through.'

They walked into absolute darkness, the grey light of the entrance receding behind them. Slowly, slowly, they went in under the immense weight of mountains, until they had to feel their way. Everything was black stillness, the air cool but not cold. The resting temperature of rock. They heard the thin distant sound of water trickling, and with every step came the fear of unseen precipitous chasms and mazy dividings of the way and the sudden touch of something alive or dead in the dark. They could not know how far they had to go. They could not know if there was a way out at the other end.

Castrel held Hope tight in her arms. Though the child was

still, she knew that her eyes were open wide, absorbing the total silence and dark. Seeing it for what it was.

At last the tunnel opened on to daylight and they were on the other side of the mountains and the road wound down and away to the south.

There was a faint warmth in the air and a trace of scents she had almost forgotten: earth and grass and sky. Far below them a misty expanse of autumn trees stretched to the horizon. The sky was a powdery blue. There were shreds of cloud and a pale, watery sun. The High Esh was behind them and they were out of the hidden country, back in the places where humans lived. Castrel felt so weak and hungry she could hardly stand, and she could see Shay was the same: so thin she could see the bones in his face. There was no strength left in either of them at all. But they had come through the mountains. Together they had done that.

They sat side by side on a slope of grass and felt the breeze and cool sunshine on their faces.

'This is a good place,' said Shay. He was hugging his knees and looking out across the landscape. Relief and hope made his tired face shine. 'The air's so much better here. It feels wholesome. It's normal, like things used to be. I'd almost forgotten what normal was like.'

And he was right. The world was different here. The currents of life were still flowing, warm and transparent and wonderful. Castrel reached out and touched the threads of vivid life. She joined with them and felt a huge, overwhelming surge of joy. The darkness in the world was gone. That terrible dying wound, that unhealable morbid corrosion she'd been feeling everywhere and in everything since the tide of alien air overwhelmed them at the gates of Sard Keeping – it was gone now.

'It's the mountains,' she said. 'I couldn't feel it when we were in the tunnel, but I can now. The last wall of mountains we came through is the frontier between here and the hidden country, and it's full of high magic. There are wardings and protections in the mountains – in the very rock itself. They're high magic, and they're rooted deep. The mountains themselves are like a huge wall of standing stones. Whatever it is that's destroying everything north of here, the mountains are holding it back and it can't cross. Look, you can see it, I think.'

Behind them, the white peaks of the High Passes shimmered as if they were edged with haze. It was faint but it was there, and beyond it to the north the sky was rising masses of dark cloud stained with streaks with purple, copper and green but south of the mountains was clear wholesome air.

'We're going to be all right now,' said Shay.

'I hope so,' said Castrel.

For the first time in many weeks she opened herself and let her awareness drift out into all that spaciousness and country and sky. She hadn't done that for so long. And all through the High Passes she had been focused tightly, relentlessly, on Hope and herself. She hadn't seen anything else.

'I'm sorry, Shay,' she said quietly. 'I didn't tell you what is happening to Hope. I let you go on by yourself. I used you to forge the way through, and I ignored you.'

'It doesn't matter,' he said.

'I did it because I knew I could. Because I knew you'd be strong and always there. I knew you'd get through without me.'

'You don't need to say any more. It doesn't matter. All that matters is that we got through, and now we have to keep going and do whatever comes next. But we're going to be fine now. It'll be better from now on.'

'Yes,' said Castrel. 'I think it will.'

But she saw how thin and weak Shay was, his face gaunt beneath a straggle of beard, his eyes sunk hollow in their sockets and bruised with exhaustion, his hair falling dirty and lifeless to his shoulders. She could see the bones of him too clearly. And she knew that she was the same. Perhaps worse. Days and days of hunger, struggle, fear and the bitter leaf had taken a heavy toll.

It struck her then how much like Khaag and Paav they were. Alone and lost and very far from home, emaciated, exhausted, terrified and sick, Khaag and Paav had outrun the darkness and come into a different country. But Khaag and Paav had died there. Castrel remembered Khaag's fierce stare and her hoarse quiet voice: *It is behind us, but it is always coming. Always. The line of shadow. The bad darkening. It follows. Sometimes it slows and you get ahead of it for a while. But it does not stop. It never, ever stops.*

But they were not like Khaag and Paav, and they would not be. Castrel felt a fierce surge of anger against the darkening of the world. They were stronger, they were fiercer, they were more determined than that. Khaag had died because in the end she despaired. Without Paav she had given up hope. But she and Shay must survive. They must keep on going. For the sake of Hope. They must not leave their daughter alone in the dark to die.

Suddenly, urgently, she had an appalling thirst for living.

'We'll be fine,' she said to Shay. 'We will come through. And I will get this thing out of Hope. I will save her from that. But I don't know how.'

'You will, Cass. You'll get your strength back and you'll find a way. I know you will. We're in a better place now.'

Perhaps it's true, she thought. *Perhaps here, perhaps now, I will find the strength to drive this thing out of Hope.*

They were in a better place. There was still life in this country, deep in the heart of things, and as long as there was still life she could use it to heal Hope and kill what was inside her. As long as there was still life. As long as the power of the barrier mountains continued to hold the darkness back.

But how long would the barrier hold? She remembered the long line of standing stones on the road out of Sard Keeping. Those stones had the same kind of strength as the barrier mountains, but when she touched them they had been dead. Empty, hollow, brittle and silent, their power destroyed by the appalling tidal wave of change. Would that happen everywhere in the end, and the whole world, all of it, be lost? Castrel pushed the thought aside. There was no point in thinking about that. All they could do was always keep on enduring, keep on going forward and never fail. Never despair. Never give up hope.

12

This is what it is like inside the mind of the child called Hope.

Everything is clean and clear, like warm water full of sunlight. No matter how deep it goes, it is no darker. The world of the child is sensation without perception, floods of vividness and colour without shape or distance.

She will learn near from far. She will learn what is Hope and what is not Hope. She will learn where she stops. She will know those borders at the edge of skin where the rest of everything begins. Soon she will learn, but not yet.

She doesn't have *before* and *after*, not yet. Everything is *now*. She has memories but she has no words for them and no special places to keep them yet, so they are everywhere. For Hope, everything that she remembers is still happening now.

When she was inside her mother everything was all reddish dim because of blood. Sunlight through flesh and blood: that was what she saw through unfocused eyes. So, red she has learned. All the tumultuous colours of the world divide for her now into red and then all the others, the undifferentiated rest that is all one colour but every one different. That is for now, but she will learn. Soon she will learn.

When she was inside her mother, everything was warm and fuzzy and dim and everything was close, but there were sounds to hear. The sounds came from outside, muffled and quiet, but she listened. So she has learned sounds. She can hear better than she can see. For now.

Inside Hope's mind there are voices speaking. They are not her voice. She hears them with the part of her brain that hears sounds, though they are not sounds. She listens although she cannot understand. She listens because she likes new things. She likes to learn.

There are many voices. They are all different, but like the colours Hope cannot tell them apart.

We have made a mistake. We should not have joined with this child. She is too young, unformed and unprepared. We have never joined with one so new before. She is not ready.

She was the last. No other would have come.

The mother would have been a better choice. The mother is gifted. The mother is strong.

Not so strong as the child. Can you not feel the strength here?

Yet the mother is strong. She fights us. She is fighting us now.

Strong enough to drive us out of the child? I do not think so.

Strong enough to harm us. We must hurry. We must build fast and dig deep.

But go carefully. No damage to the child.

Not if it can be avoided.

This is a new thing. This interests me.

I like it here.

Hope cannot tell one voice from another and she does not know what they mean.

Not yet.

But she is learning.

Part Three

13

Dawn greyed into morning, sifting mist out of dripping scrub. Condensing detail. Leaf, twig and thorn. The stony path wound between scattered boulders and sparse trees. Shay stopped at the crest of a hill and scanned the valley below for threads of smoke. There was nothing. No sign of life except a few large birds – kites and buzzards and ravens – wheeling above the woodland canopy.

They had been three days coming down out of the mountains. They walked slowly and rested often, but there was food here. Berries, roots and leaves. Every night he left snares, and once or twice there was something caught in the morning. Always they followed the ancient road south. Lanes and trackways split from it to right and left, but they didn't take them. They had no purpose now except to keep walking, to move as fast and as far as possible, and for now that was purpose enough. They were repairing their strength.

Shay let Castrel sleep as late as she could in the mornings while he scouted ahead and foraged for food, though he never went far from her and Hope. It was better here, in human country again, south of the mountains, but it was not a safe place. Nowhere was. He hadn't forgotten the broken gate at the tunnel under the mountain; the people of this country had fought to keep something out, and they had failed. He had to assume it was riders, the larger-than-human terrible riders on their six-legged beasts. Although the border magic of the High Esh was holding back the strange darkness of the other air, the light of a different sun, he knew that riders went ahead of that and did not depend on it. They had seen no riders since Sard Keeping, except perhaps some distant specks on the Chelidd Plain, but wherever he went Shay carried the axe in his hand and the dead wizard's sword strapped to the pack on his back.

Since they came out of the mountains into human country again they had seen no one at all and no sign of habitation. It was as if they were the last people left in the world.

When Shay got back to the camp, Castrel was sleeping on the ground near the ashes of the night fire, her arm across Hope for protection.

Castrel was so thin. When she walked, she walked slowly. Hunger and anxiety and the cost of what she was doing for Hope were obvious in her face, even when she slept.

'It's getting stronger,' she had said the night before. 'It's starting to change her. I can feel it.'

'What do you mean, change her? Is she getting sick now?'

Castrel shook her head.

'She's amazingly strong. I don't understand it. I'm not feeding her properly, she should be weak and hungry, but she isn't. She's growing fast.'

'It's you,' said Shay. 'It's the impossible thing that you do.'

'I wish it was that,' she said, 'but it isn't. She's becoming – I don't know how to explain it – not like an ordinary child.'

'Of course she's not ordinary. She's got the same gift as you, but she's stronger. You said so yourself.'

'That's not what I mean,' said Castrel. 'This is something else. It's as if you were in a house, and someone else was there. You never see them but you feel them there. It's like that with Hope.

I feel something there, watching me. Watching us. It's powerful, it's rooted deep and it's not human.'

'Do you think it's something to do with the dragon?' he said. 'There was that thing that happened when you went near it. Hope went so still, and you thought she was hurt. We both did. I know she seemed fine afterwards, but isn't it since then that she …?'

He didn't know how to finish the sentence, but she knew what he meant.

'It could be,' she said. 'It's possible, I suppose. I don't know. And it makes no difference, all I can do is hold on to Hope and try to keep her whole and with us, and try to hold that other thing back.'

He didn't ask her how long she could go on doing this for. He knew the answer. All the days. All the days till the end.

But she was so tired and thin, he was afraid she would be seriously ill.

He pulled the blanket up to cover them while they slept. He would keep the cold and darkness and hunger from them. Always. Somehow he would do that.

You are the strength of my strength.

Endurance and courage and trust and love. That was all he could offer them. It had to be enough.

Hope opened her eyes and looked at him. He thought she smiled. He was sure she did. In her eyes now there were bright shining flecks of purple and gold that hadn't been there before. He picked her up and hugged her.

'Hello, my darling, are you awake then? You wonderful, beautiful child.'

He wrapped her in her blanket and walked with her a while, to let Castrel sleep on. He could build the fire later.

Hope was warm in his arms and he held her close, breathing the scent of her, feeling the touch of her cheek against his. His love for her burned hot and fierce. So what if she was sick? So what? So what if some inhuman thing had got inside her? Castrel would drive it out. And if she could not? So what? So what if her life would be short? Now was all that mattered, and he loved her now.

This is my daughter, he said to the empty broken world. *See how perfect and wonderful she is.*

Castrel woke and sat up.

'Hello,' she said. 'Are you all right?'

'Yes,' he said. 'Of course. Everything's fine.'

In the afternoon the road climbed a hill through sparse hazel and thorn. At the top they paused and looked out across a wide shallow valley.

Castrel grabbed his arm and pointed.

'Shay? Look.'

A huddle of timber buildings in cleared fields near a wide, shallow river.

There was no smoke from the farmstead chimney. No livestock in the fields. No movement at all, only the flow of the river. But apart from the stillness, it was a farm like the golden memory of farms.

They stood under the trees and listened to their own breathing and the whisper of the thin breeze disturbing the thorns. Beyond the river the woodland rose again, a grey mass of trees. Low forested hills disappeared into distance and mist.

'Stay here,' said Shay. 'I'll go down and look.'

'No,' said Castrel. 'We're coming with you.'

Empty windows. Weathered timbers. Unswept fallen leaves. Shay was reluctant to break open the door. It still felt like someone's house.

There was a pair of boots inside the door. Cold ash in the stove. Shay moved quietly from room to room. He ran his hand along the back of a chair. Touched a linen bolster stuffed with hay. The beds were neatly left, though faintly musty now. He stood on a threadbare, faded piece of carpet laid across floorboards: just stood there, so he could feel it under his feet, to remember just for a moment the familiar ordinariness of doing that. Someone had put that piece of carpet just exactly there, because they liked it so.

The people of the farm were gone but their intimacy remained like a scent in the air, a voice just fallen silent. Signs and traces and things left behind. There had been parents and children here. A dog, or dogs. It was as if the family had gone into another room only moments before, but it was a room that he couldn't find.

'Shay! Shay!'

His heart lurched. Castrel was calling him from somewhere outside. Her voice sounded urgent.

'Where are you?' he shouted.

'Out here! Shay!'

He ran out, axe in hand, afraid.

'What is it? Where are you?'

She was in the yard.

'Come and see,' she said.

He followed her into the dim interior of a low stone outbuilding.

'Look.'

Even in the near-darkness he could see the radiance in her face.

Cured meat. Dried salted river-fish. Racks of apples in straw, withered but good. Turnips and carrots. Sacks of grain. Wrapped cheeses on a shelf. The room was a store of treasures beyond price.

Shay took a stone bottle from a bench, pulled the cork and put his nose to the opening. Something sweet and dark and heady. A kind of wine. He passed it to Castrel.

'Here,' he said. 'Drink.'

She took a swig from the bottle, then another. Then she took an apple from the rack and crunched it. There were no words for the joy of it. That fragile joy cut him like grief.

'We'll stay here a while,' she said.

Shay was reluctant.

'Whoever lived here, they left, Cass, and they must have been in a rush to leave all this behind. Something frightened them away.'

Or they were dead.

'But we can stay here,' she said. 'For a few days, at least. It's no more dangerous here than anywhere else. We can rest. We can eat and sleep and build up our strength.'

He saw the darkening shadows under her eyes, the edge of bones under tightening skin.

'Of course we can,' he said. 'This is a good place.'

That evening they fried meat and apples and made flat grey bread. Uncorked another stone jar from the shelf to drink. By the light of the stove, with the curtains drawn, the long day hardened into the bright-faceted jewel of all the days; the one fixed star in the field of all the stars, the one that never moves.

And then they slept, the three of them together in a bed. Shay lay with his spine against Castrel's for the warmth, and Castrel held Hope, their beautiful child, tucked in with them, close.

Shay woke early, warm in the bed. Day was drifting in through curtains at the window. He felt the silence and the early light and Castrel's quiet breathing and their daughter nested in the warmth between them. The human ordinariness of that. Not ordinary at all.

We might be the last, he thought, *for all we know. The very last people of all.*

All the uncountable generations, all the parents and all the children there had ever been: all of them had done what he was doing now; all of them had woken human and ordinary from sleep. That was what humanity was. Waking ordinary and human, again and again, through all the seasons and the days. All the thousands of centuries of that. What if it was all ended now, and this their human family waking was the very last one?

That was what 'the end of the world' meant. That.

Yet we are here, and this is also true.

He got up carefully and left Castrel and Hope to sleep on. They looked so ordinary. So human and peaceful and happy.

He emptied out their packs and carried all their clothes and blankets down to the river to wash them. Nothing had been washed since the day they left. *How long ago was that?* He didn't know any more.

The bundle of dirty linen in his arms was rich with scents and smells, and as he carried it to the river he breathed them all: there was woodsmoke; the underground room in the Keeping; the red dust of the Chelidd Plain; the cold of mountain passes; the child's soil, and the sweat and faint traces of Castrel and himself. He was carrying their story in his arms, written in grubby fabric and scent. He was taking it down to the river to wash it all away.

The river ran fast and wide and shallow over stones. The water was clear and clean, it was ice against his hands and made the linen heavy and dark.

When he had finished, he spread the wet things out on the stones of the riverbank to dry in the sun. They were like sodden grey banners unfurled for the world to see. They shouted into the silence of the valley and the wooded hills.

Here we are! There are people here!

But it could not be helped.

Halfway to the house he turned round and went back and gathered up the wet linen again.

What am I doing? We're not safe here. The road was only fifty yards away, and overlooked the river. Anyone passing would see. It could even be seen from the hill. *We should keep watch and light no fire by day. We shouldn't really stay here at all, but we have no choice. Castrel must rest and recover. And so must I.*

When he got back to the house he hung the wet things to dry in a barn, then packed their bags with food they could carry and put them by the door. They must always be ready to leave at a moment's notice.

He unwound the wrappings from the dead wizard's sword. It was a two-edged, hand-and-a-half broadsword, heavy to wield. The leather of grip and scabbard was split and crusted with mould and mildew, but the blade was long and clean and white, engraved with strange markings, its metal like the metal the White Knives used. He found a stone to hone it, but there was no need. He took it out to the yard and began going through exercises and practice swings. He needed to build arm muscle and get used again to the feel of a weapon in his hand.

Days unfolded out of days and the river raced shallow and cold out of the mountains and Castrel grew stronger and more whole. Shay kept an eye on the road but it was always empty. Nothing and no one came.

We are the last, then. There is only us now. Everyone else must have already gone further south.

Hope was growing stronger too. Larger, and heavier to hold. There was a solidness there that he hadn't felt before, and her face had a slightly different shape. She was focusing her gaze now, following him as he moved across the room. Watching him with wide expressionless eyes. Sometimes he took her down to the river and held her so that her feet were in the water and the stream went between her toes. He watched her concentration and how she moved her legs.

Everything she does is done for the first time. Everything is a wonder to her.

Her hair has grown. There's more of it now.

Being a parent meant being parent always to difference and change, and yet always to feel the same, always as raw and unready as on the first day. Shay loved his daughter with a wordless intensity that drove out thought. Almost indistinguishable from grief and fear, it transfigured both into something else, something that nourished him and made him strong.

Shay found a razor and shaved his beard and cut his hair short. He barely recognised his own face in the looking glass, he was so changed. There was a hard fierceness in his eyes that startled him.

Sometimes Castrel went out for long walks like she used to, and took Hope with her. They came back happy and smelling of outside. He watched Castrel draw lines and patterns on Hope's skin, murmuring as she worked.

'She's getting better, I think,' she said. 'She's talking to me again, in that way she has. I can still feel the thing inside her, but less now. I'm not sure I'd know it was there at all, if I wasn't looking for it. It's like a dim unease in the distance. A cloud on the horizon.'

'That's good,' he said. 'That's wonderful.'

Perhaps after all this was just some illness in their child that Castrel could heal.

When Hope looked at him now, he saw the bright shining flecks of purple and gold in her eyes. They were more obvious and the colours were deeper.

*

'I love this place,' Castrel said once. 'It's a home like we used to have. I wish we could stay here a long time. Always.'

Shay longed for that too, with all his heart, but he knew she was just idly spinning wishes and dreams.

'That would be good,' he said. 'But we're not safe yet. We'll have to leave soon.'

'Maybe we won't, Shay. We don't know that. Perhaps the wardings in the mountains are strong enough to keep us safe and keep the riders away for ever.'

'I think those riders have already come through.' He remembered the smashed gates and burned barricades at the tunnel through the mountains. 'I'm sorry. I think they're already here.'

One day Castrel sat on the bed with the papers they'd found on the dead wizard's corpse. Shay had forgotten all about them. He hadn't realised she'd brought them with her. He watched her quiet absorption as she read them through and sorted the writings into piles, while Hope lay next to her on the blanket, awake and practising quiet sounds with her tongue. Castrel's face settled into a look of abstract concentration he hadn't seen in her before. So much of her was strange country to him.

'What are you doing?' he said.

'Just looking, to see what's here. There might be something that could help us. I was wondering if there was anything about the dragon and why he killed it.'

She moved over so there was room on the bed next to her.

'Here,' she said. 'Come and have a look. You don't often get a chance to see wizards' writing.'

She gave Shay a pile of creased and stained papers. Some were torn scraps that had been crumpled and flattened out again, and some had charred edges as if they had been snatched from a fire or found among the ashes of one. Some looked very old, and the ink had faded to a faint brown. Most of them were covered with handwriting in small neat lines, but some had other markings: complicated curls and circles and patterns with words in them. Some looked like maps and drawings.

'I can't make anything of this,' he said.

'Nor can I, mostly,' said Castrel. 'A lot of it's in languages I don't know. And see how it's written in different hands? See the difference between this and this? It's all out of order, just a heap, and I can't tell for sure which bits are written by him. I think it's mostly stuff he collected, but sometimes there are notes scrawled in the margins or on the back.' She showed him. 'Like that, for instance, and those are always in the same hand, so I think that must be the wizard's own writing, where he made notes while he was reading. And then there are these, in this pile, and they're all in that same hand, so I think they must be his.'

'What are they about?'

'I'm pretty sure they're about the wars in the hidden countries that Mamser Gean told us about.'

Shay was curious.

'Really? What do they say?'

'It's hard to be sure. It's like he kept notes of what was happening, but they don't make much sense, and it's all out of order.'

'Read some to me. I want to hear.'

She picked one off a pile.

'*From Oskh, five; from Tyhe, two; from Kershmoss, one; from the Hedgeway and Soe, three; and from Ancinet, one. In total, twelve. Twelve! From the others, from Tellin even, nothing. Not one. It is not enough. Not nearly enough.*

'I think the names are places,' she said, 'but they might be people.'

She read another.

'*If we can bring the three of them together, there is still a way through even now. I must try to speak with him tonight, but how can I speak with him when all the stones are dark and cold? I don't have the strength for the other road. The risk is too great. But I must. I must.*

'There's lots like that. Most of it I don't understand.'

She sorted through the heap to find what she was looking for.

'I am leaving them here to their fate. Errish curses me and calls me a coward and worse, and perhaps she is right, but there is nothing more to be done. If I can reach the Erehold before Kint is crossed, there is still a chance. The wards still hold there, I would know if they did not. Of course I am frightened! I hurry to leave because I know what is coming and I am afraid. But reason is on my side. It is, though Errish does not see it and I am sorry for that, but it can't be helped. I must get away quickly now.'

She turned the page.

'I broke the heights behind Farraract and destroyed the Wielder there, that shambling beast, but still they will not listen to me. They despise us all openly now, because of what happened at Feierel, as if I could have prevented that. And another disaster came upon us. Tellin has fallen. She failed. I felt it happen, and feel it still. I cannot shake loose the anguish and despair. At the end they tormented her for the pleasure of it, they prolonged her pain for weeks for no other reason than because they could. Her screams. Oh, her screams. I knew it – I felt it – and could do nothing. Of the four that landed at Drouast, I am the last. We made so many mistakes. We were stupid. We assumed ... but it is too late now.'

'He sounds frightened,' said Shay, 'all the time, as if everything is always getting worse. But I've never heard of any of those places or people. Have you?'

'No, never. I have no idea what it means, but I haven't read them all yet. It may make more sense when I've finished the rest. He never puts dates on them, but perhaps I can get them in some kind of order.'

Shay left her to finish reading. A little while later she came to find him, carrying a few scraps of paper, and there was a dark, lost look in her face that wrenched his heart.

'Listen, Shay,' she said. 'Listen to this.

'*We have not the strength. After all these hundreds of centuries, it will end in our destruction and all will be lost. Everything. For ever. There will be no coming back this time. In our arrogance we grew obsessed with the enemies in the south and thought them the only threat, when we should have paid attention in the north. But who would have thought he would attempt such a thing as this? We believed him feeble and vain, but it is because he was feeble and vain that he did this, and succeeded, where greater and worse than he could not. He has done it. And it is done. The door that should not have been opened is open. It is the end ...*

'That one stops there, but there's this as well:

'*It is beyond catastrophe. The darkness is spreading from the north more quickly than I thought. I expected more time. More time! And a reprieve at the last, like always before. But now that cannot be. There is no way to reverse it, and the end will come. I did not expect to see this. I am not prepared ... Is it my failure? Did I miss my chance? No, I was not even important, though I thought I was. Do not call this defeat. It is worse than that. It is the end.*

'Oh, Shay ...' she said when she had finished. Loss and dismay in her eyes. The loss of all the world and of their future. 'It's the same, it's what the stranger told you at the Keeping ... *The door that should not have been opened is open. It is the end.*'

'It's just words, Cass. Old words on scraps of paper ... Vague rumours ...'

He was trying to reassure her, but it sounded hollow even to himself. Yet what else could they do but push it aside and keep going?

'There's something else,' she said. 'A scrawl on the back.'

She turned the paper over to read the other side.

'*I must kill her. I must kill the dragon, my beloved Vespertine. It is the last and only chance for any kind of future at all.*'

That evening, after they had eaten, Castrel laid Hope on the bed to sleep.

'I'm sorry we haven't got the crib you made for her,' she said. 'She would have liked that.'

'I'll make her another one, one day, just the same.'

'Like a boat?'

'Yes.'

They sat by the stove and talked, trying to make sense of what Castrel had read in the dead wizard's papers.

'It doesn't tell us anything we didn't already know,' said Shay. 'It only confirms it. There was a war among wizards in the hidden countries. It was going badly and then something terrible was done somewhere in the north.'

'*The door that should not have been opened is open,*' said Castrel.

'Yes,' said Shay. 'And whatever happened then, it released a terrible power which the stranger at the Keeping said is from a different world and would destroy this one.'

'The dead wizard despaired then,' said Castrel, 'because everything he was trying to do had failed. Then he killed the dragon called Vespertine and died himself.'

They went over it again and again but there was nothing more. It was no help. It didn't tell them what the thing was that had got inside Hope, or how to drive it out. It didn't tell them where they could go to be safe.

'We shouldn't stay here much longer,' said Shay. 'We have to keep moving south. We should keep looking for other people. We can't be the only ones left.'

'I know,' said Castrel. 'But this is a good place. We're not strong enough to travel again yet.'

*

That night they slept in a bed again, ordinary and human with their child.

The next day they went together to take Hope to the river. The sky was pale blue, the sun misted, watery and diffuse. Shay stood on the bank to watch Castrel bathe the child.

There was a sound behind him.

Shay looked back. Riders on six-legged beasts were coming round the bend in the road. Already they were almost upon them.

'*Cass!*'

Shay flattened himself on the slope of the riverbank. Castrel was next to him, holding Hope. Her breathing was fast and shallow. There was a wind, and the sound of the river, but he could hear the heavy footfalls of the beasts, the hooves on the road and the clank of bridles and gear.

'Did they see us?' she whispered.

'I don't think so, but they could have heard us. We were talking loud.'

'The noise of the river might have covered it.'

They waited. The pace of the riders didn't change.

'Hush, sweetheart,' Castrel was whispering to Hope. 'Please, my darling. Please. No sound.'

Shay forced himself to stay still.

Let them pass, he begged the world. *Just let them pass.*

He had the knife in his pocket and the axe at his belt. He cursed himself that he hadn't thought to bring the sword.

He crawled a few feet forward on elbow and belly.

'They'll see you,' whispered Castrel.

'They won't.'

There were three at the front, riding high on their six-legged beasts, strung out and silent. They rode upright, attentive, moving their heads from side to side. Scanning. Two more walking behind. The dirty grey cowls shrouded their faces, making their heads look bulky and too large.

Shay felt the pressure of their attention pass. He inched his way cautiously back. Castrel gripped his arm hard. It hurt.

'There's another one behind us!' she hissed. 'Coming across the field on the other side of the river. We're trapped. There's nowhere we can hide and not be seen.'

Fear crushed his chest and made his heart struggle. He wanted to breathe clear air. He wanted to run.

I will defend them. I will fight. For Castrel and Hope I will fight and kill.

He would fight. And he would die. He could not protect them, though he would try.

There was a weird shriek from the road, and the sound of footfalls stopped. A cry from across the river behind them answered it.

'They know we're here.' Castrel's voice was flat with despair.

And then Shay stood up. He would not hide, not if hiding was useless. He couldn't always be afraid.

The riders on this side of the river had dismounted. All five were coming down the slope from the road towards them. They were walking slowly and they carried foul weapons, heavy-bladed, filthy and poisonous.

Shay had the axe in his hand.

He walked out to meet them, swinging the axe, moving to one side to draw them away from Castrel and Hope.

The five walkers paused. He heard a kind of hiss from them, a ripple of anticipated pleasure. Then they divided: three peeled off towards him, and two carried on towards Castrel and Hope. Unhurried. He could not see their faces, but he knew that they smiled.

He heard a shout from behind him and looked back. The sixth

of them, the one that came from behind, was fording the river. Already he was almost upon Castrel and the child.

But this one was not grey and hooded, as he had seemed before. He was tall and bright and beautiful, slender, with fine pale hair and golden skin and honey-gold eyes, and he carried a shining sword in his hand.

The walkers paused and realigned themselves to meet the new threat. Shay sensed their consternation. Their relaxation gone.

The golden stranger from the Keeping was running towards them with an easy stride. He seemed to have no weight at all. His sword cut the heads from two with a single flickering sweep, almost too quick to see, and then he was behind them, and two more fell, their throats sliced open and oozing dark liquid.

But the one enemy still standing brought its weapon down on the golden stranger in a crashing arc, and though he rolled from the blow it crushed his right arm and shoulder. He staggered and fell to his knees, the sword dropped from his hand.

The grey hooded thing raised its weapon again for the killing blow. And died with a long white knife in its chest, a thrust from the stranger's left hand.

The golden stranger was on his knees, his head bowed. Shay could see that he was badly hurt: his right arm hung useless at a wrong angle, the shoulder slashed and torn and oozing blood. Castrel knelt beside him.

'This wound is ugly,' she said. 'I can do something for it.'

'Thank you,' the stranger said, 'but it's of no consequence. I can tend to myself.' His voice was clear and subtle and light.

'Please let me help,' said Castrel. 'It's a debt we owe you, and I want to pay it.' To Shay she said, 'Help me get him to the house.'

Shay looked doubtfully towards the road from the mountains. 'Those beasts. The creatures they rode ...'

'They are of no concern now,' said the stranger. 'Without their riders, they will turn back and return to the host.'

'You mean there are more coming?' said Shay.

The stranger shook his head, though he winced because the movement hurt him.

'There's no need for alarm,' he said. 'In time there will be many more, but these were only scouts. The rest of their horde is still coming through the mountains. They're some days away. You have time.' He was twisting his head as he talked, trying to see the wound in his shoulder. Probing it tentatively with his fingers.

'Come back to the house with us,' said Castrel.

'Yes, perhaps I should.'

Shay put a hand under the stranger's unhurt arm to lift him.

'Can you stand?' he said.

'Of course.'

Shay helped him to his feet. His lightness was surprising.

'If you would be so kind,' the stranger said to Castrel, 'perhaps you might recover my knife from that one's chest, and bring me my sword?'

Back at the house Castrel laid Hope on a pile of blankets on the bench against the wall.

'Sit at the table,' she said to the stranger. 'Please.'

He groaned when she cut the shirt from his wound.

'That's a grievous loss,' he said. 'This shirt was from Traille. It's been with me a very long time. I won't find another like it again.'

His body was slender, the muscles clear and smooth, but the wound was vicious. A long and ragged gash. Shay saw the glisten of pale bone and raw flesh. Castrel sluiced the blood away, then ran her fingers over the golden skin of his shoulder and arm, frowning in concentration.

'There are fractures, and fragments in the flesh that carry disease, but I can help it mend. Be open and let me in. If you feel me, try not to fight. It is possible to resist, but if you do there may be harm.'

'To me or to you?' The stranger smiled. Castrel ignored him.

'I'd give you an infusion to drink for the pain,' she said. 'But I don't have it. I'm sorry.'

Shay watched her work. No matter how often he saw her do this, it was always strange and wonderful to him. Even her beautiful voice was somehow unfamiliar as she half murmured, half sang the unfamiliar syllables of the hedge-tongue.

When she had finished she bound the shoulder with a strip of clean linen.

'Your bones are different,' she said. 'I think I've done them right, and I've cleaned out the wound as best I can, but that weapon took its foulness deep inside. I'm not sure—'

'It will not matter,' the stranger said. 'Injuries trouble me for a while, but infection and disease do not. Thank you for what you have done. I am grateful.'

'The gratitude is ours,' said Shay. 'If you hadn't—'

The stranger waved him aside.

'A small thing. Forget it.' He was examining the damage to his green leather coat. 'I can repair this. Not perfectly, but well enough.'

Castrel was clearing her jars from the table.

'I know who you are,' she said. 'I know you talked to Shay at the Keeping. But how is it that you are here now? Were you *following* us?'

'Alas, no,' the golden stranger said. 'I was merely following those riders, though it's not such a coincidence that we should meet again. There's only one road out of the High Esh. I did see you once before, a while ago, as it happens. I thought you might have seen me.'

'I think we did,' said Shay. 'A few days out of the Keeping, just before the rain. There were two riders behind us, and another was keeping pace with them, out of their sight. We didn't see them again. I thought then the third rider was different. Was that you?'

'It was. Those two were following you, but I destroyed them for you.' He held up his hands in mock modesty. 'You need not thank me for that, it was a pleasure.' He smiled. 'Even though you told me that you were alone at the Keeping, and you were not.'

'I ...' Shay began, but the golden stranger waved it off.

'It was a wise precaution,' he said. 'In your position I would have done the same. But I knew. Of course I did. Even before you found me, I knew the basement where you were sheltering, and I knew when your child was born.'

'You seem to be everywhere and know a lot,' said Castrel.

'I make a point of it. I try not to get involved, as a rule, though I make an exception for those riders. I take the opportunity of destroying them whenever I can.' He eased himself to his feet and pulled on his coat gingerly. 'But now I must go. My horses have been tethered alone too long. I wish you well. You left it very late to cross the mountains and I didn't expect you to make it this far. I am glad you did, but you must be quick now. The mountains are warded but the wardings will fail soon, and the horde is coming. You should leave tomorrow. At the latest, tomorrow. And travel fast.'

'Can those riders really break the protection of the mountains?' said Castrel. 'Are they really so powerful?'

'Not the riders themselves. They're foul killers only, the harvest outriders of the scavenging horde. They have no power like that. But there are other creatures that travel with them sometimes, huge shambling things. I haven't seen them closely, and I don't want to, but they have certain strengths of that kind, I believe. Perhaps very great powers indeed. I don't know for sure. I only know that the wizards feared them and called them Wielders.'

Shay remembered what they had seen at the bridge across the Skywater, when Gean died. A heavy form lumbering behind the riders, dwarfing them, struggling to follow because of the narrowness between the parapets.

'There was one of those at the bridge, when we came to the Keeping. Mamser Gean killed it.'

The golden stranger laughed with delight.

'Did he? Then your friend was a warrior indeed. But even if the Wielders can't break through the mountains, the wards will fail of their own accord soon enough. The world itself is turning against them now. The energies they draw on, the world-stuff they are rooted in, that itself is degrading. It's a fundamental corrosion. The other world is flooding this one and these bleak riders are merely the first hint of the inundation to come.'

He paused, and Shay saw real sadness in his eyes. Grief for the world that was being lost, and sympathetic sorrow for them.

'I am sorry,' the stranger said softly. 'So sorry. You are good and courageous people, I admire you and you have been gentle and kind to me. But now I must go.'

As he turned to leave, Castrel put a hand on his arm.

'Must you?' she said warmly. 'I really don't think you should travel straight away. You've been hurt, and you should give the wound time to knit. Won't you stay with us tonight? You could leave in the morning.'

The stranger looked taken aback. He hesitated. Shay thought he seemed almost shy.

'I don't know ...'

'We owe you so much,' said Castrel. 'And we'd love some company. We haven't seen anyone else for so long. No one at all.'

'This place is full of food,' said Shay, 'and if we have to leave tomorrow we can't carry it away. Why don't you stay and share some with us? We could make it a feast. There's wine here too: it's home-made stuff, but it's good and there's lots of it.'

The stranger smiled, genuinely surprised and pleased.

'Thank you,' he said. 'I will. Yes. That would be good. But first I must look to my horses. I left them across the river.'

The stranger must have moved fast. It was less than half an hour before he returned with two tall horses, slender, chestnut brown, glossy and sleek. One was saddled, the other laden with packs and satchels.

'My clothes,' he said, 'and some materials I carried off from the Keeping. And a few other possessions I've picked up over the years that are precious to me.'

Shay went out with him to show him the stable. Night had fallen. The deep sky was clear and shining black, each single star surrounded in its own faint bright cloud of mist. They seemed to hang there in luminous blackness like pure clean fruit.

'I used to think that was where other worlds might be,' said Shay, staring up at the sky.

'Out there?' said the stranger. 'No, all the worlds are here. They occupy the same place at the same time, all of them, like contrary thoughts in a single mind.'

'And you really are from somewhere else? Another world?'

'Yes. But I like this world. I've been here a long time.'

'How long?'

'About three thousand years.'

Shay stared at him in blank incomprehension.

'Three thousand years?'

'More or less. This was a more crowded world when I first came here. The first place I ever went was Far Coromance.'

'I still want to go there,' said Shay. All the long days of their walking since they left Sard Keeping, he had been weaving idle dreams in his mind of Far Coromance, a sunlit golden place, an island among islands where warm seas glittered and lemons grew.

'It was a wonderful place,' said the golden stranger. 'I saw it grow and change through thousands of years, but it was never more beautiful than the first time I was there. I wish you could have seen it. The nights were warm and scented, and the night skies were a deep purple-blue, netted with golden stars. I possessed nothing and slept in the open, but I slept on the pavements of emperors then.'

'And now you're going back to that other world you came from?'

'There'll be a crossing opened for me at a certain place and time, and if I'm there I will go back. But that will be the only crossing. There'll be no others after that. I won't get another chance. But there's plenty of time yet. I will be there.'

When they got back from the stable, Castrel had lit candles and laid out food on the table, the finest of all they had. The room smelled of fresh baked bread, and they ate and drank wine by the warmth of the stove. It was a grand feast of plenty and the best of times. Shay surrendered himself to the strange thrill of it: here he was, a boy from Harnestrand, a boat-builder's apprentice, at the table with Castrel and their child, feasting at the ending of the world with a golden man who was at least three thousand years old. A great golden warrior who had killed five monstrous riders and saved all their lives.

'We don't even know your name,' said Castrel.

The golden man smiled.

'I don't have one,' he said, 'not any more. I've lived too long. I have had names in the past, from time to time, but in the end they all wear out and fall away. Names are what the people you love call you by, and when those people are gone the names are only echoes of the past and reminders of grief. So I don't use a name. I am just myself.'

'Oh,' said Castrel. 'That's so sad.'

'Is it?' He made a neat courteous bow. 'Then I apologise profoundly. I have no wish to make you sad. Actually, I don't find it so. I find it liberating.'

'But we need to call you something,' said Castrel. 'I want to.'

'Then call me friend.'

'Yes,' she said. 'Yes. You are that.'

Their golden friend.

What's it really like in such a man's mind? thought Shay. *He behaves like us – of course he does, he's had centuries of practice, he'd be better at it than we are – but what does he see when he looks at us? How would it feel, to be him? It's an unsolvable mystery. Even if we had the answer, we couldn't understand it.*

Ask him a question you might understand the answer to, then.

Shay cut himself a piece of cheese and broke some bread.

'What's a wizard?' he said.

Their golden friend looked surprised.

'Why do you ask that?'

'It puzzles me, that's all,' said Shay. 'I mean, are wizards human? Are they one of the other peoples? They don't keep themselves secret, they don't live only in the hidden countries, but they fight wars there, and they have this magic – I saw it for myself at the Keeping – so what kind of thing are they?'

'Being a wizard is what they do, not what they are. They remake themselves as they choose. Some begin as human, some not, but they all learn to reshape their bodies and minds to some extent. They make *trades*. They extend their lives. They traffic with other worlds, and sometimes they cross from one world to another. Wizards ignore borders, they go everywhere, they choose their own ambitions and purposes and means. Some of them remain more or less wholesome and wise, but some end up as unnatural, *made* things. Artefacts. Works of art. All too often, little remains of whatever it was they began with.'

'They sound unpleasant as well as dangerous,' said Shay.

'Not all of them. The best of them are bold, far-sighted, gener-ous and wise. Others … Well, you remember those cold beasts caged in Sard Keeping? Those half-living eternal faded things? Wizards make bad choices sometimes, and ruin themselves like that. It is terrible to see.'

He turned to Castrel.

'Wizarding is not like what you do at all,' he said. 'What you do is an abundant natural gift. I envy you that.' He smiled. 'You're very good at it, by the way. I've submitted to several healers over the years, but none was as strong and quick as you, and none had your insight and imagination. You grasped my anatomy perfectly, even though you'd never seen anything like it before.'

Castrel looked uncomfortable. Shay couldn't tell whether she felt pleased or belittled. She didn't respond, except to change the subject.

'I've been thinking,' she said. 'How is it you came through the mountains behind us? We saw you just after we left the Keeping, and with a horse you'd have gone much faster. You could have been far south of here by now.'

The golden man took a sip of wine.

'I was exploring elsewhere,' he said. 'I went west to see if Tellin was still at Erehold, but it was all destroyed. There was no life there, and I couldn't find her. Apologies,' he added, 'these names mean nothing to you.'

'Tellin is dead,' said Castrel. 'She was tortured. I'm sorry. It happened a long time ago.'

Their golden friend stared at her, astonished.

'And how in the world would you know that?'

She told him about the dead wizard's body and the papers she took away with her. His eyes widened with interest.

'May I see?' he said.

'Of course.' Castrel fetched the satchel and took out the sheaves of writing. 'Here, have them. You can keep them if you like.'

He took the papers and began to leaf through them avidly.

'These are wonderful,' he said. 'A real treasure. Thank you.' He read for a moment or two. 'I wonder whose they are?'

'There isn't a name,' said Castrel. 'Well, there are lots of names, but not his.'

'We've got his sword as well,' said Shay. 'Do you want to see it?'

'I do. Yes.'

Shay brought it out from under the bed.

'This isn't a gift, though,' he said. 'I'd like to keep this.'

The golden friend smiled.

'Of course. Here, let me see it.' He unwrapped the bindings and frowned. 'I know this sword. This was Tariel's. He was my friend, if one may ever call a wizard friend. This is sad news, although not altogether a surprise. I knew Vespertine had fallen. I saw her body.'

'Vespertine was the dragon,' said Castrel.

'She was. You have an astonishing fund of knowledge for ...' His voice trailed off.

'For a hedge-witch, you mean?'

'No, no.' He looked embarrassed. Shay thought he was blushing. If a golden man could blush. 'I'm sorry,' he said. 'I didn't intend to patronise you. For a human, I was going to say, but that would have been just as rude. And stupid, since you've already shown you're neither of you usual for humans. You've been in Sard Keeping and passed through a hidden country. Nothing about you should surprise me now. All the same, what do you know of Vespertine?'

'I know that the wizard you call Tariel killed her.'

'That's impossible! That could not be.'

'He did. The dragon on the Chelidd Plain was killed by that wizard, I know the signature of his magic, and there's something in his notes about how he had to do it because it was his last chance. Last chance for what, I don't know.'

'But he simply could not have. Tariel was the most powerful of wizards, and one of the wisest and best, but even he hadn't the resources to destroy a dragon. Vespertine was in her prime. Tariel could not have attempted such a thing and lived.'

'He did not live,' Castrel pointed out.

'But he loved her. They had been bond companions for … I don't know how long. Many centuries, perhaps thousands of years. I cannot remember the time when I hadn't heard of Vespertine and Tariel.'

'You mean it was the wizard's own dragon?' said Shay.

'No, if anything it was the other way round. A dragon is immortal, and no one's, but a dragon often takes a bond companion. A wise and beloved friend. It keeps them from turning too much inwards, away from the world, and they often choose wizards because wizards' lives are long. You wouldn't choose as your best friend someone who only lived for one afternoon of your life.' He frowned. 'Yet Tariel destroyed his beloved Vespertine, though the effort cost him his life. Why would he do such a thing?' He poured himself more wine and drank it all. 'And it occurs to me that she must have permitted it. I cannot understand that.'

Hope woke then and cried out loudly because she was hungry. Castrel went to pick her up.

'There you are, my darling. You've been asleep such a long time.'

She brought her to the table, still bundled in her blanket.

'What's her name?' said their golden friend.

'Hope,' said Castrel. 'Her name is Hope.'

He smiled.

'A good name. May I see her?'

'Yes, of course.'

He moved the blanket gently away from her face to see better. Hope opened her eyes and he saw the bright shining purple and golden flecks in them. His face clouded.

'Oh,' he said. 'Oh – '

Before Castrel could stop him, he pulled the blanket right back to see Hope's shoulders and chest. Her beautiful iridescent scaling shimmered in the candlelight.

Castrel jerked Hope away and wrapped her again.

'What are you *doing*?' she said fiercely.

He stared at her. His golden eyes glittered. Inhuman golden eyes.

'This is something else,' he said. 'I was not expecting *this*.'

'What do you mean?' said Shay.

The golden man ignored him. He was focused only on Castrel.

'When you saw the body of Vespertine on the Chelidd Plain, did you go near? Did you approach? Did you touch her?'

'Yes.'

'And the child was with you? She also went near?'

'Yes. What are you saying? What do you know? Tell me!'

'I'm sorry,' he said. 'Your child is lost to you.'

'What—?'

'She has the heart of the dragon in her. She has been joined by Vespertine.'

14

As soon as she heard it, Castrel knew it was true. Catastrophic emotions surged inside her: an overwhelming flood and burn from the deepest and most ancient primal places in her heart. Horror. Anger. Disgust. Desperation. An appalling, dizzying grief. What their golden friend said accounted for everything: the elusive presence in Hope that watched her with interest but no concern; the unshiftable, incomprehensible power of it; the way Hope grew so fast and strong when even her survival through the bitter cold and starvation of the mountains was a miracle.

There is a dragon inside my daughter.

She wanted to scream and wail and thrash and fight and howl with despair.

I must get rid of it. I must get it out.

But she pushed it all back. Closed it down and shut it away. Emotion was for later. First, now, she must be cold and clear and hard. Now, she must pay attention. Now, she must learn all she could from this strange golden man who knew so much.

If I am to fight a dragon, I have to know how.

She looked at Shay. He was always so raw and open, and his face now was crumpled and empty, broken open with shock. All the feelings that Castrel was forcing down deep inside her were there, visible, all of them at once. His mouth opened to speak but he was finding nothing.

Oh, Shay.

He loved his daughter so much.

We'll look after her, Castrel wanted to say to him. *She'll be fine. We'll get her back.*

But all that must come later, too. She sat at the table with Hope in her arms, opened another bottle of wine, and filled the three cups again.

'The dragon Vespertine was dead,' she said to their golden friend. 'She had been dead for years. Her body was decayed.'

'She wasn't dead,' he said. 'I thought she might have been, when you said Tariel killed her, but now I understand that she wasn't. Vespertine's body was ruined, but the body is not the dragon. The heart is the dragon, and the heart of the dragon would still have been there.'

'I don't understand. You have to explain. We need to know everything. We have to understand.'

'All I know is what Tariel told me and what I have read.'

'Tell me,' said Castrel. 'All of it. Please.'

'I'll do my best,' he said. 'The essence of the dragon is not a body at all – or rather, you might say the dragon is a succession of bodies, an accumulation of lives. The body of the dragon is not immortal, and when the body fails, its life – its essence, its heart – chooses another person and joins with them, body and mind. Then the new body it has chosen grows and changes and becomes the body of the dragon, and the new mind becomes the mind of the dragon. And so it goes on.'

'And the heart of the dragon has chosen our daughter,' said Castrel.

'Chosen to feed on her!' said Shay. 'Chosen to kill her and steal her body!'

'I know it must seem like that to you now,' said their golden friend gently, 'but that's not how it is. Not really. When the heart of the dragon joins someone, he or she doesn't die. He or she *becomes* the dragon. It's still their mind, their will, their thoughts and choices. They *are* the dragon. They join with all the other lives in the heart of the dragon to become one life, and when eventually the new body they have grown for themselves is exhausted, the heart moves on again to another, and the process begins once more. All the lives and memories and personalities that have ever been the dragon join the new life, and the new life becomes the dragon. It is an unbroken accumulation of lives and wisdom and memories and strength that continues for ever: the heart of the dragon flows on like a river, and no part of it is ever lost; it is all kept, all accumulated into one magnificent unending beautiful life. This is what a dragon is. Now that Hope has joined with the heart of the dragon she will never die.'

'But this whole world is dying!' said Shay. 'According to you, the whole world is over! All we want is our own beautiful child for as long as we can, to love her for whatever time is left, and this dragon is taking even that from us! That's what you're saying. Isn't it?'

The golden man fell silent, watching them grieve. Small reflections of the candle flames flickered in his golden eyes. Castrel reached across the table and took Shay's hand in hers and held it.

'It's all right,' she said. 'He's telling us what he knows, that's all. We have to let him. It's not his fault, and we have to hear all of it, so we know what to do.'

'I know,' said Shay. 'I'm sorry. Please. Take no notice of me.'

'You're angry,' said their golden friend kindly, 'because your child will not be as you thought and hoped and wished her to be. I understand that. But even though this whole world is lost, your child will live on. Hope will become the first dragon of whatever new world comes in its place.'

'You mean she'll turn into some monstrous creature,' said Shay. 'Some huge and terrible thing as big as a ship. She'll have *wings!*' But he was calmer now. Holding himself together and trying to understand.

'Possibly,' said the golden man. 'But possibly it won't be like that. The girl and the dragon will shape each other as they grow.'

'What do you mean?'

'Each form the dragon takes is different, and Hope is a strong and fine child. She's still your child and always will be. She won't lose that. So who can say what kind of dragon she will choose to become? Something extraordinary, something wonderful, a new thing in the world. The dragon called Vespertine becomes the dragon called Hope: there could have been worse fates than that for your child.'

'No,' said Castrel. 'Just no. No.' She emptied her cup of wine in a single swallow and felt the warm strength of it inside her. 'You're being gentle and kind and wise,' she said, 'and you're making the best of it, like a friend should. You're trying to make this sound like a good thing. But it isn't! Hope is our child. Our human, ordinary, wonderful child and we love her and we will not let this happen. It will not happen. Just no.'

She looked at Shay and he looked at her and she could see he felt the same.

'Yes,' said Shay. 'Hope will have her own life back.'

Their friend watched them gravely, with sympathy and sadness. *He is not human*, thought Castrel. That faint glimmer of ancient sunlight in his honey-golden eyes. A glow of immortality in the shadows of the room.

'You are good people,' he said, 'and you love your daughter. I'm so sorry, but this is not yours to choose. You have no control here. None at all.'

'We do!' said Castrel fiercely. 'Hope hasn't chosen this! If she had, that would be different, but she didn't and she can't. She is an infant! A tiny newborn child! We are her parents and we have to choose for her. We can choose, and we do. My daughter will be herself, not a body for some other thing. I will drive this monster out of her. I will destroy it, if I have to. We will not have it in Hope. We simply will not.'

'There's truth in what you say,' said the golden man. 'It is not normal, I think, for the dragon to join one so very young. There is usually choice and preparation on both sides. And no dragon has ever joined a human before.'

'Exactly!' said Shay. 'This isn't *right*!'

'Never a human before?' said Castrel. 'How many dragons are there, anyway?'

'I don't know,' said the golden man. 'They are the rarest of creatures. I haven't heard of another living dragon in my time here, only Vespertine.' He paused. 'But you cannot drive the dragon out. Not even the greatest of wizards would have the strength to do that. They wouldn't even know how it could be done.'

'I will do it,' said Castrel. 'I will learn how and I will get it out of my daughter and give her back her own life.'

'Please don't try,' said their golden friend. 'I am begging you. Please do not. You must understand, what I'm telling you is what could happen in the future. The only thing certain now is that Hope has the heart of the dragon in her and she will become a dragon herself in time. But she isn't a dragon yet, and that won't come for many years: she has to grow into it. For now, and for a long time to come, she will still be your fragile human daughter, and she needs all your protection and care and love like any other child.'

Castrel could see his concern was real and his fear for Hope was honest.

'Of course I will love and care for her,' she said. 'That's what this is all about.'

'But,' he continued, 'you are a very powerful hedge-witch. Perhaps more powerful than you understand. If you try to fight the dragon, you could do your child terrible harm. The dragon is part of Hope now, for ever, and attempting to rip it out could damage her permanently. She could even die. I think she almost certainly would.'

'You can't know that for sure,' said Shay, but their golden friend pressed on.

'But death is not all that would happen to her,' he said. 'If she died, the heart of the dragon would simply wait for another mind to join, but Hope would be lost. She would be far worse than merely dead. Her mind, her soul, would be adrift for ever in the heart of the dragon. Think of that: an unformed infant mind, neither human nor dragon, never growing and never fading, but awake and aware for all eternity. That would be an appalling fate. Unimaginably terrible. That's what you would be risking if you tried to fight or destroy the dragon. And besides,' he added with a smile, 'the life of a dragon is not a bad thing. I talked with Vespertine once. She was terrifying and tremendous, but she was not cruel. She was intelligent and wise.'

'Then why did the wizard Tariel destroy her?' said Shay. 'If she was so fine and he loved her, why did he do that?'

'I don't know ...' Their golden friend looked puzzled. 'I've been thinking about that. Vespertine must have agreed to it. She must have chosen ...'

His eyes widened in sudden understanding.

'I see now,' he said. 'I see. It was done so that exactly this could happen! It was done because the world is ending and everything in it will be utterly lost and destroyed. It was done so that something could live on. It was done so the heart of the dragon could join with a human for the first and last time, and something of humanness would survive beyond the end of the world.'

'Tariel and Vespertine gave their lives for that?' said Castrel.

'It must be so! They wouldn't have known it would be your child, your Hope, not precisely; but Tariel must have freed the heart of the dragon from the body of Vespertine so it could wait for a human to cross the Chelidd Plain. It was a slim chance. It might never have happened. But it did.'

Castrel glared at him.

'So Hope is being taken from us and changed into a dragon, and it's all part of a wizard's great plan for another world to come?'

'In a way, yes. I think so.'

'Well, fuck that,' said Shay. 'It was wizards who brought this whole end of the world thing down on us in the first place. So just fuck that. We have our own lives to live.'

'We will find a way to drive this dragon out of Hope,' said Castrel. 'We will never, ever harm her, we would die first, but we will protect her from this parasite, this usurper, this *thing* that's crawled inside her mind. She did not choose this for herself. She should have been allowed to choose.'

15

After their golden friend had gone out to the stable to sleep with his horses – he insisted on that, he said he always preferred it – Shay lay awake in the dark, trying to imagine what it meant. Trying to think it through. Trying to think at all.

Our lovely little girl is changing into a dragon. She'll become a beautiful woman with blue and purple crystal scales. She'll be fifteen feet high. She'll have a wonderful voice like music, and fiery wings.

No, that was wrong. That was too small. She would be a dragon to fill a quarter of the sky. A dragon of retribution and justice and righteous terror, the dread winged wolf of the world. That would be something worth seeing. Perhaps there were indeed worse fates than that.

No, these are only dreams and imaginings of dragons.

The wizards' wars had released a terrible desolation into the world. If they believed the golden stranger – and Khaag had said the same, and it was in the dead wizard Tariel's writings too – then the desolation would never stop. It would get worse and worse and the whole world would soon die. Castrel would be dead soon. He would be dead himself soon. Everything would die, except their beautiful girl. Hope alone would live on for ever – for ever and for ever – imprisoned eternally in some foul and monstrous body.

After we die she will lumber on through the empty desolation of the world, and she will be a horror, huge and inhuman. She will be a lizard-dragon, flightless, low-slung and weighty, with a black tongue as thick as the trunk of a tree to lick bitter ashes from the ruined air. And there will be no end for her. For all the lonely dreadful duration of eternity she alone will find no release from the ruination of every-thing. She will always know it, and she will never stop feeling it, ever.

Was that a worse thing to think of, than the end of the world and the death of all things? Yes, it was lonelier than that. It made the end of the world worse. Their golden friend was wrong: there were not worse fates than becoming a dragon after the end of the world. Shay could not imagine a worse fate for his baby child.

Desolate and bitterly helpless, he lay curled up on his side in the dark and wept silent tears.

Castrel moved closer in the bed and put her arm across him.

'We'll get it out of her,' she said. Her voice was quiet in the dark. 'We'll work out how to get rid of it. We won't let this happen to her.'

'No,' he said. 'We can't let it happen.'

'I don't know how though. Not yet. I wish there was someone to help us. I wish Bremel was here. I wish I could talk to her again like I used to.'

'You'll find a way. I know you will. But what can *I* do? I can't do anything. I can't even help.'

'Be you, Shay,' said Castrel. 'That's the most important thing. Be strong and keep going and don't give up. Ever. We will keep her safe from this. We'll get her back.'

'Yes,' he said quietly. 'Yes, we will.'

But tomorrow, they would have to leave this good place and shoulder their packs and walk out onto the road again, with nowhere to go but south, and nowhere was safe. The door that should not have been opened was open. It felt to Shay as if they were already the last human people left alive in all the world. Whatever they did, they must do it alone, entirely alone, just Castrel and him, and their own strength and purpose and love was all they had. There was no help for them anywhere. None at all.

16

Castrel stood in the farmhouse doorway cradling Hope, the child's head resting warm against her shoulder, and stared north at the mountain border of the High Esh.

'It's happening again,' she said to Shay. 'The wards are failing.'

The mountains were a wall of smoking darkness against a heavy copper and purple sky, the peaks rising out of fog, illuminated by flickers of grey silent lightning. The trees on the lower slopes were burning with a pale cold fire.

'Already?' said Shay. 'So soon? I hoped we'd have more time.'

'It's the same as before,' she said. 'A darkness in the sky. It's just like when we left our own house. It comes in cycles. Surges and waves.'

The same as before, only this time we know what's coming, we know what it means, we know all the horrors that will come on us again.

The cold of the world seeped inside Castrel's clothes and touched her skin. She shivered. Another departure. Another home lost. Another small grief. Weariness and despair.

I am so very tired. I don't want to do this again. I'm not ready yet.

Their golden friend came to make his farewell. His wound had repaired itself remarkably; Castrel had never seen healing so quick before. His horses were packed and saddled and he was eager to be on his way.

'Won't you come with us?' she said. 'Travel with us, at least for a while.'

'Yes,' said Shay. 'Do.'

'No. Thank you, but I must go fast now to Barathule. There are books in the library there that I am anxious to take with me when I leave this world. Knowledge and wisdom that should not be lost.'

'Well, then …' said Shay. 'Thank you. You have done a lot for us. You've been a good friend.'

As the golden man mounted his horse, Castrel caught the scent of the subtle perfume he was wearing. It was complex and beautiful. He had found a new shirt, brighter and finer than the one that was spoiled the day before. His chestnut horses were fresh and rested and ready for the journey. He looked down on them from the saddle and smiled.

He is not human. He doesn't see the world as we do. He doesn't feel as we feel.

'Take care of your child,' he said. 'I know you will. She is a special treasure. A new thing come into the world at the very ending of the old.'

'We will,' said Castrel. 'I will drive this dragon out of her. I will kill it if I must.'

He frowned.

'Please be careful,' he said. 'I urge you again. You cannot harm the dragon, but you could do terrible damage to Hope. She is not dragon yet, and will not be for a long time. She is only a fragile child. What you have said about the injustice of it is fair enough, Hope has been chosen without making a choice herself. But please remember, the only thing Tariel and Vespertine have done is try to make a new beginning. What becomes of it will be up to Hope. What kind of dragon she becomes, where she goes and what she does, that will all be up to her. Vespertine will not control her. She will be the dragon called Hope.'

'But she won't be herself!' said Castrel. 'She may live for ever, but she won't be human any more. We must protect her from that. We are her parents. It is our duty. We have to.'

'We'll find somewhere safe where we can live,' said Shay. 'We'll keep going south until we're far away from all this, and there'll be other people there. We'll find a life for her.'

Their friend glanced at the darkening horizon behind the cold burning mountains. There was grief and sorrow in his golden eyes.

'Do not hope that,' he said gently. 'Do not wish it. There is no safe place for you. What is coming will come. It is unpreventable.' There was genuine anguish in his face. 'I do not blame you for your choice. I admire it. You love each other and you love your child. You are courageous and strong. I fear you may be among the last of your kind and your world is ending, but you are also among the finest and the best of it that I have ever seen. I truly wish that everything I have said to you was mistaken. I wish I was completely and utterly wrong. But I fear that I am not.'

They watched in silence as he rode away, leaving the three of them alone.

The road crossed the river and climbed into trees. Soon the paved way began to be lost. Broken stones sinking under ivy and mud.

'If we lose the road,' said Shay, 'we'll steer our way by the stars. I know how to do that. It's no different from a boat at sea.'

He had strapped the dead wizard's sword to the outside of his pack, and slung the axe in a loop of his belt. The path they were following took them deeper into the trees. A wild endless woodland. To Castrel it felt like a kind of coming home. The darkness had not yet broken through south of the mountains, and all the trees were deeply alive and aware, in the way that trees always were. Trees ate light with their leaves, they were made of light and water, their roots went wide and deep: root tangled with root and leaf head breathed to leaf head; trembling and flaring, they poured out scent and colour like flaming torches ignited with life. Forest tugged at the edges of her, and bits of her snagged on the trees and pulled free. Part of her spilled out into forest air, a scent cloud dispersing under the branch-head canopy. The wild woodland was the first place, original and primordial: it was how the world was before the first people came. The hedge-witch magic, ancient and simple, was rooted in the first forest and had grown there. That was where it had first been learned, where it was strongest, and where it belonged.

As she walked, Castrel opened herself to Hope and shared feelings with her. Hope's mind was like sunlight spilling through green leaves, or light seen through eyelids closed against the bright sun in summer. Her child was an endless sky. There were wide landscapes in her, the landscapes of all the possibilities of what she would become. And the endless sky was already a person, with all the feel and uniqueness of what a person was – a person like no other had ever been or would ever be. She was full of spacious and unresolved futures, but already she was as complete and distinctive and recognisable as a human voice.

Hope was a voice now. A voice that had thoughts. Slow expansive thoughts. Curious and wondering. A voice that did not yet have words but soon would.

But there was always that other thing there in Hope's mind. Far off in the distance, deep in that endless sky, there was a single bright speck of brilliance. The heart of the dragon. Castrel could see it more clearly now: the faint threads and veins of strange transformation that were spreading out from it. Filaments of light and warmth, finer than the thinnest of hairs, almost imperceptible, reaching out from the heart of the dragon and merging with Hope.

Castrel tried to drive it back, but she had no strength and no way of doing it. She wanted to erase the heart of the terrible dragon, but it was hard and deep and full of power. All she could do was watch, and with a dark eye of shadow it watched her back. She sent it a roaring thought.

You watch me and I watch you. But know this, creature. I will drive you out.

Now that she knew what her enemy was, she could think. She could make plans. She would find a way to fight it.

I wish I could talk to Bremel again.

Bremel might have known something about dragons. Bremel might have known how to do what she must do.

The track took them down into a sheltered valley where some warmth still lingered. Watery afternoon sunlight poured slant-wise through the trees.

'Over there!' said Castrel. 'See, on the brambles! Berries!' She shucked off her pack and ran. 'Come on,' she said. 'Come on.'

There was still some sweetness in them. Side by side she stood with Shay and they ate from the runners and stuffed their pockets, ignoring the sting of the thorns that scratched their hands. The juices stained their fingers a sticky, dusty blue.

'These are delicious,' said Shay. 'The best I've ever had.'

At evening, as the last light was fading, they came onto a clear rise of ground. A heavy tree had toppled there, its root-mass ripped from the grey earth.

'We could stop here for the night,' said Shay. 'This is a good place.'

Castrel watched him build a shelter. He hacked branches from the fallen tree and wove stem-lengths through them, binding a frame to lean against the trunk. Then he heaped fallen leaves on the frame, an arm's length deep, and laid more branches on top to keep the leaves in place. He left a low dark entrance-mouth at one end. He worked neatly and well. By the time he had finished the light was almost gone from the sky.

Castrel pulled the pan out of her pack and set it in the fire. A fist-sized lump of salt meat. She put a few pieces of hard bread in the pan with the meat to soften and take up the fat.

'We'll need to find our own food soon,' said Shay. 'What we're carrying won't last long.'

'We can do that. We'll be fine. There's plenty in these wood-lands.'

She knew how to set snares and which roots and leaves and mushrooms to eat. Bremel had showed her, before she first set off from Weald.

You'll need to know this, Bremel had said. *People turn mean. You can't be sure of them, and you won't always be able to pay your way.*

It was dark inside the shelter, rich with the scent of earth and leaves. Castrel squirmed in alongside Shay, with Hope between them, and pulled the blankets over them all. Shay shifted slightly to make room.

'This is good,' he said. 'I like it here.'

Castrel lay on her back with her eyes open in the dark under the low roof of branches. Listening to the leaves stir in the rising night breeze. The blanket was wrapped tight around her, rough against her face. Her knees were pulled up against her stomach, her feet against the solid weight of her pack. She breathed with her mouth, shallow and slow. She could feel the small weight and warmth of Hope resting against her. Castrel could sense her child dreaming, but not what she dreamed.

You will grow straight and true. I will heal you of this thing, my darling. I will find a way.

She hugged her child in the dark.

You are my heart. You are all of me. I live only for you. You are here with me now, and that's all that matters.

'Castrel?' Shay's voice was quiet in the darkness.

'Yes?'

'I've got a plan. I know what we should do. I know where we can go to be safe.'

She could hear the excitement in his voice.

'Where?' she said.

'I think we should go to Far Coromance.'

'What's that?'

'It's an island among islands. I saw it on the map at Sard Keeping, but I've heard of it before, and our friend told me last night when we were in the stable that he's been there many times. It's the most beautiful place in the world. There's a big city there, and it's warm and the sun always shines, and everything grows there. Lemons and olives and grapes. There'll be lots of people there, crowds, and it's way down south, far across the sea, as far from here as it's possible to go. Maybe there'll even be wizards there. I think there would be. And they'd help us deal with the dragon, if you haven't managed to do it by then. It'll be wonderful. It's everything we need, Cass. It's the solution to everything.'

'But where is it, Shay? How would we get there?'

'Thousands of miles south of here, all the way to the bottom of the continent and then a ship across the ocean. I'm not sure exactly where, but when we get to the coast we can find a ship that's going there. Or a navigator who knows the course. Or a chart, and you could read it.'

Ships? What ships? Castrel found it difficult to imagine a world where there were still ships.

'We haven't got any money to pay for a ship,' she said.

'Don't worry about that. I know boats, I can work our passage, we'll be fine. All we need to do is keep on going south till we get to the coast, and go from there.'

'I don't know ...'

'Will you come with me, Cass? Come with me to Far Coromance.'

There was so much hope in him, so much enthusiasm, and she didn't have a better idea. And in the end, all it amounted to for now was walking south, and they were going to do that anyway.

'All right,' she said. 'Yes. Fine. It's a good plan. We'll do that.'

But she didn't really believe it. It was a beautiful golden dream.

Castrel woke early and cold inside the mound of leaves and branches which was their hiding place, their little burial, their dream time, their forgetting. Then they were walking again. Walking. Always walking. Shay strode on ahead of her, strong and happy. He was delighted. He had a purpose and a goal. For him now this was the long walk to Far Coromance, and every time after they rested he set off again with a straighter back and a lighter tread and Castrel followed, carrying Hope.

It began to rain, and the rain clagged the mud underfoot and made the forest hiss and whisper. Rain plastered her face and trickled cold down her neck. She wiped her face with her hand. It made no difference. The sodden weight of her clothes, wet all the way through to her skin, was clumsy and useless, a burden. Mud clumped and dragged and weighted her boots. Every time it rained, the rain was colder. Bitter grey corroding rain. She arranged the soaked blanket to be a hood for Hope, and wrapped her tight against her own body, for the warmth and scant shelter of that. It was something.

Hope stirred and nestled closer to her without waking. She kissed her daughter's chill, wet, beautiful face. Her perfect face. She touched it with her fingers gently.

*

The land rose and then fell away and the trail descended into low, watery lands. Wide spaces opened between the trees and there were broad shallow pools that reflected the mushroom-coloured sky. Most of the ground was water now, water and fallen trees. Roots and stumps in the water. The track was a sodden mud causeway winding this way and that, sinking so they had to wade, boots filled with water, the cold numbing their feet, slipping and stumbling.

Castrel scooped up handfuls to drink. It tasted of cold earth and powdered bone. Ash in an iron hearth. Behind them through gaps in the trees she saw the rising northern sky, dark and coppery and veined with purple. Harbingers of the alien darkness that was coming after them. Moving faster than they were.

Something bad is coming. I feel it. Already it's crawling into my bones.

The feel of the forest was changing. Castrel could feel her connection with it failing, though she didn't know why. The woods were without boundary or variation, and walking brought them no nearer and no further away. Motion without movement, everything grey and brown. All the trees grey and brown. She felt small beyond insignificance.

'Shay?' she said. 'Do you feel it?'

'Feel what?'

'I don't know. Just ... something. A feeling. Everything's turning dark. I'm starting to feel ... afraid. I haven't felt anything quite like this before.'

He stopped and looked at her. Love and concern for her in his eyes. And alarm, too.

'I can't feel it,' he said. 'But that doesn't mean anything. It doesn't mean it's not real. What should we do?'

He looked around, scanning the trees.

'That's it,' she said. 'I don't *know*. I don't think we can do anything.'

'Is Hope all right?'

'Yes. I think so.'

'We'll just have to keep going, then. Shall I carry her for a while?'

'No, I'm fine. Sorry. I shouldn't have mentioned it. There's no point in worrying if we can't do anything.'

'I'm glad you did. We have to keep talking, Cass. All the time. We'll be fine. We always are in the end.'

When they stopped for the night Castrel cleared a patch of earth with her foot, scraping away moss and ground ivy and twigs, and built a fire. She used thick stumps of log so it would burn long and slow. The heat chewed at the wood, smouldering and strengthless. Watery yellow licks of flame. The smoke drifted low, clinging to her hair.

She sat side by side with Shay, their shoulders touching, and ate out of the pan: loose grey pieces of salted river-fish, the flatbread burned and flecked with embers and soot. Afterwards Shay rummaged in his pack.

'I've got something for you,' he said. 'Here.'

An apple.

The skin was wrinkled but the fruit was good, yellow and full of juice. When she bit into it, it burst on her tongue sweet and bitter like joy. She ate it slowly, carefully, getting every scrap from the core. Opening the skin of the pips with her fingers and teeth for the hard, sour, white almond seeds.

'Thank you,' she said. 'This is wonderful. I didn't think we had any left.'

'It's my pleasure,' he said and grinned. 'You're very welcome. You deserve it.'

'You're not having one?'

'Not now.'

'How many have you got?'

'A few.'

'You're not saving them all for me? I wish you wouldn't do that.'

'I'm not. I don't feel like an apple now, that's all.'

'Well ... just don't. I don't want you to do that.'

'I'm not. I won't.'

'Good.'

When they had finished eating Castrel sat in silence, staring at the bleak, fragile flames of their fire. She was remembering a page from the dead wizard's writings. She had read it so often she had learned it by heart.

The luminous beautiful creating stars, the tide and swell and shine of all the oceans of stars ... they are gone now. The smear of the stars become ordinary points of light. All is ended. All is lost. I can no longer taste the livingness and emotions of all things on my tongue. I cannot feel it, heart and blood and skin; I cannot speak it with my voice. Rivers are silent, the trees no longer watch, the anger and patience are gone from the mountains. I cannot touch the deep currents in the earth.

And what comes after will be worse. Ending after ending, ever deeper into darkness, unfolding ever colder layers of death within death. I am alone here. I have outlived the others. I wish I had not lived so long.

She remembered the carcase of the fallen dragon on the red plain. Vespertine. She remembered its enormous ruin. Its ribs like a cliff. Its wings. And she remembered the licks of fire across the earth, the long swathes of raw blackened earth, and the bodies that had burned there, charred to lumps like coal. Dust and ash.

Vespertine.

She pictured the vast dragon descending on armies, and

soldiers screaming and dying. The dragon from the air hosing the flesh from them with roaring torrents of fire. Again and again.

The heart of the dragon wanted to make her darling Hope become such a thing. With the heart of the dragon inside her, her beautiful child would grow vast and inhuman and alone, immortal and cruel, gliding for ever above the ashen desolation of the ended, emptied world, poisoned and foul.

An endlessness of lonely pain.

'I will get it out of her, Shay,' she said quietly. 'I will keep trying. All the time. Always. I will never stop. I will never think about anything else. I will rip that thing out.'

'I know you will,' he said. 'We'll find a way.'

It was becoming their ritual now. The last thing they said to each other every day.

Night thickened around them. Threads of thin mist came drifting in from under the trees. There was absolute stillness and silence beyond the light of the fire. To the north, a grey light illuminated the low belly of cloud. A pale flickering on the horizon, like white fires burning.

'That's new,' said Shay. 'What do you think it is?'

'I don't know. Nothing good. I think it's coming closer.'

Castrel lay on her side and pulled the blanket closer around her. The mist had soaked away. A few bleak stars prickled out of the sky. The fire had collapsed on itself, and flickered now, small and frail in the darkness.

'Cass? Are you still awake?'

'Yes.'

'You should sleep. You need to sleep.'

'It's all right. I will later. I'm sharing with Hope now.'

'How is she?'

'She's fine. She's happy.'

'Good.'

'I'm going to get that thing out of her, Shay.'

'Yes. I know. But sleep now. You need to sleep.'

She woke suddenly. Her heart was pounding. She wanted to scream. Fear had put a hand over her face. It covered her mouth, so it was hard to breathe. Fear gripped her heart inside her ribs and squeezed. Everything inside her was tight. She wanted to dig herself into the ground and cover herself with earth and hide. She wanted to run. She was shaking. There was a ragged, whimpering sound near her head, and it was her.

'*Shay!*' she screamed. '*Shay!*'

She panicked. *Where was Hope?* She scrabbled around in the dark until she found the child and grabbed her, holding her tight, and lurched to her feet.

'*Shay!*'

The scream hurt her throat.

Everything around them, the trees and the undergrowth and the grass and the earth itself, it was all burning with cold grey fire. The light was dim and smeary. Pale silent flames flickered under the copper night sky, and shreds of low smoke drifted across the ground. The earth was a crust over smouldering embers. The roots of the trees were burning under the ground.

Yet there was no heat in that pale fire. The touch of the flames was as cold as ice.

'*Shay!*'

She had to run! She had to escape. Get Hope away! She tried to run, but there was nowhere to go, because the burning was everywhere. It was inside her. It was inside them all. It was so cold.

She tried to hide Hope from the fire by wrapping her in the blanket, but it was no use.

She found Shay. He was turning this way and that, holding the dead wizard Tariel's sword, clumsy and useless in his hand.

Winged fear was screaming at them from the sky. High in the air, immense creatures were circling on huge flaggy wings. The shrieks of their shrill, terrible voices reached them, carried on the flames, on the cold burning air.

'Dragons!' yelled Shay. 'It's dragons! They're coming for Hope! They want to take her with them.'

'No,' said Castrel. 'This is not dragons. I don't know what it is, but it's something else. Something different.'

She could sense them, a little. Inhuman watchful minds, hungry and full of a strange warmthless elation.

'It's nothing to do with us,' she said. 'I don't think they even know we are here.'

And then suddenly Castrel felt something terrible happen inside her. She screamed. A wordless, grief-stricken terrified howl.

'*Cass!* What is it? What's wrong?'

She looked at him, blank with horror. It felt like in every part of her small wounds were being torn open inside. A thousand appalling fissures were gaping wide and defenceless. All the bitter fear and coldness of the fire that was burning the trees and the earth around them was flooding into her, and through every one of the thousand tiny internal wounds something was being taken away.

The shrill shrieking creatures of the air were feeding on her somehow. They were draining something out of her and gorging on it.

'What is it, Cass?' Shay was holding her tight and stroking her hair. 'What happened?' he was saying. 'Oh, my darling, what happened.'

'I don't know,' she said over and over again. 'I just don't know. Is Hope all right? What about Hope?'

'She's fine. You don't need to worry about her. What about you?'

The shock and anguish were fading. She had no idea what had happened, except that she was lost and confused and something had been taken from her and she didn't know what it was. But it mattered. It was the most important thing she was.

'I just don't know, Shay,' she said again. 'I just don't know.'

At last the icy fire faded in the dawn, leaving their whole world brittle and grey. Ash and bone. Everything was covered in flakes of pale cinder and dry white soot. Castrel felt the dust in her mouth and lungs. She tasted it on her tongue.

Shay doubled over, coughing, his chest heaving dry, and when the coughing fit had passed he showed her his hands. They were covered with berry-bright red. Flecks and droplets of blood.

'It's nothing,' he said. 'It's just a cough. That fire and smoke—'

'Come here and let me look at you,' said Castrel. 'I can put it right.'

She put her hand inside his clothes, touching her palm against his ribs, and let herself drift into his body, feeling for him. Feeling for his lungs, so she could gently touch and repair.

Except she could not do it.

The strength and the power of healing were gone.

All that part of her, all that she had always been able to do, the hedge-witch strength and everything that Bremel had taught her. It was lost.

No matter how she tried to reach him, Shay felt like another person, separated from her by walls of flesh and bone, and that was all.

And it was the same when she tried to open herself to Hope. All the contact, all sharing, was gone.

Her gift, her talent, the wonderful connection with life that shaped her and made her who she was: it was all lost. It was completely and absolutely dead. She was alone and cut off from the wonderful interwoven life of the world.

17

Hope perceives her parents now. She perceives the insides of their bodies and her own. She hears the music of her parents' thoughts. She feels their love for her, and for each other. She feels their sadness and despair, and that they will not give up. Also she senses weather and trees and earth. She is aware of all of that, and of the movements of magic, darkness and monsters.

Hope knows that something has happened, and that her mother is hurt and sad. She feels the change in her, and she feels her mother's pain, but the something that happened brought no pain to Hope. She absorbed it into herself and it made her stronger. It helped her grow. Everything that happens makes Hope stronger and helps her grow. She is strong and happy and curious, eternally curious, but she is not afraid. She watches and she listens.

And she can perceive the heart of the dragon.

The dragon Vespertine lay dead on the red plain for a very long time. Almost too long. The heart of the dragon was beginning to break apart, and its many minds were drifting. Separating. They had begun to argue among themselves. Perhaps the heart of the dragon was going to die at last. Some were afraid of that. And then came the child whose name was Hope.

When the heart of the dragon joined her there was a tough shell formed over it, burned all black and covered with ash, but that was a carapace, and inside the carapace now there is trans-formation and new growth happening: bright colours and warm, beautiful, shining iridescent things, fresh and young and new. The carapace is softening and breaking up, letting the inside stretch and stir and get ready to come out, and inside the carapace is not one but many. A multitude. Complex shimmering colours and light and life. This is what is inside the dragon. This, and voices.

Hope likes listening to the voices.

Vespertine should not have let the wizard Tariel kill her. I did not like being dead.

We should not have chosen a human. We have never joined with a human before.

It was our purpose. This is important. This is consequential. This is grave.

The wizard Tariel did what he thought wise.

We were in our prime. We did not need Tariel.

I miss him. He was a friend.

The young voices speak and the older ones watch the world. The older ones see long stories that the young cannot see because the long stories unfold too slowly and are too subtle. The ideas of the older ones are different: their thoughts feel like shapes and lines, complex forms in many dimensions. It seems to the young ones that the thoughts of the older ones are altogether still, though in fact the older ones are thinking very fast and all the time. Hope listens to all the voices. She does not know words, not yet, but it doesn't matter. The voices in the heart of the dragon are not words, they are something else.

This world is dying. There is no reversing what has been done.

So? It will not matter to us. We are the heart of the dragon. We do not die.

We owe this world nothing. We should leave it. We have crossed worlds before.

But none who still speak remember how we did.

It does not matter how the last crossing was made. Our story does not repeat itself. We are not wheel, we are river.

Hope grows larger and stronger every day. She grows quicker than a human child ever has. She is learning very fast.

18

Shay followed Castrel as they walked through the woods in the aftermath of the white and warmthless fire that had burned everything. He watched her go ahead of him between brittle grey skeletons of trees, carrying Hope.

A scent of cold air. A silence. Only the crunching of ash and embers underfoot, and the earth itself feeling somehow hollow. Shay felt they were treading on the crust of some great dry emptiness.

They walked until the dark of night began to gather and thicken under the trees, and when they couldn't walk any more they sat in the ash in the shelter of a fallen trunk and drank some water.

'Do you want to eat?' he said.

'No.'

'Neither do I.'

They sat with their backs against the trunk and stared ahead into nothing.

'I think we could light a fire,' said Shay. 'I think it would burn.'

'Don't,' said Castrel.

'It's fine. I think we're safe.'

'I don't want a fire, Shay. Please.'

'All right. We don't need it anyway.'

There was no wind stirring the ash and the fragile burned trees. There was nothing but silence.

'You'll get better, Cass,' he said quietly. 'It'll come back to you.'
She shook her head.

'It's gone. I don't know who I am any more. I'm nothing. Empty. Hollow and dead inside. I can't help Hope any more. How can I help her now?'

Shay wanted so much to put his arm around her and hold her close and comfort her, because it would comfort him too, but he held back. He sensed it would be an intrusion – she was grieving the loss of something he had never fully understood – and also, he half-admitted to himself, part of him was afraid of this fierce new bleakness in her. He couldn't lean on her any more. He had to step forward now. And he would, but he wasn't sure how.

'You're still you, Cass,' he said. 'I'm not saying it doesn't matter, because I know it does; I know how special and wonderful and important it was to you. And I still think it may come back. But even if it doesn't … It's not the whole of you, it was never what made you who you are. Your gift wasn't what made you a human person. It was important, but never that. It's not what I love. You're still you, and you always will be, and nothing can change that. Not unless you let it. We have to not let the darkness in.'

In the night, cloud obscured all stars and darkness was complete. Twice Shay was woken by a loud crash nearby. A heavy branch, or a whole trunk, falling.

The next day they emerged from the wasteland of brittle burned trees and found the road again. It wound away south through an expanse of open country dotted with copses of trees, stragglers of the receding wood. The thin wind in their faces unsettled Hope. Castrel patted her back as they walked and sang to her quietly, a long simple wordless tune.

*

241

They camped in a hollow away from the road and in the morning Shay woke first and climbed the rise to look. There was a cloud of dust behind them, where they had come from. It was moving. Coming closer. From the north.

He worked his way to a place where he could see and not be seen.

There were hundreds of them, travelling south in an untidy column, still small in the distance but coming closer, covering the ground fast with a kind of shambling jog, not mounted but on foot, hunched and loping and somehow like human but certainly not. When they got nearer he could hear the noise of their feet hitting the road and the loud roughness of their lungs breathing. The guttural harshness of their incomprehensible speech. They were ragged and spiked. *Thorny*, he thought, though he couldn't describe it, not really: there were no words that were right. He stayed hidden until they dwindled again to a distant cloud of dust on the skyline.

When he got back to the camp, Castrel was hunched on a grassy mound nursing Hope.

'They've come,' he said. 'They're here. I saw them on the road. Hundreds of them. Thousands. They're south of the mountains now.'

She hugged Hope closer and looked up at him and said nothing. Her eyes were dark and fierce and lonely.

All afternoon the pall of yellow smoke hung in the sky ahead of them, thinning but not dispersing. When they came near, the wind brought the smell of burning wood. And something worse. Something sour and dark.

It had been done with care. Purpose. Pleasure.

The buildings were all burned. All of them. The paddock was ringed with still-smouldering ruins. In the middle, in the area of hard-packed earth, a tree had been planted upside down, its crown buried in the ground, its torn root-clump jutting skyward.

Human bodies hung from the roots, heads downward.

'Don't go nearer,' said Castrel. 'I don't want to see. None of us should see. Those people shouldn't have stayed, Shay. They should have run long ago. Why did they stay?'

They turned away and walked on down the road.

The dog-crows carried on picking at the thing in the dust and watched them come. Shay had seen dog-crows before, but only flying. Close up they were bigger than he'd thought, more like geese, and drabber, looser-winged, raggedier than crows, with unwieldy bone-grey beaks that should have been too heavy for their heads.

Cass picked up a stone and threw it among them.

'Get away!'

The birds glared and moved a few feet off with ungainly two-footed jumps. A few hauled themselves up on flaggy wings to squat in the tree and watch.

The body on the ground was small and had no head.

'It's a child,' said Shay. 'Just a boy.'

Castrel had walked off to a clump of thorns at the roadside. He thought she didn't want to see, but she was looking at something else.

'Not a boy,' she said. 'A girl.'

The head was hanging from the thorns by the tangle of her hair. Castrel groaned quietly, leaned forward and was sick.

He touched her shoulder.

'Cass . . .' he said. 'It's—'

'Shut up! Shut up!' She wiped viscous trails from her mouth with the back of her hand. 'Please be quiet,' she said. 'You have to.'

*

Something was coming behind them, hidden by trees and a bend in the road. The sound of heavy wheels grinding across broken stone, and coarse inhuman voices.

'Hide!' Castrel hissed. 'Shay! We have to hide!'

They lurched off the road among scrubby bushes. There was no time.

He had been stupid. He should have been more careful. He had been tired – forgotten – and now it was too late. He crouched next to Castrel in a low place among the thorns, the fear rising in his throat.

Wait. Wait. Do nothing but wait.

Their cover was thin. All they could do was keep low. Low and still.

Hope was awake but made no sound. Her eyes were staring wide.

She knew.

The wagon rounded the bend, crude and low, crawling on solid iron wheels. Things on foot were hauling it with tarred, fibrous ropes. They were tall, but stooped and leaned into their work. Their heads were cased in strapped constructions of dull metal and grey wood. Cages more than masks. Cages for the head. Shay could not see their faces but he could see the faces of their cargo. Human faces, women and children and one old man, chained and staring. It seemed to Shay that one of the women was looking right into his eyes. There was no recognition there.

After that, they didn't walk on the road any more but kept it in sight, away off to the left. Shay scanned the country behind them all the time, but there was never anything.

They camped well away from the road and didn't light a fire. Hard bread and salt fish soaked cold.

'That was the last of the food,' said Castrel. 'There's none left now.'

'We'll find something,' he said. 'We always do.'

The spaciousness all around them – all the wide miles – was dark, empty and still. Wind hissed in the grass. Coarse dry blades.

'We don't belong here any more,' said Castrel. 'This isn't our world. Not any more.'

Mile after mile the road climbed slowly into harsher territories. Valleys narrowed and the hills grew steeper. Outcrops of black rock dripped trickles of water. Fern and moss spilled between gaps and over ledges, pale brown and livid green. A healthless, uncomfortable growth. The road was hard slow walking: a precarious path over gravel and loose stones, squeezing through dark, blind gullies.

Twenty yards ahead of him, Castrel crested a ridge and suddenly stopped. Ducked back and retreated. He saw her slide Hope from her shoulders and go to the ground. She eased herself forward on her elbows till she could look down on the valley without being seen. He crawled alongside her and lay flat.

'People,' she said. 'Coming this way.'

A straggling column was walking towards them. They trundled handcarts, bundled high and swaying. There were a few plodding dusty horses and a pair of oxen, hauling a heavy wagon that lurched slowly across rutted and broken paving. Parents walked with their children. Some carried younger ones on their shoulders or in arms. He could hear the shuffling of feet, the hooves of the beasts, the creaking timbers of the wagons. They walked almost in silence: only the occasional quiet voice or the crying of a child carried on the wind and reached them on the hill.

Castrel froze and pointed.

'Look,' she said.

In the shoulder of a nearer hill where the approaching column could not see, an ambush was waiting. Creatures that were not human weighed their notched knives and the ugly blades on long poles. There were riders with them, in command from the saddles of their six-legged beasts.

'We should warn them,' said Castrel.

'How?' said Shay. 'They would only come for us too.'

A cry rose from the ambush, a grating wail that seemed to come from one of the six-legged beasts, not its hooded rider. The attackers rose from hiding and surged forward.

When they realised what was upon them, the people made a sound – not a scream, more a collective groaning sigh. And then the attackers closed round them in an engulfing tide, and the screaming began. The hooded riders lumbered in, their mounts treading, trampling, the riders sweeping their blades, hacking rhythmically to right and left, reaching down sometimes to seize a small body and fling it over the heads of the crowd to be caught by their waiting troop. Killing. Harvesting. There was little resistance. They had nowhere to run.

Shay hadn't understood till then that helplessness was itself an emotion, nor that it could hurt so much. Helplessness was a bleak and horrible sickness like despair.

They didn't stay to watch any more.

'Those poor souls,' said Castrel. 'Those children.'

Shay lay on his back on the cold stony ground and stared up at the wide canopy of night. The shining darkness of the sky, cleaner and deeper and darker than all the oceans. He was tired but he could not sleep. His coughing kept him awake. Ever since they were caught in the cold fire that burned the trees, there had been something in his lungs that was not right.

Castrel had said the other day that the stars had changed, but for him they were the same. He went through their names, marking off the bright ones and their slowly wheeling constellations. Capault. Corsant. Herom and Heiem. The Harepath, the Aewelm, the Besom and the Skew. He said their names aloud to himself, quietly, like he used to do with his mother. Long ago. So many years ago. Just him and her. Warm summer nights in the garden of their house in Harnestrand, while the others slept.

Felel.

Braithe.

Fromalarim.

The Wentletrap.

The Great Mooring.

He couldn't remember his mother's face, nor anything of how she looked or moved, but he remembered the feeling of what it was like, that time when he was small and she was there with him, and she showed him the stars and taught him their names. He hoped she was not living now. He would have spared her this. Alive or not, he would not see her again. Not ever.

Everything and everyone is lost, but we are here. We are alive. Hope and Castrel and me, alive in this huge emptiness under the stars, and that's enough.

He said it quietly, aloud, like the names of the stars.

The stars in the sky made him think of other worlds. There were many, and this was only one among them all, and some were bad places but some were beautiful. Their golden friend had come from another world, a world with a brighter sun and bluer shadows, a beautiful place where everyone lived for ever. In his mind it blurred with the dream of Far Coromance. Green islands scattered across a glittering sunlit sea, lemon groves, and in the harbours a forest of golden ships. Citrus and spices in the air that filled their bright sails. They would go there, him with Castrel and Hope. They would walk all the way, and when they got there all would be well.

*

Days unravelled out of days, each bleaker than the last, and the road rolled on through the days and the nights, the hunger and the fear. Every day the palls of smoke on the horizon were further in the distance, until they saw them no more. They scavenged for what they needed among what the inhuman column that went ahead of them had left. Sometimes there were places where the cruel harvesters had not been, where it seemed that the people had fled in time. They never saw anybody alive.

Sometimes the sky in the north turned copper and flickered. Dry lightning storms. Flashes of cold grey light.

Mornings when there hadn't been rain and no stream was near, Shay woke early for the dew. He trailed his shirt through the grass and wrung it into the pan. Did it again, and again, half a cupful at a time, until there was enough to drink and some to carry.

Some nights the dew didn't come, or he slept too late.

They saved what food they carried till the night, and ate as little as they could. They were always hungry. Shay had heard once that if you didn't eat, you stopped feeling hungry in the end, but it wasn't true. Every day they woke a little weaker and walked a little slower. Castrel was so thin, it hurt him to see. He supposed he was the same.

Castrel showed him how to knot snares out of bramble stems and long grass. Always he found them empty in the morning.

'Bury them a while before you put them out,' she said. 'Cover them with earth. It will mask the smell of you.'

'I don't think there's anything out there, Cass. We don't even see birds any more.'

'Well, sometimes we do.'

*

Day followed day and always there was Castrel, silent and dark. Brooding over Hope. Grieving. Loneliness opened like a space around them both, and there were times he thought that was the worst thing of all.

One evening when they rested he went to sit by her, shoulder to shoulder like they used to.

'Let me hold Hope for a while.'

The child was getting heavier. She changed and grew every day, but still it caught him by surprise. It took his breath away.

'It doesn't seem possible that she could grow so strong and well,' he said, 'not ... not in all this ... but she does.'

His daughter's eyes were large and bright in the twilight and flecked with purple and grey and gold. The scaling on her shoulders and back was like an emperor's cloth from Far Coromance. She studied his face with a long curious stare, wise and profound and beautiful.

There was a hurting in his lungs. Sometimes when he coughed, he spat small packets of blood onto the stony dust of the road.

The noise of the surge was like distant rolling thunder. It was growing louder and closer. Castrel ran and Shay followed, stumbling, heart pounding, splashing through the stream and scrambling up the steep slope using his hands. He threw himself on the ground. Trembling. Chest tearing. Breath rasping. Punishing his lungs.

'Hush, little one,' Castrel was saying to Hope. 'Quiet now, sweetheart. Quiet. We're all here. It's all fine. That was a run, but we're safe now. All safe.'

'Cass—' Shay tried to speak and broke off, coughing.

'They can't hear,' she said. 'They're too far away.'

*

They watched the southward surge from the crest of a ridge. The surge of the appalling horde. Not an army, not disciplined and not going to fight. Thousands. Thousands. Thousands. Distance made it seem they were moving slowly, but he knew they were running. That shambling inhuman lope. Thousands, and voracious thousands more. They were a ragged, tumultuous flood. It was as if a great swollen river had burst its banks in the north. They were the scavengers of the coming extinction, spilling in their millions through the mountain passes and spreading out across the dimming southern lands.

Wave after wave they would come, and worse would follow. Somewhere in the north a gate had been opened, a tear in the curtain between worlds, a wound, and it would never be closed.

The near edge of the surge was half a mile away. Shay couldn't see the further side. It reached the skyline. The noise they made, like rolling thunder, was the pounding of their feet and the voices they raised. Shouts and barks and yells.

Riders on six-legged beasts moved among them, and there were other creatures too, huge and indistinct in the distance, crawling, misshapen and grotesque, their movements jerky and wrong. Immense flying things hovered above them: creatures like vast lacy moths that fluttered and swept low over the horde, shedding falls of ash and darkness over it from their tattered leather wings.

All day long the inundation flowed. Only at dusk did it fade into the south, and even then there were still stragglers passing when darkness fell.

That night Shay sat up and kept watch, listening in the darkness to the grunts and shuffles and quiet moaning cries. Some were very near. He kept the dead wizard's sword laid out across his knees, resting his hands on the bared blade.

He thought Castrel was sleeping, but once she spoke to him quietly.

'What have we done, Shay, bringing a child into this terrible place? We shouldn't have. Better for her if we had not.'

No words had ever caused him so much pain.

'Don't say that,' he said. 'She makes it good. She makes even this good.'

'But it never stops, Shay. There's never any rest. I'm not sure I have the strength. Not all the time. Not for ever.'

In the morning they went down from the hill. The surge had left a swathe of country churned, trampled and desolate: smouldering ruined earth and bitter dust where nothing would ever live or grow again. The stench, acid and foul, burned Shay's eyes. It snagged in his throat and brought a bad fit of coughing.

I'm sick, he thought. *I'm getting weak and sick.*

He didn't say anything about it to Castrel. There was no point. She wasn't a healer now. That was lost.

'If we'd been caught out in front of that when it came ...' she said. 'If we'd been in the open, in the middle of it ... If we'd walked nearer the road ...'

'But we didn't,' he said. 'We weren't.'

'This is not the worst. Not yet. More will come up behind us. We can't use this road any more.'

'Then we'll turn west for a while. Just for a few days. In a while we can turn south again. There'll be another road. There always is.'

In Far Coromance he would trade lemons from distant islands and grow wealthy. Then he would sit in the sun with Castrel and they would drink wine out of crystal glasses, and they would remember this terrible time and they would say: *But we came through it all, didn't we, and look at us now.* And Hope would be a young woman and walk smiling among many smiling faces, and she would wear gowns of beautiful cloth like their golden friend.

She would be taller than all of them and her eyes would shine, because she had the heart of the dragon in her but somehow she was still just the same.

On, again on, always on, into the unworsenable worst. Bitter air was moving down from the north. Each day colder, each day weaker than the last.

19

They walked west for days that Castrel didn't count into a country where the surge had not yet passed. Here there were places where they could forage for food and streams with water they could drink. Here the sun climbed thin and watery at their back and westered ahead of them in shimmers of dusty gold, and sometimes if she closed her eyes it was possible for Castrel to think that the world was not ruined, but almost as it used to be.

Every night her dreams took her mind to places her eyes had never seen, though what she saw there felt like memories. Dark observations. She saw foul seas breaking against jagged black rocks and cities lit by terrible light. She heard rancorous voices that spoke to her in strange and bitter syllables: alien tongues she didn't understand. She felt that something was hunting her. It circled ever closer and watched her while she slept and called others to do the same, summoning presences she couldn't see. Cruel hearts that were not dead because they had never been alive.

A chill, dark exhaustion was hollowing her out.

She hated the dragon-thing that had infected her child. It had climbed inside and was taking Hope away. She couldn't sense it any more but she knew it was there. She felt it watching her. It was always watching her. Once she had fought with it and tried to drive it out, but now she could not. Now she could only hate it.

She heard Shay coughing in the night. The constricting darkness that was growing in his lungs was more serious than he knew, but there was nothing she could do to help him. Once she could have, but not any more. She loved him and she loved Hope, but she could not heal them.

I must do something. I must go somewhere. I need help.

I wish Bremel was here.

Bremel could have healed Shay, at least.

The road they were following branched several times and met others at crossroads. There were many roads now, hollow lanes worn deep below the level of the hedgerows by centuries of human travelling.

'Which way, do you think?' said Shay when they came to another crossing.

'This one,' said Castrel, choosing a road that ran south and seemed broader than the rest.

It rounded a hill and descended into a rolling, thinly wooded country. To their left were some houses, set back among trees on the gentler slope of the hill. Empty houses. It was worse here, somehow: sadder, in this abandoned place where the surge had not yet come.

Suddenly Castrel realised that she knew where they were.

This is the road from Drade to Fent.

She had travelled and worked all through this country not long after she left Bremel's, and it hadn't changed much since. It was only a week or so's walk from here to Weald, where Bremel lived. Where she herself had lived, when she was a child.

Of course she knew that Bremel would not be there; nothing would be there now except memories and sadness, and it would be a mistake to go. But still she wanted to, just to look. Perhaps it was only that she wanted to go home.

She told Shay that evening what she wanted to do.

'Of course we'll go there,' he said. 'If that's what you'd like. If you're sure.' He paused. 'You know it might be bad there, don't you?'

'I know.'

'And the chances of Bremel still being there …'

'I know, Shay. She was old when I left, and that was five years ago. But I want to see her again with all my heart, just to talk to her again. I know it's too late for that now, but all I want to do is go and look.'

'Of course,' he said again. 'If that's what you want we must go.'

The road passed between hedgerows and the edge of coppices. It crossed the Harkett by a narrow plank bridge at Oldwaithe; the river there was a black seep clogged with mud and shadowed by leaning alders. There was a thin thread of smoke beyond the line of trees. A dog barking in the distance.

The house, when they reached it, was of thatch and quarried stone. It stood where the road forded a shallow stream. Across the yard was a timber barn.

The buildings were not burned.

There were no gibbeted dead. No corpse-hung tree.

They watched for a long time but nothing moved. There was a wagon canted at an angle, propped near the barn. Everything was untended ramshackle decay.

'There are people here,' said Shay, 'but they're hiding. That's what I'd do. Hide and watch.'

'Do you see anything?' she said.

'No.'

A man stepped out from behind the houses into the road. A scrawny man with a few days' growth of beard and thin greying hair falling to his shoulders. He carried a stick that was as long as he was tall, with a blade lashed at the end that looked like a big knife. He had made himself a rough shield of wood. The dog followed him, staying close, eyeing them warily. A heavy-jawed, bristle-haired barrel of a dog.

They took a few steps forward to meet them.

'That's far enough,' the man called to him. 'What do you want?'

'We're not looking for trouble,' said Shay.

'Trouble? You, trouble? There's only you and that baby she's carrying. I know, I seen you coming, all the way. You have a care, there's more of us inside.'

Castrel doubted it.

'Your wagon looks broken,' said Shay. 'I could fix it.'

'Why would you do that?'

'We help you and you help us. We've come a long way and we're hungry and tired. You could give us food.'

'We've none to spare. We don't need you. Walk on. Go your way.'

'Let's go,' said Castrel quietly to Shay. 'If he doesn't want us, he doesn't.'

'It's someone, Cass. We haven't seen anyone, not since ...'

His voice trailed off. He called to the man again.

'Don't you want me to fix the wagon? You could leave here, then. You could go south, all of you, if you've got a horse for that wagon. Have you? Got a horse?'

'Don't question him, Shay. Let's just go.'

'I told you, there's more of us inside,' the man called again. 'And there's the dog.'

'You're not safe here,' said Shay. 'You really should go. We've come from the north, and what's following behind us is bad. Believe me. We don't want to take anything from you. We want to help.'

'You're a liar. We're not stupid.'

The man picked up a stone and threw it. It hit the ground in front of Shay and skittered in the dust.

'We don't want you!' he shouted. 'Come closer and we'll kill you, all of you.'

That night in Castrel's dream there was a demon with a huge stone head and the dark red sun was bleeding out of the sky like a hole. Like an unhealable wound. The demon was squatting on the side of a black mountain and the mountain was shattered like ice. The demon was picking Hope apart like a leg of chicken, and Hope was tiny and the demon's fingers were clumsy and enormous like the trunks of stone trees.

She woke in utter terror, sweat-soaked and trembling with bitter cold, so terrified she couldn't move. Her limbs were locked and frozen, her heart racing hard, her mouth stretched wide to make a scream that did not come because her throat was closed.

Fine rain drifted into her face as she walked. It misted the distances and made everything grey.

Hope was growing quicker now, and she was finding her heavy to carry. The weight made her arms and back ache and in the evenings her shoulders hurt. When she put the child down, she would crawl away and explore. Hope was happy and all things were curious to her. She would pick up a twig or a damp fallen leaf and hold it up like a prize. She would mouth it, murmuring to herself, or sit with it, patient and busy. She gathered collections in her lap and carried them there while she moved herself around, sitting upright and hauling herself across the ground with her heels. Sometimes as she chattered to herself, frowning with concentration, she spoke syllables that sounded like words, and she looked at Castrel then and smiled because she was so pleased with herself.

One day an argument flared between her and Shay, sudden and bitter and shocking. She was exhausted, footsore and hungry, her back hurt and she felt shut out from the world. The future was a black wall. Dead brick endings in every direction.

She said something harsh to him when he stopped to talk to her, and afterwards she couldn't even remember what it was, but he responded with a sudden flood of anger and despair. Fierce bitter words, though she struggled to follow what he was saying. And she was the same. She heard herself saying cruel, stupid things she didn't mean: something dark and cruel and angry inside her was saying them with her voice.

Afterwards: 'I'm so sorry,' she said. 'It's my fault. We don't talk to each other any more, not like we used to.'

'No, it's my fault,' said Shay. 'I'm so tired. All the time I'm tired. How can we talk when there's nothing to say? We know what we have to do and we do it, every day, and that's all there is.'

'How's your chest? You cough quite a lot now.'

'It's fine,' he said. 'I'll be all right. Don't worry about me. You need to look after yourself.'

But she knew he wasn't fine.

'At least Hope's well,' he said. 'Look at her. She's strong and happy, and that's all that matters really.'

'I wanted to tell you,' said Castrel. 'I know where we are. We're not far from Weald now. We're almost there.'

They crossed the Farrow path and came out into farmland. The unploughed fields were choked with bramble and briar. They passed apple garths where fallen fruit rotted where it lay. The old Wythe House under the beeches was a shell of blind windows and greying lichenous timber.

Shay climbed a fence and waded out through long grass to gather pears from a stand of small, twisted trees. There were some they could still eat. He was pleased, though the flesh was bruised and mealy and tasted of little.

'Tell me about these places,' he said as they walked. 'Talk to me about what it was like to live here.'

But she didn't want to.

'I don't want to think about it,' she said.

'We should remember. We shouldn't forget how it used to be. It's important. It matters.'

'Of course I remember,' she said.

She remembered it was warm in the sunshine, out of the wind. She remembered a small brown butterfly like an autumn leaf nosing about. Trees cast blue shadows on the green grass. She lies on her back and gazes up at the morning sun through half-closed eyes, seeing a burst of gorse-flower light.

The sky is like an upturned bowl of milk, but blue.

There are days in your childhood when you are immersed in your life like a strong swimmer in a lake, and your hours light up like flames. You know those times. By their loss you know them. You never find your way into that bright country again.

From the top of a rise they glimpsed the roofs of Lowster away to the right, but as they came down into the valley the village disappeared behind a fold of darkened land.

The lane narrowed as it rolled on into the dusk, making for Hickle Wood and Hookforge and Anstey Hook. She knew that after Anstey Hook it would climb out of Carser Vale and wind away south-east, heading for the Lumb ferry and the borders of the Breckholt.

She stopped to rest and without thinking she tried to let her awareness reach out towards her child, looking for contact. But there was nothing. Of course there was nothing.

Shay came up behind her.

'Is Hope all right?' he said.

'Yes,' said Castrel. 'She's doing fine. She's sleeping now.'

'Can I see her?'

Shay parted Castrel's coat to look. He stroked Hope's cheek with his finger.

'Brave girl,' he said. 'Courageous small one. Tougher than you look.'

The next day they reached Weald. All was bad there, sad and lost and dying. There was no magic there, not as in her memories of it. Her old house was empty and destroyed.

'I'm sorry,' she said. 'We shouldn't have come.'

The old woman was some way off, climbing slowly up the hill ahead of them, stooped and trudging, shoving a handcart, the weight of it almost too much for her. She limped a few steps, paused, limped on again. There was something about her, in the way she held her head and the swing of her limp as she walked, that snagged at a corner of Castrel's mind.

Then she knew her, and tears were pouring down her face.

'Bremel! Bremel!'

She started to run awkwardly up the hill, clutching Hope tight, sobbing and weeping as she ran, all the grief and suffering, all the loss and the appalling sorrow of everything that had come upon them, all of it welling up suddenly and unstoppably, bursting up from the secret, wordless places where she had kept it hidden and locked away.

'Bremel?' she called. 'Wait! Stop! Bremel?' Was it even her?

The old woman turned and it was Bremel. Older and harrowed and faded, but Bremel still, frightened and puzzled; and then her face broke open with impossible joy and she was weeping too.

'Castrel? Castrel? Is it you?' Tears were spilling down her cheeks and she did not notice. 'Castrel, my darling, you've come.'

Castrel folded Bremel in her arms and breathed again her familiar scent. She had forgotten that. It was dizzying to remember, like falling from a great height into the past. But Bremel was an old woman now, so fragile and thin, so tiny and bent out of shape. Castrel hugged her and pressed her face into her neck, and then both of them were sobbing though neither of them knew.

At last Bremel pushed her gently away and looked at Hope.

'And there is a child!' she said. She could scarcely speak. 'You have a child!'

'Yes,' said Castrel. 'And this is Shay.'

He had come up behind them and was standing awkwardly a few feet off, looking out of place and not quite sure what to do or say.

'Hello,' he said, awkwardly.

Bremel went to him and gave him a hug. Her head barely reached his shoulders.

'What a darling man!' she said, beaming through her tears. 'Come home with me, both of you. Come home.'

Castrel walked with Bremel while Shay followed behind with Bremel's handcart.

'Will you give me the child to hold?' Bremel said. 'Let me carry her, just for a moment.'

'Of course, darling.'

She took Hope and cradled her in her arms, studying her closely with warm and loving attentiveness.

'What's her name?' she said.

'Her name is Hope.'

'She's beautiful, Castrel. So beautiful. You cannot know how beautiful she is. You've done a wonderful, heartbreaking, impossible thing. I didn't think it could happen again, not in this world. I've helped so many to be born ... I've been with so many women at their time ... but I thought that the having of children was finished, everywhere and for ever, and now here is one. And to think it's you, you my darling, my beloved Castrel, you've done this ...'

Bremel's face brimmed again with the burning light of joy, wet with unnoticed tears.

'We can't stay,' said Castrel. 'Not for long. We can't.'

'Of course not. But tonight. Stay with me one night, at least. You could do that.'

20

Shay sat quietly and watched Castrel and Bremel talk. Bremel was a tiny bird of a woman stooped with age, but a sharp bright intelligence burned in her eyes. There was a fierceness in her that was almost harsh. He had heard so much of her from Castrel, but he hadn't pictured her like this: he'd expected someone softer, kinder, more motherly, but in person he found her a little intimidating. She was deeply moved to see Castrel again, the joy of it illuminated her, but all the same she watched them both closely and nothing escaped her.

He looked around at her room. The bare boards of the floor were scattered with dried sprigs of herb. Things she had collected were ranged on shelves or hung from nails on the walls. Stones and branches. Feathers. The skull of a badger. She lived sparsely and had little hospitality to offer them, but what she had she brought out.

'I'm so glad you're still here,' said Castrel. 'I wanted you to be, but I didn't dare expect it. I didn't dare even hope. We've seen almost no one.'

'Most of the others left long ago, when we first heard what was happening further north,' said Bremel. 'The whole of Weald went together, everyone in a long line down the road, taking with them everything they could carry. They were going to find a better place. I hope they found it.'

'You didn't go with them?'

'I'm too old for that. I'd rather wait here for whatever comes next. A few others stayed, though I haven't seen any of them for months. They keep themselves to themselves, or they're gone now.' She frowned. 'Or dead.'

'I wish you'd gone with them,' said Castrel. 'What's coming behind us is terrible. You can't imagine it. It comes in waves, not everywhere at once, and sometimes it moves slowly, but it keeps on coming, always, and when you think you've seen the worst of it you haven't. It'll come here too. In the end the shadow always falls, and it's terrible when it comes. You should have gone with them, Bremel.'

'Well, I'm glad I stayed, because you came, and I have seen your child. How old is she? Twelve months? Fifteen?'

'Not nearly so much. I'm not sure exactly. Three months? Perhaps four.'

Shay felt Bremel's flicker of surprise. Only the movement of an eyebrow.

'She was born too soon,' said Castrel. 'I was ill for days, but Shay looked after us.' She glanced at him, and his heart leaped to see the warmth and love in her eyes. 'Hope was born so *small*, Bremel,' she said. 'She was such a tiny fragile thing. I didn't think she would live. But look at her now. Every day she grows.'

There was a long silence.

'I do know, Castrel,' said Bremel at last.

Shay saw the darkness that clouded Castrel's eyes.

'Of course you know,' she said.

'There's something different with her,' said Bremel. 'I can feel it there. Tell me what it is.'

Castrel told her then, about crossing the red plain and seeing the dead dragon, and what their golden friend said to them.

'The heart of the dragon is taking my child and there's nothing I can do to stop it. It's changing her. It's destroying her—'

'She doesn't look to me like she's being destroyed,' said Bremel gently.

'I've tried to fight it, I've tried to drive it out, but all it does is watch me. Yet I keep on trying, I keep on looking for the way, and I will never stop.' There was anguish in Castrel's face. Desperate need and hope. It cut Shay's heart. 'I was hoping you could help me,' she said. 'I thought you might know something.'

Bremel put an arm around her and hugged her. Touched her cheek and hair.

'Oh, my love,' she said gently. 'I can't do this. No more than you can. Driving out dragons is wizards' work, like your golden man said. If it can be done at all.'

'You really can't?'

'How could I? How could any of us? Our work is with the life of this world. With birthing and sickness and hurt and dying. What we do can be harsh and rough, and often is. We can be tough and dark and strong like crow's flesh. But a dragon? These are things we know nothing of. These we cannot traffic with. You know this. If you try your strength against a dragon you will hurt yourself.'

'But I would risk that,' said Castrel. 'I would at least try.'

'And would you risk harming Hope?'

'No. Of course not.'

'But your golden friend warned that you might.'

'Yes, he did.'

'Well, then, my darling heart … I think you should listen to him.'

'What, and do nothing? Nothing at all? Should I just let the dragon have Hope for its own? You didn't see it, Bremel. That foul, disgusting, monstrous carcase …'

'Don't you sometimes think,' said Bremel, 'that this terrible anguish you're feeling – this darkness and fear and corrosion – that it might be in you, not Hope?'

'No!'

'Look at this child you have, Castrel. She's wonderful. A miracle. See how beautiful and strong she's growing? In the end of everything, in the desolation of the world, in the midst of all this horror and dying, you and Shay have made a new child. It almost makes me believe that all things are not over. Love her, both of you, and find joy in what she is, not what you wish she could be. Hope is beautiful now, and whatever she becomes in time, that will be beautiful too. It will be her. Herself. You can't change that now, but then you never could have. That is not given to parents, ever. How your child grows is not yours to control. Hope will be right for whatever comes next to take this dying world's place, and she will be a good thing in it.'

'You don't know that,' said Castrel quietly.

'I think I do. Something good must come out of all this horror. I think something good already has.'

'No!' said Castrel fiercely. 'She hasn't chosen this. I will drive it out of her.'

'Please, sweetheart,' said Bremel, 'don't tear at yourself like that. Don't hurt yourself with anger, or mourning the loss of something you wanted that was never going to be. Don't make your love for Hope into a grief that will destroy both you and her.'

Castrel stared at her and said nothing.

Bremel turned to Shay.

'You're the father. What do you think?'

'I don't know anything about dragons or healing,' he said. 'The golden man said it would be years before Hope changed, and everything else he told us has turned out to be true, so far. That means we have plenty of time. Maybe we can find out more. Maybe we can find someone who can help. We should always keep searching for that.'

'Who else is there to help us if Bremel can't,' said Castrel.

'Who else could there be? A wizard? Would you trust Hope to a wizard, Shay? After what we've learned? With their wars and their experimentations and what they are?'

'No,' said Shay. 'I don't think so, not that. But we can keep searching. And we can keep loving her, Cass. We have to look after her and make her life as good as we can. What I'm afraid of is that we'll spend all our time hating the dragon and we'll lose sight of what she is now. I'm afraid we could forget how to love her because of it. We could come to fear and hate her in the end, and we can't let that happen. That's the most important thing.'

Bremel reached out and touched his hand gently, just for a second.

'You're a good man, Shay. Castrel knew what she was doing when she chose you.'

'I hope so. But she's stronger and better than I am. I know that.'

'Yes,' said Bremel with a smile. 'Of course she is. She's my Castrel.'

'So this is what both of you think?' said Castrel. 'We should accept the dragon is in Hope and just let it be, and do nothing?'

'Cass ...' said Shay quietly. 'That isn't what I'm saying ...'

Castrel sank back in her chair.

'Maybe you're right,' she said. 'I don't feel sure of anything any more. But neither of you know this thing, not like I do. You haven't watched it, digging itself deeper and deeper ...'

'He said she would become a dragon, Cass,' said Shay, 'not that the dragon would become her. He said she'd take control of what she was, and she would grow, and choose.'

'But she's only human! And she's an infant! He didn't know anything about that, except it had never happened before. We're her parents, Shay. I don't see how we can just do nothing.'

'I don't think you have to do nothing,' said Bremel. 'You can help Hope to shape herself as she grows. Work with her, Castrel.

Work with the heart of the dragon instead of fighting it. Use all your strength to help her grow strong, and then when she's old enough to go forward alone, you can step back and let her go.'

'Oh, Bremel,' said Castrel, and Shay saw her despair. 'You don't understand. You don't know. I can't do that. Even if I wanted to, I couldn't. It just isn't possible any more.'

'Why not?'

'Because I've lost the gift. Healing and touching and sharing. It's been taken away from me for ever. I've lost everything. I can't reach Hope like I used to at all.'

'No,' said Bremel. 'No. That can't be.'

Castrel told her about the pale cold fire that burned her and the shrieking creatures of the air that drained her. Fed on her. Took everything away.

'It's all gone now,' she said.

'Oh, my darling. Come here.'

Bremel put her arm round Castrel again, and Castrel leaned into her, closer, for comfort. Shay saw that Bremel closed her eyes, as if she was listening to something far away. She stayed like that for a long time, stroking Castrel's head gently with her hands.

'I see it is true,' she said at last, and her face was full of shock and loss and grief. 'Castrel. My poor, poor sweet child. I've never known this before. I wouldn't have thought it could happen.'

'But it has happened,' said Castrel.

'I wish there was something I could do.' Tears were brimming in Bremel's bright dark eyes. 'With all my heart I wish that.'

'But you can't,' said Castrel. 'And I can't work with Hope or help her. You see how I cannot.'

'Then we must trust Hope on her own. She will find her own path and fight her own battles by herself.'

'But she's a child! A tiny baby! How can she—'

'Hope is unique. She will do it, and on her own if she must.

She has her own strength, she has your strength and she has another strength too, the strength of the heart of the dragon. She is a joining of the very old with the absolutely new, and if she is to be a dragon she will be unlike any dragon this world or any other world has ever seen. She is your daughter, after all, the daughter of you both, and that's a fine thing to be.'

They talked on, late into the night, and when the candles guttered and the fire sank to embers Bremel showed them where they could make a bed on the floor. Castrel fell immediately into a profound sleep. It wasn't just exhaustion, it was something to do with coming home and being under Bremel's roof again. Shay lay awake and listened to her slow quiet breathing.

Was the heart of the dragon a parasite invading and consuming their child? Or was it a wonderful change, the beginning of a beautiful transformation? They simply could not know, and going on asking the question over and over again would tear them to shreds and destroy their child more certainly than the dragon itself ever would. Bremel was right. The only thing they could do was let the question go, and trust to Hope herself. She may be as strong as they said, but for now she was still only a small, fragile child and terrible things were happening in the world. Their duty was to love her and keep her safe. And that was enough. He saw things clearly now. For the first time since the bear-people came he felt sure he knew what they must do. He didn't know how, not yet, but that would come.

He shifted under the blanket, trying to get comfortable, and coughed. His chest was troubling him more and more. He knew by the hurt in his lungs, the blood he sometimes spat and the weakness deep in his bones, that something was wrong. He coughed again and again. He couldn't stop.

'Shay?' said Castrel sleepily. 'Are you all right?'

'Fine,' he said. 'Sorry I woke you. Go back to sleep. You need it.'

'I'll talk to Bremel in the morning. I'll ask her to look at your chest.'

'Thanks. Yes. That would be good.'

He got up from the bed and went outside until the coughing subsided, so he wouldn't disturb her again. He was sorry he hadn't thought of it before.

The next morning he was down by the little river that ran near Bremel's house when she came to him.

'Let me look at your chest,' she said. 'Will you let me?'

'Of course,' he said.

Bremel's touch wasn't like Castrel's, though he couldn't quite say how. Bremel was both gentler and firmer, sure but not so strong, a sun behind clouds, not a fire in the sky, and on her tongue the hedge-words sounded different. Dark and harsh, ancient, sibilant and strange. It was disturbing to feel her working inside him. Her touch was like faint cool roots working their way deep inside his ribs.

Then suddenly he was doubled over and coughing violently and choking and spilling foul stuff from his mouth and nose.

The agonising heave and spasm of his ribs.

He fought against panic. He was choking and drowning at once.

Afterwards, Bremel said: 'I've done what I can. It's clear now.' And he felt that it really was clear. 'But you have to be always careful in future,' she added, 'or it will come back, and if it does it will be worse.'

Careful? How can I be careful, in this world, now? How can I do that?

He thought that but he didn't say it. He could see what the effort of healing him had cost Bremel: she looked tired and strained and old.

'Thank you,' he said. 'Truly, thank you.'

She smiled and reached out to touch him lightly, putting her frail bird-like hand against his face just for a moment. It felt like a blessing.

'It's harder for me to heal people now I'm so old,' said Bremel. 'I don't have so much strength to share any more. Castrel would have done it better. She had more skill than anyone I ever knew.'

'Castrel says Hope is stronger than her, or you.'

'Hope is extraordinary,' said Bremel, 'and she doesn't inherit that only from Castrel. It's from you too.'

'Me? I'm just an ordinary man.'

'There's nothing ordinary about you. You and Castrel are the best of people. If there's any hope for the future, it's with you and your child. You have to look after Hope and Castrel now. You have to be strong.'

'I will. I try.'

'I know you will,' said Bremel. 'You're a good man.'

'Castrel never talks about her family,' said Shay. 'Only you.'

'Castrel was young when her mother died, barely older than your Hope is now, and after her mother died, her father was no good for anything or anyone. Castrel has always thought he blamed her, for her mother's death.'

'Did he really blame her?'

'She never recovered properly after Castrel's birth, but I don't suppose he truly blamed Castrel for that. I don't suppose he thought of anything much at all, beyond his own grief. But Castrel blamed herself.'

'Why would she do that?' said Shay. 'It wasn't anything to do with her. She was only a tiny child.'

'Castrel has always hated it when anything gets sick or dies. She always takes it that she could have saved them, and should have, so it's her fault if she didn't. But being a healer's not like that. There's only so much you can do.'

'What was she like, when she was a girl?' said Shay.

Bremel laughed.

'All narrow bony shoulders and large dark eyes,' she said. 'Thick hair shiny as a crow's wing, cut jaggedy short round her neck and always falling into her face. Her father scarcely fed her. When I found her she was starved to skin and bone. Wersh she was then, *wersh* – a tiny little thing and dressed all raggy like a shewel, even in the worst of winter. But fierce. There was always a wildness in her.'

'She hasn't changed so much, then.'

'No.' Bremel paused and looked at him. 'She loves you. I can see that.'

'I hope so,' said Shay. 'I love her too.'

Later, Shay looked back on that talk with Bremel as a kind of benediction on Castrel and him. An acknowledgement and a rite of joining together. He treasured it in his heart.

Day followed day and the days were all the same. The days were good. They stayed with Bremel in her house and Shay was glad of it. Castrel slept late in the mornings and sat for long hours at Bremel's table with Hope on her knee, talking. He watched her spending time with someone she knew in a place where she belonged, among all the normal feelings of life being lived. It was company, it was ordinary, and it felt like healing. He saw the fierce darkness around her beginning to lift away. Once he heard her laugh in the next room. It surprised him almost to tears.

Castrel and Bremel did small tasks together. They rummaged in wooden chests to find clothes for Hope to wear and mashed apple and carrot and potato for her to eat. The child was open-faced, happy, exploring. Taller and stronger and finer every day.

After the first night they never talked about the heart of the dragon again. Shay didn't know what Castrel was thinking, and he didn't ask her. He thought it was better to leave her alone and give her time to recover. They made no plans. They didn't talk about the future at all. For now, each day as it came was enough.

Shay felt himself outside the little circle that gathered every day around the table, the two women and the child. Not excluded, but apart. He didn't mind. He left them alone and found things to do by himself. He fixed Bremel's roof, cleaned her stove, stacked logs in the yard and gathered a last withering harvest from the orchards and barns of Weald. The work was tiring but wholesome and good. When he came into the house at twilight he was bone-chilled and hungry but there was plenty of food now, and in the evenings he sat by the stove to warm himself and hold Hope in his arms, talking to her until she fell asleep.

One evening he realised with a jolt of surprise that he was happy. He hadn't even thought about that for a very long time.

He found the boat one morning down by the river. She was moored in a dark and leaf-littered crook of the stream, half-hidden under overgrown briar and red-thorned bramble. She was shallow-bottomed, open, thirty feet long, her timbers sodden and grey.

It took him a day to hack away the growth that covered her so he could see her clearly. Her thwarts had rotted but the hull seemed sound. The sludge that had gathered in the bottom was only collected rainwater, black with the murky silt of mouldered leaves. When he cut her free, she wobbled and swung out into the current, sending ripples that slapped gently against the bank. The last thing he found when he finished baling her out was a waterlogged sail bundled and stowed in the bow.

'What's the name of that river beyond the ash trees?' he asked Bremel that evening.

'That's the Withylode,' she said.

'What happens to it after Weald? Where does it go?'

'Through Dernewood,' she said, 'and then Scarhoe and Arrish. After that it flows south-east and joins a great river called the Harricker that goes on into other countries. I've never been further than Arrish in a boat, nobody from Weald ever did that, but they say the Harricker gets broader and broader until it reaches the sea at Proud Somail, and by then it's wide and deep like a moving sea itself.'

Shay knew of Proud Somail. Even in Harnestrand there were sailors who said they'd been in that miraculous port at the edge of the southernmost ocean, thousands of miles away. From Proud Somail you could take passage on a ship to anywhere in the world. From Proud Somail you could sail to the green archipelago of Far Coromance.

Hope and excitement welled up inside him. From almost outside Bremel's own door there was a waterway that could take them all the way to Far Coromance. And there was a boat, and he knew how to handle boats. He was born to it. The boat needed fixing, but he knew how to do that too.

It was only a chance, a flimsy chance: he knew how long and hard such a journey would be. But it would be a lot better than walking.

The next morning he spread out the sodden sail on the bank. It dried stiff and dirty-brown, stained and streaked like a corpse-sheet, but strong and free of rot.

He did all he could to make the boat good. He fitted her with new thwarts, and cut an ash pole to serve as a new mast. Ash wasn't the best wood for a mast – it would bend like a bow in a strong wind – but it was the best he could find. It should be good enough for river work. They would need to find something else for the ocean when they got there. At Proud Somail they would find a ship.

He bodged a crude iron rowlock and fitted it at the stern for the steering-paddle. Then he built a frame of bent withies across the middle of the boat, which he covered with oilcloth sheets to make a shelter against the weather. It would be a kind of floating tent. He rigged a length of rope with a heavy rock for an anchor.

Bremel came to see him once or twice while he was down by the river. He saw her notice the boat, but she said nothing and neither did he. He didn't say anything to Castrel either. He wanted to finish it first.

It took him many days that he didn't count, and when at last it was done he had a boat that was too broad and shallow, that wallowed fatly and swung off course in the slightest crosswind. But she would do. He and Castrel could manage her together, just, at least while they were going downstream and the current was with them.

There would be room for Bremel too.

And then one night the darkness was torn apart by flashes of distant lightning, silent and bitter grey, and in the morning the whole vastness of the northern horizon loomed dark purple and copper beyond the trees. A thin rain was falling like fine gritty ash from the sky and all that day it never grew properly light, though by the calendar and the lengthening of the daylight hours the season should have been unfolding into early summer.

The ending of all things was coming for them again, as they had known in their hearts that one day it must. Already it was almost upon them.

'We have to leave now,' Shay said to Castrel. 'I'm sorry, but we must. We have to get moving again.'

'Yes,' she said. 'I know. We've been lucky to stay here so long.'

They were standing side by side in Bremel's yard, the two of them on their own, watching the darkening sky.

'Whenever we come somewhere,' she said, 'it always follows us in the end. A few days or weeks and then everything begins to die all over again. Sometimes I feel as if it's us. Are we the bringers of all this death, Shay? Are we the carriers of this plague? Sometimes I think we must be.'

'We didn't make it happen,' he said. 'I don't know what did, but it wasn't us. We may be the last spark in the darkness, but the end won't come until we're gone. Not till then. That's why we have to burn brightly while we can and never let the bitterness in. If we have to be the last, we can also be the best.'

'Come with us, Bremel,' said Shay. 'Don't stay here on your own. You can come with us. You'd be welcome, you know that. There's room in the boat.'

Bremel was standing on the bank of the Withylode watching him provision the boat. There was a line of blue-grey mist on the northern horizon, the smoke of distant cold fires burning, and a sour grey snow like ash was falling thinly. It settled on her shoulders and in her hair. Castrel wasn't there. She was in the house with Hope.

'No,' said Bremel. 'I won't come with you. Castrel asked me the same. All my life has been at Weald, that's been the shape of it, and I don't want to see other places now. I only want to see this one through.'

'But, Bremel—'

'Please, Shay. No more of this. I will not come with you. I'm old and I will only get older, and in the end you and Castrel would have to care for me, and you mustn't do that. The old must loosen their hold on the world when their time comes, and be ready to die. The young must not be sacrificed to care for us; you must be left free to find your own way. That's how it has to be. Always. Look to your child, only to her.'

'Castrel won't want to leave without you.'

'Castrel and I understand each other. We have said what we need to say. She'll go without me. Of course she will.'

*

When they were ready to leave, Bremel couldn't be found. Shay searched for her but she was gone.

'I wanted to say goodbye,' he said. 'I wanted to thank her.'

'She's taken herself off somewhere else,' said Castrel. 'She's walked away into the woods until we're gone. It's all right, Shay. That's the way she is.'

There was a package on the table, a parting gift. Wort-soap and candles. Shay watched Castrel read the note Bremel had left with it. He didn't ask her what it said. There were tears in her eyes, and the pain in her face, the grief he saw there, cut him to the heart.

When they were ready Shay untied the boat and pushed away from the bank and raised the dirty sail. It shook out and snapped taut with the breeze and the boat surged downstream, ploughing a wake through thick dark water. Sliding between coarse grass banks and dying trees. He showed Castrel how to use the paddle in the stern to steer. It felt good to be in a boat again.

River flowed into river, wider and wider, always southwards, thousands of miles, all the way to Proud Somail. The bleak wind from the north would help them now. Darkness was coming, but they would outrun it yet. At least for a while. And a while could be good. A while could be a very long time.

21

Hope listened to all the voices in the heart of the dragon. They were sharing their memories with her, and the memories were becoming Hope's memories too.

Hope remembered flying on outstretched wings above a great shining city. Slender towers of marble and gold gleamed in the bright morning sun, and many faces looked up at her from wide paved squares. The people were smiling and shouting, and some of their faces she knew and loved. Her name was Hoon then, and that city was Belavaresse.

Hope remembered sleeping on the side of a grassy hill in the rain, and an old man was with her. He was sleeping too. He had been her friend for a long time, but he was ageing now and would die soon. His death didn't matter to him because he had done everything he wanted to do and learned what he wanted to know. That happened when her name was Deep Lake.

Hope remembered swimming deep in a cold black ocean, far from any shore. She swam fast with her mouth gaping open to swallow huge shoals of silver fish. The fish filled her belly – they were sweet and delicious – and she was young and life was new. The next day she would fight a fierce battle that she was going to win, and her victory would taste sweeter than all the fish of the ocean. That battle happened when her name was Calamitous Dragon.

These things and many others happened a long time ago, and some of them were in other worlds. But in the endless mind of the heart of the dragon – so old it could no longer remember its own beginning – all of it was happening still, and now, and always.

And Hope remembered all of it. She was learning fast. Her body grew taller and stronger every day.

Part Four

22

Castrel sat at the back of the boat and steered it with one hand on the paddle. The Withylode was wider than she remembered, the waters surging deeper, faster, dark and cold. There was a low drifting early morning mist that seeped into her bones and smelled of raw wet earth. The willows on the banks were dry and brittle.

The Withylode had flowed all through her childhood, a river of warm sunlight and cool green depths, out of somewhere and on to somewhere else, from for ever to for ever, moody and changeable as the sky. She used to swim in it every day, and sometimes she would dive down deep and touch the bottom, and when she looked up she could see the surface of the river shimmering and shining high above her. It was like another sky.

Everything important that she had ever known could be learned from the river.

The surface of the river wasn't a solid wall, it was only the place where two different worlds touched – the world of water and the world of air – and the surface was the place where you passed between them. That was how the healing gift worked.

Every living thing in the world had a surface like the river, and none of the surfaces were really there. They seemed like walls but they weren't walls. The surfaces of living things shimmered and shone but a swim or a dive would take her through. When she came to a surface, all she had to do was keep on going, right on through, and then she would be somewhere else, and she could look back and watch the world she had left from the other side. And she belonged everywhere. Every time she passed through a living surface, part of her was left behind, but another part of her was already waiting on the other side.

But now all of that was changed. Her gift, her sight, her healing touch were gone, lost in the cold fire that burned the trees and the shrieking of cold flying beasts high in the air. Now all the surfaces of the world were unbreachable walls, and all the parts of her that were behind the walls were gone, and Bremel was gone, and she grieved for it all. Again the sky in the north was a rising darkness of copper and lurid green; the waves and surges of desolation and horror were still following them, slowly and fitfully consuming the world and bringing all good things to an end, though they kept running before it and always she hoped they would escape it at the last. It was all appalling, unhealable loss. But most of all she grieved for the loss of the sharing times with Hope. What hurt her worst was the silence of her child, that lost landscape where she used to go. She grieved for that all the time.

Yet Hope was still with her. Her child was not lost. Castrel watched her now, crawling in the bottom of the boat, hauling herself upright, taking her first unstable steps. When she fell she laughed, because she was happy. Hope was growing fast, she was learning, she was strong. Much taller now, more slender, there was a definite shape to her face. A structure to her cheeks and chin. Her face was somewhat long and narrow like Shay's. The dragonish scales on her back and shoulders were bright and beautiful and many-coloured, and her eyes were flecked with shards of purple and grey and gold. When Hope looked at her there was wisdom and knowledge there, far beyond her years, and sometimes her look was grave and sometimes it was glad and burned with fierce joy.

Hope was still with her, and so was Shay, and that was all that counted in the darkening world. She had so nearly forgotten that.

Trust the child, Bremel had said. *Let her find her own path.*

The heart of the dragon was in her and the thought of that still brought Castrel anguish and almost physical pain, but she could not fight it any more.

Love Hope and care for her and keep her safe and let her find her own way.

They all said that, in their different ways, all of them, Shay and Bremel and the Golden Friend. They were her friends, and Hope's friends, and they were wise in their different ways, and she was resolved to put her trust in them. She tried to let go and be free, though it was hard.

I wish I could reach out and touch Hope and hear her, like I used to do. Then Hope could tell me herself. Then I would know, I would really know.

That was the loss she grieved for most of all.

'When we were children we used to make leaf-boats,' Castrel said to Shay. 'We loaded them with berries and little scoops of earth and sticks with names. Mostly they'd get nowhere, they'd only get stuck in the roots along the bank, but sometimes one of them would sail right off, far away and out of sight for ever. We always wondered where they went. We used to say they went all the way to the ocean and a hundred years later they'd be there, bobbing about on deep waves far out of sight of the land.'

They named their boat *Apple Leaf* to remind them of home, of all their homes, of all their lost short seasons of home.

Castrel swam with Shay in the cold dark waters of the Withylode, and then they washed with Bremel's soap. The faint scent of lavender was like memory.

She watched him standing in a shallow place near the bank. He had his back to her and he was naked. He took a few steps and crouched so he could dip his arms in deep, sluicing the water over his hair and shoulders and back. He shaved his beard with the knife and cut his hair. His legs were so thin, sinew and bone, and his shoulders were sharp and prominent like a boy's. There was a fading bruise on one thigh.

Her love for him flared, sudden and incandescent. It hurt like pity and need. He was so raw, so defenceless, so stripped away in the cold, till there was nothing left of him but loneliness and courage.

When he swam back to the boat and hauled himself over the side she was waiting for him and wrapped him in the blanket.

'You are beautiful,' she said. 'I'm glad you're here.'

Nights she listened to the sounds of the river against the boat. The river used to have a voice, but now it was just noises. Only the slop and trickle of moving water.

Sometimes she walked along the bank, keeping pace with the boat. Hope was too heavy to carry in her arms but she couldn't walk far, so Shay fixed one of the backpacks with a sling for a seat and the child rode up high on her back, chattering without words, holding tight fistfuls of Castrel's hair in her small fists.

Castrel collected small things as she walked. Smooth greenish stones from the bed of a stream. Twigs. Cones. Galls and cankers. A trail of dark ivy stem, rough with root-hair. A piece of bark like a mossy face. Feathers. Scraps that snagged her gaze, instinctive and wordless. She picked them up and put them in her pocket, and when she was back on the boat she took the small things and shaped them. Knotted them together with grass. Threaded them. Fixed them with dabs of sticky mud and resin smears. She was making strange objects. Each small thing was a tiny part of herself, and into each one she put something small but very specific. An expression. A vessel. A distillation. She didn't know why she did this but it felt right.

The Withylode took them into a sheltered valley where watery light spilled through the trees. The northern sky was still darkening, the approaching wave-crest rising always, but they ignored it now. Let it be. What might come was not here yet, and *now* – this day, this hour, this moment – was all that counted. Trust to the now. Precious fleeting eternities of now.

That evening they let down the sides of the canopy to turn the boat into a closed-in, low-roofed secret place, and in the twilight Castrel set out all Bremel's candles, all of them, inside it.

'We'll burn them all,' she said. 'One night of abundance. A festival. One normal, special time. One good memory when everything is nice.'

They crowded together with Hope in the tented canopy. Outside was the cold and empty dark of the night, but inside they were snug in a perfumed golden candlelight. They ate the last of the food Bremel had given them, sharing it with Hope. The child's eyes laughed, wide and flecked with slate and gold, and the dragon-scales on her neck and shoulders shone with warm colour like jewels. Like preciousness and magic.

'Isn't she a wonder?' said Shay.

'Yes,' said Castrel. 'She is a wonder. Beautiful and strange.'

In the morning Castrel came awake to the first glimmer of grey dawn through the canopy and the lingering scent of guttered candles. Shay and Hope were warm bodies against her, still asleep. For the first time, she woke entirely without dread. No fear. None.

Trees on both banks leaned across the water, their branches merging, shadowing the river. While Hope and Shay slept, Castrel made a leaf-boat. She pinned it into shape with thorns and ballasted it with a pebble. Then she took one of the small figures she had made out of twigs and moss and berries. She held it up close to her eye so she could see the tiny markings on the bark, the exact complexity of the grass-stem knots, the russets of old moss and the lichen like the marks on moth wings. Then she put it in the leaf-boat, leaned over the side and put the boat on the water, and let it go.

The tiny leaf-vessel wobbled and turned, listing to one side, uncertain, testing the way, then settled and righted itself. Castrel watched the stream carry it clear of the banks. It grew tinier and tinier under the shadow of the trees, until it rounded a bend in the river and went beyond where she could see. Then she stooped back in under the canopy and found Hope awake.

The child was sitting upright and looking intently at her hands. Moving her fingers. Her hair was a wispy tangle and her eyes were bright. She was making quiet noises in her throat, a kind of humming. When Castrel came in, Hope looked up and met her gaze. There was a light in her face, a kind of gentle illumination, a calm triumph.

And suddenly Castrel felt the touch of Hope's awareness reaching out to her, and joy burst open inside.

She had thought she had lost it for ever, but now it was there again, warm and strong, because Hope was doing it by herself. The child's awareness was passing easily through all the surfaces that Castrel herself could no longer breach. Hope went through the walls between them as if they were not there.

And then Castrel felt the voice of her daughter speaking, a quiet simple voice, not from throat and mouth and tongue but from Hope herself, mind touching mind. She could not reach Hope, but Hope could reach her.

Mother, hello, mother, I'm hungry, pick me up.

Castrel sat among the blankets under the canopy on the boat with tears of joy pouring down her face. Hope was in her arms, and she was cradling her, rocking her from side to side. She wasn't thinking at all. She couldn't remember how to think. Such joy as this, such explosions of joy, were entirely outside thought.

'Oh, my darling,' she murmured, again and again, 'my darling, my darling, my wonderful child.'

When Shay woke he found her sitting next to him and holding Hope, weeping with happiness.

23

Every day Shay expected that they would break out of narrow waters, that one morning the *Apple Leaf* would round a bend in the stream and he would swing her out wide and free, her sail bellying full, out into the deep brown currents of a broad and mighty river like Bremel had described, a river that would roll on southwards, majestic, to Proud Somail and the faraway ocean. The Harricker, Bremel had called it. Shay realised it must be the same river Mamser Gean talked about, the Arker, whose source was the Skywater lake to the north of Sard Keeping.

But it never happened. They never found the great river. Somewhere among all the channels and small islands, the tall marsh grasses, the riverbanks higher than their mast and ribbed with the exposed roots of trees, the brief widenings of the stream into pools and shallow lakes, somewhere among all that, the *Apple Leaf* must have left the Withylode behind and entered some other nameless dying river sliding between dying hills.

The nameless river carried them through countries where the darkness had already arrived ahead of them, and through other countries where it had not yet come. Almost each day was different. Sometimes they woke to darkening copper skies and a rain of bitter ash. Sometimes the skies were wide and bleak and swept with high grey winds. The whole world seemed patchwork now, a perpetual borderland, a cross-hatched country divided between the places of the doomed and the places of the already dead.

Somewhere deep in his heart Shay knew and accepted that their human world was over. If he and Castrel and Hope were not the last people left alive now, it felt that way. The door that should not have been opened was open, and it would never be closed again.

He didn't say this to Castrel, but he sensed she knew it too. There was no need to speak of it. The times of anguish and searching for answers and places of safety, all those agonising and exhausting swings between hope and anger and despair, were finished. This was their life now. Day after day the nameless river carried them south, always south. Day after day their beautiful child with the shining iridescent scales on her back and the heart of a dragon grew more clever and strong.

Shay sat in the bow of the *Apple Leaf* in the last grey light of evening. She was drifting on a slack wind, barely faster than the current. He held the sail-sheet lightly, a water-stained rope end, fibrous, grey and thicker than his thumb. The dead wizard's sword unsheathed beside him along the thwart.

He was watching wolves in tree-shadow on the bank. They were silent. Indistinct as moths. One turned its face towards him. Wolf eyes. Unhurried. Considering. The wolves were larger than a wolf should be. Ox-shouldered and pale.

He wondered if they were really wolves at all.

He would fight them if he had to. He would fight the wolves with bare hands and sword.

He imagined wolf jaws on his face. His arm in a wolf mouth. His fingers gripping a wolf throat, digging. The blade of the sword sliding into wolf belly. Blood and more blood.

Without hope he would fight them.

'Wolves', he said to Castrel in a low voice.

'There are more on the other bank,' she said. 'They've been there a while.'

He jerked round, but there was nothing he could see. Only deep shadows and tangled branches.

'I can't see them,' he said.

'When they want us, they will come.'

'I don't think wolves swim.'

'If they're hungry they will swim.'

'They're just watching.'

'They're following us,' said Castrel.

'Why would they do that?'

'Because they're wolves.'

Castrel sat for a long time, staring into the deepening dark.

'There's worse than wolves out there,' she said quietly.

After the wolves they anchored in mid-stream and kept a night watch, taking turns to sleep in the day.

Sometimes at night Shay heard strange sounds in the woods. Alien cries and the moans of unknown creatures. Almost-human screams. Almost voices. Almost words. In the dark he saw lights moving a long way off among the trees and the glow of dull red fires on distant hills.

Sometimes by day there was a thread of smoke on the horizon, and the whole vast heaviness of the sky was green and copper. It cast a lurid light.

Evenings the sun showed red and misty, westering into the quiet, and Shay guided the boat beneath the shadow of great trees that passed like ghosts, their thick roots twisting down into the water through gathering shreds of fog.

*

'What do you miss the most?' Castrel asked him once.

'What?' said Shay, taken by surprise.

They were sitting in the dark and she had wrapped a blanket round her shoulders against the cold. It was pulled up over her head like a hood so he couldn't make out her face in the shadow. Hope was sleeping under the canopy. The child had stayed awake late: the anxiety on the boat unsettled her. She noticed that kind of thing now.

'I mean,' said Castrel, 'if the old life came back, just for one day, what would you do?'

'I don't want to think about it. It's gone.'

'Don't you think we should remember?' she said. 'So we can tell Hope how things used to be, and everything we used to do then. If we don't remember and don't tell her, then she'll never know. She'll grow up not knowing.'

'Maybe that's good,' he said. 'Her world won't be like ours.'

'I try to tell her things. When she comes to talk to me in my head. I don't think she understands yet, though. She can show me her thoughts, if they're simple, but she doesn't have words. It's more like, she looks at me and I know what she's feeling, and she knows what I'm feeling, and that's all.'

They both fell silent for a while.

'So?' she said at last.

'So, what?'

'So tell me something you remember. It's important, Shay.'

He saw that she was right. Every day that passed was putting the gone time further behind them, and they needed to keep hold of it, tighter and tighter all the time. If they didn't, the past would fade and fall away behind them into being something different, something lesser and dead.

'All right,' he said.

He told Castrel about a morning when the horizon was flushed and the sun was lifting fast and hot out of the sea's rim.

He was in a needle boat, coming out of the west, sail full out and taut with a driving wind. She crested the swell and dropped, stern lifted high, prow slicing the downslope and jabbing the oncoming shoulder of sea in a salt slew of spray. She was forty miles off the coast, and her name was *Cormorant*. She was all strain. Every smack against the sea jarred her to the stem, every surge forward creaked her, joint and seam. Cabinless, a coastal trader built for a crew of twenty, the *Cormorant* carried only three, Shay and Galla and Moar, all reckless, racing high, yawing and skittish on the shelterless ocean under a sky-coloured sail.

Shay was fully alive that day. His body and mind were one thing, and the wind and the sea sang in him.

'I want to see the sea again, Cass,' he said. 'I want to show it to you and Hope.'

That night a blast of searing white light scorched Shay from sleep. He burst awake, lashing out and shouting, heart hammering in his chest. It was the middle of the night but a shocking, brilliant, bone-white glare flooded the world. A torrential searing stare. The abolition of all darkness and shade. Light poured out of everywhere. Though his eyes were tight shut it scorched his brain. Everything and everywhere was flooded in stinging blue-white light, a continuous unceasing lightning-burn that didn't flicker or fade. There were no shadows. When he held his own hands before his face they poured unbearable, impossible light into his eyes. He could see the insides of his hands. He could see the insides of everything, lucid and skeletal. The whole world and everything in it was screaming light.

And with the light came fear. Not fear of something in particular, but fear of all things. A raw, distilled purity of terror: dumbfounding, sourceless, unbearable, unfaceable fear. There was no running, no hiding, no turning away, because the fear was everywhere and the fear was of everything. He couldn't move and he couldn't remain still.

He was holding Hope in his arms and she was screaming, eyes stretched wide open, glaring into the light. He couldn't tell whether she was screaming in terror or joy. The shards of slate and purple and gold in her eyes burned like flakes of jewelled flame.

Shay stared at Castrel and she stared back at him, blank with horror.

This was the end, then. It had come for them all, and there was nothing to be done but be together and hold their shrieking child and meet it when it came.

When whatever was coming came.

Yet minutes passed, then hours that felt like eternities, and nothing else came. Only the light burned on, and the terror pressed and tightened, sickening, choking, driving the air from his lungs.

And then at last with the dawn the light faded to a grey exhausted calm. Shay's whole body was left trembling. Exhausted. Drained. After-images of orange and pale blue skeletal burn ghosted in his eyes, drifting and twisting across everything he saw.

Day rolled out of day, each day different, each day the same, unfolding the unravelling patchwork cross-hatching of the slowly collapsing world.

Something bumped heavily against the hull of the boat and swam slowly away. Shay saw a slick barrel of darkness breach the river. Saw the flick of a roping tail as thick as his arm at the shoulder. It left behind a trail of oil glistening on the rippled water.

After that there were others: shadows sliding deep; the coil of submerging eels. The prow of the boat nosing forward parted pale, jellied shoals. Once a wide mouth gaped at him, broad and flattened, forested with fine green needle teeth.

Rafts of wet ash and rotting weeds turned slowly in their wake.

'We shouldn't wade out to wash,' said Shay, 'not any more. We mustn't swim. Don't let Hope trail her hand in the water.'

Everything was getting worse.

Sometimes in the evenings they saw in the distant sky huge tatter-winged creatures that looked like vast moths. They were flying low on the far horizon, a kind of circling dance, shedding clouds of dust.

Shay went to their diminished food store in the stern and found it rotting. All crumbled and oozing black sticky slime and covered with a mesh of fine white threads. Sickened, he picked through what he could rescue, then tipped the rest over the gunwale and left it floating in their wake.

The nameless river broadened and they passed the mouths of other waters flowing into it. The *Apple Leaf* nosed through thickets of pale reeds that shut out all view of distance. Marsh and fen. The dark bent plumes of tall grasses hissed soft and harsh. Single dead trees stood knee-deep in pooled and sodden ground. The sky was wide and low.

Shay saw riders, half a mile off to the left, moving slowly along a low ridge: cowled misty figures on six-legged beasts. The riders saw them and turned in pursuit, urging their beasts down the slope at a gallop, splashing out onto grey flooded levels, raising clouds of spray. He heard their wailing cries like birds above the rain, but the *Apple Leaf* was already ahead of them and the river left them behind.

*

Uncounted and unmeasured, days and nights and miles passed empty like hunger. They drank but could not eat, because there was nothing.

Shay had made nets and hooks and lines for fish but he didn't use them – he suspected that to eat such creatures as they now saw moving in the water would be death – so they trailed their hands in the current and scooped up trails of weed and put it in their mouths and grew weaker and thinner. The *Apple Leaf* was their famine vessel. He crouched in the stern and scanned the skyline, the dead wizard's sword drawn and gripped tight in his fist.

There was always green and purple and dull copper now in the sky. The light was never right and the air they breathed was always thin and cold. Sometimes it tasted faintly metallic. Nights fell absolute and total black. No ashen glimmer of stars.

Without trees for mooring they drove pegs into the soft ground of the riverbank and roped the boat, keeping anxious watch, prepared to cut loose at the first sound or glimmer of light.

Shay wanted to keep moving through the night, but it was impossible. They tried it once, sailing on through the utter blackness by the light of a burning torch, but all the torchlight showed them was river and rain. That point of fire in the darkness was a beacon they dared not show again.

When it was his turn to rest Shay would hold Hope while she slept. Her hair was long now, and he would move it away from her face, and his love for her then was like a warm sea filled with light. It completed him.

But most of the time he stayed outside at the stern, steering. He was Hope's boatman and she was his precious fragile cargo. He watched over her as the rain-swollen river carried them always south, further and further into the sad, weakening, hungered emptiness of the ending world.

They passed through a country full of the signs of ancient wars: earthworks gouged into the sides of hills; leaning timber towers and weathered palisades; low burial mounds at the edge of flat ground; swathes of burned land where no growth had returned. Places where battles had been fought years ago: the fading murder-grounds of abandoned victories and forgotten defeats, all the armies long dead.

The *Apple Leaf* drifted between the ruins of ancient embankments. Both banks of the river were lined with walls of massive stone, overgrown with thorn and moss. In places the walls had collapsed into the water, spilling grassy earth. Small trees were rooted among the crevices.

The river was taking them ever deeper into the ruins of a fallen city. They sailed between high jetties and the stumps of squat lichenous towers. The silent relics of an older land. Strange haunted constructions of forgotten purpose.

Newer things had been built on top of the old: crude broken frames of iron and wood; lean-to shanties; precarious walkways of plank and rope; metal cages and wheels; timbers caulked and pitched till they were slick and creased like lacquered leather. Like a sea crow's throat. All those things too had been abandoned to weather and rust long ago.

'Do you think we're back in a hidden country again?' said Shay.

'I don't think so,' said Castrel. 'I think these ruins are older than that. This city goes back to the time before the human settlers came, when the other peoples were everywhere, before they withdrew to the hidden countries.'

'This is so much greater than anything humans have built. I wonder why the other peoples hid. Were they really trying to protect themselves from us? Why would they think they needed to, when they could build like this?'

'More likely they did it protect the humans. To protect us from their wizards and the wars.'

'So that worked well, then,' said Shay.

For the last hour of the evening, the rain fell mixed with grey ash. It turned the river whitely opaque, like thinned milk. Heavy raindrops marked the boat with splashes of grey.

'There's something moving,' said Shay. 'On the top of the high wall. Over there. Way back in the city.'

Figures were silhouetted for a moment against the sky. A line of them, small in the distance, ragged and insectile, crossing the gap of sky between distant broken fortifications.

'They're here, then,' he said. 'They're already here.'

'I know,' said Castrel. 'We're not running ahead of darkness and change any more. We haven't been for a while. It's ahead of us now as well, and we're going further into it all the time.'

'The golden man said the riders were only the first. Wave after wave will come after, each worse than the last.'

Later, in the twilight, he heard a single cry, a long raking call from somewhere up high, like a watcher giving the alarm. There was no answering call, and no lights were lit in the city as it faded into thickening night, but after that Shay always felt himself observed. Always the prickle of attention on the back of his neck.

The world had turned strange, but sometimes Shay felt that in truth now he and Castrel were the strangers: intruders from another time and place that didn't exist any more.

He kept the first watch while Castrel slept. Things he couldn't see were moving out there in the emptied city. He stood with his back to the mast, the dead wizard's sword unsheathed and ready in his hand, listening for the quiet dip of oars in the river, the shuffle and pad of bare feet on damp stone. But even though he was listening, when Castrel came to relieve him and take her turn he didn't hear her come. She could move in the dark without making a sound.

That night Shay dreamed of a huge creature in the depths of dark moving water. A creature with staring eyes, colourless and sightless as pearl, trailing long appendages. A creature transparent as the cold black water, black-veined, with transparent flesh. Transparent entrails. Transparent bones. A black transparent pumping heart. The vast creature sensed him and stirred, turning in the black water, turning towards him with wide dangerous eyes of lidless pearl. The creature was in his mind, and also not in his mind but out there, watchful and oceanic in the deepest of all dark rivers.

Dawn brought a sullen copper sky in the north and distant cold fires. White smoke like mist was bleeding up out of the horizon. The river thickened and slowed and dark writhing weeds, long tendrils as thick as fingers and wrists, attacked the boat. Shay hacked at them with axe and sword. Where the weeds were cut they oozed and bled thick oily slime.

There was no wind so he furled the stained sail and let the boat move through the ruined city at the pace of the river. Castrel was at the stern, steering. She had a knack for it. She had a feel for the quiet currents and the barely perceptible shifts of the keel. Occasional light touches at the paddle was all it took.

Hope was playing with Castrel's figures, the ones she had made with bits and pieces of stuff she picked up as she walked. He watched her put them down and pick them up again, frowning in concentration. She was wearing the brown woollen garment Bremel had found for her. It had been too large for her when they left Weald but now it fitted her well.

Their daughter was so tall and strong and beautiful now, it seemed almost wrong she didn't yet speak. It was hard to remember she was less than a year old, perhaps much less – he'd lost track of months and seasons. Time didn't pass for Hope as it did for other children. The growing and learning she was doing were all her own, and very fast.

Shay watched Hope often as she sat high in the bow of the *Apple Leaf* hugging her knees, looking forward. She was watching the future come and the river flow under the boat and behind, and she wasn't afraid. Sometimes Shay saw her smiling quietly to herself.

24

Rain fell in sheets. Blind downpours of dead grey water spilled from the sky, relentless and enclosing. The *Apple Leaf*'s canopy thundered and shook with the shock of the falling weight of the rain and shed water in streaming curtains. Water poured into the shelter and pooled in the bottom of the boat. The noise of the rain drowned the sound of the river. They had to raise their voices to be heard. The loudness of the rain closed in around them, shutting them in like a box. They piled blankets and clothes and whatever they could save up on the thwarts, but everything they had was soaked.

Castrel, her bare head plastered numb under the rain, sat at the back of the boat and hauled at the steering paddle. She heard Shay yelling above the noise.

'The river's rising!'

She struggled to hold a straight course. The current ran fast and urgent, brown, irresistible, roped and muscular, raking the bank with foam-edged waves. Her arms and shoulder ached. The skin of her hands was rubbed and blistered. She snatched a moment to wipe the rain from her face. Her clothes were sodden through, heavy with water, bitter cold and chafing her skin. The bow swung and tipped and the stern slewed sideways beneath her.

Shay was leaning out at the front of the boat, fending off

obstacles with a wooden pole, as she steered between huge lumps of ruin collapsed into the river. Pieces of slumped wall and the treacherous columns of collapsed bridges breached the racing surface of the water. Heavy branches and whole fallen trees turned in the current and lodged against the embankments.

Hour after hour the river surged on through the ruined city, of which there seemed no end. Buildings, taller now and more numerous, crowded the banks, blurred in the rain. Tower piled on broken tower. Massive masonry shapes, pinnacled and buttressed. Slate. Brick. Iron. Tile. Broken columns and blank vaulted windows. Swelling curtain walls. Stone-pathed moss gardens flowing down the slopes of low hills to the banks of the river, and everything slicked and darkened, streaming, obscure in the rain.

She saw that Shay was pointing at something. He was shouting but she couldn't hear what he said. She looked where he showed her and caught sight of a lone figure, hooded against the rain, moving fast along a parapet. It was just a glimpse in a gap between buildings, but she couldn't shake the feeling that the figure had a purpose. That it was following them.

The rain eased a little at last, so they could hear themselves speak, but the river was in full flood, brimming its banks and racing wildly onward. The *Apple Leaf* was barely under control.

They swept round a curve and Castrel saw a bridge spanning the stream ahead, unfallen.

'Bridge! Bridge!'

Shay was calling to her. She heard the edge of panic in his voice. The swollen river was hurling itself with high shoulders of dark foaming water against the squat pillars of the bridge and surging between them, churning and roaring under the low arches.

They were coming towards it too fast.

The mast was too tall to pass under the arches.

Shay scrambled to take down the mast, fumbling at the fixings, while Castrel leaned all her weight against the steering paddle. Trying to keep a line through the centre of the middle arch. It seemed impossible they would not crash, but somehow she found the course and held it, and the *Apple Leaf* passed through, rocking wildly and swinging sideways.

They were safe. They were through.

But as they emerged from the other side of the bridge something heavy dropped from the parapet above.

A man.

He crashed into the boat, sending it tipping wildly. Shay lunged for the dead wizard's sword where it lay in the bow, but the man was too quick and nimble. Ignoring Shay, he jumped over the thwarts and ducked in under the canopy. Where Hope was.

He must have known she was there. He must have been watching them. Waiting. Planning his moves. He was the one they had seen before, following them along the bank.

'*No!*'

Castrel screamed and scrambled forward.

'Hope! *Hope!* Get out! Get out! Get away from her!'

Castrel ducked under the canopy from the back of the boat. Shay was already at the other entrance, the sword in his fist. The intruder was crouching between them with one arm hooked around the mast. Hope was sleeping in a bundle of blankets. Perhaps he hadn't seen her yet.

'Get off our boat!' said Shay. 'Get away from us! Now!'

The intruder shook his head, staring wildly from Shay to Castrel. His eyes were wide and hunted, blank with desperation and fear, but Castrel sensed an edge of cunning there. Wariness. Threat. And she could smell him. Stale sweat. Foul clothes. And something else, strong and sour, that she could not name. He was large and broad. Thick wrists and heavy hands. A wide slab of a face, gaunt and sunk with hunger, and a big tangle of beard and hair falling to the shoulders, plastered with rain. A rain-dark stained leather jacket and heavy boots.

Castrel stepped forward and picked up Hope and held her close. When the intruder saw that, his eyes widened in surprise. Perhaps he hadn't been after her, like she'd thought. She couldn't be sure. He said something. A few words in an unfamiliar language. It seemed to be a question. His voice was deep and hoarse. He had bad teeth.

Castrel felt the *Apple Leaf* slew and tip under her feet. It was turning, unsteered, in the surging river.

She looked at Shay and their eyes met and she saw they were both thinking the same. They didn't know what to do. They had to steer the boat or she would crash. They couldn't take their eyes off this man. They had to do something with him. But what? There was no time to think. They had to act. Now.

Castrel felt panic rising. She didn't know what to do.

The intruder reached into his pocket. Shay shouted and raised the sword, but the man smiled broadly and held up a small stone bottle. He uncorked it with his teeth and took a swig, then wiped the neck with his sleeve and held it out towards Castrel with a wink. She shook her head. The man turned and jabbed the bottle towards Shay.

'No,' said Shay. 'Get off our boat.'

The man shrugged, took another swig and put the bottle away.

Castrel wanted him off the boat. He filled it with rank smell and danger. Hope was awake now and moving in her arms, protesting.

'We have nothing to give you,' said Castrel. 'Nothing. You have to go.'

'I don't think he understands,' said Shay.

She felt the boat slide sideways again. There was a heavy collision that almost made her fall. It came again. They were bumping against something in the river. Maybe a large branch floating.

'We've got to get rid of him,' she said.

'How?' said Shay. 'How?'

'I come with you,' the man said. The words came clumsily. Awkward in his mouth. 'You give food. I help.'

There was another crash and the whole boat shuddered.

'Out,' said Shay, gesturing with the sword. 'All of us. Now. Cass, go to the stern and take the steering paddle. I'll watch him. We need to get this thing under control.'

Keeping her eyes fixed on the intruder, Castrel backed outside.

The intruder started to follow her but Shay gestured with the sword.

'Not yet,' he said. 'Wait.'

Castrel caught a sideways look in the man's eye. Watchful and wary.

He is a predator, she thought. She was sure of it now.

The *Apple Leaf* was careering slantwise towards a blind bend of the river. With the steering paddle in one hand and Hope next to her on the bench, she leaned hard and felt the boat slowly straighten.

The intruder was standing in the canopy entrance, and Shay was behind him. The man was taller than she had thought. Solid shoulders and heavy legs. He was a danger to them all. He was carrying nothing and seemed to have no weapon. That wasn't right. Such a man would. Anyone would.

She wondered if Shay would stab him in the back. She would have done it then, if she could. This man was a mortal danger to them.

It would have to be a stab: there was no room to swing the

blade wide from the side, or lift it and bring it down on his neck. But was it the kind of sword you could stab with? No, it was too long. You'd need distance and balance to make the lunge. Where Shay was standing now, the sword was next to useless. Even she knew that, and that meant the intruder would definitely know it too.

The wind was throwing rain into her face, blurring her vision, but she had no hand free to wipe it away.

Shay was too close behind the intruder. The intruder was bigger and stronger than he was. Castrel knew what was going to happen.

'*Shay!*'

She screamed the warning too late.

The intruder swung his elbow hard and sudden into Shay's face, sending him stumbling backwards out of her sight. Then he lunged for Castrel, and suddenly there was a knife in his hand. She saw the vicious black jagged broken blade.

He came in low and to the side, and she knew then what he was going to do. He would hit her hard with his shoulder and seize Hope and hold the knife against Hope's throat. He would press the blade-edge hard against her skin, and he would hold her in front of him, and then he would be able to tell them what to do.

He would make Shay give up the sword.

Then he would take the boat.

And then he would kill them all.

Castrel wasn't going to let that happen.

She screamed at the intruder, harsh words in the hedge-tongue, shrieking into the rain, and she made the signs of seizure and killing at him with her hands.

The words and gestures had no real power or meaning, not even if she'd still had her gift, but people were superstitious about hedge-witches, and the hedge-witches had encouraged that for centuries. It was a protection for them, and there was some use in it: sometimes sudden fear could open ways to get inside a person's mind quickly and confuse it.

If the intruder was superstitious, perhaps her fakery would still have power though her gift did not.

She saw his sudden shock of fear. He hesitated. It had to be enough. She moved fast.

She launched herself at him, fingers clawed rigid, jabbing him deep under the ribs in the place she knew that would cause sudden agony and make muscles weak.

She didn't catch him quite true, but he staggered and swayed and she shoved him then with all her weight, sending him stumbling to the side of the boat. She pushed again and he tipped backwards over the edge into murky turbulent water.

The current carried him along beside them, a few yards off the boat and just out of reach. He thrashed and cried out, furious, pleading, desperate. He was struggling to swim, but his clothes were heavy and dragging him down. Her attack had left him weak. His arms and legs weren't working right.

Castrel sat in the stern in the pouring rain, one hand on the steering paddle. She stared into the drowning man's face. She was fierce and glad. Shay was standing next to her; thick blood was streaming from his nose in the rain. One eye was swelling, already almost shut.

'He'll drown,' he said. 'He's going to die.'

'Yes,' said Castrel. 'I know.'

'Maybe he thought we were going to kill him. He could have thought that.'

'We weren't going to kill him. He didn't believe that.'

'We could save him?' said Shay. It was a question.

She was still staring into the man's face. Fixing his eye with hers. He was the first person they had seen since they left Weald, and he had done what he did. He did not need to. But he did.

'No,' said Castrel. 'No. We will not save him.'

'You would kill him, then?' said Shay quietly. It wasn't a challenge.

'I will wait here and watch until I know that he is dead. Until I know he will not come again. So I'm sure.'

'He was a person. He might have had someone. He might have thought he was doing the only thing he could.'

'So? It wasn't the only thing he could have done. He attacked you, he attacked me. He was going to hurt Hope, Shay, and we have to keep her safe. Nothing else matters, only that. To save her I would kill and kill again, till there is nothing left in the world but blood.'

Shay looked at her.

'Yes,' he said. 'You're right.'

They stayed at the back of the *Apple Leaf* and watched the relentless clatter of rain on the surface of the river, the strong muddy surge of the floodwater current, until there was nothing else to see except that.

All day the rain continued, heavy, bleak and chill, a dreary relentless punishing of the world. At last the city thinned and faded and they left it behind. The land rose and the river narrowed and surging floodwater carried them between tight ravines, grey turbulent water swelling over boulders, mounds of loud water tumbling and churning. The *Apple Leaf* jarred and rocked and there was nothing they could do any more to slow her or steer a straight course.

Castrel picked up Hope and held her on her knee, breathing the smell of her skin and hair in the rain. The warmth of it, wonderful and real. She was heavy now, a larger person, whole and alive.

'You're safe, my darling,' she said quietly. 'The bad man is gone. I'm sorry it isn't better for you than this, but we will find a way. We will do whatever must be done. I promise.'

There was a thud and the boat lurched and shuddered and spun and tipped, up and sideways, spilling Castrel backwards into the water.

'*Hope! Hope!*'

Her shout was a desperate scream, cut off by water in her throat.

Hope had fallen out of the boat with her. At first she was holding Hope's arm but the force of the icy current was too strong for her. It dragged the child from her grip. Then something struck Castrel in the back and the crash of pain against her spine burst brilliant and blinding inside her head and drove the air from her lungs. She sank under the water.

She kicked and clawed to the surface, retching and choking.

Shay was leaning over the side of the boat, reaching for her.

'Take my hand!' he was yelling.

But Castrel would not.

'No! Not me!' she screamed at him. 'Save Hope! Find Hope! I've lost her! You have to find her!'

She fought against rising panic, struggling to keep her face out of the water, looking around desperately.

Where was Hope? She couldn't see her. The child was gone under the river.

The last thing Castrel saw before she went under again was Shay jumping over the side into the water and the *Apple Leaf* lurching and swinging away out of reach.

25

The shock of immersion was an iron band tight around Shay's chest. His face went under the water and a vice of cold gripped his skull. He could see nothing but green-black hurtling darkness. He sank, dragged deeper by the weight of his boots. He kicked his legs but they were sluggish and full of weight, like in a dream.

There was no end to the depth of the river, no bottom, no end of sinking, and the current was a strong force. Hard water dragged him. He felt his hair rise and his shirt billow. He kicked again, harder, and came up coughing and spitting against a slippery hardness of rock, the weight of the surging water pressed against his chest, its force bearing down on his shoulders and hurling into his face, the noise of it filling his mouth and nose and thundering in his ears.

He got mouth and nose almost clear, dragged air and water into his lungs, and went under again. Fought his way back to the surface, floundering, chest heaving, gasping, retching, exhausted. Shuddering with the bitter, impossible cold.

'*Hope!*' he screamed. '*Hope!*'

He choked on the words, desperately searching the small visible area between the rocks in the surging water. He saw nothing. He scrabbled and thrashed to stay afloat.

He couldn't find his child.

He was close to a steep slope of riverbank at the surging edge of the water, a gap between rocks filled with gravel and mud. He lunged for it, kicking and scrabbling with clawed fingers and bruised knees. Somehow he gained purchase there and hauled himself out. From the bank he could see the *Apple Leaf* was spinning slowly, obscured by spray and high water near the further shore. The shape of her was wrong. Somehow she was lifted and canted over on her side. He could see more of the inside of the boat than he should have.

Where was Castrel?

Where was Hope?

The river roared and broke over rocks and flowed on into the blurred distance.

'*Castrel!*' he yelled. '*Hope!*'

Please. Please. Oh, please.

Then he glimpsed the child, a small bundle floating face down in the water, a small body turning in the current downstream of where he was.

He slid back into the river and tried to swim but he was weak, there was no strength in his arms or legs. Icy cold went all the way to the heart of him, draining his body feeble, and the river hauled him under again, down deep, eyes shut and lungs bursting. He smashed against rock. His lungs collapsed and he felt the air leaving them, driving back up his throat and out into the water in a great burst of hopelessness. A voiceless gasp of pain.

Somehow he surfaced, all direction lost. He did not know where he was, where the bank was, where the place was where he had last seen Hope. He lashed out wildly, hitting fist and elbow against water and stone. Knowing she was gone.

He slipped away from the rock and the current bore him downstream, dizzy and swallowing bitter water. He tried to clear his head, but he wasn't really thinking any more.

Then suddenly she was near him, his child, a dark shape wedged between boulders, and he grabbed her with one numb strengthless hand. His head sank beneath the surface and he panicked and floundered and lost her. Then found her again.

Pushing her ahead of him as he swam, he worked his way along the face of the rocks, scraping skin from his fingers, and pushed out into the stream, kicking weakly for the shore where the bank was lower.

He seemed to be in the river with Hope for many hours. He struggled to swim, hauling himself one-handed against the water, holding the weight of the child, river-blinded, all distance reduced to inches, getting nowhere at all. And then, at last, exhausted, stupefied, his feet touched a slope of mud and he was dragging himself and Hope out of the river and onto a stony piece of shore. He sank to his knees, coughing, spilling water and other stuff from his mouth.

He turned the child's small body on her back. Her eyes were closed and her face was still. Hair was slicked across her face.

He could find no life there. None at all.

Shay's whole body was bruised and broken and filled with the dark cold weight of the river. He sank to his knees on the shore, lungs full of water, and there was no strength left in him. There was a sharp aching deep in his chest. The last thing he knew was Castrel leaning over him, her wet hair falling forward, blood on her face, her hand cold on his shoulder. He looked up into her face and she was there. Her eyes. The love and the grief in them. Her mouth was open and moving as if she was speaking, but he could not hear. The river was the only noise in his ears.

And then the shore and the river and Castrel all slid sideways into a deep and quiet distance and he was gone.

When awareness returned – it might have been moments or hours, he never knew – Castrel was sitting on the sloping gravel shore holding Hope in her arms. They seemed far off in the distance, but it was only some yards.

His daughter was dead.

Was she?

He hauled himself to his feet and walked across to them.

'Castrel?' he said. 'How is she?'

His legs were trembling, his whole body shaking. It was a struggle to stay standing, but he must and he would.

'She's alive,' she said. 'At least ... she is not dead.'

He kneeled heavily beside them. Hope was limp and unresponsive. There was a bruise on her face, and an angry swollen lump on her temple. A matted and darkly bloody place was crushed into the side of her skull. Her breathing was shallow. A weak fluttering pulse.

'This is bad,' he said. 'Isn't it?'

'Yes.'

'Really bad.'

There was a long graze down the side of Castrel's face, still oozing blood. He reached out to move a strand of hair that was stuck there.

'And you?' he said. 'What about you?'

'I'm fine.'

Cass. Oh, Cass. Look at our poor lovely child. She's hurt and she's dying.

Shay pulled himself to his feet. The effort made him giddy. He was so weak. Exhausted and hurt.

'Where are you going?' said Castrel.

'The boat.'

The weight of the river was holding the *Apple Leaf* wedged against rocks a few yards off the bank. She was tipped at a steep angle, the mast gone and the canopy collapsed.

'You can't,' said Castrel. 'It's not safe. I think she's going to break up.'

'There are things we need.'

He didn't want to go back into the river again. He feared it. It was nothing but dark cold death. But he must. He slid into the water and let the current carry him till he could catch the prow and pull himself onto the boat. Three times he did it, until he had saved what there was to save and the last of his strength was gone.

Soaked to the skin, bruised, aching, exhausted and freezing cold, he built a small fire kindled with handfuls of coarse grass pulled from the bank. The fire spat and smoked and burned weakly. It didn't stop him shivering. He was trembling deep inside.

'Let me hold Hope a while,' he said.

The child's face was calm and simple, as if she was sleeping. He could feel her breathing, the rise and fall of her ribs, shallow, uneven and too fast. He stroked her hair and brushed his fingers gently against her injured skull. He only wanted her to move. Just open her eyes and come back. The whole of the side of her head was viciously swollen and darkly bruised.

'Is there nothing you can do?' he said to Castrel.

'You think I haven't tried?'

'I know you have. I'm sorry.'

Later Shay made an inventory of all they had. All that he had rescued from the wreck of the *Apple Leaf*. Two backpacks, the one for things and the one for Hope; two water-skins; fire-steel, knife and axe; the dented brass bowl; three soaked blankets and a length of wet canopy; the dead wizard's sword. And that was all. That, and the sodden clothes on their backs and the unconscious weight of their broken child.

They would stay there that night and wait out the dark with the fire, and in the morning they would walk.

'Where should we go?' he said.

'South,' said Castrel. 'Follow the river till we find a road.'

The country rose around them into stony hills – gravel slopes marked with outcrops of raw naked rock. Since they had left the ancient ruined city behind them they had seen nothing but scant coarse grass, dead trees, stone, gravel and earth, but he couldn't shake the feeling of being overlooked from high places. He was oppressed by the prickling sense that danger was always close; that there were predators following, invisible hunters for whom Hope and Castrel and he were the visible, obvious, undefended prey. Perhaps the hunters were imagined. He saw nothing and did not know.

Hope remained unconscious and unresponsive.

'I can't feed her,' said Castrel. She was holding a damp cloth at the child's mouth, squeezing a trickle of water between her parted lips. 'She's not being nourished. I can't help her at all. There's nothing that keeps her alive. I don't know why she isn't dead.'

Shay filled the brass bowl with water and set it in the fire to warm, like he used to do in Sard Keeping in the first days after Hope was born. When it was ready they washed together the living body of their child. The water made the dragon scales on her back and shoulders shine with the shimmering brilliance of jewels.

He woke in the thick blackness of the night. His heart was a clenched fist in his ribs and the darkness around him a weight that pressed him down. Everything he had done was weak and stupid and wrong. Everything he had done, it would have been much better if he had not, and the only thing the future held was a dark horror.

Castrel was sleeping beside him, her warmth against his under the blanket, but she might as well have been a thousand miles away. She had gone far off and deep down into her own darkness, mining the black seams and silent ores of her grief for their dying daughter who did not die.

Every day Castrel carried her, an inert and floppy weight. She was too large for carrying really, but there was no choice. Every night they took turns to hold her and watch over her. They expected her to die.

They didn't talk much. All words were ashes in their mouths. All purposes trivial. They grieved for her, each silently and alone. Grieved for what she had been and all that they had lost. They had failed Hope. They had not protected her as they had promised her they would, and she would die. All that was left to them was to keep on walking, because to do otherwise would have meant making a choice and they could not make any more choices. All their choices were bad.

On, always on, into unworsenable days.

But Hope did not die.

One evening they stopped at the top of a hill and looked down as the last sour light of day faded from a city spread out below.

The road before them wound on down to the city's edge through a tumble of shacks and ravines and bridges made tiny by distance. There was an open gate in a high ruined wall, and beyond the wall the city sprawled on across further hills and away into the distance.

The city was huge.

From somewhere a single thin thread of smoke was drifting upwards, and far off a single bell was tolling, quiet and thin. Tenuous echoes chased the sound, skittered and faded. Then the bell suddenly ceased, leaving holes in the silence that slowly healed and closed.

'There are people there,' said Castrel.

'Someone, at least. We should be careful.'

'Yes, but we have to look.'

'Tomorrow,' he said. 'It'll be night soon. We'll camp here and go in the morning.'

Shay woke in black darkness, coughing. The old trouble in his chest was beginning to come back: he could feel it as a kind of distant ache, though he paid it little attention. It was a small thing compared to all the rest. He didn't know how many hours it was till dawn, but he knew he wouldn't sleep again. He pushed back the blanket and hauled himself stiffly to his feet. Felt for his boots and pulled them on. Found his pack and the dead wizard's sword that was always near to hand.

He left Castrel and Hope asleep and walked quietly away, out into the enfolding dark, down the hill towards the city, alone. If there was food there, he would find it and bring it back, and if there were people, he would see what kind of people there were.

26

The heart of the dragon builds and shapes the child, working fierce and fast. All the slow growing she would have done over many years must be done in weeks. They are changing her, body and mind. Building muscle and bone, flesh, sinew, nerve and vein. Laying foundations of strength and power. Weaving her so she will sing inside with light and fire. They are making her articulate, magical and strange. It is an endragoning. They are building scale and wing. They are consumed by their work. They have done this before. They know how. But never have they worked so fast.

The child has been badly broken. The mother and father are failing too.
    They are trivial. Let them die.
    We need them for now. This body is too hurt to be alone.
    We cannot keep them alive. They will die.
    Then we must make the child strong quickly or she will also die.
    We must make her as we choose. She is too new and weak to shape herself.
    Haste, then! Haste! Years into days! We must be dragon again.

Hope listens to the voices. She understands now, and walks towards them. She is walking across clear water and grass and sky. She is a child, smiling. Fine and sure. She is large here, strong and wise. She has already learned much. Already she remembers the memories of many dragons. This is her place.

Hello, she says. I am Hope.

We know. We are Vespertine.

What are you doing? says Hope.

We are the heart of the dragon in you, and you are dragon now. We speak to you and you are our voice. Our shape. Our form in the world. You will be magnificent, rough and beautiful.

Not like this, says Hope. I do not want this. I do not want scale and wing.

Listen. She is strong.

She has the heart of the dragon in her. Of course she is strong.

We are making you like Vespertine, they say to Hope. *A hard dragon, a late dragon, a dragon late in time, born into hardness and battle when much has already been lost.*

We are the flying mountain.

We are the furnace and the fire that burns.

We are the dragon. We are Vespertine.

Dragon is dragon. We do as we do.

You were the dragon, says Hope, but I am the dragon now. I will grow as I choose.

You are young. Do you yet know who you are?

I will know. I will be chooser, learner and change.

And then Hope speaks with her dragon voice.

I AM HOPE AND I AM THE DRAGON NOW AND I WILL DECIDE.

Hope is a good name. Keep it.

27

Castrel woke and found Shay gone, and his pack and sword and axe gone too, but she wasn't troubled by it. He often went in the first grey of dawn to forage, or to scout the way ahead. He would be back soon.

Their camp was near a stream. She undressed Hope and washed her as best she could, though the water was bitterly cold. She took her child's hands in hers one by one and touched her small fingers. Washed her feet. Wiped her arms and legs and body with the dampened corner of a cloth, rubbed her gently dry, and ran her fingers through the fine long tangle of hair. Hope gave no sign and did not stir. Last of all she washed her face, carefully putting the cloth to her slightly open lips and wiping the delicate translucence of the lids of her eyes. Those beautiful eyes that were closed.

She bathed her daughter at the beginning of every day. It was a sacrament at morning time. A grave and speechless prayer.

Hours passed and grey cloud hung lower in the sky and cold wind carried fine drifts of rain and Shay did not return. Castrel told herself not to worry. Shay knew what he was doing. He would be all right.

She sat on a stone to wait and cradled Hope in her arms. Her beautiful daughter, destroyed. Her skull broken like an egg, her brain damaged beyond repair, she was a warm, soft sack of bones with lungs that still breathed. Her eyes would never open again.

Castrel's grieving was a slow hourly death inside, and still Shay did not return.

These were dark hours. Some of the darkest there had been.

At midday she started to look for Shay. She circled the camp in widening circles and scanned the country in all directions from the top of the hill, not wanting to go too far, not wanting to miss him if he returned. The huge city sprawled across hills to the south, disappearing into misting rain and distance. There was no sign of life there. None at all.

What happened, Shay? What did you do?

She imagined him lost somewhere, wandering, not knowing how to get back. She imagined him fallen. Hurt. Stuck. He might be lying injured close by now, and she didn't know. If she found him, she could help him. But if she did not ... She circled as widely as she dared, calling his name louder than felt safe.

Shay did not come, and Castrel didn't know what to do. She could not stay here on this hillside for ever, but if she walked away from the camp and Shay returned and she was not there, what would he do then? That way, they might lose each other for ever. That could happen, in this empty world.

She couldn't walk on alone, and find food for herself, and carry Hope on her back, and care for her. She just could not do all that.

She tried to think more clearly but she could not. She decided to wait the next night through, and if Shay had not come by then she would make plans in the morning.

28

Shay walked alone down towards the great sprawling city spread across many hills. He went because he would find something there. He went because things could not go on as they were and he had to make a change. He didn't know what he was hoping for, he didn't think about that, he didn't think about anything much at all. This was not about thought any more. He did it because something must be done, and he must do it, and this was something. This was the only thing.

The cloud settled low and resolved to soft insistent rain, slicking his face, trickling down his neck and soaking his shirt across his shoulders. There was no smoke thread rising among the rooftops now. No sign of life at all.

The city was larger than any he had ever seen before. He followed streets at random. Bladed iron buttresses and verdigrised cupolas. Narrow lanes and alleyways, wide squares, and halls with lichened, statued gardens. The aftermath of foundries, and the stump-roots of aborted towers where ferns had taken grip on the jag-toothed tops. Closed doorways, weathered timbers, skewed lintels.

Empty windows reflected his head and the dull sky and towers behind him. He pressed his face against the panes and looked in at abandoned rooms, bare boards, faded furnishings. There were doors that were closed, and instinct warned him against entering there. There were gates of bronze and iron he could not pass.

He disturbed a carved stone head buried among dead ivy. The head was white like marble, large and weighty as a bull, weather-pitted and bird-excrement-splashed and seamed with dark veins. It had pointed ears like a dog but a man's flattened face, and it returned his gaze with a patient, wanting stare. The rain was falling heavier now. It dripped from the stone head, but the gusher-spout in its mouth was stopped up with a mess of wet dead leaves.

He tried a door. It was locked. He pushed at it, but it didn't move. It felt heavy and solidly bolted. He broke it down. Inside, the flagstone floor lay under a gritty covering of dust thick enough to leave footmarks in. He made a finger-trail along the windowsill that came up grey and stained his hand. There were no marks in the dust except the ones he was leaving now.

A pitcher on a table still held water. He was thirsty and poured copiously into a chipped earthen wash bowl and bent to scoop and drink. The water was icy and tasted of ashes. He sluiced his face and head, cupping and splashing, shuddering at the shock of the cold. The water he spilled made a puddle at his feet, blackening the dust. His boots trod it to sparse mud-streaks. He went back outside.

There was nothing in this city, and he had gone further than he meant. Castrel would be awake by now. She would have been awake for hours. Castrel and Hope on the hillside alone in the rain, wondering where he had gone.

He had made a terrible mistake.

I'm sorry, Cass. So very sorry. I shouldn't have done this. I shouldn't have left you alone. I wish you were here with me now.

He had to go back.

He must hurry. All he wanted to do was go home.

But he had come too far, and he didn't know the way back to

the gate and the road. There were many gates and many roads. He was lost.

He jogged from street to street with nothing to steer by, hoping he was moving north, back to Castrel and Hope, but there was no way to know. Perhaps he was only circling. There were many hills in the city, and he seemed to be always climbing.

And there were small sounds now: footfalls; perhaps voices. The quiet slithering noise of something heavy being dragged. He became more and more certain that something was following him.

He caught a movement somewhere behind him in the corner of his eye. Heard the strike of hooves on paving somewhere far away, echoing off high walls. Were there riders here, then? Riders, cowled and searching and larger than human, harvesters of the coming desolation, saddled high on their monstrous six-legged beasts?

He had been stupid. He could not believe how stupid he had been. And now he would die.

I'm so sorry, Cass.

He crossed a bridge over a black, churning sluice way. The alley he was following took him through a canopied conduit-house where running water was channelled into mechanisms – cisterns and chutes and spilling pipes turning heavy, rumbling gears. The water levels were lower than they should be. Much of the engineering was seized up, rusted and broken, but some still ground away slowly at inscrutable functions.

He was in a place now where the very fabric of the city was ruinous and decayed. Wood had rotted soft and black here. Stone crumbled to grit and dust. Iron corroded. He found a well inside a rough shed, but the rope had rotted away. The only growing things that flourished anywhere were black creeping vines like overground roots, and pale fungal growths and threads that spread across everything.

He came to high railing-gates, and beyond them a shadowy woodland growing within walls. It appeared to go back much further than made sense. He peered in at dense, tangled thickets of immeasurably ancient trees, oak, beech and ash – not tall, few overtopped the wall – and a dense understorey of hazel and thorn. He heard noises deep within: the kee-wick cries of owls; the long shriek of some small animal, dying in the hunter's bite. A cat slipped out past his legs and away, the first living thing he had seen since he could not remember when.

The gate into the woodland was chained shut, but he would not have entered if he could. He sensed larger creatures in there, snouting and padding between the trees. Ranging, slavering dogs. Boar and wolf.

Shay walked on, searching. Hoping to find some place he would recognise. Somewhere he had been before.

Something is following me. I am sure of it now. The hunted always knows the feel of the predator's gaze.

Heart beating hard, mouth dry, close to panic, he jogged faster. A dry cough troubled him.

He found himself in a street that had no exit. It ended in a wide apron of steps that climbed to a large building with an open door. The towered and pinnacled roof that rose above it seemed familiar: he was sure he had seen the same building before, but from a different angle.

He dared not turn back to face the hunter he knew was behind him somewhere, so he climbed the steps and went inside.

*

He was in a great hall. Columns rose in ranks and arcades like the trees of a forest, climbing to a vaulted ceiling vague in the high shadows. He saw that all the angles were slightly out of true. The pillars and columns were splayed, leaning outwards as if under the weight of many towers above, and the floor was bowed and sunk in many places: an acreage of white and brown tiles in complex geometries, a gently undulating chequered dim forest floor, its edge lost beyond the reach of the last fading light.

Shay's footfalls echoed in the silence as he went deeper in. Trickles of rain found their way down from the floors above and dripped, puddling underfoot. He saw staircases leading down but he did not go. He knew that down there somewhere there were endless subterranean tunnels and cavernous rooms: catacombs; ancient dungeons and oubliettes.

There was something in this dim forest-hall with him. It was a cold hunting beast. He couldn't see it clearly, but he could hear it. He could smell it. He could feel the chill of its breath on the back of his neck.

It tracked him from the shadows. It was large and strong.

Fear tightened its grip in belly and throat.

Why did I come here? What have I done?

It crossed his mind that he should stand and fight. He could set his back against a pillar and draw the dead wizard's sword.

But he knew that if he tried that, he would die.

Ahead of him, Shay saw a glimmer of daylight through a distant archway, and made for it. When he was almost there, he looked back.

The pursuer was almost upon him.

It was pacing after him with a heavy quietness. He saw a dark hunch of rags, a heavy swing of muzzle and bunched shoulder. It fixed him with wide pale eyes. Shay felt the force of its gaze pulling him. Drawing at him. All his strength and purpose being drained away. The stench was overwhelming.

It was real. It was there.

It was ready to charge and spring.

Shay ran.

Bursting out into the sudden glare of daylight he raced blindly on, directionless. Whenever he looked back, the terrible, pale-eyed shambling pursuer was still there, neither closer nor further behind. It dogged him, driving him always onward towards the end. He could feel its hunger, its steady breathing, its dark intent. It was on his trail. Coming for him. It would wait for him to tire; it could not be shaken off and it would never stop.

He came suddenly to a broken parapet at the brink of a high precipice and pulled up short. There was a sheer ravine that cut across the city, running for many miles in either direction, and he had come to the brink of it.

He looked down over the edge and saw a wall plunging away downwards from his feet. It was vertiginously high. Ledges and balconies and roofs and oriel towers jutted out far below, dizzyingly small. Bastions and drum towers and collapsing wooden bartizans.

From the foot of the wall, way below him, the city began again. It spread away to the horizon. It was another city, a city within the city, much larger than the first.

A black river wound through it. He saw bridges and the miniaturised wharfs of a faraway dock, and beyond that the city-within-the-city rose and fell with the landscape, scale-less, measureless, pale and mist-horizoned.

It was raining again. Fine drifting rain.

He coughed and spat a small splatter of stuff on the pavement. It was finely marbled with blood.

*

Shay looked behind him. His pursuer was crouching twenty yards off, smoking like a mirage, observing him with milk-pale patient eyes. The reek of it was strong, sharp and sour. The smell of carrion and rot.

It began to move towards him. He could hear the steady drag and scrape of its coming. The clack and tap of heavy nails or claws. The feel of it closing in on him filled his mind, pushing thought to the margins, leaving room for nothing but the desperate need to escape and survive.

There was a place where a huge tree crawled up from below and spilled over the edge of the wall. He would climb down it. There was no other way.

Fear rose in his throat and knotted his belly. Confusing. Distracting.

Focus!

Shay let himself down from the broken parapet and clambered out into the branches of the immense tree.

The tree was an oak, but it had climbed the wall like a tremendous unstoppable vine to the height of ten trees – twenty – gripping the rough surface like ivy with spreads of limb and grim adhering roots, driving arm-thick branches burrowing into the cracks between stones. Boulder-sized and boulder-hard cankers fruited from the boughs. Whorled intricate patterns in the bark.

Looking down Shay could see nothing but a darkening well of branches and leaves and he was glad of that. The streets of the city within the city were far away below.

The fine cool rain shivered ragged leaves, plastered his hair across his forehead and filled the air with tree smells. He kneeled and gripped a branch with his hand and reached a leg down, searching with his foot for somewhere to stand. It was too far and he had to let himself drop, unbalanced for a moment, and catch himself again. Heart racing. Hands slick with sweat.

The branch that he was on sloped downwards. He crouched and lay along it, hugged it and let himself slide till he was caught in a crook and had to edge round past that and down. He reached the place where the tree touched the wall and fanned out, burrowing into it and spreading, digging in with fibrous root-growth. It was as if the vast tree sucked sustenance from the hewn stone itself.

He could climb better now. It was like descending the rigging of a great stone sail. Hand under hand, foot following foot, he made steady progress.

Never look over your shoulder. Never look below.

The pursuer was following him down the tree. He could hear it somewhere above him, disturbing the leaves and branches as it came. It wasn't fast but it would never give up, he knew that, as he knew that his own strength would fail.

He felt again the sickening touch of fear and despair.

Rain dripped into his eyes and trickled down the wall. Damp lichens, patterned like moth-wings, crumbled under his touch. Crooks in the boughs cupped cushions of wet, earth-scented moss. Small cranny-plants had found footholds: somehow they grew up there, rain-soaked to a dark waxy green.

Keeping close to the wall he worked steadily, using elbows and knees, not trusting the strength of his grip. There were places where the tree had grown around ledges and sills in the wall as if it had flowed into them. The roots and branches had pulled rusting gutters from their fixings and snapped them off. There were lead cisterns and moss-furred pipes with trickling water.

Shay was aware all the time that he was not climbing down a cliff but the outside of a huge mass of buildings, unthinkably vast. Sometimes there were windows, but he could not get in – always they were out of reach, or barred.

And overhead, slow shifting continents of rain cloud. Deep

miles of grey-dark vapour. The sky a lowering weight he could feel.

His arms ached and his legs were beginning to tremble. The ground below seemed no closer. Climbing was all there was, it was an end in itself, an everness, the only thing in his world. The climbing stretched from everlasting to everlasting, without beginning or end, without any progress except towards the coming exhaustion and fall. The ache in his chest was a sharp pain now. It made breathing hurt. He needed to rest. But always the heavy climber above him pursued him down.

Shay reached the point where he could do no more. All strength was gone, and below him there was nothing he could reach. Nowhere left to go.

He hung over yawning space a moment, gripping with aching hands the last branch of all and then, despairing, lost his hold and let himself drop away.

He slipped and fell, sliding and tumbling, faster and faster, out of control, crashing and breaking through the branches of the huge climbing oak and hurtling out into a long open fall through air to the streets below.

Long he fell, long enough to feel suspended, to feel he was not falling but hanging motionless in the air, waiting for the end.

The end that came.

His legs were not ready. Nothing was ready, nothing was prepared for that collision, not when it came, as it must come. All that hurt, that break, that split across blackness, that pain that was strangely like a flash of light, a bursting shatter of light in the darkness of his mind. All that hurt.

*

He was lying on his back in a white roar of pain. The wall loomed high above him and the pursuer was coming down it, working its limbs, crawling impossibly, head first down the sheer stone face, descending on him. There was nothing left to do. All that remained now was terror. Terror, hurt and blood.

On. Somehow on. He tried to roll over and crawl away. He was lying on lumps of stuff. There was a warm pooling wetness, a mess of that.

On. Somehow on. He was trying to crawl away through fear and pain and racking, heaving coughs, but his legs would not do it. His legs would do nothing. He tried to crawl away, but in the end there was nothing to be done, there was only hurt and sorrow getting further and further away, and then the collapse towards dark extinction.

Castrel. Hope. I'm so sorry.

The pursuer hunched close, leaning in towards him.

Its pale blank murky eyes.

And then its head split open in a gash of dark watery blood and it was dead.

Shay struggled to focus through the pain. Everything was vague and blurred and lurched sickeningly, sliding away sideways and down. His leg was sharp agony and would not move. He tried to lift himself, but there was no strength in him. The whole world hurt.

A tall slender figure was standing over him, wiping his blade. He had long fine pale hair and his skin was gold and beautiful. He wore beautiful clothes, fine silken fabrics that shimmered with shifting colour even in the rain. Golden yellow eyes, inhuman eyes bright with the illumination of their own immortality, looked down on him and they were smiling.

He was their friend. Their golden friend.

And behind him, watching patiently, were two tall and beautiful horses.

29

Although Castrel was watching, she didn't see them come. Forms solidified from nowhere on the empty road at dusk, as if a gate had opened almost in front of her that she hadn't known was there, and they walked through. Two tall and beautiful chestnut horses carrying their burdens lightly, and a tall slender figure leading them. Their friend. Their golden friend.

The first horse carried bags and satchels; the second, a man, slouched and awkward, obviously hurt. It took Castrel a moment to realise it was Shay. *Shay.* Her heart lurched with a dizzying rush of joy and relief. She hadn't thought she would feel such happiness ever again.

She helped their golden friend get him down from the saddle.

'He is a little dazed,' he said. 'And he has injured his leg. Nothing worse than that. He was fortunate.'

His voice was subtle and weightless, full of warmth and strangeness, the music of alien sunlit waters. She remembered that.

They settled Shay on the ground with his back against a wall. He opened his eyes and looked at her, struggling to focus, as if waking from heavy sleep.

'Castrel?' he said hoarsely. 'Cass?' And then: 'How is Hope? Is she all right?'

'The same. Nothing's changed. Let me look at your leg.'

She touched his ankle and he groaned.

'You can repair the injury,' said their golden friend. 'He will recover and be fine.'

'I can't heal this,' she said. 'Something happened. I've lost the gift, I can't heal anything any more, it's beyond me now.'

The golden friend frowned. His eyes were filled with compassion and regret.

'I see,' he said. 'I didn't know.'

Castrel brought Shay a cup of water. He took it and drank. His face was grazed and bruised, but his eyes were beginning to focus better now. She ran her hands more thoroughly, gently, along his leg. The bone didn't seem to be broken. He would be all right in time.

'I'm sorry, Cass,' he said hoarsely.

'Why did you go into the city by yourself, Shay? I was worried.'

He shook his head as if to clear it, and winced because the movement hurt.

'I'm not sure. I shouldn't have. It was stupid. I wasn't thinking straight. I guess I wanted to do something good. It didn't work out like that though. I'm sorry.'

She could hear the strain and hurting in his voice. She reached out and put her hand on his arm.

'You don't have to prove anything to me,' she said. 'Not ever. Nothing at all.'

'Not to you, maybe, but to myself. I've messed everything up. Always. Ever since the beginning.'

'No,' she said. 'No. You haven't. I need you with me, Shay. We can do this together, but I can't do it on my own.'

'I know. I'm sorry. I won't do anything like that again.'

*

Castrel lit a small fire for warmth and Shay fell into a heavy sleep, his breathing irregular and loud. Their golden friend laid out his fine fabrics on the ground and made himself a place to rest.

'I may stay with you for this night?' he said. 'I can travel in the dark, but my horses do not like it.'

'Of course,' she said. 'I'm sorry we have nothing to offer you.'

'Nor I you, though if I had food I would share gladly.'

'Tomorrow we'll find food.'

'Perhaps, but not here. Here there is none to find. Here is not safe, and you should move on. But you know that already.'

'Yes.'

'Yet Shay cannot walk.'

'He'll manage.'

'Tomorrow? Will he be strong enough so soon?'

'He must. There is no other way. I'll splint his leg and make him a crutch. He can lean on me.'

'And Hope? She is hurt. What happened?'

'We had a boat on the river. There was a storm and a flood and we were attacked, and the boat was wrecked. Hope hit her head on a rock.'

'Is she all right?'

'I don't think so.' Castrel felt all the grief and hopelessness rising inside her again. 'If you must know, I don't understand why she hasn't already died.'

'She has the heart of the dragon in her, and that makes her stronger than you could know.'

'Perhaps.'

'So,' he said. 'Just so that I understand. Tomorrow you will carry Hope, and Shay will lean on you, and you will travel again, and you will keep the three of you safe, and you will find food. And you will do all this by yourself?'

'I will do it, yes!' Castrel could not keep the anger from her voice.

Their golden friend was silent. She could not see his face clearly in the flickering shadows of the fire.

'I could travel with you a while,' he said at last. 'If you would allow it. Shay could ride, and Hope could ride with him. You could ride too if you wish. You could all recover your strength a little.'

Castrel's heart lifted a little.

'Really? You would do that for us?'

'Of course. There's a hard road ahead, but I know this country a little.'

'Thank you,' she said. 'You are a good friend. You're the only friend we have.'

He smiled and his golden eyes were warm and kind in the firelight.

'This is our third fortuitous meeting,' he said. 'It begins to seem that our paths are intertwined.'

'Are you saying you believe in destiny?'

He laughed.

'I've lived too long and seen too much to think that. Alas, there is no providence in our lives, only random event and happenstance.'

'Are you really three thousand years old?'

'Three thousand years is how long I have been in this world, though I would not choose the word *old*. Ageing is a human concept.' He paused. 'But I am coming to love your little family. You are courageous and good.'

'We try to keep going and look after Hope, that's all.' She thought of the intruder on the *Apple Leaf*. How they watched him drown. 'I'm not sure we are good people though. We've had to do some bad things to survive.'

The golden friend waved the thought away.

'Actually, you have taken me aback,' he said. 'Detachment is something I've come to prize in myself. I am only here to observe and learn, but I've been thinking of you often since I saw you last. You have affected me. To be honest I didn't expect to see you again, but I'm glad we've met once more, and I'll try to help you if I can.'

'Thank you,' she said. 'That means a lot.'

He made a brief neat courteous bow where he sat, hands across his chest. It struck her as a glimpse of a different time and place, a long-lost, kinder country where she had never lived, but wished she had.

'Have you seen many others?' she said. 'Other people like us, I mean. While you were travelling.'

'A few. None still looking for a future. None like you.'

'Surely we can't be the only ones left? Sometimes it feels like that.'

'Perhaps not the only ones, but there are not many and I fear none of you has much time now, not even in the terms of your brief existences.' He looked suddenly ashamed. 'I apologise. I am truly sorry. That was harsh. I forgot myself. Please forgive me.'

In the night Castrel lay awake on the cold hard ground, eyes wide in the dark, a few dim stars scattered across the aching sky. For the first time in so long she couldn't remember, the day had ended better than it began. Shay was back and they had a friend. At least for a day or so they would not be on their own. But Hope was so badly hurt. Castrel was afraid she was lost to them for ever. The only reason she was not dead was the dragon inside her. Was a body for the dragon really all that she would now be?

Castrel was struck dumb by sudden overwhelming tides of grief. Grief for Hope, grief for Shay, grief for herself, grief for the loss of all humanity and everything good in the world. Grief for sunshine and clean water and green spring grass. How much longer must this go on for? She couldn't bear it patiently any more. She could no longer hold grief in. But she must. Always she must.

Why our own beautiful child? Why us? Why now and not later? Why could this not have come some other time? What did we do, that our time must be the worst of all and we must see the end?

She couldn't protect Hope from what was coming. She did not know how. To have a child was to make a promise, and she had made a promise she could not keep.

Bitter silent tears streamed down her face in the night.

'Castrel?'

Shay was awake too, his voice close to her, speaking so quietly she could hardly hear.

'What?'

'She's only alive because of you, and so am I. You're extra-ordinary and precious and wonderful and all in all to me. My trusted friend. I love you, and I have to say that. So that you know. Only so that you know.'

She didn't say anything, but she reached for Shay's hand and held it in the dark.

The next day Shay rode high on a beautiful chestnut horse, hold-ing Hope in his arms. The horse needed no leading but went on steadily ahead down the road, and Castrel followed, walking with their golden friend. His fine pale hair lifted on the breeze, glossy and fresh and faintly perfumed. He walked without visible effort, long slender legs elegantly covering the ground. The road they followed skirted the edge of the empty city spread across distant hills.

'What city is that?' said Shay.

'You have strayed out of human country into hidden lands again,' said their golden friend. 'That is the Hidden City of Barathule. You may remember I told you I was going there. Barathule was the city of cities once, long ago. A wizards' great city. In fact it was many cities existing simultaneously in many times and many worlds. What you see now is merely the desolate wreck of it, stranded like a broken ship on a beach. I had hoped to find more there than I did. Alas it is all empty now.'

'There was something there,' said Shay. 'That thing you killed that was hunting me. What was it?'

'That? It was not really a fully living thing, but something like those caged abominations at Sard Keeping. Think of it as a guard dog of a kind, left behind and alone centuries since but still doing its duty.'

Hour after hour the road skirted the city of Barathule. Sometimes they passed large country estates and landscaped gardens long fallen into ruin and disrepair. It must all have been so beautiful once. Lives had been lived here of a richness and civility that she and Shay had never known, or even seen at all. But overhead the sky was thinned, greenish and sour, the sun a watery pink stain bleeding through vague mist and shedding no warmth.

'It's all so sad,' said Castrel. 'Why did they do this? What was the point of all their appalling wars? What were they fighting for?'

Their golden friend shrugged indifferently.

'Does it matter now? It was just a war between people you didn't know and who didn't know you, fighting over things even they didn't fully understand. The details are merely echoes of the fall. Embers from a fire drifting on the wind. Their story is finished. Their book is closed. Their magic is gone. They failed. All of them failed.' He turned to face her. His golden eyes looked into hers and his face brimmed with emotion. 'What matters now is not that this world and everything in it is dying, but that your daughter is not. The question that matters is: what to do about that? I don't know the answer yet, but I will think.'

*

They made camp in the middle of the afternoon in the ruins of a walled garden on the slope of a hill, under the branches of dying cherry trees that bore no fruit.

'Enough travelling for one day,' said their golden friend. 'You need to rebuild your strength. I'll ride on a little and scout ahead. Perhaps I can find a little food.'

He rode out through the rusted gate and faded away. Castrel didn't hear the footfall of his horse on the broken road.

After he had gone Shay rebound the strip of cloth round his ankle and tied a branch against his leg from foot to knee as a splint. Then he cut a longer branch for a crutch. Castrel watched him test it. Hobble and swing. He winced.

'It'll do,' he said. 'I can walk. It's fine.'

'You should ride as long as you can.'

'I won't be carried any more. I'm not useless. I'm not baggage.'

He limped about in circles so she would see that he could do it, but his face showed the pain.

'I'm going to fetch some wood for a fire,' he said.

When he had gone, Castrel sat in rough grass next to a dry overgrown fountain. There was a strange statue there, crusted with lichen. She settled Hope in her lap. The terrible bruise on Hope's face had faded to a sickly green but the side of her head was swollen out of shape. She touched the hurt gently with her fingers, moistened earth and ash and drew patterns on the child's face and neck and spoke hedge-words, but there was no life in them. The only thing with any life at all was the bright iridescence across Hope's back and neck. There was more of it, and it was hardly scales any more. A shimmering skin of colours.

The body of her daughter lived, but the child inside was ruined and gone. The dragon was taking her. Castrel closed up Hope's clothes and wrapped the blanket round her again. She was her beautiful child, and the love she felt for her was still like hunger and need, but it was made of entirely of sadness now.

I will stay with you as long as I can. I will wait with you until the end.

That was her purpose now, the only one she had. There was nothing else she could do. And then Hope opened her eyes and looked at her.

Eyes that were alive and shone with a wonderful intelligence. Eyes flecked with slate and gold and purple, brighter than ever, and shards of shining translucent green like sunlight through leaves. Castrel felt a rush of joy and love and relief go through her like a shock.

Suddenly there were words in her mind. The voice of her child speaking a few simple words. Clear like a bell in the morning, though there was no sound.

Hello Castrel Mother I am Hope.

Castrel stood up and she was trembling; she was weak with joy and she could not think and she was shouting.

'Shay! Shay! Where are you? Come here! Quickly! *Shay!* She's back! Hope is back!'

Their golden friend returned when night was falling and set a bag of provisions on the ground.

'I rode far and fast,' he said. 'Another day's walk takes us out into open country again, and the road is clear and good for a while. But after that it is bad. A darkening shadow is falling in the south, much worse than here.'

Then he saw the change in Hope and he grinned, full of infectious warmth and pleasure. He looked suddenly young, almost boyish. He hugged them both.

'How wonderful! She is awake again! Oh, this is marvellous! May I see her?'

He studied Hope closely. Ran a finger along her cheek.

'She is changing,' he said. 'Her injury is repairing itself and she is reshaping her form. This is all happening much faster than I would have expected. And differently.'

'Differently?' said Castrel.

'The dragon is strong in her, but so is the human, too. Much stronger and more resilient than is normal for such transformations, I believe. I have been reading everything I could find about endragoning in the libraries of Barathule, but this is not a dragon-forming exactly as they describe. I would have expected – I don't know how best to put it – more *dragon* by now. But see how fine and human the bones in her face still are? Her limbs seem unaffected, except they are strong and large for her age, and her scaling is becoming skin.' He paused and looked at them, his face thoughtful and serious. 'None of the authorities I've read discuss the endragoning of a human, of course. I really am sure now that it's never happened before. I can't say exactly how the changes will progress from here, or what will be the outcome for Hope in the end, but there is one thing I'm almost sure of. As certain as I can be. Now that she has come through this crisis, I think she is safe. She will not ever die, not now.'

'Oh ...' said Shay.

Castrel could see he was feeling the same as she was. Joy and grief and happiness and terrible loss. Hope was safe but they were losing her again, in a different way. Their brief future now held only a slowly widening gulf of separation and distance, and then Hope would be left eternally alone without them in this terrible, darkened, emptied, cruel and futureless different world. They didn't doubt their golden friend was right. They could already see for themselves that it was true.

'Which means we have to talk,' their golden friend was saying. 'I'm sorry, but there is no good moment for this and time is short for me. I wasn't sure before, but now that Hope is so much recovered I feel I must speak. You have to make your decision now.'

'Decision?' said Castrel. 'What decision? What do you mean?'

'I've been thinking a lot about Hope today, while I was on the road, and I have a proposition to put to you. Will you hear me out?'

'Of course,' said Castrel. 'We're listening.'

Their friend sat with them at the fire, cross-legged in the coarse brittle grass. There was faint starshine in his golden eyes, and firelight shadows made the trees behind him seem to move in the dark. Castrel was more aware than ever that he was not human at all, and not of their world but just passing through.

'This world is dying,' he said. 'It is finished. You know this. Both of you. In your hearts you know. There is no real hope for you in going further south. The jaws of the trap are closing, and soon there will be nothing on any side but strangeness and horror and death. All the things you know are ending. The world of humans is over. Their life force has been consumed and spent.'

He paused.

'And that is true of you, too.' He looked at Shay. 'It is. You are lame. Your lungs are bad.'

He turned to Castrel.

'And you,' he said, 'you can no longer heal. You have lost that. Both of you are weakening fast. You must see that you are on the brink. If I had not been there yesterday and rescued Shay in Barathule, what condition would you all be in now?'

'We go on,' said Shay. 'We always do.'

'You have courage. You are the finest of people, and I have come to love you, all of you, really and truly I have, to an extent that shocks me, because it is not my way. So it pains me now to speak sharply, but you must see that you cannot care for your child for much longer. What more can you give her now? She has the heart of the dragon in her. You will die, and soon, and she will not. She will live on in the form she is making now, perhaps for thousands of years, and after that she will still always be the heart of the dragon. She will have other forms, other lives, for ever. But think of it. What will become of her, in this ended world? This is not a place to be immortal in. All she will find here is aloneness. An immortality of coldness and ruin and dread.'

Castrel could feel Shay's anger rising. She touched his arm.

Listen. Let him speak.

'You said you had a proposition,' she said. 'What is it?'

'I am leaving this world. The last bridge will open for me, and I will go to meet it. Soon I will go, and the place where I am going is not dying. There is no death there at all. I am going home. And if you wish me to, I will take Hope with me when I go. That is what I propose.'

Castrel felt a surge of anger and protectiveness. Nobody would take their child away from them. Not ever.

No! No! I won't let you! She wanted to shout at him. *I will not let this happen. She is my child. She is my beloved girl no matter what.*

She wanted to say it, but she didn't. Not yet.

'Hope has the heart of the dragon in her,' their golden friend was saying. 'Child and dragon will grow together, and she will become ... I do not know what, but something new in the world. Something magnificent. She needs to be allowed to live in a better world than this.' He paused. 'So let me take her with me when I leave. I will take her somewhere where she can heal her injury and grow freely. Where she can become all that she can be.'

'Take Castrel too,' said Shay quietly. 'Hope is still a child. She needs her mother. Take Castrel with you when you go.'

'Take us all!' said Castrel. 'The three of us. Together. We will come.'

'Alas, I cannot do that.'

'Why not?' she said.

'I'm so sorry. It simply isn't possible. A human could not

survive the crossing. You would die, and it wouldn't be a pleasant death. You would be lost in the liminal borderlands, in a drifting agony of slowly dissipating awareness. And your presence at the crossing could also endanger Hope and myself.'

'No,' said Shay. 'Surely ...'

Their golden friend spread his hands wide in a gesture of despair.

'I'm sorry, but there is no doubt about this. On this subject, I know what I am talking about. I would not have suggested taking Hope with me before, but now that she's come through this crisis and the endragoning has progressed so far and so quickly, I believe she could survive the crossing. Dragons have crossed between worlds before, it is in their nature. They are born to it, in a way. But you simply could not. No, you cannot cross. I can take only her, it's all I can do. And I will do it, if you wish me to. Let me take Hope with me. I believe this is for the best, but of course the choice is yours.'

'Hope is our *daughter*,' said Castrel.

'I understand the price I am asking you to pay.'

'How can you understand?' said Shay. 'You're not human. You're immortal, or almost. Do you have a child?'

'No.'

'Hope is our child,' said Shay. 'She is ours, and we will love her and be with her till the end, whenever and whatever it is. No one will take her from us. Never.'

'But where will you go? What will you do? Do you not see the falling of the world?'

'We'll carry on south to Proud Somail,' said Shay. 'And from there we'll take a ship to Far Coromance.'

Oh, Shay, thought Castrel. *You say that, and it's brave, but you don't believe it any more, and nor do I.*

The golden man turned to her.

'Castrel? What do you say?'

I don't know. The thought was anguish. *I just don't know.* Doubt. Uncertainty. The impossible choice. His way, Hope would have a chance to live, if what he said was true. But a parent cannot simply give up a child. It was not possible. And though he was their friend, he was almost a stranger. He wasn't even *human*. He didn't think or feel the way they did. How could he love their human child as she needed to be loved, now more than ever?

'I don't know,' she said. 'I just don't know. I need time to think.'

'There is no time. There are still tasks for me elsewhere in this world before I leave, things that I must search for and try to bring away with me when I go, and then I have to go to the crossing. If I am not there at the appointed time, it will close, and it will be the last. Let me take Hope with me. I will take care of her while she needs it, I promise you that. Let me take her out of this ended world to a better one for her.'

Castrel knew then what she must do. It wasn't a thought; it came from somewhere much deeper than that. She looked at Shay and saw he felt the same. They didn't need to talk about it. They both knew.

'No,' she said quietly. 'We can't let her go. She is a child, a tiny helpless infant. I know you mean well, and I believe you would care for her as well as you could. But you couldn't love her, not as a small child needs. How could you? She's our child, and we love her, always, whatever she becomes. No matter what horrors come, we'll protect her and love her. We'll survive as long we need to do that. We'll keep on going. I don't know how, but we'll do it. For Hope, we'll find a way. Always. First and last. We would die for our daughter, but we couldn't give her away to someone else. We will not do that. It's impossible.'

Their golden friend looked at them both with love and sadness, in his way, but it was not a human way.

'You are good people,' he said. 'The very best. Of course, it's your decision. I understand your choice, and I will not say that you are wrong. On the contrary, I hope that I am wrong. But I must leave you now. I wish you only well.'

He saddled his beautiful horse and prepared to leave. When he was ready and mounted in the saddle, they went to make their farewells. Castrel rested her hand on his chestnut horse's neck, feeling the warmth and muscle there.

'You mean well,' said Shay. 'We know that. Are you sure you won't stay with us, at least for tonight?'

'It's best I do not. The country to the south is rapidly getting worse, and I must hurry. I have to reach the Voulge Keeping while I still can, and it's many miles east of here. But my offer stands. I will take Hope with me if you wish.'

'No,' said Castrel. 'We thank you, but no.'

'So be it, then. But if you change your mind, take the road that runs west at the great crossroads south of Barathule and walk till you reach the sea, then follow the coast. Keep going west. There is a wide bay with high black rocks at both ends. The eastern rock is like a tower that stands, and the rock at the western end is like a tower that has fallen. Wait for me there. When Capault rises in the constellation of the Great Mooring, I will be at that place and the crossing will open. You know the Great Mooring?'

'Of course,' said Castrel.

'Well, good. I will be there at that time. If you bring Hope then, I will take her.'

'Thank you,' she said. 'For all that you have done. You have been our friend.'

'Remember the place I have told you.'

'I hope you reach it safely. Think well of us. We will not see you again.'

Part Five

30

Alone again, the three of them together, Hope, Castrel and Shay, they followed their chosen road. South, always south, folded in the warmth and brightness and certainty of their endurance and love, a small and fragile point of illumination moving slowly through all the vast cold darkening of the broken world. Their wonderful child was the fire that warmed them and lit their way. She was their purpose. In all the horror and loneliness and desolation, every day they still walked on, and Hope was their reason why.

'Did we do right?' Shay asked Castrel once. 'To keep her, I mean?'

'Yes.'

'You don't think we were selfish? You don't think we should have let her go? For her own sake?'

'You can't ask a mother to give away her child to a stranger and never see her again. No one can ever ask that.'

Shay didn't doubt her choice. Their choice. They didn't speak of it again.

On they walked, always on, somehow on, onward always into the worsening unworsenable days. All as of old, only worse now, worse than before, weaker, more hurt, more exhausted, gaunter and frailer on the hungry road, into the mortal deepening of the cold and dark that was to come – there they were going. Because they must. Carrying their child Hope with them because they would not let her go. They would never be separated from her.

Shay knew that Castrel talked with Hope as they walked, in that way they had which wasn't words and he didn't fully understand, and sometimes she told him what their child was saying to her. Simple, happy things. Hope was a shining dragon with jewelled flecks in her eyes, but she was also their infant child.

Nights they slept by the side of the road without shelter. Blankets under the empty darkness and the stars, when there were stars. They built a small fire in the evenings if there was something to burn. The skies were always misty, threaded with purple and copper and green, and they cast a weak cadaverous light. Under those sad pale skies, all things were dying.

For weeks Shay went on crutches but at last he threw them away, though he still walked with a limp.

Somewhere they must have crossed out of the hidden lands again and into a country where humans had lived. There was a small house, little more than a cabin, on its own in a valley.

The door was weathered grey wood. Shay broke it open with the axe and entered a room filled with dim light. His boots echoed on bare timber boards and a thin, faded carpet. He could feel the emptiness there. Dawn sifted in through drawn curtains at the window, and the curtains were threadbare and frayed. He paused a moment to let his eyes adjust to the quiet twilight. The corpse of the woman was laid out on the bed under a single blanket folded under her chin. She had died some time ago, so that even the odour of her death had faded into the smell of abandonment and dust.

He went through into the other room, where the windows, uncurtained, were smeared and cobwebbed, the sills grey with drifts of stone-dust and grit. Whoever had left the woman there had left food with her, enough to last much longer than she had. She must have laid herself out like that. Herself, alone, perhaps on the very day her companions went. She had got onto the bed and tucked the blanket around herself neatly and stared at the ceiling and waited for the end to come.

Shay searched through the provisions. Fruits and vegetables, mouldered to the general dust. A piece of meat hung from a ceiling hook, dried now but sunken and foul beyond eating, and beneath it a dark mess on the floor where its putrefaction had dripped. In the cupboard he found sackcloth bags of grey flour and wrinkled dry beans. On the way out he thought of taking the blanket from the woman's bed. It would have been a wise thing to do, but he could not carry a corpse-cloth to the living.

Uncounted days later in some dusty late afternoon two men and a woman stepped out in front of them in the road. Hoarse grey humans, neither young nor old, sick and weak and wearing rags. They made threats and demanded food but Shay drew the dead wizard's sword and they sloped away, back into the ruins, cursing. He kept watch for several days but never saw them again. It was almost illusory, like something in a dream, and afterwards he wanted to ask Castrel if she had seen them but he dared not, in case she didn't remember at all.

Sometimes in the evenings they saw vast leathery moth-like creatures, their wings wider than the sails of the biggest ships, hovering and dipping overhead, shedding clouds of dust and ash from their ragged wings. When they swept down, low and close, Shay saw that each trailed twin tails, long fluttering pennants on the wind. The tails made them look like vast and tattered kites, or the shadowy stingrays that used to ripple and slide under the hulls of boats in the clear sunlit water off the coast of Harnestrand.

Nights were lit by the flicker of dry silent lightning and they heard the screaming of distant beasts.

The road wound on through the villages and small towns of the human dead: all the human places, ruined and emptied. Stones and dust. So it was everywhere. Shay accepted it at last. What was befalling the world had brought with it the ending of humankind. It was the same elsewhere and always as it was here and now. It was finished. They were the last. Everyone was gone. Everyone was dead. A continent of the dead. All the sparse scattered thousands of the silent dead. There would be no ships at Proud Somail to take them across the ocean, and there would be no Far Coromance. No sunlit islands in the bitter and poisoned sea under a bitter and poisoned sky.

Shay limped and coughed and spat in the road, and sometimes he left little rosy packets of blood in the dust. How much longer could they keep on walking like this? He was ill and getting worse. Where was it all going? What was really the point any more? What good was all this doing for Hope?

31

Days unfolded out of days, and each day bleaker than the last. The road crawled forward across shelterless uplands, a wearying stony track picking its way through levels of bracken and heath. They were in a brown country littered with stumps of grey rock. Dead trees. Black masses of fern, like the charred skeletons of leaves that had burned. Mires of lurid green bog that dragged at their feet and filthied their legs.

As they walked ever deeper into the horror and blankness of the ending world, Hope grew stronger, stranger and more wonderful. She was much changed now, her legs and arms longer, the structure of bones in her face clear, triangular and strong. All mark of the hideous injury to her skull was gone. There was a muscularity under her skin and shimmers of fine colouring at the base of her throat and across her shoulders and back, no longer dragonish scales but weavings of subtle glimmer and brightness, soft and warm to the touch.

Too heavy and tall to carry, no longer an infant child but a girl, she walked beside them sure and unafraid, an inextinguishable light in the darkness, watching the world with fierce jewel-shards of slate and purple and gold and green in blazing confident eyes. It was hard to remember how young she really was. Still not a year old. It began to feel odd that she didn't speak yet, at least not with words.

In her way, Hope talked with Castrel often as they walked. Sharing thoughts, inviting her mother into her mind. Although Castrel had lost all power to do this herself, it still seemed possible for Hope to reach her, perhaps because of some residual shaping in Castrel's brain that hadn't been shrivelled and torn away in cold alien fire. Hope remained mute and blank to Shay, although she smiled at him and walked with him often and held his hand as they went. Castrel's heart went out to him; she could see he felt sad and excluded by his daughter's silence.

'Don't worry,' she said to him. 'Remember she's young. It's normal for children not to start talking for a long time yet.'

'But she talks to you. I don't resent it, of course I don't, it's marvellous, what you and she have. I just wish ...'

'It's not talking, not really. There are no words as such. It's like what I used to be able to do, sharing feelings – it's just that Hope's gift is very strong, and her thoughts and feelings are simple and clear. I'm really not sure how much of what I'm thinking gets through clearly to her.'

'What kind of things does she tell you?'

'Simple things. What she likes, what she notices. Whether she's hungry or tired. She points out things that catch her attention. She's happy, Shay. She doesn't worry about the future. She likes us and she's glad we're here and she wants to be with us. She loves you very much, and when you're out of sight she wonders where you are, and when you come back she goes to you and says hello.'

Castrel tried to explain it to Shay, but she felt she wasn't doing it right. She couldn't fully communicate to him the wonderfulness of their daughter's mind, the clean spaciousness and wisdom and slow easy strength that she felt when Hope shared with her. And Castrel didn't tell Shay that she felt these things she shared with Hope were just glimpses, and there was much more in her that she could not reach or share.

It was as if there were rich and complex thoughts in Hope's mind, whole continents of knowledge and wisdom and memory and power that were just out of sight beyond further hills, and some of it was very ancient and very strange. Sometimes Castrel wondered if Hope was hiding this from her, but more often she was sure it was all just somewhere else, untapped and not yet fully articulated potential. The connections between the different parts of Hope's mind weren't yet fully grown, the threads in the weave not yet fully woven. But Hope was learning and growing fast.

'And what about the dragon, Cass? Does Hope talk about that?'

'We don't talk about it, no. I don't try to ask her. I don't like to, and I'm not sure how I could. I don't want to frighten her, I don't want her to get the idea we think there's something wrong with her, but when she talks to me I watch for it, and I know it's still there. In a way.'

When Hope shared her feelings and thoughts with her, Castrel still perceived the dragon-ness in her child. It was always there, as strange as ever, that ancient and terrible power. She couldn't communicate with it, but she felt it everywhere, in every part of Hope. Yet it was changed. No longer withdrawn, a walled and hidden watcher, almost furtive, defensive, the dragon was interwoven and absorbed now into everything that Hope was.

'Things are different with her now,' she said to Shay. 'It's not like there's a dragon inside her as a separate thing. It doesn't feel like she's been invaded by a monster any more. It's more like – I don't know, it's hard to put into words … It's as if Hope is a girl with the heart of a dragon, as if she is the dragon now, and the dragon is her. She's still a human girl, she's absolutely that, with a very strong hedge-witch gift, and she's a dragon too. She's all those things, all at once. They're all one thing in her now, not separate at all. Do you see what I mean?'

'I think so,' he said. 'I'm not sure I really understand. But I can see she's happy and strong and well, and that's all that matters.'

'And she's still changing, Shay. What I've said is what it's like now, but she's changing all the time, and very fast. We don't know how this is going to end. I can't see that, not yet.'

And still they walked on, following the high and lonely road into the endless south. Rain closed in, dismal and cold and unrelenting, erasing horizons, cleansing nothing. Walking was labour against walls of ashen rain.

Castrel stopped and pushed back her woollen hood to let the rain cool her, to feel the air in her face, and wait for Shay. The wide sound of the rain falling. Expanses of rain for miles and miles in all directions. The hiss of brown moorland under the rain.

Shay was a small dark figure, laborious in the distance, far back down the road. Castrel watched him approach. He was still limping after his fall in Barathule. He walked now with an unnatural straightness of the knee, and she supposed he always would.

He paused, coughing. His chest was not right. She knew that, but there was nothing she could do.

When he got closer she saw the pained concentration in his face, the struggle to keep walking day after day. With his wild straggling beard, his long hair tied back and the gaunt anxiety that lined his face, he looked like an older man than he was. Diminished. Aged. The darkness and desolation of these times was burning his store of life quickly. She supposed that she must be the same.

Shay's will was strong. Absolute and unbreakable determination: that was the essence and truth of him, when all else had been stripped away. She saw it in him every day, and still it could astonish her. It was the root of her love for him: that, and the courage, and the unbending iron honesty of his love for Hope and his love for her that would not ever fail. For her and for his daughter, Shay would endure, everything and always. He would keep going on. But she knew that his body was weakening, and in truth it was only stubbornness that bore him forward. And she was the same. She knew that, too.

Was it all stubbornness now, and only that? Was that what she and Shay were coming to, now? Love and courage becoming stubbornness, and stubbornness becoming narrow and blind? How much longer could this continue?

Hope is not dying. She is a dragon and will never die.

Stubborn and unseeing they were ploughing on south, wilfully walking slowly into inevitable catastrophe and taking Hope with them because they could not change now. It was too late and they were too tired to change.

The world was dying, and she grieved for it. She grieved for Bremel and Stalwart and Mamser Gean.

They would never go back to Allerdrade and Ersett again. Ersett had burned long ago and everyone there was dead. Weald was destroyed, and the *Apple Leaf* was lost, and they would never get to Far Coromance. Their golden friend was gone, and she and Shay could not protect Hope from what was coming. They did not know how.

And we will die.

I will die and Shay will die.

If not yet, then soon.

But Hope would not die. She would never die. Hope would have to find a place, immortal, isolated and entirely alone, the only one of her kind, in all the bitter, ruinous darkness and cold that was coming.

Castrel knew then that she had made a terrible mistake. Her instinct to keep and protect her own child had been wrong. She should have let her go with their golden friend to a better world, where she could live fully as the fine dragon-woman she would soon become. To live where there were other good people like their golden friend – a whole world of people like him.

Castrel's heart almost burst then with sadness and dismay.

Oh, Shay, she thought, *my beautiful, darling, courageous man. What have we done to our daughter? We have made a terrible, terrible mistake. Is it too late? If we turn back now, can we find him? Can we reach the crossing place in time?*

That night they made a fire of dead gorse-stump and woody root, gnarled and twisted like tiny ancient trees. The pile smoked thickly but mustered little heat, and on that sickly seethe of small pale flame they cooked carrion, the dark meat of something with wings that had died. Roasted in gorse-smoke, it was like chewing charred and bitter rope.

'Shay?' said Castrel. 'I think we've made a mistake.'

He looked at her, puzzled.

'What do you mean?' he said.

'This thing we're doing, this always grimly going on, always walking south, keeping Hope with us and holding on to her tight … I think it's for us, Shay. Not for her. Not any more. We're keeping hold of her because we need her. Because she makes our lives worth living. We haven't sacrificed ourselves for her, we've sacrificed her for us.'

'You think that?' he said quietly. 'Really? You think we should have let him take her?'

'I didn't think so at the time, but everything's changed now. She's learning so fast and becoming so strong and so strange. You probably don't see that in her as much as I do, not yet, but you will. I think our friend always knew that, and that's why he suggested he should take her, but we didn't understand. I don't blame us for that, but now I think we were wrong. We have to protect her, Shay, but we're going to die, and she won't.'

We're going to leave her alone, and probably soon. It'll be awful if we leave her alone in a world where nothing good grows. Look around you. How can anything good live in this?'

Shay didn't say anything, but stared for a long time at the fire.

'Shay …?' she said at last. 'What do you think? Do you think I'm wrong? Don't be angry. Tell me what you think. I'll listen.'

'All the time, Cass,' he said at last, so quiet she could hardly hear him, 'always, day after day, I hobble along behind you, watching you and Hope walking, and there's me dragging lamely after you, always struggling to keep up and always falling further behind. Knowing you have to stop and wait for me now. Every day I keep going, and every day my leg gets no better and my lungs feel a little bit worse. I'm getting more and more useless every day. Weaker. Feebler. More tired. Do you think I don't know this? Do you think I can't see what's coming?'

'Shay …' She put her hand on his arm in the growing dark. 'Please. I didn't mean that … I didn't mean you're not good enough, I didn't mean I wish I'd chosen a different man to be Hope's father because of that … You're—'

'That's not what I'm saying, Cass. I know what you mean. This isn't about me or you at all any more. Our time with Hope is nearly over. What I'm saying is, I think you're right.'

'Do you?'

'Yes. It's been obvious for a long time, hasn't it? Only we were hiding from it. Not admitting it even to ourselves. We just can't keep on with this, not any more. I think we should turn back. I think we should try to find the crossing place he told us about, and try to meet him there. I hope we find him. I hope we're not too late. And if we do find him, then when the time comes I will stand aside and let Hope go on without me. I think I can find the courage even for that.'

'I don't know if we've still got time,' she said.

'Nor do I. How could we know? There are no seasons now and

we've hardly seen stars in the sky for months. We don't know where we are, or even when. But we can turn back and look for the place. At least we can try.'

Castrel put another gorse root on the fire. She was glad. They had something to hope for now, something to make all their determination and endurance worthwhile in the end.

We will find our golden friend again, she thought, *and he will take Hope with him to a better world, and Hope will grow fine and wonderful. The time of humans is finished, but in the country of golden friends she won't be alone. She will become the brightest and finest of them all. The beautiful immortal woman with the dragon's heart.*

She sat with Shay in the thickening dark by light of the fading fire, side by side, their arms around each other, close and intimate and warm. Shay held Hope on his lap, wrapped in her blanket, and she was sleeping.

'We'll find him, Shay,' she said. 'I'm sure we will.'

32

Shay's leg still hurt and his chest was still bad, but it mattered less now. Every day he pushed further and faster. Days counted. They must reach the meeting place before it was too late.

'When Capault rises in the Great Mooring, that's when he said he would come,' said Castrel. 'We haven't seen stars for months, but the year feels older than that.'

'We'll be in time,' said Shay, 'and he will be there.'

The sky lay heavy and copper on broken hills – low silhouettes of jagged shattering where cold fires burned – and elsewhere scavenging tides were surging across dying plains, illuminated by silent lightning. But they would evade and outpace it all, as they always had. When it was night they nested together among blankets in the vastness of the enfolding dark and they were warm, and though the next day they would always be walking again, now they had somewhere to go, and that made all the difference.

They reached the crossroads south of Barathule and turned west, as their golden friend had said. Now they were walking towards the sea again, not south towards distant Proud Somail but to some good nearer shore and a happy meeting.

'I've never seen the sea,' said Castrel. 'When I was young, the thought of it always terrified me.'

'You'll love the sea, Cass. It's like the sky, huge and deep and different every day. When I lived at Harnestrand I used to climb up to a high place where I could look out over it, just so I could feel the wind and the sun and listen to the birds and watch the sea glitter and move.'

He remembered how the shimmering surface of the ocean rolled out and away for ever. Boats sailed on the sunlit surface but when storms came the deep water was a fist that could kill.

'I want to see it again,' he said. 'I want to show you the sea.'

Whatever happened to the world, there would still be oceans.

'Yes,' said Castrel. 'That'll be good.'

But Shay felt the sadness in what she said. When they reached the sea, Hope would leave them and they would be alone, just the two of them standing together on the shore.

Having a child means losing in the end, he thought. *That's what it is. We do what we can, and then our time is over and she slips away out of our reach and goes forward on her own. That's how it will be. But that's how it should be, in the end. It's natural. The whole point of fighting is to lose.*

Every day Hope grew stronger, more beautiful and strange. At last she had begun to talk in words, and Shay could talk to her.

Hope didn't start talking by making single sounds and hesitant stumblings like other children did. She simply one day started to speak. She spilled out whole rivers of words. Some of what she said Shay and Castrel understood, but much of it seemed to be in other languages, with sounds and meanings they didn't know. Sometimes all they listened to was the music of Hope's mysterious, wonderful voice.

'It's as if she already knows lots of different languages,' said Castrel, 'and she's talking to us in all of them at once. She doesn't keep them apart in her mind because they're all one language as far as she's concerned. She's swimming in an ocean of words.'

And the sounds Hope made weren't the whole of her music:

her voice was emotion, unmediated and direct. She wove what she said with what she felt, so that even Shay could feel it too, fluent and simple and strong.

Sometimes she laughed when she talked. A child's sudden laughter in the bleak ruination of the world.

It was Shay's best happiness now that he could simply walk down the road hand in hand with his daughter and talk with her. And the more he walked with Hope, the more he absorbed and copied her fluent and unconstrained talkiness and let himself chatter on too. After a while he found that it came easily, as if the world was still an ordinary living place and desolation hadn't come at all.

He could never tell how much of what he said to her Hope fully understood, but it didn't really matter because the whole point was just to be talking and walking together hand in hand. Sometimes he would chatter on for ages and think Hope wasn't even paying attention, and then she would suddenly say something that surprised him because it showed how much she listened, and how much she already knew.

'When I was a boy I used to live in a small village by the sea called Harnestrand,' he told Hope once, 'and when I was older I learned how to make boats. We took trees from the woods and split them and put them together with nails in the right shape to go on the water. We made ropes and sails too, and nets, and we sailed out onto the sea to catch fish.'

'Did you catch lots of fish?'

'Loads and loads of fish. The fish were silver and heavy in the nets, and white birds came to try to steal them, but that didn't matter. We let them have some because we had caught so many. When we brought the fish home there was always a feast and everybody came and there was wine and dancing. The sun shone all day and it was always bright and hot. There were smells of fruit and grass and cooking fish, and children played on the beach and everybody swam in the sea.'

'Fish are sweet and cold and delicious,' said Hope. 'I swallowed whole rivers of fish in a single swallow when I was Calamitous.'

Shay looked at her in surprise. She said those odd things sometimes.

'Was that a dream you had?' he said.

'No.'

'Your mother was very beautiful when I saw her first,' Shay told Hope once. 'She still is beautiful. This wasn't very long ago. Her eyes were dark and bright and wise and she had hair that shone like blackcurrants. I loved her very much as soon as I saw her and I still do love her very much.'

Another time, he found himself telling Hope about the White Knives.

'I saw ten thousand horses all together on a long beach by the sea, and that was the most wonderful thing I've ever seen. They came to the beach in ships and they were all tall and beautiful and their riders had banners and they had white knives in their belts. And then they rode away. I don't know where they came from, somewhere very far away, I don't know where.'

'To fight in a war,' said Hope.

'Yes,' he said. 'To fight in a war, somewhere.' He paused. 'We had our own horse once,' he went on after a while, 'you and your mother and me. She wasn't beautiful and she was only small, not like those other horses, but she had a courageous heart and that matters most of all. We had a cart and she used to pull it every day and you rode in it with your mother. Do you remember that, Hope? Her name was Stalwart, and you used to stroke her. But you were very tiny then, not much bigger than a kitten. I could hold you in one of my hands.'

'I remember you killed Stalwart and put her under all those stones,' said Hope. 'I remember that.'

'Yes,' said Shay. 'I did.'

Sometimes Hope would look at him with a profound and ancient understanding. Like a leviathan it surfaced from some-where very deep. The ferocious justice of dragons. It measured him. The glitter of immortality in darkness.

The road rounded the edge of a leafless brittle woodland and began a slow descent. Ahead was rolling country under low bleak skies, and in a notch cut between distant hills Shay caught sight of a band of dark purple, glittering with grey-green light.

'Look!' he said. 'The sea. The sea.'

His heart lurched with the joy of excitement and remember-ing. It was almost like coming home. A feeling of being young again. He coughed and hawked and spat in the mud of the road. Small jewels seamed with pink and crimson blood. There was a dark tightness in his chest. He didn't think about that.

33

In the late afternoon they came down on a small shore of mud and reddish sand. Mounded sea-wrack stank when they walked on it, their feet breaking crust and crunching into ooze and blackness. Castrel picked up a length of strap and bulb. It was as strong as leather. Unbreakable. It smelled of stagnation and left her fingers lubricated with the odour of the dying sea. On the beach were ruined trees: storm-beached carcases, salt-grey and rotting inside. They seemed to be trying to lift themselves from the sand on branch-stumps and matted clumps of root.

Shay walked down to the ocean's edge and stood for a long time watching the weak slide, slap and withdrawal of thickened, bitter waves. The same hopelessness was in him as was in the fallen trees. She went to stand by him.

'This isn't the sea, Cass. Not as I remember it. This isn't what I wanted you to see.'

He coughed and she could hear the wheezing in his chest.

'It doesn't matter,' she said, but Shay's disappointment was close to despair.

'He isn't here,' he said. 'He won't be coming. We're too late.'

'We don't know that,' said Castrel. 'And this isn't the place. We're looking for a wide bay between high black rocks, one like a tower standing and the other like a tower that's fallen.'

'There could be so many places like that,' said Shay. 'Half the shores of the world must look like that.'

'He meant us to know it when we saw it, and I'm sure we will, or he would have said something else.'

'He doesn't think like us. He doesn't see the world the same.'

'We'll know it when we get there,' she said. 'We just have to keep looking until we do.'

'How far? Did he say how far?'

'No. But west. We have to keep going west.'

A bend of bay and a long grey reach of sand under spacious light, the tide a distant brown edge. This place was different. Some things were living here still.

Two seabirds offshore, diving. Hang and then fall. Silent white bullets plunging against the weight of the sky.

When did they last see any birds?

'Gannets,' said Shay. 'They're gannets.'

'There's life here,' said Castrel. 'This is a better place to be.'

A man was riding along the beach, still far off and small, leaning forward, hunkered down and shoulders sloping, and the horse was moving slow, dragging a heavy mounded burden without wheels. He was not their golden friend, but he was a living person when they had thought there was no one else left.

They descended the slope of rough tussock and stood at the edge of the sand to wait. The rider slowed and watched them for a moment, then came on. No change of direction. Shay walked out onto wide damp sand, an intercepting trajectory, sword not drawn. Castrel followed him with Hope.

The horse was rib and sinew, a reddish coat once but greying now, salt-bleached. The sled it hauled was stacked high with sea-wrack and lengths of driftwood. The horse looked at them without interest – eyes like dulled fruits – then dropped its muzzle, as if its skull was suddenly too heavy for its neck, to browse the ungrazeable sand.

The rider was old like the horse and held the reins loose in weathered, knotted hands. Grey-white stubble in the folds of chin and neck.

'Tide's been poor,' he said. 'Nothing of interest here. I'm not selling. Just picking. Just for me.'

'We don't want to buy,' said Castrel. 'We don't have money.'

The old man shrugged.

"Course not. Who does?' He turned away from her. 'Where you from?' he said to Shay.

Shay gestured vaguely behind him.

'North. Along the shore.'

'Only I thought I seen your face before. Something in it familiar.'

'I don't think so. We're looking for a long beach with black rocks at each end. At one end the rock's like a tower, and at the other end the rock's like a tower that's fallen. Do you know a place like that?'

'Don't remember it. Far as I know there isn't such a place. I don't go along the shore more than a day, though, not either way, but no one ever said they'd seen a place like that. Not that I ever heard of, and I been here all my life.'

He heeled the horse in the ribs and it walked on a pace or two and stopped. The old man twisted, looking back.

'Not looking for work, are you?'

'No.'

'Only I could offer you that. I could use a hand. Nothing too hard. There's samphire back there on the cliff, only I'm too creaky to go up and get it, and there's better mackerel comes in round the other head, they're the kind you can eat, if you've got the weight to go up against the tide. Nothing more than that. Isn't hardly work at all. I see you got a wife and child. I could use them too. You'd get fed and peace for your trouble.'

'We're not looking for that,' said Castrel.

The old man ignored her.

'Come back anyhow,' he said to Shay. 'We'll feed you up. Try us and see how it suits. We burn a good fire. It's not more than a step along the bay.'

'No. Thank you. No.'

He rested his hand on the hilt of the dead wizard's sword. The old man eyed it narrowly.

'Ah, well then,' he said.

He dug his heels in the horse's withered ribs and moved off, dragging his reeking beach-haul.

'There isn't no place like you said, though,' he said over his shoulder. 'I never heard of it.'

'You did right,' said Castrel to Shay after the old man had gone. 'I didn't trust him at all.'

'No,' said Shay. 'I don't think anything he said was true.'

The last shore was their only road now, and day after day they followed it west.

The formation of rock rose out of white sand at the edge of surf. It was separate from the cliff, a high needle, tapering, jagged and blue-black, a hundred feet high. When they got close, Castrel saw that the black was seamed with fine mineral veins of whitish translucence. The sand at the foot of the needle was matted with purple wrack and barnacled with a crust of chalky dead shells.

A pale crescent of empty sand curved away west and at the further end, misted by fine rain and distance, the broken stump of a twin formation prodded the horizon. The rest of it had toppled like a fallen tree and lay where it fell, reaching out into the surf. Waves were breaking against it in rhythms of white spray.

'This is the place,' said Shay.

'Yes,' said Castrel. 'I think it must be.'

Thick banks of cloud closed in the sky from horizon to horizon, weighing dark and low, spilling an oppressive dim greenish coppery shade that tinged the sea the same. Out in the bay, beyond the tip of the fallen tower, the sea seethed and churned among low rocks and broke against the broken timbers of a wrecked ship. Its prow, still intact, lifted above the waves, its angles ruined and wrong.

They walked towards the wreck along the beach, close to the sea. The wet sand under their feet was many colours, browns, ambers and greys, mostly pale fine greys, arranged by the ebbed waves in delicate, rhythmed patterns like fish-bone weaves. Back from the sea's edge where the sand was dry it was almost white: soft low mounds that sifted in the breeze and made the work of walking hard. Further back, the mounds became dunes.

Castrel walked with Shay and Hope walked on his other side, holding his hand. The endless sound of the surf was blank and white like wind among trees.

At the back of the beach about halfway along, tucked into a sheltered corner out of the wind, there were three timber huts, long abandoned and empty. Sand-scoured and bleached bone-grey by decades of light and salt. One had lost the shingles from its roof, but the others would keep out rain.

Castrel chose one and opened the door and they went in. A small, windowed room filled with quiet air and wide ocean light. The floor planks were gritty underfoot and drifts of dry sand were piled in the corners. She closed the door and slid the heavy pack from her shoulders. Leaned it against the wall.

'This one,' she said. 'No more walking. We'll live here.'

No more road to walk. Nowhere else to go. Here they would wait for their golden friend. If this was the right place. If the time for that meeting had not already gone.

34

We have fire, says Hope to the heart of the dragon. I remember that. Fierce dragonfire that burns.

You cannot have that, says Fellimbre. *Dragonfire comes from within like a furnace. You must have dragon ribs and dragon lungs and dragon wings for the fire, you must be mighty and huge, and you have not chosen that.*

That's for fire breath and fire blast, Fellimbre, says Hope. But it's not the seed and the spark of the fire. That's everywhere, that's in our blood and bone. Show me how to do it. I want to have fire.

What's the use of seed and spark if it's only within us?

You forget who I am born, Fellimbre. You forget my mother. I am not only dragon, walled inside my own self by skin and scale. I am born open. I am born sharer and reacher-inside and healer. I am born toucher of life.

I don't understand.

I am Hope. I am learner and change. Show me how to spark dragonfire and I will learn how to reach out and make anything burn.

Yes, says Fellimbre. *I see now. Now I understand.*

35

Shay was so tired. Nights he slept long and woke slowly with a weary dullness he could never shake. Want of nourishment weakened him, but what they had – the little Castrel scrabbled out of the ground or they picked up from the shoreline – he made himself eat without savour or desire, and always he left the larger share for Castrel and Hope, though they did not know it.

One day he stumbled and twisted his ankle, and it brought all the old pain back. After that he took to sitting by himself high on the shore and watching Castrel play with Hope in the sea. The dark tightness was in his chest all the time now. Death had got into his lungs. It had got in his mouth and eyes and under his skin as well. When he paused in the day to rest he would lapse into sleep and wake confused.

The ebb and flow of the tide brought no one. No wind. No stars. The clouds shed always the same strange dark greenish-coppery end-of-the-world light across their days, and blanketed their nights always in a thick darkness. The nights were illuminated only by the dim green phosphorescence of the waves.

The hut where they slept was filled with the pale ceaseless sound of the sea.

They were the final family, beachcombing the last days of the world.

*

Shay woke in the afternoon to the long roar of waves in his head, flat out on a bank of shingle, his arm hooked under his body, awkwardly numb. There was a jagged pain behind his eyes, his tongue swollen and clumsy, the taste in his mouth gone sour. He wasn't sure where he was.

Castrel was standing over him. She looked panicked.

'Where's Hope?' she said. 'Where did she go?'

'Um … What …? I don't know.'

'I can't find her, Shay. We were over by the trees and I was looking at something, and when I turned round she wasn't there any more. I've been looking for her. I've been shouting. I can't find her. She's lost. She's gone.'

'She can't be gone.'

'She is.'

He hauled himself stiffly to his feet. Wiping his face with his hand. Trying to clear his head.

'She can't have gone far,' he said. 'We'll find her.'

Fear dinned in his head, louder than the sea. Sickening possibilities of a horror that could not be borne. From such a loss there could be no afterwards, no survival, no going on. And the responsibility would be his, because he had been weak, because he had left it all to Castrel. Because he slept. He broke into a spasm of coughing. The tightened pain of his ribs and lungs made him lean into it, bending forward. He coughed tiny jewelled spatters, rose red like anemones on the sand.

Hope came walking towards them, out from under the shadow of the trees. She was carrying something white in her arms. Castrel ran and scooped her up, hugging her tight.

'Hope!' she said. 'Oh, Hope, where did you go? We were looking for you, we didn't know …'

Relief made Shay's whole body feel weightless. He wanted to

shout light-headed joy to the world, but he hung back, limping up slowly behind Castrel to greet the child, suddenly tongue-tied, surprised by shyness.

'I was playing,' she said.

'We were so worried,' said Cass. 'Don't do that ever again. You mustn't go somewhere we can't see you. It's not safe, sweetheart. You have to stay with us always, so we can look after you.'

'What have you got there?' said Shay.

Hope showed him. It was a bird, young and white. A seabird. Its wing hung slack and broken.

'He's hurt,' said Hope. 'His mother and his father have gone. He's my friend.'

Sometimes Shay lay whole days inside on the floor. He shivered and sweated, lost in fever dreams.

Hope found shells on the shore and carried them home. She laid them out in rows on the floor and lined them along the sills. Shay didn't know how she found so many. He rarely saw one on the beach at all.

'He's not coming,' Shay said to Castrel. 'He's not, is he?'

'We don't know that. He might. Any day.'

'I don't think so. Not now.'

'We're all right here, anyway. This is a good place to be. There's nowhere better.'

'We could look for him, though.'

'Where?' said Castrel. 'This is the place. If he's coming he'll find us here.'

One morning Shay woke to a speck on the ocean horizon. A tiny mark of white. A sail.

'Castrel!' he called to her. 'Castrel! Look! There's a ship!'

For hours they watched it grow, tacking slowly in towards the coast against faint offshore breezes. A three-masted ship, riding light in the water. Two miles out, it dropped sail and came no closer.

Shay remembered the ships the White Knives came in. The most beautiful ships he had seen. A thousand of them, crowding the reach off Harnestrand, bringing ten thousand beautiful horses and their riders. And this ship was the same.

Perhaps.

It lay too far off to be sure. But it was a ship.

A ship to Far Coromance.

'We have to make it see us,' he said to Castrel. 'Help me, we must have a signal. A fire.'

He hobbled up the beach and found the axe. Carried it to one of the empty huts and began to swing at the planks of it, clumsy and desperate. Dragging at the timbers, splitting hinges and tearing nails. Heaping the wood. He cursed himself as he worked. He should have thought of this before. He should have got a big fire ready in case there was a ship.

'I don't know,' said Castrel. 'We should be careful. We should think before we attract attention like this.'

'We'll think later,' said Shay. 'We can't just stay here and wait for the end. Help me.'

They built a woodpile taller than themselves, and fetched a smouldering branch from the cooking fire to light it.

'It won't burn!' said Shay.

He stuffed the hot tinder deep inside the beacon-pile, but all that came from it was a slow charring and feeble feathers and threads of smoke. He blew on it, and packed it with leaves, but it made no difference.

'It'll catch eventually,' said Castrel. 'We just need to be patient.'

'It could take hours. If it ever does. We haven't got the time. What if they go?'

Hope was standing with them, watching.

'I'll help,' she said.

Shay looked at her in surprise.

'If you want to, of course you can,' he said. 'But I don't think you can make any difference.'

Hope picked up a dry branch and held it in her hand.

'You need to put it in the fire to set it alight,' said Castrel. She showed her how. 'Like this.'

But Hope didn't do that. She held the branch in her hand for a while and nothing happened. She looked disappointed, as if she had expected something more.

'Wood is dead,' she said.

'Don't worry,' said Shay. 'It doesn't matter. We'll manage.'

There was a spiky stand of sea-thorn growing near the beacon. Thick pale blue stems, ribbed and fibrous, prickled with sharp hairs. It was one of the few things that grew on the beach. Hope walked over to it.

'Be careful,' said Castrel. 'Don't touch that. It's got sharp hooky thorns that'll hurt you.'

'I won't touch it,' said Hope.

She stood there and watched the sea-thorn for a while, frowning in concentration.

Whoomph!

Suddenly it exploded in fierce white-hot cascades of seething fire. Shay felt the heat like a hot wind in his face.

Castrel yelled, 'Hope!'

She grabbed the child and pulled her away from the flames which were billowing towards her.

'Oh, my darling. Are you all right? Your clothes are smouldering. Are you hurt? Are you burned?'

Hope was smiling with happy triumph.

'It doesn't hurt me,' said Hope. 'Dragons don't burn.'

Shay stared at her, and she looked at him. The shards of colour in her eyes, slate-grey and purple and gold and green, shone brilliant like tiny flakes of fire.

'Was that you, Hope?' he said. 'Did you do that?'

'I've been learning,' said Hope. 'I wanted to see if I could.'

That evening Shay and Castrel sat side by side on the sand with their backs against the wall of their seashore house and watched their daughter. Hope was away down at the sea's edge, walking alone in the surf, tall and shining and strong, carrying her injured bird under her arm. A thick pall of black smoke was still rising from the beacon-fire. It had burned all afternoon but no boat came. The ship gave no sign, and after a few hours it had raised sail and gone from the bay.

'How did she do that, Cass?' said Shay. 'How did she set that bush on fire?'

Their daughter had done that. It was strange and wonderful and disturbing. What could they feel or think of that?

'She's got the heart of a dragon,' said Castrel.

Shay thought of wide furrows of scorching on the Chelidd Plain and the hundreds of soldiers burned to an agonising death.

'But dragons breathe sheets of flame. Streams of fire. She's not a dragon and she didn't do that. She just looked at the bush and it burned. How could that happen? Magic? Is she some kind of wizard too?'

Castrel shook her head.

'There was no magic in that. I don't have the healing gift any more, but I'm sure I would have known.'

'Then how?'

'She couldn't burn the branch,' said Castrel, 'but she burned the living bush. I think perhaps it might be that. Everything that lives is filled with light and warmth. That's how healing and sharing work. If she can reach that, and somehow make it go … I don't know, somehow *faster*. Set all that life loose all at once.

379

Perhaps that would make it burn. A dragon must have some way of making its fire, and if it does it like that, then maybe Hope can get other living things to do it too.'

'You mean, Hope made that bush set itself on fire?'

'I don't know. Maybe. I'm just thinking how it could be.'

They fell silent and watched their daughter walking alone at the edge of the shore.

'We have to get her out of here,' said Shay. 'This is bad. This, here and now, this is bad.'

The world's long age of life was over. It had crossed a threshold and entered the endless age of death. Their daughter was becoming a strange and beautiful dragon girl who would live for ever, and she would be alone.

'We should have let him take her when we had the chance.'

'We always did our best, Shay,' said Castrel. 'We made the best choices for her that we could at the time, with what we knew then. We can't go back and make it different now, and we mustn't blame ourselves because we didn't understand.'

Shay shrugged.

'It doesn't matter now. He's not going to come. It's too late. And there'll be no more walking now. I can't do that any more. I'll have to stay here until the end. But you should go on, Cass. You and Hope. Go on further. Maybe there's something else we don't know yet, something we haven't found. Leave me here and go.'

For a long time Castrel was quiet, watching the sea.

'You are a good man,' she said at last. 'You are the best of men, and you do your best. I will never leave you. Please don't ask me again.'

Shay turned to look at her and she was beautiful. Still and always beautiful.

'Every day with you …' he said. 'Nothing else. I never wanted anything else. I would choose even these bad days with you over good days and everything right again and you not here.'

The next day Shay rose with the dawn and went back to the hut he'd half-dismantled to build the beacon fire, and began to demolish the rest. Working methodically, with slow thoughtful care, he separated the timbers and sorted them by size. Hefted the roof beams, substantial and strong, so heavy he must drag them across the sand. Prised out each peg and nail and set them aside. One day soon he would go up into the woods and cut a mast. He would worry later about rope and tar.

Castrel came down to see him when she woke.

'What are you doing?' she said.

'Building a boat,' he said. 'I still know how to do that.'

If they could walk no further, and if there was to be no crossing for Hope to a different world of immortal golden friends, and if no ship would come for them, then he would build their own boat. He had built her a crib like a boat before she was born, but he had lost it. So now he would make her another and better one. Who knew, perhaps there was some wonderful place across the ocean where Hope could live happily for ever, and they could take her there or at least set her on her way. At least they could try. He wasn't going to sit on the sand and wait to die.

But he was weak and ailing. Seriously ill. The exhaustion was heavier to carry every day. There was a wrongness in his chest and his own body was turning against him.

36

Castrel woke early in the bleached timber room furnished only with sand and immersed in ocean light. The sound of the sea on the shore.

The waves will continue for ever the same although all else is gone.

The sea was too near. Its vastness unnerved her; her imagination drifted on it; she dared not dive in it and swim.

She pushed back the blanket and went out.

At the far end of the bay, where a shallow stream from the dunes spread out across shingle and sank into sand, livid green sea wrack still grew on the rocks. Castrel gathered handfuls of it. When she spread the wet leaves on her palm she could see her skin through them. The wrack was edible when it was boiled, though the mush was thin and pale and tasted of little but slime and salt.

There were shells on the rock: shells the colour rain clouds used to be, shaped like sharp-edged tears. They contained small purses of gritty blue and yellow meat. Collecting the shells she sliced and grazed her fingers, and the salt water stung in the cuts.

She was cold and worked slowly, stooping and stiff. Her back hurt.

*

Hope was sitting among the dunes and sharp grasses, nursing her injured bird. The child gripped the threads of its weakening life in her fierce tight fists and would not let it die. Even through the numbness of her ruined perceptions, Castrel could see the strength of the girl's power to do that: to hold on grimly to life and never let it go. Every day Hope worked at the fine shattered bones in the wing, patiently trying to remake them whole, though she didn't yet know how. She would work it out. Her determination was like a rock in the sea.

Castrel recognised the syllables that Hope murmured and sang under her breath. They were fragments of what she had herself learned from Bremel when she was a child: hedge-words of weaving and growing and making whole. Hope didn't have them quite right, not all of them, but strength and life flowed in her speaking. How had Hope learned that? She must have absorbed it somehow. Found them in Castrel's mind.

What is our daughter becoming? Have I ever really understood?

Hope looked up.

'Help me,' she said. Her voice was in Castrel's mind, the shared knowing, not mouth sounds. 'Teach me to do this. I want to learn.'

'I can't do it myself any more,' said Castrel. 'But I'll try to show you how.'

Every day Shay laboured at building his boat. He spoke little and bent to his work with slow care, reshaping the aged and weathered timbers of the demolished hut into a hull.

Shay spotted an ancient shipwreck at the western end of the beach, out at the tip of the fallen tower of rock that stretched out into the bay. There wasn't much left of it that could be seen from the shore. The long swell of the ocean rose and surged green shoulders of water against the rocks, foaming and bursting clouds of spray that spilled across the few visible timbers, so far away that the sound of the crashing waves couldn't be heard above the general sound of wind and sea.

'I'm going to go and look at it,' said Shay. 'Maybe there'll be things out there that I can use.'

'Like what?' said Castrel.

'I don't know. Spars. Barrels. Rope.'

'Are you sure you want to do that? It looks dangerous.'

'Better to try than to sit here and look at it and wonder.'

'But—'

'Don't try to stop me, Cass,' he said quietly. 'Please.'

She stood on the beach and watched him scramble clumsily out along the jagged edge of rock, drenched under breaking waves, dragging his hurt leg. At the far end he let himself down into the water and swam the last few yards to the wreck and hauled himself out. She could see what the struggle was costing him. He almost couldn't do it at all.

When at last he returned he was carrying a single chunk of wood under his arm. His face was full of exhaustion and disgust.

'Look,' he said.

The timber was sea-black and swollen and bored through with smooth holes wide enough to take her thumb.

'The worms of the sea,' said Shay.

He pushed his knife into it. The wood was soft, like dark fibrous butter.

As it took shape, Castrel saw how small Shay's boat would be.

'She'll be strong,' he said. 'She'll ride out the waves well enough. You'll see.' He coughed.

How thin he was. How his hands trembled. How many rests he must take. How the sweat stuck strings of hair across his brow. The growing distance in his eyes.

Oh, Shay.

'When it's finished,' she asked him, 'where will we go?'

He gestured towards the south-western skyline.

'Out there. Along the coast till we find a better place. That ship we saw came from somewhere.'

Don't do this, she wanted to say to him. *Don't think it. Don't say it, even to yourself. You've already done more than enough, Shay. You've finished now. There's nothing else you can do.*

But after she had said that, what? What followed?

So she said nothing, and day after day from dawn till dark he laboured, pushing himself further into exhaustion.

One evening they sat on the sand by a driftwood fire. The four of them: Castrel, Shay, Hope, and Hope's white nursling bird. The bird watched them from its place in Hope's lap. Its eye was a bright living bead, the colour of the lost blue sky.

Two huge winged creatures that were not birds wheeled and mewed far out over the sea. They climbed high, circling each other in a kind of sweeping spiral dance, then plunged swooping and arcing low across the darkening bay on flaggy wings.

Hope pointed east along the shore.

'Over there,' she said. 'What's that?'

A lone figure was approaching along the surf line. Still far off, it looked like a man walking, limping and slow. Shay rose with a grunt of pain and went to fetch the dead wizard Tariel's sword. When he came back he stood leaning on it, digging its point into the sand, watching the walker come closer.

Twilight closed in and the unfed fire sank to smoulders among the ash. It was a long time before the figure was near enough for them to make him out clearly. Then they could see the colours of his beautiful clothes. Then they could see the long fine hair spread pale across his shoulders.

Their golden friend.

'He looks hurt,' said Castrel. 'See how he's holding his side.'

'He's lost his horses,' said Shay. 'Something's happened.'

'Yes. But he's come.'

Castrel felt a faint stirring of joy: the hesitant coming-to-life of possibilities she had given up long ago. Cautiously, hopeful futures were waking. She walked down the beach with Shay and Hope to meet him, and hugged him warmly.

He was weak. Exhausted. Hurt. His face gaunt with pain, his clothes stained with dirt and crusted with dark blood.

'I had bad luck at the Voulge Keeping,' he said. 'Misfortune and much delay. My horses are dead, my possessions are lost, and I've had to come far on foot. It was slow walking.'

'We've been waiting for you,' said Shay.

'Yes,' said Castrel. 'It's good to see you again. We're so glad you've come.'

She hugged him then, and felt him flinch. Under the delicate fabric of his shirt, his body was airy and fragile. Slender, like a tall child. She lifted her face to kiss his cheek and his skin felt cool and soft against her mouth.

'Come with us,' she said. 'We have a house, and you can sleep there. Come and sit by our fire. Let me look at where you're hurt.'

There was an ugly wound in his side: a long ragged gash, crusted and angry. He winced when she brushed it with her fingers, though she tried to be gentle.

'I'm sorry,' she said. 'There must be a lot of pain.'

'It hurts, but it will not kill me. It is possible that in time the pain will subside.'

The wound was healing slowly and wrong. There were weals of scar tissue, lumpy and not where they should be. Castrel did what she could to clean and rebind it, but there was nothing useful to be done.

'It should have mended quickly,' he said. 'Something has changed. Nothing is as it should be now.'

'How long ago did it happen?' she said.

'I do not know for certain. Some weeks, at least. Perhaps much more. For a time after the fighting I couldn't think clearly. I wandered, I think, or perhaps I slept. I do not remember much. I miss my horses. They were my good companions, but I fear they suffered at the end.'

'We thought we'd missed you,' said Castrel. 'We thought you had already been here and gone. We haven't seen the stars for months. Every day is the same now. There are no seasons any more. But now that you're here …'

Their golden friend shook his head.

'I'm sorry,' he said. 'I have arrived too late. If my friends were here, then they have gone, the threshold is closed and there will not be another.'

He stood for a long time in silence, staring out at the wide darkening emptiness of the ocean.

'My world is so very close,' he said at last. 'Even now, we are in it. Even now, we are standing there.' He spread his arms wide in a wild despairing gesture. 'It is here. It is *here*! *Now*! And yet so very far away. Invisible, inaudible, intangible, more unreachable than the distantmost star, yet closer than this breath of wind against my cheek. In that other world, my home, I have watched another sun westering beyond a different, darker sea. I wish you could have seen my home, all of you. There, the setting sun swells and reddens as the cloud-ranges slide up to meet it and the clouds glow like hot metal. The sun that shines on my world burns hotter than yours. Warmer and fiercer by just the faintest margin, but enough. The shadows there are deeper, the brilliances harsher, the contrasts more pronounced. It is my home! My beautiful home, that I have not seen or touched for so long. So very long. And now I will never go there again.'

'We saw a ship out in the bay,' said Castrel. 'It stayed for a day and then it went. We lit a big fire on the beach, and they must have seen it, but they didn't come. Perhaps it was them? Perhaps they saw you weren't here, so they went away, just for a while? Perhaps they'll come back?'

'No. That is not the way, not a ship. If they ever did come for me, they have gone long ago. There will be no second chance. I cannot escape now, and I cannot take Hope away from here with me.'

The tide of days rose and fell, slow and empty like the tides of the thickening ocean, like the roll and withdrawing of waves on the sand. The sound of the sea was ceaseless and dark like the pulse in the deep arteries of the ear.

Hope walked on the shore and collected shells and carried her nursling bird tucked inside the wool of her shirt against her skin. Still she held on fiercely to the thread of its life and would not let it go, though she could not yet heal its broken wing.

'Your child is strong,' said their golden friend. 'She will grow beautiful and true, it cannot be otherwise now. I am sure of that.' Grief rose in Castrel, unbearably sad. *My poor wonderful child.* And Shay was so ill. She wasn't sure how much time he had left, but it couldn't be long, and when he was gone she and Hope would live on this shore by themselves, and she would grow old like Bremel. But how could that be? The days were already dark and cold.

'She'll be left all alone by herself in this terrible place,' she said.

'I am sorry. I truly would have taken her with me. It was a promise I meant to keep. I would have done that, if I could, and not because of the dragon in her, but because of Hope herself, and because of you and Shay.'

He paused, and his eyes were focused somewhere else, somewhere very far away.

'I have known this world and loved it for thirty centuries,' he said. 'I have seen the bright fresh glories of the world's morning and the glories of its noontide splendour. I found a sad loveliness in the long decline of its autumn evening, and I have seen the appalling slow destruction and spreading emptiness of its twilight wars. I have witnessed the final closing of darkness and night and the drawing of the curtains. I have known empresses, wizards and kings. Admirals of war fleets and captains of the guard. I have dined at the tables of travellers, merchants and scholars, and listened to their talk. I have studied for a hundred years in the endless libraries of Barathule and swum alone through the caves of Persillian. I have slept under emerald canopies in the peacock gardens of Yi. I have heard the singers of Oskhandy and walked ten miles through the galleried treasure houses of Far Coromance.

'But I have never known finer people than you, Castrel: you and Shay. Never have I known stronger, truer, more loving and courageous hearts. You are the last and finest flowering of humankind, come at the hour of its dying. You have taken my cherished detachment and smashed it completely to pieces. Taken it utterly away. I have been an observer for three thousand years, but from you I have learned better wisdom, and there is nothing and no one I would rather preserve from this catastrophe than your beautiful child, if I could. I would do it as a parting gift to you, a tribute to your love for her, and most of all as some small sign of my love for you all.'

Castrel took his cool-skinned golden hand and held it in hers. 'Stay with us now,' she said. 'Stay with Hope.'

When he looked at her there was despair in his golden eyes.

'No. I cannot stay here. I know what is coming, I know how bad it will be. This is not it, this is just the beginning. The opening of the doors. Far worse is coming, and I will not live through it. I refuse. I will choose death rather than that.'

'Don't,' said Castrel. 'Whatever else you do, don't do that. Any kind of life is better than despair.'

*

The next morning she woke late. Shay was sitting hunched on a stack of planks, digging at the sand with his heel, gouging a furrow. He didn't look up when she joined him. She sat next to him, her arm touching his, warm and intimate. Finding nothing to say.

'I can't build this boat, Cass,' he said at last, quietly. 'I just can't do it. I've built her all wrong. If she ever put out to sea she'd ship water at the first swell and come apart in the first wind. I could never have sailed her anyway, and where would we go? There is nowhere. There never was. And watch this.'

He took hold of the edge of the boat and broke a piece of wood away with his hand. It came easily, shedding dust.

'All the timbers of the house are the same.'

He showed her the head of the axe. It was dusted with a fine gritty coating of grey crystals, like salt leaching from the metal. The edge was notched and broken. He struck it against a pebble and a sliver of blade split away.

'But the sword is still strong,' he said.

'That's something,' she said. 'That's good.'

Heavy with weariness, Shay shook his head.

'What are we doing, Cass?' he said. 'Well, what are we? I'm no use any more, and everything I tried to do went wrong in the end.'

She loved him so much it hurt.

'I chose *you*,' she said to him then. 'Even Hope was a gift I didn't choose. The only person I ever actually chose was *you*.'

She stood up and dragged him to his feet and they went together slowly, hand in hand, to the edge of the ocean where their child was walking, and they joined her there.

The emptiness of the ocean and the heavy darkening silence of the sky. The wide pale sand. The endless surge and drag of bitter surf against the shore. These were the last days of the world: a quiet and melancholy final folding away of all life and of everything that had ever happened.

Castrel woke to the shriek of a huge flying creature. She stood in the doorway and watched it come sweeping in across the bay, so low she could hear the slow beat of its wing. Feel the chill dark of its shadow.

It saw us! The signs of us on the beach! It must have!

She felt almost resigned, too exhausted for terror now. There was nowhere else to go. So she went outside and sat with her back against the wall, the blanket round her shoulders, and watched the light of dawn harden across the beach.

As the sun she could not see rose higher, the belly of the cloud was stained copper and lit from within by flickers of dry silent lightning. On all sides now lightning ringed the horizon and the dark row of distant hills across the bay was edged with a thin line of white. The vapour of cold fires burning.

Their golden friend was standing at the edge of the ocean, staring out.

She heard his voice shouting.

'Castrel! Castrel! Come!'

He was waving to her. There was a sudden urgency in his voice.

'Look!' he called to her. 'Can you see?'

She walked down the beach to where he was standing. At first she could see nothing where he was pointing except the murky darkness of the thickened sea, and the thin green and copper of the low, dying sky. But then she saw a faint brightness in the distance towards the skyline, and as she watched it grew clearer.

There was a faint, misty island in the sea where there had been no island before. It was some distance away. Perhaps a mile. It seemed to be floating just above the water, though that must have been an illusion. As it grew brighter and more solidly present in their world, she could make out the shapes of green hills and tall slender towers that glimmered red and gold and blue. The towers of a city lit by a different sun.

'It is the crossing!' said her golden friend, and he was illuminated with joy. His subtle, beautiful voice trembled. His face, his whole body shone. 'The passage is opening. I did not come too late.'

Castrel wanted to shout and weep and run for Shay and Hope, but she could not move. She wasn't sure. There were doubts. Was it possible that after everything was lost, what they had hoped for and longed for and given up hoping was at last here? She could not quite think it.

If it was so, then Hope would leave them now and they must let her go. The pain of that cut her heart, so she could hardly speak.

'Is it real?' she said.

'Yes.'

'But … it's so far away. Miles across the sea. How …?'

'There will be a bridge. It will take some time. Hours. Perhaps the whole of the day. But it will come. You can see it now, it is beginning.'

It was true. The island city lit by different light was already fully real and there, and between it and the shore the sea was calming and turning a cleaner shade of green and blue. A glitter like sunlight on a lake. A path of light like the reflection of the sun. Slowly a way across the water was forming.

'You will let her come with me?' said their golden friend gently. 'If I can do that, I will have done something worth doing though everything else has failed. If she comes with me, all of this world will not have been lost, and she will have life elsewhere. Will you let her come with me? I understand what you will lose. I know the pain of it. But for her it is the better thing to do.'

392

'Yes,' said Castrel. 'I want that. But we need Shay. I know he feels the same, but he must choose.'

But she didn't go to find him, not straight away. She stayed a while and watched the light and sunshine growing stronger across the water. Her golden friend walked a little way off and left her alone, and she was glad of that. Just a few moments by herself to mourn the loss of her child.

A voice crashed suddenly into her head, a voice but not a sound. Hope's voice in her head. But different. Magnified. A child's voice, but also ancient and complex and commanding. A voice full of understanding and power. A voice like the sun if it spoke. A dragon voice.

DANGER! DEFEND YOURSELF! THEY HAVE COME! THEY ARE HERE!

Castrel swung round and stared up the beach behind her.

Hope was a hundred yards away, standing near their cabin where the stream flowed out of the dunes. It was Hope, but she was changed like her voice. Taller. Stronger. Illuminated. She opened her arms and something large and white lifted up from her and away. Her injured seabird, that she had been tending for so long. The white bird circled and flew west along the beach, flying low on wide strong wings.

And then Castrel saw what was coming towards Hope from the east, lumbering out of the dunes and along the beach.

The rider on the six-legged beast was moving at a fast lope, the hooves of its mount striking heavily, kicking up clouds of grey sand. Castrel could not see the rider's face under its hood. It was sitting tall in the high saddle, leaning forward, intent. The clang of harness. She heard the loudness of the beast's flared muzzle, breathing. The working of heavy lungs.

It was covering ground quickly, making for Hope.

'*Hope!*' she screamed. '*Hope!*'

The rider heard her and turned his head towards her, then looked away. He would attend to her later.

And behind the rider came something else. Something larger, moving clumsily, a huge awkward lumbering creature. Castrel couldn't see it clearly; it seemed to smoke with pale cold fire and darkness, and it left trails like clouds of shadow behind it as it came. Its head swung heavy and low between massive shoulders. All its movement was ungainly, but as it came it was staring at Castrel with cold, sharp, clever eyes.

She felt the overwhelming force of its gaze. It was as if it knew everything about her and could see into all the grief and weakness inside. There were no secrets in her that it didn't know. It made her want to cringe, to sink to her knees and give up all the fight in her and accept her end. Shay's end. Hope's end.

Their golden friend was standing at her shoulder, staring horror-struck at the thing that came.

'It is a Wielder,' he said, 'a strong one. An intelligence. It comes to prevent the crossing and close the breach. I was afraid of this. They are terrible. I cannot fight it. Not this.'

A look of sudden horror crossed his face.

'No! I see it now. I understand. It is worse than I thought. Its ambition is huge. The Wielder intends to cross the bridge in my place and take another world.' He looked at her in despair. 'My world. I cannot stop it. Nothing can.'

The rider was ahead of the Wielder, and closing fast on the child.

Castrel screamed.

'*Hope!*'

Castrel shook herself free of the submission that the Wielder's gaze had crushed her with, and she was running. But it was too far. The rider was already nearer Hope than she was and her feet were clumsy, slowed by the soft damp sand.

Shay came round the corner of the house, the dead wizard's

sword in his hand, moving as fast as he could, limping on his injured leg. Moving in silence. Saving his breath. He was closer to Hope than she was. The blade of Tariel's sword caught grey light and glinted like the sea.

Shay was slow but it would be enough. He would come between the six-legged beast and Hope. He would cut the rider off.

The rider saw the danger and raised its weapon and the mount made a lunge sideways, dropping its leading shoulder towards Shay. The rider's weapon swept wide in a low reaping arc and caught Shay across his shoulders and upper back.

Shay fell hard on his face in the sand and lay still, his arms and legs all wrong, blood oozing through the cloth of his shirt.

Then the rider picked up pace again and rode on towards Hope.

The child stood and faced it. She was standing bareheaded, legs set wide, her back against the pale bleakness of the dunes.

Castrel ran. Screams shredding her throat.

'*Hope! I'm coming! Hope!*'

On harder sand, she ran faster now.

'*Hope!*'

Their golden friend overtook her, racing lightly, almost weightless, ignoring the rider and hurling himself towards the Wielder, but his movements were awkward because of the wound in his side, and he carried no weapon. The Wielder seemed to glance at him briefly with a sideways twitch of its head. The golden friend tumbled and collapsed like a puppet when the strings are cut.

Hope was standing in front of the oncoming rider and Wielder. She was a fierce slender dragon of a child. A roaring rainbow of colour and light. But rider and Wielder were almost upon her and they would ride her down, and Castrel would not get there in time.

*

Castrel reached the place where Shay lay motionless and broken. The sand he lay on was stained with his blood. She snatched up Tariel's sword.

But she was too late, there was no time, and nothing she could do to save her child.

She felt the Wielder's attention on her again. Closer now, she could see that its shoulders were taller than she was, its shaggy head larger and heavier than a bull's, and she felt the full force of its intelligence and power. With a thought it could strike her down, and it would. But not quite yet. Anticipation was pleasure. First, the child.

Castrel felt a roar in her head – an impossible shout that wasn't a sound and wasn't a voice. It was a force ... a shrieking storm-wind in her mind.

The voice of Hope.

The heart of the dragon speaking.

STOP!

The rider's six-legged beast tumbled and collapsed heavily, carried forward and down under its own momentum, suddenly devastated, as if the tendons in its legs had been sliced through. It was dead. The corpse was smouldering and smoking. There was a fire burning inside.

But its rider sprang free and landed safely, with an agility and speed that wasn't human. Its limbs didn't move in human ways. It was close to Castrel. It jumped forward and lunged at her with its weapon. Jabbing for her chest.

The rider was fast, but Castrel was faster.

Slipping inside the reach of its weapon, with the dead wizard Tariel's sword she killed it. She plunged the sword into the rider's inhuman body again and again as the foul creature shrieked and spasmed. The blade of the sword had a power that was more than forged metal: it sang and leaped in her hand, drinking the life it took. Drawing into itself all the darkness of that cruel thing's terrible soul.

Castrel was screaming at it as it died.

'*You will not touch my child! I will not let you do that!*'

She had never killed with a weapon before, not a man nor a thing that resembled a man, but it felt easy. It was a visceral triumphant joy. She could not tell if the joy was hers or if it belonged to the dead wizard's living sword. She did not care.

Then she looked for her child.

'*Hope!*'

Castrel's yell was hoarse and ragged. The Wielder was shambling closer to her daughter. It loomed above her head.

Then Hope's dragon voice spoke again.

NO MORE STOP NOW END YOU ALSO DIE.

The Wielder erupted into blinding white incandescent flames of dragonfire. The heat of the explosion was a searing wind. Every part of it was burning.

With an escaping sigh like wind among trees it slumped to its knees and died. It was a massive mound of flickering white fire on the sand. A blackening fleshy lump of burning rock.

Castrel scooped up her child in her arms.

'Oh, my darling, my darling, it's all right. You are safe now. Those things are dead.'

Hope smiled at her.

'Yes,' she said with her human voice. 'They're dead now.'

She was still her daughter, though she seemed taller than before and warmer than human to hold. Hope's hair smelled beautiful against Castrel's face, like summer wind and scorched iron. Her eyes were illuminated and flecked with slate and gold and summer-leaf green.

She was girl and she was dragon. They were the same thing now.

*

Castrel and their golden friend carried Shay into the hut and laid him on blankets on the sandy timber floor.

'I'll leave you with him and take Hope to the shore,' said their friend. 'The child should not see this. And the threshold bridge is nearly complete.'

'How long will it remain?' said Castrel.

'Not long. I'll come and tell you when we're ready to cross. And then Hope and I must go.'

And then her child would be gone and she would be alone with Shay on the abandoned shore of the world.

The blow from the rider's weapon had done Shay terrible damage. Castrel cleaned his wound as well as she could, but the blade had poisoned him terribly. The wide gash in him was already beginning to smell bad, and she couldn't stop it oozing. There was nothing she could do.

Shay opened his eyes and saw her there.

'It hurts a little,' he said. 'It hurts quite a lot.'

He coughed, and winced. The dark wheezing rattle in his chest.

'There's no need to talk,' she said. 'I'm here. Hope is near. We're all safe now.'

'I did what I could, Cass. And always I have loved you.'

He reached for her hand and she let him take it.

'And I love you,' she said. 'So much. Always so much. Always that.'

'I wanted to see Hope set on her way. I wanted to see her strong and ready.'

'You have. She is. The way out of this world is opening for her.'

'Is it?' He smiled. 'That's good. That's wonderful. Then she will be safe.'

'Our golden friend is with her on the beach. She'll have to go very soon. The way won't stay open long.'

'Go with them.'

She shook her head.

'I don't want to, Shay. I want to stay with you.'

'That's silly. You should go.'

'I would not go, even if I could,' she said, 'but you know I can't.'

He closed his eyes. His breathing was ragged. His face felt feverishly hot to the touch of her hand.

The pain of Castrel's grief was appalling.

There was a sound behind her and she turned and Hope was standing in the door. She came in and squatted beside her father, watching him gravely. The glimmer of a dragon's immortality in her eyes.

'I can help him,' she said. 'I can heal this. I can make him strong again.'

'Don't say that, Hope,' said Castrel gently. 'I'm sorry, but he's too badly hurt. Even when I was whole I could never have mended this. He understands that.'

Shay reached out and took his daughter's hand.

'Everything's fine,' he said. 'You don't need to be sad, my beautiful sweetheart. Not too much. I'm glad for everything. I'm glad I've spent so much time with you. You are my daughter and will always be. But now it's time for you to go to a good place, far away from this awful world. You're wonderful and I love you and I'm so proud of you, but we have to say goodbye now. Have your life. That's all I want for you.'

I SAID I CAN HEAL YOU.

The dragon voice of Hope seemed to fill the room.

I CANNOT HOLD YOUR HAND IN THE FIRE OF LIFE FOR EVER, BUT STAY WITH ME FOR NOW.

*

Their golden friend ducked into the room. Already he looked stronger, as if his wounds were healing. His clothes swirled subtle colours in the twilight shadows of the house, and his eyes gleamed less human.

'It is time to go,' he said. 'It must be now. We have little time. The way will not stay open long.' He turned to Hope. 'Come.'

Castrel stood up to say farewell to her daughter. She didn't know she would do that. She wasn't sure she had the strength. She looked at Shay.

'Leave me here,' he said to her. 'Go with them down to the shore and see them go. I'll be fine.'

YOU HAVE NOT ASKED ME WHAT I WISH. I AM NOT GOING.

Castrel stared at Hope. The fierce and terrible judgement of dragons glinted deep in her eyes. Jewels of immortality in darkness.

'Oh, my darling,' she said, 'I don't want you to go, I can't bear to lose you. But you need to go. It's the only thing to do. We'll die soon, and then you'd be here all alone. Going across the bridge to the other world is the way to have a better life for you. It hurts now, but you'll understand why one day.'

'Now is one day,' said Hope. 'This is one day. Here is one day.'

She was speaking with her child's light voice, but her words were rich with nuance and understanding far older than her years.

'You believe you're making the best choice,' she said, 'but it is my choice to make, not yours, and I will not go.'

'Please,' said Shay. 'You have to go. It's the only way.'

'I won't leave you to die,' she said.

'No!' said Shay, horrified. 'Not that, please don't say that. Don't think it, Hope. You mustn't sacrifice yourself for me. No child should do that for their parent. Never—'

But Hope hadn't finished.

'That is not all,' she said. 'Even if I could not heal you, I would not leave. This is my world and I belong here. I will not be driven out and let foul shadow have it.'

Castrel stared at her strange, courageous, beautiful daughter. She had the heart of the dragon in her, but she was so young. Courage and beauty, but even the courage and beauty of a dragon couldn't change the world. It couldn't turn back what was coming. She wouldn't allow her child to sacrifice herself for that lost cause.

'Do you think you can change what's happening here?' she said. 'Do you think you can turn it all back to how it was?'

'No,' said Hope. 'I don't think anyone or anything can do that. But this is my world. I will stay.'

'But ...' Shay began.

NO MORE. I AM HOPE AND I AM THE HEART OF THE DRAGON AND I WILL DECIDE. I AM THE CHOOSER OF WORLDS AND I CHOOSE THIS AND I WILL STAY.

Castrel realized then that what Hope wanted would happen and there was no changing it. She turned to their golden friend.

'We owe you so much,' she said. 'All we can say is thank you, though it's not enough.'

Their golden friend looked at Hope.

'What will you do?' he said to her. 'Where will you go?'

'I don't know,' she said.

'I'm not sure how much time you have left, before the final darkness falls. I think not much.'

Hope regarded him with her jewel-flecked dragon eyes. She was more dragon now and less child. Glittering and golden. A small column of ancientness and insight in that wooden hut at the edge of the ending world. She seemed to change from one thing to another, from child to dragon to child, like the flicker of a candle flame in a draught.

'No darkness, however deep, endures for ever,' she said, 'and no world will outlast the heart of the dragon. I am chooser and learner and change. I am Hope.'

Their golden friend said nothing then, but only looked at her.

'And you?' Hope said to him. 'You will leave now?'

'Yes. This is my only crossing. I must take it now.'

'Are you sure?' said Hope. 'I wish you would stay, at least for a while.'

He stared at the dragon-child.

'What?'

'Loneliness is painful. The heart of the dragon needs a bond companion. Someone whose time is not brief like humans, someone who can see things at least a little as we do, and be our adviser and friend. Vespertine had the wizard Tariel, and I would choose you, if you would have me. You are a wise heart and good. I do not think your time here is finished yet: there is more for you to be. So I ask this of you. Please. Of course, I'll outlive you in the end, but not yet.'

Their golden friend was studying Hope and there was something in his face that was alive and new and almost like joy.

He is not human, Castrel thought. *He doesn't think or feel like we do. But then, neither does Hope.*

'It would be intriguing,' he said. 'And foolish. And dangerous. I expect only an early and painful death. Yet I have lived here long and come to love this world, and now here is a new thing in it. Better perhaps this, than leaving here and remembering it all from somewhere else.' He bowed courteously and smiled. 'Yes. I will do this. I will stay. And gladly.'

'Good!' said Hope, and hugged him like a child. Then she stood back and studied him. 'I wish I knew your name. I know you remember it really.'

'Rook,' said their golden friend. He grinned like the youth he had once been. 'My name is Rook.'

*

Hope spent some time with Shay, and set his wound on its way to healing. Castrel watched her do it. It seemed to her that when Hope touched him, Shay's body shimmered with a kind of gentle dragonfire. She had seen nothing like it before. The wheeze and coughing deep in his chest grew steadily less and less.

That night they slept in the hut on the beach, and the next morning dawned bleak and cold. The sky was copper and greenish-dark and cast a weak, watery gloom. Huge leathery moth-like creatures danced slowly on the horizon, shedding clouds of dust. The carcases of the Wielder, the rider and the six-legged beast still smouldered on the beach. The tide was in. The slopping of thick, black waters.

After breakfast, they packed their bags and turned east along the shore, the four of them walking towards the darkness. Shay slipped his hand into Castrel's without speaking. She took it and held it tight, and together they walked slowly away from the beach, side by side, fragile and weak, following behind their dragon child.

Their task was finished now and their story done: the door that had been opened could not be closed, and the world they had known was gone for ever; but Hope would make her own way in this new world that she had chosen for her own, and she would be fine and beautiful. She would be human, the last and the first, and she would also be dragon. She would live for ever, a strange eternal life they could not understand or have a part in, but she would not be alone. She would have a golden friend. And though Castrel and Shay might live for a few years more, they had done all they needed to do and they could rest when the time for that came; but for a while yet they would still be together, and they would see their child go on into this new life, just a little further; at least they would see it begin, and that was good. That was enough.

THE END